A NEW HOME FOR SOULS

BY
PAUL POLAKIS

This book is dedicated to those who believe there's a half a chance our universe has a creator.

PART 1

CHAPTER 1

THE OLDEST ROCK

Jack Whinston's boots crunched over the brittle terrain of the Isua Greenstone Belt in southwestern Greenland. It was a balmy fifty-degree Saturday in late July. Jack's thinning gray hair was moonlighting as a weathervane in the blustery wind, whipping northeast with each gust. He adjusted his wire-rimmed glasses and peered at the massive thrust sheets poking out over the northern horizon. As if he were touching the peak of each rocky nappe, his index finger bounced in the air as he counted them off. He struck a short course to the west, stopped, and pointed north. His scruffy beard rode up his cheeks, exposing his angled yellow teeth in what was either a smile or a grimace. "There it is," he grunted.

"There's what?" asked Alex. "This is mostly igneous. Where's the sedimentary rock? I'm looking for fossils, man."

Jack sidled up to a rugged sheet of metamorphic rock, removed his pack, and inverted it. Dropping on stone, the dissonant clanking of chisels sounded like wind chimes. Alex hated wind chimes. They reminded him of horror movies, where their spooky peal signaled an impending murder. And it didn't help that he felt like murdering Jack right now. He had taken a break from his faculty position at the University of Chicago to fulfill his dream of accompanying the world-renowned geologist in a quest for ancient rocks in the Isua Greenstone Belt. That dream now seemed more like a nightmare, and Jack was looking more and more like Freddy Krueger.

The crusty geologist had at least twenty years on the youthful Alex. But Jack's relentless pace over the rugged terrain had left Alex gulping the crisp air. They had already hiked several miles from the helicopter drop zone. Jack had changed course countless times, compounding the distance. Alex trudged behind, his ankles turning sideways over the uneven gneiss. His gimpy rugby knee mocked him for skipping physical therapy.

Alex removed his stocking hat, uncovering a thick crop of jet-black hair that seemed impervious to the wind. He wrinkled his brow. His crystal blue eyes narrowed as he looked at the face of the unremarkable stone Jack was about to waylay with a pickax. Alex smiled tightly. It was not his charm smile. That smile, along with his perfectly placed dimples, square chin, and rugged cheekbones had opened many doors—including that of his ex-wife. But that door had slammed shut when he opened the one to their bedroom. Arriving home early, he had wanted to surprise her. She was surprised.

His current smile, the one with pursed lips, paired with a wrinkled forehead, was one of incredulity. He was irked by Jack's departure from the route prescribed by officials at the Greenland Institute for Natural Resources. They had seemed pretty adamant about their restrictions. Yet here they were, on the blazing-red part of the map that an official had repeatedly rubbed his thick finger over while shaking his head sideways. Numb to Alex's objections, Jack had forged on. After all, he was with Jack Whinston, the Stanford professor who had won everything short of a Nobel Prize for his novel methods for dating biogenic sediment. Alex had little choice but to trust him.

Alex opened his tool bag, and both men hammered and chiseled away for a couple of hours to no avail. Most of the rock there seemed pretty deformed and unlikely to represent the original crust that the greenstone belt was famous for.

"It's getting cold," said Alex. "When does the helicopter come back for us?" Jack slammed his pick hammer into the gneiss with more enthusiasm than usual. "Find something?" queried Alex. He looked closely at the newly exposed stone.

"Yeah, I thought I saw your face on that rock." Jack's shoulders slumped in resignation. His hammer dropped to the ground. He pushed up his safety glasses long enough to chafe Alex with his eyes. His sour smirk parted; words poured out. "Why did you come out here, Alex? You practically begged me to take you along this time, and all you've done is complain about the cold, the wind, your sore hand. And for the last time, no! You can't get a fucking beer out here! We're in the middle of the Isua Greenstone Belt. Look around. It's nothing but ice and rock. That's why we're here."

The barren landscape sculpted by eons of tectonic regurgitation and receding glaciers was both beautiful and haunting. It was at once a fantastical animation and a creepy art installation. Perfectly striped chunks of striated bedrock were strewn around like giant blocks of candy. Iron banding patterns painted the distant facades with alternating swaths of orange and black. Narrow rays of sun that snuck through the mostly cloudy sky lit up patches of the jagged plutons while leaving the rest stark and lifeless.

"Well, we're not supposed to be exactly here. That was your idea, Jack. And we better not be exactly here when the copter returns. If the pilot tells the GINR guys, we could end up in jail. We're supposed to stay north of the fault, remember?"

"There's nothing north of the fault that I'm interested in. And, for your information, the Greenland Institute for Natural Resources is clueless. They're just happy to milk the visiting geologists for mining fees so they can buy a new espresso machine for their cushy office."

"Mmmm, espresso," waxed Alex. "Can I get an espresso around here?"

"Alex! These are the oldest rocks on the planet, and you're a paleontologist, one of the world's finest."

"Well, not exactly. Despite my affiliation at UC, I'm not really a paleontologist, I just play one on TV. I guess that makes me a Playleontologist." Alex issued a hollow chuckle at his own joke. "I'm really just a biochemist who happens to have a thing for old life."

"And a thing for young life, too, by what I've gathered from your colleagues. Whatever you call yourself, you should be excited about excavating here. You could discover signs of the most ancient life. Life nearly as old as the planet itself. This is where three-point-seven-billion-year-old stromatolites were discovered."

"Again, not exactly here," Alex retorted. "Allen found those in sedimentary rock a few miles from here. Which, technically, isn't here, because it's over there. Why are we over here? This rock is significantly more deformed than those near Allen's site. Most of the crust here isn't that old, and the metamorphic stone mostly originated from lava protoliths. We're not going to find any protolithic sediment here, Jack."

Jack answered by dropping his goggles over his eyes and picking up his hammer. He stepped away slowly, feeling the rock as though it were Braille. He stopped at a sizable crevice, where he poked his hand into the gash. It swallowed his arm up to his elbow until he quickly retracted it as if bit by something. He grabbed a large rock hammer and slammed it against the lip of the crevice. The rock exploded, transforming the gash into a gaping hole. He pushed up his googles again, unclipped his flashlight from his vest, and peered into the lit hole.

"The oldest stones are here, Alex. They don't just jump out at you. We have to uncover them. We're looking for something special here. Something no one else would find. And Allen lucked out because the ice had melted away, exposing his stromatolites. He barely had to dig. Some have argued that they're not even real stromatolites. Some of the mounds appear to have grown downward. How could bacteria do that?"

"I don't know, but I analyzed samples of metasedimentary rock from that field myself. The stable isotope ratios are consistent with biologic activity over three point seven billion years ago. But, again, those samples weren't from here, which makes me wonder why we are over—"

"Bingo!" shouted Jack, uncorking his head from the hole. "Graphitic shale. Nicely layered, too. And I'm not a petrographer, but it sure looks like pre-metamorphic dolomite to me. Not supposed to be any biogenic-looking stone in this area, huh? Here's your ocean floor right here, doubter. Let's grab some of this."

Alex poked his head into the hole. "Wow! For real, Jack! What the hell?" He scraped a wire brush over the surface and swiped it with his gloved hand. "That is some good-looking clay. Holy shit!" he shouted. "This section looks fossilized!"

Jack poked in his Maglite, lighting up the profile that Alex was inspecting. Etched into the laminated rock, he could see what looked like layered sine waves, each bump about a centimeter high and separated from the next by two or three centimeters. Multiple horizontal waves were stacked vertically, in phase, creating a pleated pattern of alternating dark and light stripes.

"More fake stromatolites?" goaded Jack.

"This is unreal," replied Alex. "I've never seen anything like this. Look at the bottom of the stack here." Alex pointed out a feature that tracked horizontally under the bottom-most series of waves. It looked like a string of beads with a tiny bead positioned precisely under each wave's crest. "We'll need isotope ratios for confirmation," he said. He positioned Jack's light on the alleged stromatolites. "I challenge anyone to tell me how these formed in the absence of a living organism. And this, this stuff, these little spheres at the bottom. What are those?"

Forgetting the time, they busied themselves chiseling out samples of the coveted sedimentary stone, carefully preserving the fossilized features. Finally, a strong gust of northerly wind relieved Alex of his hat and reminded them of their rendezvous with the helicopter. They had at least an hour walk if they hustled, and toting their hefty booty wouldn't make it any faster. Jack looked shocked upon realizing the time. Usually meticulous, he hastily shoveled his dirty tools into his pack while prompting Alex to get a move on. The helicopter would wait for them, but Jack was more concerned about the pilot spotting them than arriving late.

"Let's move," said Jack. "We can make it if we double-time it. Remind me to tip the pilot handsomely, especially if he spots us before we get there."

"Fifteen thousand dollars for a hundred-and-fifty-mile round trip and we need to tip him, too?"

"We're tipping him to keep his mouth shut," replied Jack.

Still a mile from the pickup site, and clearly out of bounds, the two men scrambling across the darkened terrain stood out like polar bears on black-top. The pilot even mistook them for wildlife until he drew close enough to spot their bulging packs and flailing arms. They looked like they were on a prison break with dogs in pursuit. Considering bears might actually be chasing them, the pilot executed a sweeping 360-degree turn to check. Finding none, he continued to the pickup site to await them.

"Sorry we're a bit late, Buzz," wheezed Jack, as he tossed his pack in first. "We got a little lost, I guess. Everything kind of looks the same when you get out there."

"Break your compass?" grunted Buzz. "Or did the north pole move?"

"Yeah, the second one," quipped Alex, clambering in. "You know, the magnetic field actually does move, Buzz. Besides, why does the north pole of a compass needle point north in the first place? Shouldn't it point to the south? Opposites attract, right? I think that's what confused us. We had the whole world upside down."

Buzz's leathery face looked to be eternally frozen in a state of irritation. His tiny black eyes punctuated a pair of bushy gray eyebrows that matched the tone of his unruly beard. The nine remaining hairs on his balding head were wrapped in a ponytail that fluttered around in the turbulence like a shredded flag. The origin of Buzz's name was unknown to Alex, but right now he was pretty sure it was due to the unwavering stare cutting through him like a saw. Buzz eventually turned his attention to the controls, and before his two passengers could get buckled into their seats, he launched a gut-curdling ascent. Alex and Jack rocked back in their seats, both reaching for anything to hold on to. As they leveled off, Jack flashed a derisive glare at Alex for his flippant comments to Buzz. Alex just shrugged and rolled his eyes.

The short flight to Nuuk took less than an hour but dragged on in silence until Jack broke in, elaborating on his apology. "Seriously, Buzz, sorry we made you wait. We let the time slip away. It was careless. We'll make it up to you, bud." The saw looked straight ahead, cutting through the granite butte between them and the airport.

"You weren't just late," Buzz replied. "You weren't lost, either. And for your information, smart-ass, a compass points north. I can lose my license if the GINR finds my passengers hiking off-limits in the Isua. I can't take you out there anymore, Dr. Whinston. You'll have to find another way. I'd recommend leaving your dipshit partner behind next time, too."

"Aw, c'mon Buzz," said Alex. "What gives with the cranky pants? Can't find a rubber patch for your inflatable sex doll?"

Alex coughed up a wince that Jack's pointed elbow coaxed out of him. Buzz stared straight ahead, silent, eyes measuring the remaining meters between them and the airport.

On arrival, the chopper landed hard, tilting sharply to the left and launching the passengers toward the exit hatch. The shoulder harness cut into Alex until the helicopter settled evenly again. "Is that a hint, Buzz?" he asked.

The saw. That's all Buzz really needed to send the message, but he punctuated it with a terse, "Get out!"

Jack fumbled with another apology, but the saw was having none of it.

"Well, there goes your tip for fast and friendly service, Buzzster," quipped Alex. "Does the local bordello accept credit?"

Buzz bent over, and a flash of black metal emerged from under his seat as he withdrew his sidearm.

"And we're good as gone," said Alex, spotting the handgun.

Jack's eyes popped. "Holy shit, Buzz, take it easy! Alex is just joking."

"I'm not," replied Buzz, still looking straight ahead.

The two men tossed their packs onto the tarmac and jumped down from the chopper. Neither looked back as they struck a brisk pace for the terminal. Cutting past the baggage carousel, Jack veered toward the restroom, telling Alex he would meet him out front. Alex exited the building. He squeezed between some parked cars and waited on the street for a duration well beyond that required to take a pee. He stared blankly at the aqua-colored storage trailers resting on concrete blocks across the road. A few decommissioned snowmobiles sat idle on the dry gravel flanked by two large treaded vehicles equipped with snowplows.

Alex was beginning to wonder if the snow would return before Jack did when he suddenly appeared alongside him. Studying the lonely steel light post doubling as a street sign, Alex asked, "Hey, Jack, who names a street...Awk-es-ek-ara-jook?"

Jack had no reply. Alex expected none. After some silence, Jack checked his watch and said, "Sten should be here shortly to take us back to the hotel."

"Great. Can we get a beer there?"

Jack cringed. He looked down at the concrete and took a few halting steps forward. Alex thought Jack was just distancing himself until he spotted their approaching van. Jack greeted Sten with a perfunctory smile and ensured him that they were all set to go.

Heading along Siaqqinneq Road, Alex spotted a couple of inconspicuous one-story white buildings. "Dang!" Alex shouted. "Is that a golf course? It says Nuuk Golf Club on the sign. When's the season, Sten? July tenth, one to four p.m.? Do they use snowmobiles instead of carts?"

Sten was old enough to drive, but barely. He initiated a polite response to Alex, but Jack quickly butted in. "Please, Sten, pay no attention to the asshole next to me."

"How about the one under me?" retorted Alex. He elevated one side of his buttocks, but his flatulence failed him.

They sat in silence the remainder of the way until Sten turned onto Aqqusinersuaq and eased up to the Hotel Hans Egede. It was a rectangular, sturdy blue and white three-story building that looked more like an institute than a hotel.

"I hope they have our cells ready for us," said Alex. He took in the structure's sterile glass and metal face. "I could use a quick nap before my execution."

Sten only smiled and asked if they needed any assistance with their packs. Jack paid him and proceeded briskly toward the hotel, leaving Alex behind.

Alex, still standing near the van, squinted at the block letters, *PISIFFIK*, posted above an entrance to the building.

"Are you pisiffik'd off at me, Jack?" he asked loudly.

Without looking back, Jack replied, "I'll be eating in my room, alone."

Alex took a few quick steps to catch Jack. "Aw, what's up, man? That Buzz is a dick. I don't even know why you do business with him. He deserved it."

Jack spun on his heel to face Alex. "Because he's the only business that can get me out there. And if he's pisiffik'd off enough, he's going straight to the GINR and tell them where he saw us today. That means we can't take the samples home. That means I came here for nothing. When you add all that up, it means you're the dick."

"He doesn't know if we have any samples. We just have to avoid the GINR until 3:15 tomorrow when we depart for Reykjavík."

"It's not so easy to avoid people here, Alex."

It was true. And Alex made no effort to avoid people, either. After finishing dinner in the hotel restaurant, he returned to his room, where he grew restless as the daylight dimmed. He tried the television. The lone station, KNR, was broadcasting in Greenlandic—an Eskimo language spoken by only fifty thousand people in the entire world. Alex was not one of them. From what he could surmise, the lead story was a riveting report about an eleven-million-ton glacier threatening a tiny village south of Nuuk. Maintaining an interest in the not so torrid advance of glaciers required a lot of patience. Alex had little.

The next piece kept his attention, though. A stout, ruby-faced native woman, adorned in animal skins and wearing as many colored beads as there were tons of ice in the menacing glacier, was describing a new drink. The Greenlandic coffee was sweeping the nation. The concoction of black coffee, whiskey, and coffee liqueur, topped with whipped cream, looked suspiciously like an Irish coffee to Alex. Nevertheless, the key ingredient, whiskey, had piqued his interest.

It was nine o'clock, too early to sleep, and the TV had little left to offer Alex. As directed, he stepped out onto Aqqusinersuaq Street and headed south toward the Mutten. Having inquired about local bars at his hotel, the receptionist had pronounced it *Moo-tin*, which made it seem far more appealing than the flesh of an adult sheep. Within crawling distance from the hotel, the low-lying, homey-looking watering hole sported bright yellow vertical siding, white trim, and a series of neatly arced white awnings accenting the windows and doors. Painted on the exterior wall near the front entrance were silhouettes of people dancing. Built on a small rise directly behind the Mutten, the monolithic, stark-white Hans Egede Church cast a shadow over the bar. Alex warmed to Greenland upon realizing that the three-hundred-foot rule for separation of church and bar was likely not in effect there.

The music grew louder as Alex approached the front deck of the Mutten. The band's boisterous cover of the Eagle's "Already Gone" spilled out onto the deck when he opened the door. He felt immediately at home. True to the silhouettes, people were indeed dancing. The dim yellow lighting, the low ceiling, the aged wood paneling, and the garish red the-atre carpeting spoke to him. More importantly, the spirits lining the shelves behind the bar screamed to him. With his eyes on a vacant barstool, he wiggled his way through the dancers, oblivious to the long-ing stares he elicited from the women he passed.

"How about a whiskey sour?" Alex shouted to the bartender. He pulled a crumpled hundred-krone note from his pocket, smoothing it out as he awaited his drink. The bartender returned with an oversized glass filled nearly to the brim. It proved rich in whiskey. Alex licked his stinging lips after taking a sip. "Wow!" he exclaimed. "It's hammer time."

The Danish bartender spoke good English, but not grasping the refer-ence, he frowned and asked Alex if he was on his way to work and wondered what it was he was building.

Alex tried to explain the phrase *getting hammered* and MC Hammer, the former Oakland rapper, which only escalated the confusion. Finally, he blurted out that he was not a carpenter at all, but a paleobiologist.

"Ya, we get a lot of scientists in here during the summer," explained the bartender. "Greenland has the world's oldest crust," he continued. "Here's a piece of it from the Greenbelt," he said, presenting a glass jar with a chunk of reddish-brown rock in it. "Dr. Jack Whinston gave it to me. He's a famous geologist."

"Never heard of him," replied Alex. He turned the jar around a few times, assessing the rock. It looked highly deformed and couldn't have been more than a couple billion years old post-transformation. "Yeah, that's a beauty," he said. "Does the GINR know you have this?"

"They don't care much about it," he answered. "Well, at least they didn't. There's a couple new guys there now that seem pretty strict. Especially if you're out rock hunting too far south of the fault. Nice enough guys, but they will lock you up. Seen 'em do it."

Alex downed a couple more big-gulp whiskey sours at the bar. He was politely turning down a local's invitation to dance when the front door slammed behind a couple of fastidious-looking men in gray suits. Both had short cropped dark hair, were cleanly shaven, slim, and stood equal in height at about six foot even. A bearded shorter man behind them— a pit bull in a parka—pulled off his hat to reveal a bald head with just a wisp of a ponytail.

"Oh, shit, here we go," Alex mumbled under his breath. The beard swiveled on its post until it stopped, pointing directly at Alex, along with a finger attached to the same body. A brief huddle ensued until all three men proceeded toward Alex.

They drew close. "Hey, Buzz. What's up? You passing out Bibles with your new Nuuk-el-head friends?" asked Alex. "C'mon, man, I'll buy you a drink and we can all pray together."

Staring straight at Alex, full *saw*, Buzz addressed the suits next to him. "That's him," he groused.

The suits stepped forward, flanking Alex while Buzz remained at center. Feeling boxed in, Alex spun a one-eighty on his stool to face the bar but couldn't escape the image of the men in the mirror, still meeting his gaze. He tried ordering another drink, but the bartender, along with his gift rock from the famous Dr. Whinston, was nowhere in sight.

"Dr. Sina?" asked one of the suits. "Are you Alex Sina?"

Alex wheeled back around on his stool. Facing the suits yet still ignoring them, he tilted his head while watching the dancers stomping along to Michael Jackson's "Bad." "That's not the moonwalk. You have to slide on your toes," he shouted to no one in particular.

"Dr. Sina! May I have your attention, please?"

Alex finally took in the two men, surveying both from head to toe. He leaned in and casually straightened the black necktie worn by the one closest to him. He gave it little tug. "Whoa! Not a clip-on, eh? Jehovahs are so formal. You'd get more converts if you just loosened up a bit. Get out there, Jonas," he said to the closer one, "Let me see your moonwalk, man." If nothing else, the suits were calm and collected. Their blank expressions perfectly accessorized their attire. And they were not taking the bait, either. Alex casted again. "Oh, wait, that's right. The Watch Tower Society forbids dancing. Hey, can you have sex standing up, or is that still considered dancing?"

One of the suits spoke. "Dr. Sina, I am Noah Sorrenson, and this is Emil Pedersen. We are from the Greenland Institute for Natural Resources, and we have been informed that you and your partner, Dr. Jack Whinston, were harvesting stone from an off-limits area in the greenstone belt zone. This is a preserved area, and we cannot allow you to take any rocks collected from it."

"Who on earth told you such a thing?" cried Alex with mock exasperation. He slapped his palms to his cheeks and jerked his head toward Buzz, then back to the suit, then back to Buzz. "Wait, was it Buzz? Buzz, you little snitch, you. If you weren't so damn cute, I'd drop you off at the animal shelter right now."

Just then Buzz pushed his furry face between the two men and closed hard on Alex. His breath smelled like garlic and old socks as it hissed over the handful of tobacco-stained teeth still populating his mouth. "Look around, fuck face!" Buzz seethed. "You're outnumbered here. Start cooperating or the chief of police, a.k.a. my brother-in-law, will make sure you don't go home for a while."

"Holy Jesus, there's a female with your DNA out there somewhere?" asked Alex. "I'm picturing a heavily whiskered sea lion with at least six fingers on each flipper. She must be a master at balancing on a beach ball."

With surprising agility, Noah arrested the hand en route to Alex's throat. He clutched Buzz's wrist, turning it gently in a way that caused the assailant to take a step back. Emil then stepped between Buzz and Alex, allowing Noah a moment to calm Buzz down. The brief commotion attracted some attention from a few patrons, who turned away when the excitement subsided.

Emil then tried again. "Dr. Sina, please," he urged, "we only want the rocks returned. Whatever issues you have with the pilot have nothing to do with this. We just want the samples back."

"Well, geez! Why didn't you just say so?" said Alex. "You could have left your dog at home." He tilted his head far enough to smirk at Buzz, still standing behind Emil.

"Where are they, Dr. Sina?"

"Oh, yeah, the rocks. I don't have them. See? Easy-peasy. We're done here, and Buzz didn't have to bite anybody."

"Dr. Whinston informed us that you do indeed have them or know where they are. He also correctly guessed that we would find you here, at a bar."

"What? Jack told you I have samples from the Isua?"

"That's correct. We spoke to him at the hotel. He allowed us to search his room and all his bags. We are certain that they are not in his possession. Nor are they in your room."

"You were in—"

"We have that authority, Dr. Sina."

Alex stood up. He felt a little wobbly and questioned whether downing that third bucket of whiskey sour was a good move. He slapped his hands against his pants pockets. "Nope, no rocks there," he explained. "I think we should proceed to the restroom for a cavity search. The cavity between Buzz's ears, that is. Gotta be some rocks in there." Alex looked at Buzz's bald head and likened it to a mood dome. It seemed to glow red whenever Alex struck a nerve.

In his recollection, which was decidedly hazy, Alex wasn't sure what happened next. The events unfolded quite quickly, except for one, which seemed to occur in slow motion. Nuka, the cheerful, round-faced Greenlander, had returned for another run at Alex, asking again if he would dance with her. She barged in, wedging herself between Alex and Noah, her big smile just inches from Alex's face. "Come on, sexy, it's a love song." Alex smiled back. He truly found her charming in some innocent way but again demurred, claiming scoliosis had robbed him of his once legendary dance moves.

"May I suggest an alternative?" he said to Nuka, as well as to anyone within earshot. "The Jevovahs here are respectfully off-limits," he explained, nodding at Noah and Emil. "But how about Buzz?" he said, pointing to the beard behind Emil. "The guy can dance like his crotch is on fire. Because it probably is."

Nuka turned to Buzz, giggled, and spun back toward Alex. She came in close again, "He's homoq," she said into his ear and backed away smiling.

"Homoq?" queried Alex, all too loudly. At least loud enough for Buzz to hear. "As in gay?" Alex continued, at a volume now loud enough for everyone to hear. Attracting a few spectators, he glanced back and forth at Buzz and then Nuka, who was nodding with one hand covering her mouth. "Buzz, you sly dog." Buzz's mood dome lit up brightly this time. His head darted around, taking in the gawkers. "Seriously, Buzzster? It's the twenty-first century. Why don't you just come out?" shouted Alex, addressing Buzz as well as the onlookers. "Anybody want a cuddly old bear?" he asked. "He's not my type."

It wasn't just a cliché. The music really did stop right before a bar fight. In the middle of Loudon Wainwright's "Dead Skunk," where the singer sings, *should've looked left / should've looked right,* the band trailed off at *should've looked.* The drummer was last to catch the drift. His final snare tap hung in the air like a hyphen waiting for a word to follow. The immobilized dancers looked first at each other, then at the band, and finally at the melee evolving near the bar. "That's it!" were the last intelligible syllables they could make out in the rising din. They were also the last that Buzz would utter for a while.

Buzz was not to be denied this time. He was a hungry pit bull and Alex was a Milk-Bone. Both Noah and Emil were forced back by his sudden advance. They tried to recover, but it was too late. Alex could feel the bar rail pushing hard into his spine as Buzz grasped the lapels of his coat and drove him backward. Hysterical, poor Nuka slapped helplessly at both of their shoulders while screaming, "Stop it!" But it didn't stop. Pinned to the bar, Alex felt trapped. Buzz's contorted face, a couple inches from his own, exuded a genuine madness. An image of Buzz's gun bubbled up in Alex's mind.

Alex's next move was entirely unexpected—most of all to him. It might have been an act of desperation, but was more likely one of drunkenness. He would later deny any aspersions by his friends that there was something deep in his psyche that he refused to confront. As far as he was concerned, it just happened. Unable to raise his arms high enough to repel Buzz, he tipped his head forward and kissed him on the mouth. Repulsed, Buzz recoiled long enough for Alex to free an arm and deliver a sharp uppercut into Buzz's chin. This drove his face upward, exposing his throat, where Alex punched him next.

Buzz's knees buckled. Bent over at the waist, he grasped at his throat and fell directly backward. He dropped to the floor on his rump and bounced ever so slightly before slowly rolling onto his side. It reminded Alex of the Red Lobster commercial where the grilled shrimp bounces in slow motion off the moistened bed of lettuce. The perimeter around Buzz's prone body cleared out as patrons made room for the new mass crumpled at their feet. Frantically massaging his throat, Buzz struggled to gather his breath. Dark red blood trickled from the corner of his gaping mouth and pooled on the floor beneath it. A small white and brown nugget, later identified as a tooth, waded in the pool.

By now, Noah and Emil each had a hold of Alex, who showed little interest in resisting. Nuka had dropped to her knees to attend to the gulping Buzz. The bartender reappeared. A good bartender can smell the rise in testosterone and calls the cops before the fight even starts. He was a good bartender. Looking toward the newly opened door, he was pointing out Alex and the suited custodians restraining him. The officers worked their way over to the bar, where one of them knelt down to check on Buzz. He was breathing laboriously but still unable to speak. "It's Christine's brother," one of the cops said. "Should we call the chief?" The other just shrugged and suggested that they try to figure out what happened first.

After questioning a number of witnesses, the police determined that Alex had acted out of self-defense. They knew Buzz well enough, too. He was a card-carrying hothead, and it wasn't the first time the chief had been embarrassed by his brother-in-law's lack of self-control in a public place. By now, Buzz was back on his feet, albeit wobbly. His breathing was hoarse but regular. A few unintelligible syllables rose wildly in pitch when Alex suggested that they should just kiss and make up. The officers explained that both of them, at minimum, were guilty of disturbing the peace. Alex considered this an impossibility since none existed in the Mutten prior to the fight. But he kept his mouth shut. Accordingly, the officer told them they could be arrested and spend the night in jail. Or they could agree to peacefully exit the bar and have no further interaction with each other. This proposal was further sweetened by the officers' offer to give Buzz a lift home.

The patrons began to shuffle back to their tables. The clinking of glasses resumed, as did the chatter, until it was drowned out by the band busting into a rollicking version of the Stones' "Street Fighting Man." As Buzz was escorted out by one officer, the second started to lead Alex out by the arm when Noah and Emil interjected. They hastily tried to explain their beef with the wayward scientist, claiming that Alex should be placed in their custody for the time being.

"Noah," said the officer, "if he is not in possession of stolen property and you have no real evidence that he even stole it, I can't detain him. And neither can the GINR, unless you want a harassment suit on your hands."

Alex looked at Noah and Emil. "Well, there you have it, boys. Unless you guys have a Bible for me, I see no further need for your services."

The two men looked dejected. It was true; Alex didn't have any stones with him. They weren't in his room, nor were they with Jack. But Noah and Emil would never recover them if they couldn't question the thieves who knew of their whereabouts. "I'm sorry, guys," said the officer, "you have to let him go."

With that, Alex was released into the chilly night air. He promised the police he was headed straight for his room, but he really wanted to beat down Jack's door for lying about the rocks and siccing the suits on him. It was well after midnight when he plodded north down Aqqusinersuaq toward the Hotel Hans Egede. In the lingering twilight, he could make out his hotel just a few hundred feet down the road. As he neared the building, his rumbling stomach hijacked his legs, angling him toward the entrance of a dark and lifeless Thai restaurant adjacent to his hotel.

He stood at the door of the eatery for a few seconds until his whiskey-addled brain regained control of his legs. He stumbled back and read aloud the sign above the door, "Restaurant Charoen Porn." He chuckled like a fifth grader hearing his first dirty joke. Still laughing, he staggered sideways a few steps, threw his head back, and shouted, "I'd like an order of Pad Thigh, a little Som Tom Booby, and a double order of Khao Poo Tang."

"They're closed," came a distant reply from across the street at the city center bus stop.

Alex just waved loosely at the man. He was still too drunk to be embarrassed by his adolescent behavior but sober enough to call it a night. He entered the hotel and made a beeline for the receptionist. The sweet odor of alcohol escaped with each word as he insisted she provide him with Jack Whinston's room number. She gave Alex a calculating appraisal. She added the smell of liquor to his disheveled hair, then multiplied his unbuttoned shirt by his lacerated knuckles, and arrived at drunk and disorderly.

With one finger hovering over the hidden emergency button, she suggested calling Jack's room if it was indeed an emergency.

"Oh, it's an emergency, all right," said Alex. "At least it will be after I get my hands on him."

The button pressed, she stalled while fumbling through the directory, pretending to look for Jack's room number. A very large man in an undersized suit—because none were made in his size—entered the lobby. He took brisk, choppy steps toward the reception desk. His thick arms, appended to his prodigious frame, seemed too short, projecting outward at an angle as they sliced back and forth with his penguin-like gait.

"Can I help you?" he asked Alex.

Alex looked up at the massive yeti and mentally substituted the word *kill* for *help*. The shadow cast by the human refrigerator awakened his sense of accommodation. "Actually, sir, I am residing at this fine establishment and am just trying to locate a friend also staying here," he said.

"Well," interjected the receptionist, "it appears your friend, Mr. Whinston, already checked out. Around nine p.m. I remember him now. The concierge called for a car to take him to the airport."

"Airport?" asked Alex. "There are no flights out of here at nine p.m."

"We explained that to him, but he said he had a friend working for a cargo service that was headed to Copenhagen tonight. He was hitching a ride with them."

Alex pounded the desk with his fist, instantly regretting it as he rubbed his bruised knuckles. He smiled contritely at the anxious yeti. "Okay, then," he said. "Thanks for your help." He trudged up the single flight of stairs to his floor, ambled down the hall, turned the corner, and unbelievably, there stood Noah and Emil outside his door.

"Oh, my god, you can't be serious!" he shrieked. "You guys are killing me. I'm calling the cops. You heard what they said."

"No, please, Dr. Sina," Noah said in a hushed tone. "We just have one more question. We know the rocks aren't here and that Dr. Whinston is gone. We know you don't have them, either."

"And?" asked Alex.

"Were they obtained south of the fault? From a layer of sediment accessible through a crevice in the igneous rock?"

Alex stood blinking at them in silence, trying to put it together. "How did…no, wait, who are you guys, really?" he finally asked. "Do I look like Indiana Jones to you? So, you think Jack and I found the grail or something? Or did we accidentally pull the plug on Greenland and the whole island is going to sink now? Look, I just followed Jack. I wanted to go northeast from the drop, but he insisted we go south. Out there, he's the expert. Okay? At least, he acted like he knew where he was going."

"He knew where he was going?"

"Well, yeah. Sort of. As we hiked, he would stop and count the nappes on the horizon and then adjust course and continue. Not exactly cartography, but he'd been there before. You could tell he was following a course of some sort."

Noah and Emil looked concerned. "Did you take anything from the crevice?"

"Not much. A few chunks of dolomite."

Both men registered alarm.

"Wow! Really?" Alex said. "They're just rocks, you guys. Is Greenland going to sink?"

"Thank you, Dr. Sina. I wish you a pleasant flight home," replied Noah.

"I'm looking forward to it," said Alex. "Unless some idiot opens the Ark of the Covenant and my face melts off."

CHAPTER 2

AN UNEARTHLY ROCK

Emma Curtis sat across from her parents at a McDonald's in Tempe, Arizona. It was a bit late for dinner, but the Joaquin Bustoz Math-Science Honors Summer Program for high school students was an all-day affair. The enrollees, mostly incoming seniors, were expected to live on campus for the entire program, but Emma was only thirteen. Although delighted with their daughter's admission, Emma's parents had reservations about leaving her alone on the ASU campus for three weeks. So, they dutifully picked her up after the program's group dinner and returned her early the next morning. Occasionally, she skipped the dinner to finish her work and instead ate with her parents on the way home. Tonight, they found themselves at a McDonald's on South Rural Road, a half-mile south of the university.

Emma leaned into her fish sandwich, letting her black-rimmed glasses slide down her slender nose. She tucked her thick red hair behind her oversized ears, exposing more of her freckled alabaster skin. Her rosy cheeks climbed even higher when she smiled, exposing the perfect teeth that had set her doting parents back about five house payments. They were convinced that she was nothing short of a beauty queen. Not that either could take credit for her comeliness; she had inherited none of their DNA.

Emma's father, Ron, suffered from cystic fibrosis, a crippling genetic disorder that left him infertile and likely not long for this world. Her mother, Amelia, clung to the hope that a new treatment would soon be discovered, and Ron would go on to see their adopted daughter graduate from high school and college, get married, and deliver some grandchildren. Ron harbored no such illusions about his health. He simply maintained that they had hit the jackpot with Emma and savored every moment he could spend with her.

Ron cleared his throat, coaxing the ever-present phlegm from his bronchial tubes. "What did our young genius do at school today?" he wheezed.

"I'm hardly a genius, Dad. Remember, I forgot my backpack this morning and you had to bring in for me?"

"So what? Einstein probably forgot his, too. You know he couldn't even drive a car?"

"Well, I can't, either, but that's about the only thing I have in common with Einstein."

"Honey," Amelia broke in, "we just couldn't be more pleased with the young lady you've become. You shouldn't feel any less proud of yourself than we do. You are the youngest student who qualified for the program. The counselor was already talking to us about college scholarships, and you've barely started high school. You know you can skip a grade whenever you want, sweetie."

"I don't think so, Mom. I want to stay in my grade with kids my own age. The older students just talk about parties and drinking and who they want to make out with."

"Whoa, there! Your mother and I didn't make out until we were eighteen."

Emma stalled mid-bite into her sandwich, withdrew it from her open mouth, and stared at her parents. "I don't want to hear about you and Mom making out, either."

"Oh, yeah?" chirped Ron. He pulled Amelia closer and kissed her.

Emma just shook her head and returned to her meal.

"So, really, what did you do today?" Ron continued. "Did you solve Riemann's hypothesis?"

"Do you even know what that is, Dad?"

"Not a clue, except that it remains unsolved, and that's where you come in."

"The Riemann hypothesis posits that all nontrivial zeros of the zeta function—"

Ron would have welcomed any interruption at this point, barring the one they actually got. As Emma tried to expound on the impossibility of solving Riemann's hypothesis, the street outside their window suddenly lit up with a pulsating, eerie orange glow that rapidly intensified. The strange illumination was accompanied by crackling and popping noises that sounded like a string of firecrackers going off. The noise reached a crescendo with a deafening blast that shattered windows and punched a hole through the roof. The ensuing chaos included screams, crying, smoke, a loud building alarm, and a shower released from overhead sprinklers. Through the haze, a gaping hole in the ceiling afforded a view of the starry night.

Convinced they were under attack, Ron corralled his family under the table. They peeked out cautiously at the battlefield. The floor was littered with fragments of roofing tile, glass shards, broken ceiling lights, and assorted unfinished food items. Ron's eyes followed a trail of scorched floor tiles to the corner of the room where thick black smoke was pouring out.

It grew quieter as the initial shock wore off and the sprinklers ceased sprinkling. The whimper of a toddler wafted over the varied chatter of frightened adults trying to make sense of the bombardment. Amelia poked her head out first. She reached for her phone and called for assistance. Emma had hers out, too, but only to take photographs of what was likely a monumental event in her mind.

"Is anyone hurt?" an anonymous voice boomed from somewhere behind the serving counter.

Amazingly, no one claimed to be, and the handful of patrons who were in the restaurant were all conscious and seemingly alert.

Ron and Amelia emerged from under the table, crunching over the glass and ceiling tile littering the floor. Emma followed. She shook off Ron's warning and rose to her feet, scanning the wreckage while snapping images of the ceiling, the broken windows, and the smoldering corner of the room.

Others were up, too, searching each other for clues. Emma followed the smoke to its source, a glowing football-sized rock hissing on the blackened floor. Others gathered around the searing projectile—an unremarkable black rock that could have been mistaken for a landscaping stone.

"It's sabotage," said a young man hosting a greasy mullet under a backwards baseball cap. "Terrorism," he said.

A vet who had spent a tour in Afghanistan disagreed. It did not look like military ordnance to him. It looked like a rock.

Emma contemplated the so-called rock while snapping a few more photos. No one could have hurled a steaming-hot rock like that through the roof, she thought. It probably weighed over forty pounds. It could have dropped from an airplane, but it wouldn't get that hot on the way down. It wasn't volcanic. Emma knew the nearest volcano was Sunset Crater, a hundred and fifty miles away and dormant.

"It's a meteorite!" she shouted.

"The girl's right," said the vet.

"Darn right, she's right," said Ron, claiming his daughter with his hands on her shoulders. "She's a genius!"

Emma glared up at her dad for a couple seconds before returning her gaze to the alleged space rock.

The police, firemen, and an EMT unit had arrived in short order. They worked their way through a crowd of curious onlookers huddled on the street near ground zero. Some of the more adventurous gawkers had filed inside to have a look before the cops cordoned off the area. Sergeant Morales from the TPD waded in and approached the rock. It had cooled considerably since entry but was still simmering. He registered only blank stares when he asked if anyone had been injured. He looked at the hole in the ceiling, the broken windows, then back at the ominous, forty-pound space invader. He looked incredulous. "Seriously? Nobody hurt?" he asked again and was met with silence.

A fireman clutching an extinguisher pushed his way in and asked the crowd to step back as he doused the hissing rock with retardant. Sergeant Morales questioned several people who had witnessed the rock attack. He recorded increasingly dramatic accounts, trending toward apocalyptic, until he arrived at Emma.

"She called it," said the vet. "That little genius girl knew it was a meteor right away."

"Is that right?" responded Morales, trying to conceal his amusement. He crouched to meet Emma's eyes. "So, it's a meteor, eh, little lady?"

"No," replied Emma. "It's a meteorite."

"I see. A small meteor, then."

"No." Emma struggled to hide her exasperation. "It's called a meteorite because it survives a fall through the atmosphere and strikes Earth. Meteors don't make it to Earth.

Sergeant Morales looked around. Acknowledging the onlookers, he nodded with approval while pointing at Emma. "Is this your little girl?" he asked the hovering Ron.

"Darn right. She's a genius," Ron said.

"So I've heard." Looking straight at Emma, Sergeant Morales said, "I guess we need to notify a meteorologist, then."

Emma stared at him in stunned silence until he finally broke into a smile. "That's a joke, little lady," he said.

"Oh. Good. I mean, that's funny," said Emma after too long of a pause. "Actually, you should call the Center for Meteorite Studies at ASU. Ask for Professor Wadhwa. She would be thrilled to help out."

"We'll do that," he said. He looked around again and noticed that the news crews had arrived. He spotted the glowing red lamp on the KPNX 12 camera aimed in his direction. Not one to shy away from a prime PR moment, he summoned a fireman over and asked to borrow a chisel and hammer dangling from his tool belt. He crouched down and asked Emma, "How'd you like to take home a chunk of meteorite?"

Emma's blue eyes popped. She smiled brightly, her head bouncing up and down. The onlookers swooned. They were in love with her.

Sergeant Morales briefly touched the rock and found it still damp with fire retardant but only warm to the touch. He located a small crevice with a lip protruding from it and placed the chisel at the narrowest point and struck it. Surprisingly, a thumb-sized piece fell away easily and bounced off the floor, where he recovered it. Still crouching, he gently turned Emma toward the camera and smiled broadly while handing her the fragment. "Should we give the meteorite a name?" he asked her.

"Well, meteorites are usually named after where they land," she said. Emma glanced at the remnants of a smooshed burger sticking out from under the rock. "Let's call it Big Mac," she announced, evoking immediate laughter and applause from the onlookers.

"Big Mac, it is," said Officer Morales. He then rose to full height and asked that all of those not there in an official capacity to please vacate the building.

Later that evening, Ron was bouncing off the walls of his living room as he recorded the eleven p.m. KPNX news feature in which his genius daughter was schooling the police sergeant about meteorites. "Nerd, huh?" he said aloud, contesting the moniker his bespectacled daughter had endured for years.

Emma was still awake, busy in her room studying the chunk of rock with a magnifying glass and drawing what she observed on a sketch pad. She finally felt the exhaustion settling in and looked for a place to shelf her space rock. Drawn to her terrarium, she opened it and dropped the rock between some spiderwort and golden club moss. Some worms, placed in the terrarium to aerate the soil, wriggled away from it and burrowed into the dirt. Still clothed, she plopped down on her bed and drifted off, dreaming of planets, stars, and asteroids until the morning light crept in through the window shades.

Chapter 3

Rocks of a Feather

It was late. Her postdocs had all gone home. With the stereo turned off, the monotonous hum of ventilators echoed through the vacant laboratory. The singular remaining sound was the faint tapping of Dr. Ashley Woodsum's fingers on a keyboard. She sat in her office adjoining the lab. Always the lone survivor, she stayed late enough to be familiar with the janitors on the graveyard shift. It was quiet and lonely, but she didn't mind. Her lab seemed more inviting than her lifeless apartment in North Central Pasadena. Ashley had landed at Caltech a few years ago when NASA's Jet Propulsion Laboratory recruited her to study extremophiles in hypothermal vents. At twenty-nine, she was already a champion in the field, having published landmark studies describing non-equilibrium electron gradients on the ocean floor. Those papers had sent her career skyrocketing and her phone ringing with multiple job offers.

Moving to the JPL, she had continued her work on Earth's most primordial organisms. But as of late, her interest in life on Earth was dimming. Having cracked open the vault guarding the secrets to life on her own planet, she now wanted to look for life elsewhere. This required thickening her skin to the baggage attached to her new field of study.

Exobiology sounded a bit kooky to some, especially the reverent, who were confident God had chosen Earth as life's sole dominion. An op-ed attack piece, penned by local evangelicals, hung from a tack on her office wall. And there was no shortage of playful ridicule. Some prankster had even plastered an Area 51 poster on her lab door. She left it there. She honestly—and to a fault—couldn't care less about what others thought.

These days, she told anyone who dared ask that she was an alien sent here to study earthlings.

A microbiologist by training, Ashley had wandered off into the galaxy looking for signs of life. But to study life on other worlds, she would need samples. Since it was difficult to reach other worlds, the samples had to be delivered. Not by UPS but by meteorites, some of which were thought to originate from other planets. At the JPL, she had worked on Black Beauty, a Martian meteorite found in the Sahara Desert. It was nearly as old as the solar system and contained far more water than any of the other two-hundred-odd Martian rocks discovered on Earth. Based on the elemental and molecular composition of the Martian stone, she had constructed simulated environments to see if they would yield life's basic building blocks. Demonstrating life on Mars would be monumental but hardly surprising to her. Life had evolved so rapidly following Earth's formation, she was confident it had occurred on other planets, as well.

Hoping for anything resembling nucleic acids, she stared at the spikes on the chromatogram rolling across the monitor. A shuffling near the doorway distracted her until she noticed Jay, the delivery guy from Shipping, dropping a package in her bin. "It's same-day, marked urgent, Dr. Ash," he announced. "I figured you would still be here, so I brought it up." Ashley returned her gaze to the monitor, sans any acknowledgement whatsoever of Jay.

"Geez, girl! Maybe a thanks or even a grunt in my direction would be appropriate. I ain't no robot."

Ashley looked up again and stared blankly at Jay. It was a curious look, as if he was an out-of-place object in her otherwise orderly world. "Okay, just leave it there," she said, again returning to her chromatogram.

It was wasted on her, but Jay kept frowning her way all the same. He was a tall, lanky African American man in his early twenties. In the summer, he worked in the Shipping Department at the JPL to offset his tuition at the Occidental College. He'd been up to Ashley's lab on countless occasions and was well aware of her distant persona. Nevertheless, he liked her, maybe more out of sympathy than anything else. He was gregarious and well-liked among his co-workers, fellow students, and parishioners at his church. His natural charisma he considered a gift, and he felt a calling to educate Ashley in the ways of proper human interaction. So far, it was like teaching a cat to swim.

Appearance-wise, Ashley had nothing to hide, although she did her best to do so. Dressed in flat-fronted gray slacks and a pale navy cotton shirt, she looked like a cadet. Rarely bothering with makeup, she cut her platinum-blond hair herself, and it showed. But Jay could see through it, and so could everyone else. She was attractive. She had an engaging, bright smile, although she typically reserved it for admiring good data. At five-nine, she was slim but still had all the curves. Her milky, unblemished complexion, full lips, delicate chin, and large silvery eyes did not go unnoticed, although any such admirers were typically rebuffed.

Most had given up on her. She even struggled with casual friendships, but Jay was undeterred. He thought it wasn't too late for her to join the human race, she just needed some pointers. He approached her desk and stood motionless at her side for at least a full minute. Still glued to her monitor, with Jay in her peripheral vision, she finally asked, "Are we going to do this again, Jay?"

"Hello, Ashley. How are you today?"

"Fine."

"Try, 'I'm fine, thank you.' I realize it's too many words, but it's just one of those things, you know."

"I'm fine. Thank you."

"Super! Now, you ask me a question. What is it?"

"Why are you still standing here?"

"Come on, Dr. Ash. You don't have to feel it, but you could at least act it. In fact, most people don't feel fine but still say it out of politeness. It's an okay lie, you know, like we talked about before."

This time she turned toward him but not fully, her eyes still askance at the monitor. "How are you today, Jay?" she said flatly.

"I'm fine, thanks for asking."

"No, you're not. You're worried about money for tuition next fall, your girlfriend might have another boyfriend, and your piece-of-shit car broke down again. All your words. So how can you be fine?"

"Damn." Jay just hung his head for a moment before looking up again. "I'm still fine because of the people in my life. The people I love and who love me back."

"I'm autistic, Jay. Always have been. I was autistic before it was fashionable."

"So what? So's Bill Gates. He has friends. He's got cool friends. He hangs out with Bono. He cares about people, too. All those poor folks he helps out with his Gates Foundation. And you're not autistic, anyway. You said you were on the spectrum. I looked that shit up. Says you are socially awkward—no duh—and have restricted interests."

"Look," she deadpanned while pointing to the monitor, "this peak indicates the possible formation of nucleic acids." She turned away to conceal a hint of a smile.

"Oh, you're pranking me, right? You're such a whack job, I can't even tell, anymore."

"I'm not a robot, either, Jay. I have a sense of humor. I just don't see the point in idle chitchat or that nonsensical blabber that people pass off as conversation."

"That nonsensical blabber is how people reveal things about themselves, or about you, the things that make us human."

Ashley sat soundless in a brief reverie, looking neither at Jay nor her monitor.

"Yeah, you're thinking about that, huh? Maybe we just had a breakthrough. Now let's work on how to say a proper goodbye." Jay turned deliberately toward the door, hesitated, and then looked back to Ashley. "I've got to go now. See you later, Dr. Ash. Have a nice evening."

"Bye," she barked, her eyes glued to the monitor.

Jay stopped dead and hung his head again. Then he looked up and spotted the sly curl of her lips.

"Is that how you laugh? Is that laughing?" he probed. "At me, huh? That's okay, though. You made a joke. That's a good start."

"Have a pleasant evening, Jay," she said. Then, with barely enough breath to be audible, "And thanks."

"Whoa! What's that?" responded Jay, with a mixture of mock and genuine surprise. "Human race, I would like you to meet our newest member, Dr. Ashley Woodsum!"

He dared not jeopardize the magic moment with another word, so he hustled out of the lab in silence.

Ashley watched her monitor until he was out of sight and then ambled over to her shipping bin to collect her package. She deciphered the handwritten scribble on the return label. It was from Dr. Jack Whinston, Geological Sciences Department at Stanford University. Jack had told her little about the samples he had excavated in Greenland but assured her she would be delighted with the contents of the package. Equally scant information accompanied the material. Inside the box she found a note bearing a single inscription that read, *by Ar-K, over 3900 Ma.* Apparently, Jack had performed argon-potassium radio dating on the rock and had determined its age at nearly four billion years.

Having worked on rocks of comparable vintage, Ashley was unmoved by their age until she removed the dolomite and saw the rippling waves decorating its smooth face. Shocked, she nearly dropped the sample. On the smooth face of the rock, the stacked, alternating layers of dark and light sediment snaked up and down like little waves. "No way," she said aloud, "can't be."

Then she noticed what looked like a string of beads running horizontally under the base of the waves. Its position seemed purposeful. Each bead sat directly under the crest of a wave whose trough reached down to the intervening string. She pulled out the small jeweler's loupe she kept in her pocket. Each of the beads was actually comprised of embedded, concentric circles, like the cross section of an onion. "What the hell?" she whispered. She immediately called Jack at Stanford but realized her folly when she checked the time. It was well after ten. Jack had a family and was probably home, possibly even in bed by now. She left a pointed message at the tone. "I want answers. Call me."

She dashed back to her forgotten chromatogram and looked at the tracing. She scribbled a quick description in her notebook—*polyaromatics, no nucleic acids.* Normally, she would have been disappointed by another negative result, but the failure barely registered above the fireworks set off by Jack's surprise. Still holding the rock in her left hand, she studied it again. Something glistened in the center of one of the onion beads. "Condensation?" she wondered. But the lab was climate-controlled and maintained very dry. She picked up a rubber spatula and scraped at the moisture on the bead. More seeped out behind it. She wiped the spatula on a slide and examined it under low magnification on her optical microscope.

It looked like oil, dark and translucent, until she dialed up the magnification and spotted the tiny grains. About a micron in length, they were several times larger than even the largest of known viruses but smaller than the most primitive of cells. Ashley moved the stage around and found a small clump of structures that looked more rounded and larger than the little hexagons. One more shift, and she found still larger forms, several microns in length, elongated and connected end to end like a string of sausages.

She wondered if they were bacteria, or possibly archaea, since they were hard to distinguish visually. "Come on, Jack," she said aloud. She backed away from the scope and smirked. "This is a joke, right?" Live bacteria in a four-billion-year-old rock? Even the alleged fossils couldn't survive that. She knew Jack, but perhaps not well enough. She sat for a minute, unsettled by her potential role as a patsy in a game. "Okay, Whinston, two can play at this." She took one more swipe at the bead with the spatula and smeared it over some agar media plated on a culture dish. She placed the dish in a thirty-degree incubator alongside some E. coli she had transfected earlier. Only the hum of ventilators bid her good night as she turned out the lights and made her way to the elevators.

It was late, and she knew her fridge was empty, so she drove down to the Kings Row Gastropub in Old Town Pasadena, where she could pick up a decent Cobb salad. Awaiting her takeout, she sat at the end of the bar, staring at a television to avoid the gaze of normal humans enjoying themselves. On TV, she watched a little red-haired girl with thick, black-rimmed glasses standing next to a crouching cop. He was pointing at a rock sitting on a floor surrounded by debris. A banner below the image read, *Big Mac meteorite slams into McDonald's restaurant in Tempe, Arizona*. Although thousands of meteorites struck Earth every year, Ashley was impressed by the size of this one. The camera briefly zoomed in on the rock. Without realizing it, she was off her stool and around the bar, her face parked a couple feet from the television. "What the fuck?" she said.

"Exactly," repeated the approaching bartender. "Took the words right out of my mouth. You can't come behind the bar, miss. I'm sorry. Employees only."

Unmoved and transfixed on the TV, she demanded, "Turn it up!"

"Okay," he said, and then screamed, "You can't come behind the bar!" This got some attention, from her and everyone else in the bar.

Finally aware of her position, and that of the irate bartender at her side, she muttered, "Oh, oops." She looked at him for only a second before returning her gaze to the television as she retreated to her stool. The red-haired girl on TV said something that made everyone around her laugh and clap. Then the news anchor returned, smiling broadly as he introduced Oscar the weatherman.

Ashley questioned her faculties. It was late, and she was exhausted. But crazy? She would be the first to acknowledge her mental issues, and even wore them as a badge, at times. But hallucinations? Never. She had no patience for things unreal. It was a grainy closeup on a TV, shown only for a moment, but she'd seen what she'd seen on Big Mac. There, near the bottom of that stone, she saw the little waves. She saw the little string of beads below them.

Oscar the weatherman prattled on about a high-pressure system. He was pointing at the colorful map behind him when someone said, "Your salad, miss."

From a smiling waiter at her side, Ashley accepted the bag, expressionless and silent. Foregoing any acknowledgment of him whatsoever, she turned toward the exit to leave. After a few steps, she hesitated before turning back toward the perplexed waiter still glaring after her. "Thank you," she said quietly, "and have a pleasant evening."

CHAPTER 4

THE SUITS

Alex Sina sat alone in his office at the Henry Hinds Laboratory for Geophysical Sciences. He looked out his window at the Searle Chemistry Building across the street. He would have to go outside into the searing heat of a Chicago July afternoon to get over there. He cut though the lab. "We need to install an enclosed walkway connecting us to the Searle," he grumbled absently.

A graduate student hunched over a bench looked up, her memory jarred. "There were a couple guys looking for you earlier. They started nosing around, so I asked them to leave until you came in. I told them you usually don't come in until after ten."

"It's still before ten. The second one, at least. What did they look like?"

"I don't know, just plain-looking guys. They even looked alike. Maybe six-foot, gray suits. Probably in their fifties."

"Hmmm. Probably not the cops. I already paid them. Did they say when they would come back?"

"Yes. I told them... Wait, there they go right there."

Alex followed her gaze into the hallway. Sure enough, there they were. He couldn't believe his eyes. The two men entered the lab, breezed past the centrifuges, and headed straight toward him. At least he was pretty sure it was them, the dauntless duo from the GINR. They wore the same suits and ties, and although their faces had lost some color and gained some wrinkles, it was unmistakably them. It had to be.

"Dr. Sina, I am Noah Sorrenson and this is Emil Pedersen. We are—"

"Yeah, I know who you are," Alex interrupted. "We met only a few days ago. You left a lasting impression. Not like the one I left on Buzz's face, but you are hard to forget." He studied them both, trading glances with Noah and then Emil. They looked older. Their dark hair had grayed and thinned. Their pink skin had gone pallid. Once stick-like in posture, they were angled slightly at the waist. Despite the air conditioning, both were respiring heavily. "Are you guys okay?" asked Alex. "You look ill. Rough flight, maybe? You *are* Emil and Noah?"

"The flight was fine, Dr. Sina. Perhaps it's the light, but it is indeed us. We need a word with you. Please."

Still puzzled, Alex nodded cautiously and tipped his head toward his office. He walked backward the entire distance, still taking them in from head to toe. The three of them settled into chairs around a small round table.

Noah spoke first. "We know some rocks were excavated from an off-limits area in the Isua, and we are certain that you and Dr. Whinston took those samples. We are not here to prosecute either you or Dr. Whinston, but we do need the rocks returned. It's a matter of national interest."

"Yours or mine?" Alex asked.

"Both," replied Emil.

"Actually, all," added Noah.

"What?" said Alex, laughing at their gravity over some chiseled rocks. "So, the world ends if you don't find your rocks?"

"Not immediately," said Noah.

"Okay, you guys are officially creeping me out now. Some part of me wants to call security, but then I won't learn how the world ends. Decisions, decisions. All right, I give. Tell me, how will humanity perish if you don't find the rocks? Fire? Flood? Thanos? Damn it! It *is* Thanos, isn't it? If he hadn't gotten all cozy with Mistress Death, we would have been just fine. There's always a woman in there somewhere, huh, guys?"

The two men looked at each other, both baffled by what neither understood to be playful banter. Noah looked down and rubbed the back of his hand with his thumb. A dried patch of dead skin rolled up and drifted to the floor. "There isn't much time, Dr. Sina. Please."

"You're right," said Alex. "My grant application is due by the end of this week. If I don't submit it on time, Amy, over there at the lab bench, won't get her stipend check. Without that, she won't be able to afford beer, or anything else, in that order. Now, if you don't give me at least one plausible explanation for why you so desperately need your precious stones returned, I'll have to ask you to leave. Go ahead now. Let's hear it. Maybe you could just go nuts and tell me the truth. I'm all ears."

Noah and Emil looked exhausted, leaning heavily on the table with their elbows, heads bobbing, eyelids wavering. They turned away from Alex and held a brief conference in whispers before breaking apart to face him again.

Noah spoke first. "The rocks contain the Siru for Dagon. If he assembles and meets Shala now, all of the Zumru and Bar from Ross will come, but they will all die. It is too soon. The time is not yet right. They cannot survive here. Shala's Siru has fallen. But it will not direct her assembly unless Dagon's Siru is exposed first. We believe it was exposed when you excavated the rock. Dagon and Shala should not meet. We need the rocks to prevent that."

Alex looked back and forth at the two men. They were dead serious. He pushed back his thick black locks with his fingers and tried to make sense of it. A long pause ensued. It reminded him of poker. Did he want to see their cards, or should he fold and call security? He finally broke into a smile. "Are you guys Scientologists? If you are, I don't need any cleansing today. Okay? I like my engrams. We're drinking buddies. Seriously, don't waste your time on me. Go audit somebody else."

"I don't understand," said Noah.

"*You* don't understand?" said Alex. "Did you hear what you just said to me? That Shala-dragon-Zoro nonsense? Bar was the only word I understood. Look, if we took some rocks, and I'm saying *if*, I don't have them, okay?"

"We know," said Emil.

"How do you know? I mean, that's another thing right there. It's not like they're radioactive, or at least not enough to be detected easily. How do you know they're not in my desk drawer right here? Do you have X-ray vision? I thought you needed special glasses for that? And don't get any ideas. You know those X-ray specs are fake, right? You can't actually see the bones in your hand as advertised. Although that's not why people bought them. I wish they worked. Never mind that. Look, I would like to help you guys, but I don't know where your rocks are. Jack left Greenland ahead of me. You saw him before he left, and he didn't have any rocks. You told me that. Remember? Then, that fucker lied and told you I had them. Which I did not. And, again, you confirmed that. So, that leaves one question. Why are you here?"

"We already visited Jack at Stanford. The rocks were once there, in his laboratory, but not anymore. We found fragments remaining from his analysis. He then admitted to taking them. He said he had sent off what remained of the samples to you. That is why we are here."

Alex's wry smile should have said it all, but it only drew blank stares. "Are you familiar with the concept of lying?" Alex asked. "You should be by now, because Jack is a tenured professor in the department of lying. And you're flunking his master class. He had already lied to you once, and you knew that. Here's what I find truly stunning. He not only lied to you again, but he used the exact same lie, and you fell for it. Again! Hey, you know what, guys? I just remembered where the rocks are." Sparked with anticipation, the duo leaned forward. "I sent them to Jack."

"But we were just there," said Emil, "and the rocks were not. When did you send them?"

"You have got to be kidding me!" cried Alex. "Who are you guys? Really! What the hell is going on here?"

Noah looked sad and confused. "So, you didn't send the rocks back to Jack?"

"No! I didn't. I am lying. Look it up. You'll find a picture of Jack in the definition."

"Jack is a definition?" asked Emil.

"Oh, my god! I feel like I'm talking to a couple of three-year-olds."

"I am at least six," said Noah proudly. "My oldest habitants are more than six."

Alex studied him, a grimace spread across his face. "You're six years old now? This has gone far enough. In fact, way too far."

"Not six of your years," said Emil. He touched his fingertips briefly while his lips moved. "More than eight billion of your years." He hesitated, frowned a bit, and then smiled. "But then there were no years here. There was no star yet."

Alex was standing now. He took a few steps toward the door and opened it, his palm extended toward the exit. "Why don't we continue our game of interstellar Dungeons and Dragons later, guys? Like I said, I have a deadline to meet. Please. Out!"

Both men looked dismayed by Alex's sudden change in demeanor. They rose and shuffled out into the lab, taking turns looking back at Alex. Noah stalled briefly behind Amy and looked over her shoulder onto her bench top. She was marking the peaks on a mass spectrogram spread out across her bench.

Noah said, "The delta-13-C and delta-15-N values are not in agreement." He leaned in and pointed to a pair of small bumps just registering above baseline on the chart. "There is some strontium here," he said. "It should prove more reliable than the carbon or nitrogen isotopes."

Amy only stared at the back of his head as he and Emil continued past the centrifuges and out into the hallway. She jumped at the sound of Alex's voice, who was standing directly behind her. "What did he say?" he asked.

"He said I should use the strontium signal and pointed to these." She poked at the pair of tiny peaks with her pencil.

"What? That's… I thought those were noise. Have you done a spike-in with a strontium reference?"

"Not in a while. You told me not to bother for these samples. I have an old one, though." She thumbed back through her notebook and stopped on a page containing a screenshot of a spectrogram labelled 86-Sr/87-Sr.

Alex looked at it briefly and mumbled something under his breath. "Do a spike-in on the new ones," he said. "Can I borrow your phone, Amy? I need to call Jack Whinston, and he won't answer if he knows it's me." Amy smiled dubiously and handed her phone to Alex.

He walked back to his office, closed the door, and dialed up Jack. He must have caught him unawares as Jack picked up on the first ring. "Jack Whinston, Geology."

"Oh, really? I thought your new name was lying sack of shit," responded Alex. "Don't hang up, Jack, or I'll come there and personally cram some jagged igneous rocks up your volcano hole. I want some answers."

"Alex, I was hoping you would call."

"Yeah? From where? A jail in Nuuk? What's up with these suits from the GINR, Jack? Why are they acting like their fucking rocks have the Ten Commandments written on them? These guys are nuts. They were just here, blabbering on about some cosmic crap and the end of the world and how they need the stones to prevent it."

"Okay, first the lying. I'm sorry, but you left me little choice. Remember, it was you and your smart-ass mouth that brought the authorities on us in the first place. I had to lie. I needed a diversion so I could leave with the rocks. I think they contain the oldest fossils ever found, by a long shot, Alex. I dated the surrounding material. They're almost four billion years old."

"How did you get them out of Greenland? The GINR said you didn't have them."

"I didn't when they asked. The samples were already at the airport. I left them there while you were out waiting for the shuttle. I actually did use the restroom, so it wasn't a complete lie. I know someone who flies a cargo service out of Nuuk to Copenhagen. He's an amateur rock hound, so he likes me. We talk. Anyway, he put them on his plane, and I went back later and flew out with him. No big deal. It worked. Right?"

"What worked? They're here now, and I get the impression they're not leaving. I don't know what their next move is, but I'm sure they have one."

"Don't tell them anything for the time being. But if you do, they'll believe you. They're kind of dumb like that."

"Not that dumb. They took a five-second glance at one of my spectrograms and schooled me on my own work. I'd totally missed it. These guys aren't normal, Jack. Not even close. You should have heard them. They're like Jehovah's Witnesses from Alpha Centauri or something. They're kooks."

"What did they say?"

"I don't know. I didn't really get it all. Something about a dragon and a girl named Shala and a bar. They want the rocks to prevent a meeting of some sort. Who cares? They're insane. I just want them out of my hair." There was no response for some time. "Jack, are you still there?"

"Yes. That does sound pretty weird. Are you sure it was a dragon?"

"What? Are you serious? It might as well have been a kraken. What's the difference? These guys are whack jobs. But somehow, it seems like they know if the stones are nearby. They knew I didn't have them without even looking. They knew you used to have them because they found some fragments. Right? Which brings me to my last question. Where are they now? And if you lie to me again, I've got an igneous arrowhead with your ass's name on it."

"Well, this is precisely why I needed to speak to you. I sent them to Ashley Woodsum at the JPL. I was hoping you would collaborate with her by running the stable isotope analysis on the fossilized material."

"Woodsum? Space Lady? She's an astrobiologist. She thinks ET is going to fly in on the next meteorite. Jesus, Jack. This just gets weirder and weirder. Why her?"

"Well, she's actually a microbiologist. One who looks at ancient life. If there was ever any archaebacteria alive in those stones, she can help us look for it. You should pay her a visit. She's kind of autistic, you know. You two might hit it off."

"What? I'm not autistic. I love people. I embrace them. Sometimes in a choke hold, but that's their fault. She's at the JPL now? She must have left Penn State. Four billion years old? Really?"

"Really. If you want to be on TV again, this is your chance."

"Maybe I'll give her a call."

CHAPTER 5

EMMA'S ANIMAL

"Let's go, Emma! Twenty minutes and counting, and the 101 is already backed up." Amelia Curtis pounded on her daughter's bedroom door again. "Does this have to happen every morning? This is exactly why they want the students to stay on campus. They did us a favor, Emma. Don't let them down. Dad will feed your hamster and let the dog out after he gets up."

Despite their best intentions, every morning turned into a fire drill. The sense of alarm would escalate until Emma finally smelled the smoke and hopped to it. But this morning was different. Her mother's flames were licking at her door, but she wasn't budging. Emma's books, notes, pens, protractors, and the like remained scattered across her desktop. Her backpack, unloaded, sat crumpled on the floor. She could hear her mom. She felt the heat, but the beckoning seemed distant and hollow, its gravity no match for the attraction in her terrarium. Emma sat transfixed, unblinking, mouth slightly ajar. She had picked up a pencil to draw but was too stunned to drag it across the paper.

A glistening black and red worm-like creature was slinking over the soil between the spiderwort and her chunk of meteorite. It was long, slender, and shiny like the earthworms she had added to aerate the soil. But that's where the resemblance ended. Two small buds, protruding from each side of its body, moved independently, pushing away dirt as it wiggled past the club moss. Emma knew worms didn't have legs. She knew worms didn't have eyes, either. But there they were, little black beads, darting around, mounted on opposite sides of a V-shaped snout. "A salamander?" Emma wondered. They frequented her neighborhood, but she kept a lid on the terrarium, and screens on her windows. She ruled out salamander. Through her magnifying glass, she saw a distinct, bushy patch of bright copper-colored hair decorating the creature's backside. With her own locks dangling into the open terrarium, she couldn't help but notice the similarity in hue.

Her mother thundered again, loud enough to scare Emma's slumbering dog. Zephyr leapt from the bed and barked rabidly at the bedroom door. "I'm leaving!" she heard her mother shout. The front door slammed. Emma secured the terrarium, crammed her materials into the backpack, and bolted out of her room. Her mother, steaming, was already behind the wheel when she piled into the idling vehicle. Oblivious to her mom's ear-scalding tirade, Emma stared straight ahead. Her furious mom finally paused to take note of Emma's stupor. "Are you okay, Em? I don't want to yell at you, but it drives me crazy. We have all the time in the world, but we still leave late. What was it this morning? A missing book? Couldn't find your glasses?"

Barely audible, Emma murmured, "The world's smallest mammal."

"The world's smallest mammal?" her mother repeated. "Well, I can't wait to see it."

She dropped Emma at the ASU Science Center with barely a minute to spare. "New record," she said. She kissed her daughter goodbye and sped off to work.

———

Home alone, Ron Curtis awoke and started grinding through his morning routine. The purring of his air-pulse generator echoed throughout the empty house. He shut off the machine, removed the inflatable vest, and huffed up as much phlegm as he could. He stood up only to find that he needed to sit. There he gathered what breath he needed for a walk to the kitchen. "Above average." He repeated it like a mantra. That's how his doctor described his chances of besting the average life expectancy for a cystic fibrosis patient. He didn't feel above average. He felt like he was slowly drowning. He wheezed, hocked up another lung bomb, and rose to his feet.

Zephyr practically attacked him as he shuffled into the kitchen. "Nobody let you out yet, huh?" The anxious beagle was frantic. She ran a few tight circles before rising up on her hind legs and slapping her front paws on Ron's knees. She dropped, wheeled around, and ran a few more laps. "Take it easy, Z," said Ron, "I'm on it." He hobbled over to the back door and sprung it open. He expected the canine to bolt over the threshold, but Zephyr just stared at him, her stubby tail vibrating like a strip of tempered metal. "Come on, girl, I don't have all day," he pleaded.

Zephyr ran from the kitchen into the hallway, rounded back to the kitchen and down the hallway again. Ron let the back door slam and trudged after the animated beagle. He followed the sound of barking to Emma's room, where Zephyr was sounding off at the terrarium from every possible angle. "What's up, Z? Someone drop a Milk-Bone in there?" Ron padded toward the terrarium but stopped a few feet short and reared up. "What the hell?"

He leaned over the box and peered through the glass lid at the little orange fuzz ball balancing on its haunches. It was munching on the shoot of an uprooted spiderwort. It sucked in the last purple blossom and returned to digging. It pulled up a wriggling earthworm and devoured it whole. The terrarium was a wreck. A few mangled roots scattered about the soil were all that remained of any plant life. By the looks of it, the miniature orange Godzilla was about to become the last living thing in the box. "Uh-oh. The hamster," groused Ron. "Who let him out, Zeph?"

Hardly fond of Emma's pet, Ron tolerated the varmint because his precious daughter had wanted one. She had even picked a bright orange Syrian hamster to match the color of her hair. Ron went to the kitchen, donned an oven glove, and returned to deal with the errant rodent. He removed the lid and studied the furry animal. It studied him right back. He picked it up without incident and transferred the chunky little beast to the hamster cage. "There you go, work it off." He placed it on the exercise wheel. The animal stared at him without pause, only looking away to take in Zephyr when she barked. "Let's go, Z. You can't stay in here." Zephyr was still barking at the hamster cage when Ron shooed her out. As the bedroom door was closing, he could hear the rattle of the exercise wheel followed by some frenzied clanging and squealing. Ron smirked. "Incarceration is tough after a taste of freedom. Eh, Zeph? Let that be a lesson to you, girl."

Emma was anxious. That evening, she insisted her mom take her straight home from ASU. Along the way, she finished up a sketch of the hairy salamander she had drawn from memory at lunch. She readied the door handle and seat buckle as they rolled into the driveway. Two clicks later, she leapt from the car and stormed straight to her bedroom with nary a *hi, Dad* as she blasted by him in the living room. Ron was struggling to stand when he heard Emma's cry echoing down the hall. Angry at himself for not intercepting her, he made his way to her room to explain the wreckage.

Emma stood over the terrarium, lid off, hands sifting through the soil. She picked up the meteorite and dug underneath it. "Honey, I'm sorry," she heard Ron say. "There was nothing I could do. The hamster got loose and had his way with your plants. He even ate the worms. I put him back in his cage as soon as I found him, sweetie."

Emma wasn't sure how to respond to that. She ruminated, busying herself with the ruins of her terrarium. Should she tell her dad about the hairy salamander that had appeared out of nowhere? Would he believe her? And how did her hamster get into a closed terrarium? It opened it, climbed in, closed the lid, and ate the salamander along with everything else? The inexplicable did not sit well with Emma. Math and science gave her answers. If not answers, at least possibilities. Here, she had none. She could barely find the dots, let alone connect them. She couldn't blame her father. Ron looked so contrite, his hands clasped in front of him, frowning at the rubble behind the glass.

"What a crazy week," Emma finally said. "First a meteorite, then a hamster attack." Ron returned a sheepish nod. "It's okay, Dad. It wasn't your fault. I must have left the hamster cage open, and it snuck in somehow when I had the lid off." None of that was even remotely possible. She was very careful with the hamster, and even in its prime, it could not scale the sheer wall of the glass terrarium.

She had forgotten the rock was still in her hand when she felt a dampness in her palm. Turning it over, she noticed a small bead of moisture leaking from the center of it. *A meteorite that leaks?* she wondered. Water molecules could be trapped in the mineral lattice of a meteorite, but not liquid, running water. She threw that observation onto the growing stack of oddities. Offering his condolences, Ron insisted he would help her start a new terrarium. He left Emma to grieve, quietly pulling the door shut behind him.

The instant the door latch clicked, Emma dashed to the hamster cage. She started to unlatch the door when a large mound of bedding shifted and two button-sized eyes and a wet black snout poked out from under the shavings. Startled, Emma leapt back but kept her eyes on the plump animal that emerged, shaking off loose bedding. It was about the size of a small guinea pig, but with shorter hair, a narrower body, much longer legs, and huge floppy ears. Its head was orange with a stripe of white that ran between the eyes and expanded around its mouth and nose. The markings strongly resembled Zephyr's. It shook itself again, wagged a nub of a tail, and let out a pitched yap that brought both of Emma's hands to her mouth.

The little creature danced around excitedly in the confines of the habitat. It capsized the empty food bowl, sending up a plume of wood shavings. Emma noted a chocolate-colored stain covering some of the displaced bedding. On closer inspection, a number of delicate, chalk-white sticks lay mixed in the discolored material. They were clearly bone fragments, some with small tufts of orange hair pasted to them. In the corner of the terrarium, a smooth white dome with telltale suture lines lay partially exposed. Horrified, Emma backed away. The bizarre carnivore sat up on its haunches and yapped again, its eyes fixed on Emma's, calling to her.

Both hands now on top of her head, eyes agog, mouth open, she stared in disbelief at the beckoning creature. It executed a pointing maneuver with its head, reminiscent of Zephyr's trademark food-begging move. It shifted sideways and pushed the inverted food bowl upright again. It looked at Emma and ratted its stubby tail. She approached once again. The animal shifted to the far side of the cage and placed a paw on the spout of the emptied water bottle. Looking at Emma, it pushed down on the spout and the bottle rattled against the side of the cage.

She wanted to cry for her dead hamster. She wanted to scream at the freakish salamander-hamster-dog thing. She wanted to run to her mom and bury her spinning head in her bosom. She felt like doing all of those things, but then what would become of the most curious creature she had ever encountered in her young life? *Would someone take it away?* she wondered. *Would they dissect or destroy it?* Whatever it was, it was hers, and she felt an odd sense of responsibility for it. It was still a living thing, after all. That it had eaten the hamster was horrifying, but she was well aware that animals ate each other all the time in nature. *Maybe just keep it a secret for a little while*, she thought.

Emma approached the cage again and dropped to her knees, her face within inches of the wire. The creature settled onto all fours, wagging away, mouth open, its pink tongue bouncing with each pant. It resembled a dog more than anything else, but its dagger-like front teeth, beady eyes, and grasping paws were distinctly hamster. Some hairless, shiny black skin on its belly was all that remained of any salamander features. It turned sideways, picked up the food bowl with its mouth, and dropped it in front of Emma. She grabbed the bag of hamster chow and pushed a few pellets through the cage slats. They were eaten immediately. The creature pointed at the bag on the floor, its nose forward, tail extended, and ears down. Emma dropped some pellets though the top of the cage. The ravenous carnivore lunged upward, artfully snagging them in midair.

She tried some dog food next, but it wouldn't fit through the narrow cage slats. She put some on a piece of paper and folded it over to push it through the cage door if opened just a crack. Donning the oven glove left by her father, she clumsily pinched the folded paper with her thumb and forefinger. With her free hand, she slowly pulled back the door latch as she readied the food. The creature sat quietly, listening, studying the door latch as Emma grasped it. Cued by the click of the latch, it hurled itself at the door just as Emma opened it. She gasped. As she recoiled onto her back, the uncaged beast landed on the floor by her side. She pushed her gloved hand forward as the animal attacked, scrambling up her torso, mouth open, tongue wagging wildly. Emma sucked in the breath for a scream when the animal placed its front paws on her chin and commenced licking her nose and cheeks. It tickled. It wasn't eating her.

Its tail wagging madly, the animal bounded around on Emma's lap. The little yapping noises sounded like pure joy. It scrambled forward to resume its licking. She petted its head and it rolled over, exposing its belly to invite more petting. *That's just what Zephyr does*, thought Emma. *It even looks like a miniature Zephyr.* Then she considered whether the two would get along. The creature seemed so friendly and happy. But it had eaten a hamster. *Would he try to eat Zephyr?* she wondered. *Would Zephyr try to eat it?* Maybe it was a good time to find out.

She snuck the creature out the back door and over to Zephyr's kennel. Excited, Zephyr was clearly aware of the animal before Emma revealed it. She looked eager, as though a treat was in store. Emma presented the animal outside the kennel at first. Zephyr jumped for joy as the two animals chirped away at each other. She opened the kennel door a crack and the creature wiggled from her grasp and darted straight in.

Zephyr backed away at first, until the overzealous critter stopped advancing. Posturing for Zephyr to play, it crouched down and shook its little head from side to side. The two animals looked like one as they rolled around, locked together. They broke apart, took turns lunging at each other, then rolled some more. Emma stood in wonder, giggling at their raucous play. It was love at first sight, she concluded. One would not eat the other, and there was plenty of food for two. Zephyr only ate if she was hungry, so they conveniently kept a month's supply in her kennel. Satisfied with their fast friendship, Emma returned to her room to clean up, leaving the two chums to exhaust each other.

Sitting on the edge of her bed, Emma quietly contemplated the day's events. Some part of her grasped the impossibility of what she had experienced. She was thirteen, well over Santa Claus and the Tooth Fairy and any other fantastical pranks adults enjoyed playing on kids. But her youthful sense of what was possible was still broader than that of an adult. Maybe strange stuff like this happened to other people, too, she considered. She just hadn't been made aware of it yet. She lay back on her bed, imagining all likes of beasts with mismatched anatomies and magical abilities. She imagined a horse with wings. She rode it into outer space, racing the meteors.

CHAPTER 6

ASHLEY'S ANIMAL

Ashley Woodsum felt some compensation for her insomnia. If a prime parking spot was a worm, she was the early bird. It was dark when she had left the JPL last night, and the sky was only beginning to lighten when she swiped her card key at the entrance to building 183. Her lab was dark and still but her mind ablaze with images of the meteorite she had seen on TV at the gastropub. She opened her computer on a lab bench and located the grainy images of Big Mac captured by the KPNX news crew. She took screenshots and blew up an image containing the beady, circular etchings near the base of the rock. It was not the best resolution but enough to make her gut rattle. The onion-like layers embedded in the circles looked very familiar. She rolled Jack's meteorite over in her hand and studied the circles on its flat face. She held it up, comparing it to the image on the monitor. She hadn't imagined it. They were there—the circles within circles. Even the thin lines connecting adjacent circles were present on both rocks.

She reconsidered the notion of a prank, but Jack had sent the rock well before the news of Big Mac had broken on TV. He couldn't have been aware of the circular etchings on the meteorite. Her mind wandered until it slammed into the rectangular black cabinet at the end of the bench. "The incubator!" she blurted aloud. Dashing across the lab, she retrieved the culture dish she had placed in it the night before. She held it up to the light. A lawn of opaque white plaques was spread across the entire dish.

"No way," she mumbled. She had only streaked a few lines of the goo seeping from Jack's rock, yet the plaques were everywhere. *How?* she wondered. Plaques were expected when a replicating virus infected bacteria cells. The accumulating viral particles would burst the bacterial cells, leaving behind small clumps of cellular debris, or plaques. And there were lots of them. But there weren't many bacterial cells in the goo to begin with, and she certainly hadn't inoculated them with any virus. A contaminating virus could have infected the scant supply of bacteria, but there were so few of them. Even if that were the case, the plaques should only appear where she had streaked the plate, not over the entire dish.

She plopped the dish on the stage of an inverted microscope, dialed in the 20x objective, and leaned in to look. Her head practically bounced off the eyepiece at first glance. She found herself standing, her eyes blinking at the scope, numb to the sound of a toppled chair now resting on its back behind her. Her mind reeled, but the instrument summoned. The eyepiece called. It drew her forward, sucking at her eyes. She peeked and pulled away again. Finally, steadying herself, she righted the chair and sat, immersing herself in the implausible nanoverse.

They really were moving. Whatever they were. *Worms?* she wondered. Nearly a millimeter in length, the squiggly, transparent, presumed nematodes were busy chewing their way through the agar medium in the culture dish. She recalled Janet Harley, the geneticist down the hall, who had occasionally used C. elegans, a nematode popular with the genetics jocks. Sometimes Janet would share Ashley's incubator space when hers was full. That might explain the worms. Except Janet had moved her lab to UCLA months ago. Ashley rotated the dish, observing mounds of debris that strongly resembled mammalian cells decimated by a virus. She dialed up the magnification and slid the dish around some more, stopping on a sizable clump of cells suspended in the agar. The individual cells were large and nucleated, and they were organized spherically, with a hollow center. She found a still larger clump, containing over a hundred cells, that was taking on an extended tubular shape.

If this was a trick, she desperately wanted to know how it was done. Hands shaking, she mounted the camera and snapped a few images of some of the magnified structures. She attached some frames to an email addressed to Janet Harley, including only a subject line, *Your Worms?*

Janet called within minutes. She knew Ashley well enough to skip over the small talk and launched into an excited diatribe. "Worms don't do that," were Janet's first words. "I am unaware of any nematode that develops like that," she continued. "The spheres look like blastocysts. Mammals do that, not worms. There's even a trophoblast layer of cells on the outside. That trophoblast becomes the placenta. Again, worms don't grow placentas. The cells look mammalian. They shouldn't even grow on your plates. Animal cells need complex media and serum and thirty-seven degrees, not thirty, like your incubators. And the worms? They're not mine. They're definitely not C. elegans or any kind of worm, for that matter. There are limb buds on some of them. Worms don't grow legs, Ashley. Where did these cells come from?"

"I don't know."

"You don't know? They just appeared? Like spontaneous generation? You are aware that maggots don't arise spontaneously from rotting meat. Pasteur and Tyndall solved that one about a hundred and fifty years ago."

"Stop it, Janet. I mean I'm not sure. I streaked a swipe I took off a rock that a geologist sent to me. I thought it was a prank. He said he had dated the rock to four billion years. It looked fossilized, so he sent it to me to check out."

"Is he cute?"

"What?"

"You know how a fifth-grade boy teases the girl that he actually likes? This geologist, is he, like, hot for you and trying to get your attention? You are Space Lady, right? Why not have a little fun with that?"

"What? God, no. He's old and married with kids. Definitely no."

"Okay, then. Let's say it's not a prank. Since one cannot recover living cells from a four-billion-year-old rock, it must be contamination."

"Yes. That's why I contacted you. You used to share my incubators."

"Months ago, and I definitely did not put worms in there. I just grew E. coli to amplify worm DNA. I suppose some of that DNA might have rubbed off on your oven, but such tiny amounts would be inconsequential."

"Why do the things on my plate look like worms, then? Transparent worms, like your C. elegans."

"Admittedly, that is very strange. Maybe you should bring the dish over here and we'll take a quick look at the DNA? I've got loads of PCR primer sets for C. elegans genes. We can at least see if there are any worm genes." A short silence was followed by a dial tone. "I guess that's a yes," Janet said to herself.

Ashley taped shut the lid on the tissue culture dish and placed it in an insulated box. She hustled down to her car and sped off north to the Ventura highway. In less than an hour, she was at Janet's lab in the Biomedical Sciences Research Building at UCLA. Greetings aside, they proceeded to a microscope to pick samples off the dish for the DNA analysis. Janet looked first, shoving the plate around on the stage until she stopped abruptly. She twiddled the focus knob up, then down, and up again until she froze in place for moment. She pulled away from the scope, glanced at Ashley, and dove back in for another look before standing up.

"What's this?" Janet asked. She stepped away to let Ashley settle her eyes on the oculars.

Ashley felt a rock take shape in her gut. She couldn't have missed it earlier. She had scanned the entire plate. It was huge. Visible to the naked eye. A few millimeters long, and although worm-like, it was clearly distinct from the transparent nematodes she had observed earlier. A defined body plan was emerging, with a putative torso in the center, from which black, stem-like appendages were budding. The ovular anterior section, pinched off from the central torso, resembled a head with regularly arranged pairs of indentations and extensions. The rear of the animal was unremarkable, but only because it still looked like the strange worms she had observed earlier.

"Definitely not my worm," said Janet, "or anyone's, for that matter." Her voice came from far away. It seemed unconnected to the gentle force nudging Ashley off the scope. "I'll pluck a few of the spherical structures to run some reactions." She gouged a few divots into the agar, dropped the scrapings into a small plastic tube, and handed it to her technician. "Kenji, can you run the group A panel of elegans primers on this?"

"Uh-oh!" Janet's voice, still distant to Ashley, gathered some urgency. She squeezed Ashley's elbow. "Warning. Player alert! Here comes Rex Shelton."

A tall, sandy-haired, distinguished-looking man who clearly spent too much time and money trying to look that way wandered into Janet's lab. He took the shortest route toward the women. His glossy, black Fendi shoes tapped briskly on the tile as he approached. A manicured hand adjusted his already meticulous hair while the overhead lighting bounced off his Patek Philippe watch. His Burberry suit looked far too tight to be comfortable, and its rusty orange color argued with his lavender tie. He smiled broadly at the women, revealing a history of bleaching that could give the Hyatt's laundry service a run for its money. He was handsome enough, but the shiny wrapper suggested that something inside was spoiled.

"What's up, Rex?" said Janet.

"Well, I wanted to show you this," he replied. He presented a small block of wax with some tiny insects pasted to it. "We put your elegans homeobox gene into my mutant flies, and now they grow wings again. It rescued our deletion."

"That's fabulous, Rex!" Janet said. "What else do we need to write it up?"

"We need to discuss that. I was thinking maybe over dinner tonight." Rex straightened his tie and leaned forward. His trimmed eyebrows were up, anticipating an answer.

"Geez, can't do it tonight, Rex. You see, my husband, Ray, the guy I married, I'm having dinner with him tonight. So, how about tomorrow morning in my office, right here, where the light is good."

"It's a date, then."

"No, it's not. It's a collaboration."

"Sure. Whatever." He pivoted to Ashley and took a quick visual stroll over her. "Hi, I'm Rex Shelton. I run the drosophila fly lab down the hall. I don't believe we have ever met."

"No," Ashley replied flatly, studying the floor tiles.

"No? No, we haven't met?"

"I think she means no to everything, Rex," offered Janet.

Rex looked confused while Ashley tried to hide her amusement.

"Rex, this is Ashley Woodsum. She's a microbiologist from the JPL. She's in the Astrobiology division."

"How exciting!" gushed Rex. His hand was a little sticky to the touch as Ashley shook it, still facing the floor. She glanced at him only long enough to notice makeup brushed over a wine stain under his right eye that vaguely resembled a scrotum and penis. "I just love astral biology," he said. "Any chance I could hear about your work over din—"

"We're super busy right now, Rex," interjected Janet. "So, you and I should get together tomorrow, like I said. But right now, Ashley and I need to get going on the grant we're writing."

"Sounds good," he said, rather meagerly. "I'll leave the fly block at your microscope table. Be sure to look at them before we meet." With that, he left the lab.

Once he was out of earshot, Ashley asked, "What is the grant we're writing?"

"Seriously?"

Ashley looked dumbfounded.

"I was lying. To shoo him away. He's a good scientist, Ashley, but he's far more interested in your anatomy than in your *astral biology*," she said, impersonating Rex. "Honestly, there isn't much we can do about your whacky worms until we see the PCR results. We should talk again after that. Maybe tomorrow afternoon? Do you mind leaving the dish in case we need another sample?"

"No. It's fine. Keep it here."

Ashley spent the remainder of the day at the JPL deciphering the arcane instructions for a strategic university research proposal. She was hoping to fund an additional student in her lab to start work on Hypatia. The project involved the reconstitution of an environment based on the composition of an exceedingly rare meteorite thought to outdate our own solar system. Although Hypatia was fascinating, Ashley kept drifting back to Jack's stone and its relationship to Big Mac. It was getting late. She sat staring for too long at a single paragraph of her proposal when the phone startled her. It was Janet at UCLA. Ashley could hear the phone chirping in her hand as she raised it. An unintelligible torrent poured into her ear.

Ashley held the phone at a distance for few seconds, then returned it to her ear. "Uh, hello?" she said. "Slow down, Janet. I'm getting about every third word."

"Definitely not worms!" Janet heaved. "But definitely part worm. The PCR primers specific for C. elegans genes worked. They amplified products of the correct size. We even sequenced a couple, and they are definitely worm genes."

"What? But it doesn't look like a worm. How—"

"No, wait! That's not even the weird part. Then we used random PCR primers to see what else we could amplify up. We got some products and sequenced them. We found a couple more worm genes, but also some photosynthetic genes from plant chloroplasts. We found mammalian skin genes, like keratin, human keratin. Some rodent genes, probably mouse. There's also some fly genes, including a homeobox gene that Rex had engineered in his lab. It contains the exact mutation he had engineered into it. So, the gene had to have come from his engineered fly. And by the way, your leggy worm with a head thing is now sprouting wings, transparent wings, like a fruit fly's, except green, like a plant leaf. And they're making chlorophyll. I have no—"

"Wait, wait, wait…I don't understand. How is this—"

"Possible? It's not! And it can't be a prank, unless God is playing it on us. No human could possibly arrange for this, Ashley. Genes from at least five different species, including plants. All in a single cell line that forms a blastocyst on a dish of agar, develops into a nematode, then sprouts legs, a head, and wings and appears to have photosynthetic capability. You need to come over here now and see this for yourself. I need a witness, Ashley. And a therapist. I can't believe my eyes, but I don't want to tell anyone else, either. Especially Rex."

Ashley looked ghostly, a spectral trail drifting past her postdocs on the way out of the lab. Immune to the rumblings in her stomach, she fought the remnants of rush-hour traffic on her drive back to UCLA. She parked in a handicap spot in front of the Biomedical Research Center and raced up to Janet's lab. Hovering over a laptop computer on a lab bench, Janet was interrogating a research associate. He looked on the verge of tears.

Janet threw her arms about, gesticulating wildly, drilling him over the veracity of his data. Ashley, his savior at last, distracted the shrill harpy wrinkling his ears.

Janet spotted her, then looked back to the associate. "Thanks, Kenji. Sorry about the screaming. I just need to know that it's right."

"It's right," he said, happily dismissing himself.

"More DNA sequence," said Janet, still looking at the monitor and then finally at Ashley. Janet looked as if she had been abducted by aliens, her face a shifting palette of befuddlement. Ashley experienced an unfamiliar urge to comfort her. "This is so messed up, Ashley. I like new science. I live for it, but this isn't, I mean, it's something else. We picked a new sample off the dish to confirm the presence of the photosynthetic genes, but they're not in the new sample. We tried random primers again and amplified a whole new set of genes. Still some worm there. Some human genes, too, but also a single stretch of DNA coding for bits of human, fly, and worm genes. All contiguous, aligned end to end."

"That's so strange."

"Strange? You haven't seen strange! The human segment in that stretch of DNA codes for part of the alcohol dehydrogenase gene."

"Alcohol dehydrogenase?"

"Yes, ALDH2, and it contains a variant codon commonly found in the Japanese population. The variant alters the metabolism of alcohol, resulting in increased sensitivity to it. If you've ever been in Tokyo at night, you've seen the phenotype—a stumbling man in a suit clutching a briefcase. Some time ago, we sequenced Kenji's ALDH2 for the fun of it. He gets drunk on a single beer. Sure enough, he carries the variant. This variant!" shouted Janet, poking her finger at monitor. "The cells from the dish carry his mutant gene!"

Both women stood blinking at each other.

"And Rex's exact mutant fly gene, too," Janet continued, "the one he has never loaned out. The only place in the world you would find that DNA is here, in this building, right down the hall in—" Janet stopped abruptly, walked over to the microscope table, and looked down at the flies stuck to the block Rex had left there. "Or in my lab," she said.

"It's picking up genes from its surroundings?" asked Ashley.

"Not unheard of," replied Janet. "It happens all the time with bacteria, right?"

"You mean horizontal transfer? Sure, they can do that when crowded together, especially if they're challenged with radiation or antibiotics. But how could they get access to worm genes or human genes? And how could they stitch together chunks of different genes?"

"Well, that's about the only thing that makes some sense," said Janet. "We did find DNA sequences that were common between the first sample and the second. They were mostly DNA repair genes. Like PARPs and ERCCs. The RAD genes. MutS, MutL, ligases, nucleases, recombinases. Not whole genes, just parts of them, but the important parts. Almost a quarter of the genes we found are associated with the manipulation of DNA—breaking it, filling it in, sticking ends together. These cells, they're like DNA chop shops. It's as if they grab DNA out of thin air and use their machinery to shuffle it around to make their own genes."

"This seems way too weird to publish, Janet. But I feel like we should report it somehow? Maybe tell the CDC or the NIH."

"Or the CIA," added Janet. "I don't know. I'm inclined to just keep it quiet for now. Remember cold fusion in the 1980s? The Fleischmann-Pons experiment? It defied the rules of chemistry, but they rushed to a press release and published it. No one could reproduce it, and it blew up into an embarrassing spectacle. The *New York Times* called it a circus. We don't want a circus. We need to rule out all artifacts, especially contamination. Someone could even be hacking our servers and messing with our data."

"Hacking data? Did they also paste green wings on the worm thing? Come on, Janet."

"I know, I know. Let's at least get more DNA sequence first. I think we should sequence the entire genome. So far, we have only looked at cDNAs primed off of messenger RNA transcripts. We need to look at genomic sequences directly to see what's in between the coding regions, the intronic DNA."

"We'll need more cells for that. What's left on the dish?"

"There's plenty. It's literally covered with life now. Take a look." Janet walked over to the thirty-degree incubator, opened the door, and froze. She slowly withdrew the dish. It was open. The lid had been removed. Nothing remained in it apart from a few scraps of dried agar clinging to its sides. Scratch marks resembling tracks crisscrossed over the bottom of the dish. It looked as if a tiny bulldozer had run amok over it.

Ashley approached. "Where's the lid?" she asked. "Who did this?"

Mesmerized by the empty dish, Janet barely noticed Ashley opening wide the incubator door and peering into it. The lid sat inverted in a corner. Ashley reached for it and screamed. She only caught a glimpse of the dark, shaggy creature huddled in the opposite corner of the incubator. She likened it to a tiny bat, but with green translucent wings, large antennae, red compound eyes, and a tail that looked part worm at its base and more like a mouse at the far end. Janet dropped the dish in time to watch Ashley leap back as the fuzzy animal sprang from the incubator and took flight. Its wings made an odd crackling noise, much like the crumpling of stiff paper. It was gone in an instant, exiting the lab and whisking off down the hallway.

The two women, speechless, just stared at each other, eyes wide, mouths agape.

"Cold fusion?" asked Ashley.

CHAPTER 7

SUITS IN PURSUIT

The long shadows were pointing west when Jack Whinston exited the Mitchell Earth Sciences Building at Stanford University. He wrenched his bike out of the rack lining the sidewalk and pedaled down the deserted Panama Mall toward the Coupa Cafe. Ahead in the distance, two gangly men in gray suits were loping toward him. They stood out like a two-pin split on a bowling alley. Jack veered off the mall and ducked into the courtyard behind the engineering center, where he watched the men pass. He sized them up. It was them, all right. Same suits, same build, same mechanical gait, but aged considerably since their first visit. They proceeded directly to his building and disappeared through the entryway.

Jack took a few steps into the courtyard and dialed up Alex Sina. He sounded groggy when he answered. "Have some respect for the dead, Jack," croaked Alex. "It's only nine a.m. here."

"Well, it's seven a.m. here."

"Yeah? I think that's when I went to bed. Do you love me, Jack? Is that why you called?"

Jack could overhear some rustling in the background followed by a whispered, "Jack loves you?"

"The GINR are back, Alex. I just saw them go into my building. What did you tell them?"

"I already told you. I told them I didn't have them. But they already knew that. Then they told me you used to have them but didn't

59

anymore. They left abruptly and didn't file a flight plan with me. So, I don't know what they're up to or why they returned to Stanford. I told you they were persistent. Believe me now? By the way, do they look older to you than they did in Greenland?"

"I didn't notice that. I'm sure it was them, though. Have you called Woodsum at the JPL yet?"

"Yeah, yesterday. Quite a sparkling personality. I asked her about the weather in Pasadena and she told me to look it up. Then she said the JPL wasn't really even in Pasadena. It's actually in La Cañada Flintridge. She said she was surprised that I didn't even know that. Do you know at what age her parents abandoned her to be raised by wolves?"

"She's an excellent microbiologist, Alex. We need her. I trust her work. And you need to help her characterize those fossils. The carbon isotope ratios are key, and she doesn't have a lot of experience with recovery. Did she say anything about the rocks?"

"She just said that she had received them. But she seemed kind of cagey, like there was something off, but she wasn't letting on. I don't know why, but she asked me if you were known for practical jokes. I told her you loved rocks because you shared their sense of humor."

"So, what did you decide? I think you need to go out there to kindle our collaboration."

"From first impressions, I don't think kindling would be sufficient. It might take a flamethrower. But yes, I am heading out there today. There's a big story here somewhere, Jack. It's those bloodhounds in gray suits. They're keeping my interest. They remind me of the smoking man on the old *X-Files* show. I'll be Mulder and you be Scully, okay?"

"I don't know what that means, nor care, but be sure to call me after you meet with Woodsum."

"I've got to go, Scully. But remember, the truth is out there."

Jack looked at his phone, put it to his ear again, then turned it off. He crept back toward the mall for a look at his building but decided against any fur-ther interaction with Noah and Emil. Back on his bike, he rolled east down the mall, setting his sights on the Coupa Cafe. At that same instant, Emil and Noah exited the Earth Sciences building and plodded west to Duena Street, where they stopped momentarily. Noah looked at his open palms, rubbed them together, and threw them up like he was releasing a bird to flight. The two men pivoted left, headed south down Duena and into the courtyard, where they zigzagged through a maze of picnic tables. The men hesitated again, looking east, then north. Noah rubbed his palms and released another invisible bird. He nodded to Emil, and the two of them scaled a low-lying fence behind the FedEx shipping center.

"Here," said Noah, pointing at a small dock extending from the back of the building.

They tried the door and found it unlocked. Entering, they worked their way through the stacks of boxes to a computer sitting on a small desk. Emil tapped the keyboard and scrolled his way through spreadsheets until he stopped and pointed to a line on the monitor: *Dr. Ashley Woodsum, Jet Propulsion Laboratory, Building 183, 4800 Oak Drive, Pasadena CA, 91109.* "They went there," he said.

The two of them turned to leave when the back door opened. A comically mismatched pair of campus police officers entered the room. They looked like a beanpole and a tree stump in uniforms that fit neither. Hands readied at their sides, they crouched briefly but relaxed at the sight of the aged, befuddled trespassers.

"Do you guys work here?" asked Beanpole.

"We work for the GINR," said Emil.

The two officers looked at each other before Stump said, "Okay, but do you work for F-E-D-E-X? Because if you don't, you're in T-R-O-U-B-L-E." They turned to each other and chuckled, a steep slope connecting their eyes.

"We are here on the authority of Greenland's Institute of Natural Resources," said Emil.

"Well, we are in here on the authority of the Stanford Police," said Stump.

"And Smith and Wesson," echoed Beanpole, tapping his holster and grinning at Stump.

The ride to the police station was uneventful. Emil and Noah sat quietly behind the cage wire separating them from the officers, who had given up interrogating them. From the replies they had received so far, it was apparent there were mental issues at hand. They would either transfer the pair to a psychiatric outpatient clinic or release them to family, should anyone claim them.

At the police station, Emil and Noah sat straight up, unmoving in their stiff plastic chairs. They blinked at the young female officer who had been summoned due to her training in psychiatry. "Do you men know where you are right now?" she asked.

"We are in T-R-O-U-B-L-E," said Noah.

The officer's ruby lips curled up slightly at the edges. "No, you're not," she said gently. "Everything's fine. We just want to help. Why were you in the FedEx building? Were you lost?"

"Not anymore," said Emil. "We found it. We want to go to 4800 Oak Drive, Pasadena, please. We want to see Ashley."

"Okay. Is she related to you?"

"Probably," replied Noah, "we are related to many people here. Maybe all."

"Hmmm. Okay. I mean, is this Ashley your sister or daughter or someone who can help you?"

"She can help us. She has Dagon. We need to recover him soon."

Beanpole and Stump, hovering nearby, glanced at each other. "I told you, it's *dagon*, not dragon," said Stump.

"Well, we can't take you to Pasadena. Can you call someone to come and get you?"

"Okay," said Emil. He looked down at his hands and pushed the matching fingers together.

"Uh, the phone is right there," she said, pointing to the desk next to them.

"Okay," said Emil. He smiled blithely at her, then reached over and rested a hand on top of the receiver.

"You have to pick it up and enter a number," she instructed. "Do you have a number?"

"Eight billion!" announced Noah, beaming. "At least eight billion." Then he shifted his attention to the door. "Ekur is here for us now," he said.

"Eeee...what?"

The door pushed open, and a tall, nondescript man in a gray suit, toting a black briefcase, entered the room. No one spoke as he plopped his bag on the table, rummaged through it, and produced a folder. "Hello, I'm Eric Smith from Las Encinas Hospital in Pasadena. I'm their custodian. I apologize for any trouble." He opened the folder and presented it to the officers. They perused the very official-looking contents, which presented the identification and case logs for his charges at large.

The cops, far more satisfied than suspicious, were more than happy to accommodate the custodian. But he and his charges were long gone before someone asked how the custodian knew where to find them. "GPS," offered Stump. "Oh, yeah, right," confirmed Beanpole.

"Pasadena. Is that right?" asked Ekur, studying the two men in the rear-view mirror of the Lincoln Navigator. "I can take you to the airport, where you will fly to Burbank. The tickets are set." He looked hard at Noah and Emil. They looked weak and pale. Folds of loose flesh hung from their cheeks. Deep furrows in their foreheads ran above their unruly caterpillar eyebrows. "You two okay? How much time do you have left? Maybe you need new Zumru now."

"We should wait," said Emil. "It costs too much. We have at least one more day. We can make it to Pasadena."

"And you are certain Dagon is there?"

"His Siru was sent there, but we don't think he has assembled yet."

"Shala is coming," said Ekur. "She has fallen and is assembling now. Her Zumru is strengthening. She cannot be stopped, but Dagon can. There isn't much time."

"We understand, Ekur," said Noah, "but the people here do not. They will not listen to us. They will not help us even as we try to help them."

"They are grounders, Sukka. Zumru is sacred to them. They still honor and mourn its loss. It is all they know."

"But all will be lost. If Shala and Dagon call for our Zumru, it will expire quickly. Look at us. The gas is too strong here. We cannot renew quickly enough to hold all of the inhabitants. Bar will drift away. The congregations will dissolve. All will expire, empty."

"Stop it, Sukka. You have to be strong. It's up to you to prevent it. You were chosen. You are the scouts. Find the progenitors and stop the union." Ekur guided the car to the curb at the airport and opened the doors.

Chapter 8

Smart Girl

Emma Curtis arose early to the sound of rustling in the dog kennel. She pulled on a robe and tiptoed past her slumbering parents' bedroom. The familiar squeak of the screen door alerted Zephyr. She bounded up, panting wildly and pawing at the kennel door. Emma looked beyond Zephyr as she poked a finger through the wire mesh, absently scratching the beagle's head. "Where's your little buddy, Zeph?" She frowned at the dry water bowl behind her dog. Beyond that, the overturned food bucket sat next to the doghouse, devoid of the thirty pounds of chow she had dumped in it. Although the dog was spunky, she knew Zephyr couldn't have budged it. Even if she had, there was no evidence of spilled food. Zephyr spun around and barked loudly. What resembled a beagle, albeit larger, sprang from the doghouse and slammed its oversized paws onto the kennel door.

Emma reared back. Although alarmed at the sheer size of the beast, she was stunned by its otherwise remarkable similarity to Zephyr. Both girls, they looked like scaled versions of each other. Even their tails wagged in time. Emma gave the larger animal's head a nervous scratch. "Hey, girl. How did you get so big?" The animal backed away, circled over to the empty food bucket, and nudged it with her nose. Emma's jaw went slack. "Looks like you're out of water, too," she tried. The curious canine looked her way while placing a foot on the end of the hose. "Oh, my god!" Emma shouted.

The screen door squeaked again, and Emma turned to see her mother shuffling toward her. Amelia's eyes, still puffy from sleep, were clearly focused on the new dog in the kennel as she approached. "Who's this?" she asked.

Emma flushed. She couldn't possibly explain it. She couldn't even explain it to herself. Her mom would take her straight to a doctor if she tried. "Um, a stray beagle," she replied. "I found her out front. She looked so hungry, so I fed her. Zephyr loves her. They play together."

"Sweetie, one dog is enough. We can't keep her for long. Okay? Right now, you need to get ready for program, and I have to go to work, so let's get a move on."

"Sure. I just need to get some more dog food from the garage."

———

Ron got up a bit later than usual. He worked his way into his breathing vest and endured the ventilator once again. He pulled open the end table drawer where he kept his menagerie of drugs, enzyme supplements, vasodilators, and mucolytics. He gobbled down his morning regimen. He was willing himself to inhale when he heard a deep, hoarse bark coming from the backyard. After steeling himself to rise, he padded toward the kennel, pushing open the squeaky screen door. He studied the offending hinge. Contemplating the whereabouts of his 3-in-One oil, he stiffened at the sight of the enormous dog romping in the kennel. It stopped and stared back at him, its tail wagging, pink tongue dangling. It raised a paw, tapped on the kennel door, ran a circle, and tapped again. Zephyr stood in its shadow, eager and waiting. Appended to the kennel, Ron discovered his wife's note explaining the stray.

"Well, who are you?" Ron asked aloud. The behemoth dwarfed little Zephyr. Ron sized it up, estimating its weight at seventy pounds. "You're too big to be a beagle. Are you a foxhound?" Ron noticed the overturned food bucket. "Did you clean out all the dog food?" The animal ran to the bucket and carried it over, dropping it in front of Ron at the kennel door.

"Wow! Smart girl," Ron said. She seemed friendly enough to him. He felt little harm could come from letting her out. He sprung the kennel door latch, and both dogs darted out. The larger one pawed at Ron's legs, licking at his face as he leaned forward to pet it. He opened the squeaking door, and both animals bolted through the kitchen and commenced with some lively combat on the living room floor.

Ron chuckled at the rollicking dogs as he settled into his big chair. But his smile faded when he felt a familiar tightening in his chest and the shortness of breath that usually followed. Hocking up some loose phlegm, he was overcome by a coughing fit and struggled to regain his breath. As he pounded on his chest, his face turned scarlet, and he curled forward. Heaving still harder, his constricted airways refused to cooperate. The dogs had ceased their play and were staring at him. The big one disappeared from the room and quickly returned. She dropped a small metal canister in front of Ron. The room was beginning to darken for him, but between coughs, he could make out the bronchodilator resting between his feet.

A few puffs later, his airways relaxed, and what he had learned to accept as normal breathing resumed. As his head cleared, he looked at the dilator in his hand, then at the animals sitting side by side, both patiently taking him in. He knew he shouldn't stand up quite yet, but he launched an adrenaline-fueled effort and staggered into the bedroom. He stared in absolute wonder at the open drawer. He was sure he had closed it after taking his meds. He was sure the bronchodilator—the one he still clutched in his hand—was in it when he had closed it. He returned to the living room to find the two dogs resting, Zephyr's head flopped over the flank of the larger critter.

Ron plopped down into a chair next to the canines and scrutinized the larger one, comparing it to Zephyr. The digits on its front paws were extremely long and flexible while the rear paw digits remained stubby. Adjacent to the fourth digit on each paw, a nub protruded, hinting at a fifth. Overall, its face seemed flatter than Zephyr's. Its snout was retracted and its forehead more vertical and broader. Some of the fur on its belly had receded, revealing a smooth pink flesh. Ron considered taking her to the vet when he realized he was late for his own doctor's appointment. He wrestled into his clothes, then into his car and set out for the Cystic Fibrosis Center at Children's Hospital in Phoenix.

Ron's car had been equipped with a portable oxygen concentrator so he could sip from a tube attached to his steering wheel when needed. But, oddly, he didn't need it this morning. Heading west on the 202 Loop, he began to feel downright chipper and more alert than he had in ages. His wheezing had subsided, allowing him longer and deeper inhales. He picked up a cup to spit but emitted only a small amount of phlegm that appeared clear and watery. He breathed in hard and watched his chest expand like a new balloon. Impulsively lowering his window in the ninety-degree heat, he poked his head out and screamed, "I can breathe!" He grinned at the wide-eyed children in the station wagon next to him.

————

"Well, Ronald, this is all good news," said Dr. Gerald Berthstein, retracting his stethoscope. "I certainly can't say I understand it, but your lungs have improved remarkably since your last visit."

"I've been trying some new vitamin supplements. Maybe they're working," replied Ron.

"Maybe. We'll need some sputum for analysis. And is it okay if we take a blood draw for my research lab?"

"Sure, Doc. You could take a gallon today."

CHAPTER 9

THE MEETING

Alex Sina parked his rented Buick in the JPL visitors' lot. He leashed himself to the blue dot on Google Maps and followed it to building 183. Arriving, he accepted the challenge posted at the locked entrance: *Visitors must ring reception to gain entry.* He rummaged through his bag, searching for a nonexistent key card until a student arrived with a real one. Slipping in behind the young grad, he flashed his YMCA card at the incredulous student. Alex approached the elevator and ran his finger down the registry until it landed on Ashley Woodsum, RM 413, fourth floor.

He was comfortably surprised at the sight of the Area 51 poster decorating her door. Traipsing through the lab like he owned it, he encountered a graduate student toiling at a bench stacked with culture dishes. Alex flashed his YMCA card along with a dour expression of mock concern. "Hi, I'm Agent Mulder, is Scully here?"

The befuddled student, likely born after the *X-files* had died, replied, "This is Dr. Woodsum's lab. Is there a problem?"

"You shape-shifters can't fool me," said Alex. "What have you done with her?"

"Shape what?" asked the student.

"Please ignore him," came a third voice entering the lab. "Dr. Sina is a collaborator visiting from the University of Chicago. He will be working with us on the new Greenland rocks from Dr. Whinston."

Intent on continuing his charade, Alex wheeled around to face Ashley, but his jaw locked up. A sensation he had utterly failed to anticipate flushed over him. Although she was attractive by any measure, he wasn't so much smitten by her looks as he was by her look. He knew it well. He knew the depths of it. It was his look—his *alone* look. It was the look that stared back at him in a mirror. The image that reflected his empty history as a socially disengaged human. It mocked him for his failed marriage, his string of casual relationships, his distant father, and a lack of offspring that so disappointed his lonely mother. He had never met Ashley, but that common thread was undeniable. Her mournful, rudderless aura had just rammed him broadside.

Flummoxed by his misplaced sense of longing, Alex idled, still taking her in. Her comeliness, at first an afterthought, began to grow as he backed out of his reverie and perused the surface. He took in her milky-white skin, puffy lower lip, delicate chin, and supple, hollowed cheeks. His reptilian brain awoke, turning up the temperature, kicking at his heart and lungs. She was beautiful, he opined, but not in a glamorous way. That was his ex-wife, and he wasn't about to fall for that again. Ashley would look out of place on one of those vapid magazine covers. She was more suited for *National Geographic*, searching and surrounded by natural splendor.

Alex felt convinced that whatever he said next could impact his future. An awkward pause ensued, during which Ashley only tipped her head slightly, as if to ask, *so?* Finally, Alex broke. "Is this your lab?" he said, and then immediately went red from the sheer stupidity of the question.

Of course, Ashley knew a stupid question when she heard one. She was never shy about calling it out, either, typically skewering the questioner. But something stopped her. It was an odd and barely familiar sensation. It might have been pity. He looked so shy and afraid, like a kid in a new school. She held her tongue. She didn't know why. Maybe it was Jay, her ad hoc "Mr. Manners" instructor from Shipping who had recently welcomed her to the human race. Either way, she curbed her impulses and tapped into her new status as a human being. "Yes, I'm Ashley Woodsum, and this is Jeffery, a graduate student from Caltech. Welcome." She commanded her cheek muscles to exact a smile.

Alex smiled back all too effortlessly, and perhaps for too long, at least long enough for Jeffery to raise an eyebrow in Ashley's direction. "Alex Sina," he said. "I've read your work on electron gradients on the ocean floor. Great stuff. You were at Penn State then, right?"

Without answering, Ashley took a few steps forward and robotically extended her right hand. "Pleased to meet you," she said.

Her hand was cool and dry to the touch. The chill of it ran up Alex's arm and brushed over his neck like an ocean breeze. "Absolutely," he replied, "I mean, I've really been looking forward to our collaboration." He noted her svelte stature and the lab coat that didn't entirely hide how nicely she was put together. Alex struggled to rein in his uncooperative eyes. He scanned the lab, looking for something to focus on. "So you have Jack's rocks? The ones he sent to you," he said, and then quickly added, "I mean, I guess you have them if he sent them to you." His eyes found a floor tile.

Ashley squinted at the skittish man. She was wholly surprised by his demeanor. His notoriety warranted some swagger, which she had fully anticipated, but he actually came off as halting and timid. His handsome, rugged good looks hadn't escaped her purview, but years of fending off predators had desensitized her to that. She had metaphorically slapped more than one good-looking man with bad-looking intentions.

"Let's go to my office, and I'll fill you in on what we have so far," she said, matter-of-factly.

Alex followed her to a small room built into the corner of the lab. She indicated a chair across from her desk. Alex lowered himself into the seat while scanning the austere room. He was struck by the lack of personal effects typically displayed in offices. There were no family photos, no artwork by precocious children, no greeting cards, no goofy souvenirs from tropical vacations, no commemorative gift plaques, not even a diploma. The off-white cinder block walls were devoid of any decoration whatsoever. He envisioned a toilet in the corner and bars on the door. He wanted to ask what she had done to deserve solitary, but he bit his lip and focused on the monitor she had swiveled in his direction.

It was Ashley's turn to feel nervous, but for a different reason. She had to tread carefully. She knew she couldn't just jump in with a little rock goo that grew into mammalian cells, then formed a blastocyst that turned into a worm-fly-mouse-bat-plant thing and flew away. She started by reviewing pictures of the rock that Alex had already seen. "These little impressions, the repeating peaks, they look enough like stromatolites, right?" Alex nodded silently. "But underneath each crest, we see these odd, spherical impressions that, upon closer inspection, are constituted of concentric rings."

"Yeah, I saw those when we found the rocks. I have no idea what they are, though."

She zoomed in and pointed with a pencil. "I noticed some moisture in the center, so I swabbed and plated it."

"Wait. Why are you plating anything from a four-billion-year-old rock? It's pretty dead. Guaranteed."

"Agreed. But I thought your friend Jack was playing a trick on me, so I was going to play along."

"A, he's not my friend. B, he wouldn't do that. And C, he's not my friend."

"Well. Perhaps you should suspend all rational thinking momentarily while we look over the following data."

Uh-oh, here comes Space Lady, thought Alex. *I knew it was too good to be true.*

Ashley brought up a high magnification image of the goo. "All I could find in the initial swipe was an odd, grainy particulate, tiny hexagon-shaped bits, each about a micron in length. And then this." She pointed to a string of tiny sausage-like figures strung end to end. "Looks like bacteria, or maybe archaea. Yes, I know. It couldn't have survived four billion years."

Alex was getting restless. "Contamination. Next," was all he said.

"Well, I plated it on LB medium in agar at thirty degrees and the next morning saw this." She switched to a 40x image of two adjoined cells that looked mammalian in origin. "See how the two cells already look different from each other after a single division? One is polarized and flat looking, the other is columnar and symmetric. Now when—"

"Hang on, hang on, hang on," interrupted Alex. "You actually believe that an animal cell originating from the rock divided, resulting in two cells, that then immediately differentiated into distinct lineages?"

"I know what you're thinking."

"No, you don't. You'd punch me if you did. With all due respect—"

"Please hold that thought. Here is another cellular structure I found on the dish. It looks like a blastocyst, right? Trophoblastic layer, inner lumen."

"Come on. Just stop it." Alex was standing now. "You're growing mammalian embryos on lysogenic broth for bacteria at thirty degrees centigrade? And when are you going to show me the little green men with antennae and big eyes? I flew all the way out here because—" Alex checked himself. "Look, I— What the hell is that?"

Ashley was fixed on the image of the worm-like creature she had discovered on the culture dish. "No green men," she said, "but transparent worms, eating the agar. Look at the backside. There are tiny limb buds emerging. At first, I thought they were C. elegans, from a lab down the hall. But the investigator had moved to UCLA months ago, and they're not elegans. Here's what showed up on the dish only hours later. And I know it wasn't there the first time I looked." Ashley displayed the image taken in Janet's lab—the little creature with a distinct torso, legs or arms or both, and a head, but still part worm in the rear, except with hair.

Alex was not a zoologist, but he knew an animal when he saw one, and this wasn't one. He looked for seams in the image, or misplaced shadows or lines indicative of photoshopping, but found none. "What the hell?" he said.

While staring straight at Alex, Ashley calmly said, "Then it turned into a furry bat-like thing with green wings and flew away," at which point she spun around in her chair to face the window. She shouldn't have said it but couldn't help it. She knew she wasn't crazy but would appear so to anyone listening to her. It was simply too much to hold in. But it was real. Then her shoulders starting heaving as she buried her head in her hands.

Alex froze. Regardless of how absurd it all seemed, she was, above all, sincere. He felt ashamed for his terse comments. He was certain now that it wasn't a hoax, at least not one Ashley perpetrated. He considered that the images had been doctored, but she took most of them herself. He came around the desk and cautiously placed a hand on Ashley's shoulder. It startled her. "It's all right," he said, "we'll get to the bottom of this. It's just not at all what I had expected. It's difficult to believe. Something's going on, but we'll figure it out. Okay?"

Ashley wiped her cheeks with the back of her hand and lifted her head. "I don't believe it, either," she sniveled, "but I saw it with my own eyes." She was still visibly trembling. Her voice was hoarse. "I would have committed myself if Janet hadn't seen it, too. She's as freaked out as I am. Maybe more. She PCR'd some mRNA transcripts from the cells and identified human sequences, mouse sequences, worm, fly, name it. One of the human genes coded for an ALDH2 variant that Janet's lab tech carries in his genome. One of the genes contained a unique mutation that her collaborator engineered. A gene that doesn't even exist in nature. There is no rational explanation."

"There's got to be. Who's this Janet? Do you trust her?"

"Of course. She has no reason nor the time to do something like this. She's a geneticist. She told me that a lot of the genes she identified were related to enzymes and proteins involved in the modification and repair of DNA. She made a new extract to confirm the findings but failed to find some of the genes identified in the first round. They were gone, but parts of them were found in new genes that she hadn't found the first time. She said it was like the organism was creating new genes in real time, and it was somehow collecting the code from its surroundings. That's how it got the unique worm sequence and her tech's ALDH2 variant."

"Well, some bacteria have natural gene editing capabilities. That's where the idea for CRISPR gene editing technology came from. Maybe the cells are infected with an unidentified exotic microbe. This could be the discovery of the century."

"Sounds nice, but there is something I haven't mentioned. Oddly, it keeps me sane even though it makes the whole situation even weirder.

Have you seen the recent news about the so-called Big Mac meteorite that crashed in Arizona?"

"Sure, it was unavoidable. Adorable red-haired little genius girl discovers a space rock. What news agency isn't going to run with that?"

"Did you see the meteorite?"

"It was a sixty-second piece, forty-five longer than my attention span."

Ashley returned to the computer and clicked open a split-screen image of two stones. "This is the rock Jack sent, blown up about 10x. Again, the concentric circles I described earlier are here, positioned under each presumed stromatolite. There's also a wiggly line that seems to connect them. Now, I know it's a bit grainy but here's—"

"What's that?" Alex blurted. He was already ahead of Ashley, gazing back and forth, comparing the two close-ups. "That's the Big Mac meteorite?" he asked, pointing to the image at right. "The circles."

"Exactly."

"What the fuck?"

"That, too."

Alex's spine stiffened, and his face blanched. He pushed open the office door and strode into the lab, pacing nervously between a couple benches. Rubbing his chin, he looked in all directions as if the answers to impossible questions were written on the walls. He found only more questions, one on Jeffery's face that asked, *Should I call security now?* He returned to the office, to the only person in the world who could understand him.

Very pointedly, he looked at Ashley and asked, "So, this flying thing in Janet's lab. Where did it go?"

"We don't know. She hasn't found it and doesn't want to tell others about it yet. I mean, maybe it didn't come from the dish, after all. Maybe it just got in there when someone opened the incubator. We don't want to scare people. We could end up looking like kooks."

"Can we go there? I want to talk to her. I'll be nice. I promise."

"Not today. She's hosting an all-day site visit by her granting authority. She needs to make a good impression. But we could go tomorrow."

"That's fine, I guess. Maybe for the time being we can just pretend there's nothing unusual. Is that okay? We scrape the sample from Jack and try to get a carbon isotope ratio like we had originally planned. I think it's still important to do that. Let's do that."

"Sounds good," said Ashley. "I need some work to keep my mind off it."

Ashley rose from her chair, and the two briefly collided as they simultaneously approached the exit from her small office. Although she used none, Alex's head swirled at the smell of what he thought was her delicious perfume. "After you," both said, again together. Stalled in place, their faces only inches apart, neither made an honest effort to disjoin. Alex finally smiled nervously. He felt himself blush before stepping back into the office to afford Ashley an exit.

Once in the lab, Ashley recovered the rock from a freezer. The two scientists then hunkered down, speaking only when needed, and performed the painstaking preparation and analysis. They worked through the day, avoiding the thousand-pound gorilla sitting on the centrifuge.

The sky was dimming when they finally locked up the lab. On the way out, Alex asked some tactical questions concerning their follow-up activities. But he was only stalling. He couldn't find the words or the moment to ask her. He'd grown accustomed to them asking him. Moreover, he was there in a professional capacity, as a collaborator, and she was all business while they worked. He considered just asking her to recommend a restaurant, but she would see right through it. They went silent as the elevator opened on the ground floor, where Jay from Shipping awaited it. His amicable voice filled the void, "Good evening, Dr. Ash."

"Hi, Jay," responded Ashley. Then after a brief pause, "How are you?"

"Nice!" gushed Jay. "I'm fine, and yourself?"

"Fine. Good night, Jay."

"Good night, Dr. Human," said Jay, flashing a fat, knowing smile.

Exiting the building, Alex said, "Dr. Human?"

"Just a joke. He's a really nice man."

They stood for a few seconds with Ashley looking down. Alex looked over the top of her head. "Well, I'm in the visitors' lot, so I guess—"

"Hungry?" she asked, looking up and meeting his eyes, if only for a second.

"Famished! I'm hungry enough to eat a flying mouse-bat-worm thing," he said, instantly regretting it.

Ashley's face turned red and her eyes widened as if she had been slapped. "Are you mocking me?" she asked.

"No. Not at all. I'm so sorry. Please, I didn't mean anything by it. There's just this tension, you know. It's like this building's on fire, and we're both just ignoring it. I'm sorry. I believe everything you told me, Ashley. I'm with you all the way. It's just so crazy. I can't keep it inside, anymore."

His bumbling sincerity took her by surprise. She almost felt sorry for the groveling man. "Meet me at the Kings Row Gastropub on Colorado, just off Fair Oaks," she said.

————

The room was relatively quiet. They seated themselves at a two-top in the corner. Alex's foot landed on top of Ashley's as they pulled their chairs in. He sat up quickly, jerked his feet in, pushed his chair back a few inches, then forward a couple more. His elbows slid off the table until only his wrists rested on the edge. He checked his shirt sleeves, then his shirt front, shoved his hair back, and examined the backs of his hands. He finally noticed Ashley, who was quietly observing her twitching subject. "Comfortable?" she asked.

"Yeah. It's great. I like all the red brick and mortar. Nice place. Thanks for the invitation. I wouldn't know where to go."

"Good salads on the menu, but no flying worm-bat things."

"Hey, okay. Yeah, sorry about that again."

"It was my fault. I've been told I take things too seriously."

"Did that Dr. Human guy tell you that?"

"Jay? I suppose. He tells me lots of things. He says I lack common courtesy and that he's teaching me how to better interact with people. I suppose he's right. It's just hard to do if you don't really feel it."

"Maybe you do feel it. You felt bad for me because I acted so stupidly when we first met."

Ashley squirmed inside. Most people didn't know what she felt, and she liked it that way. Her lack of expression was like a veil. It concealed her thoughts and gave her the upper hand. It was unsettling to her that this stranger could already see behind the curtain.

But he could. He could see through it. He knew it well, having constructed his own curtain over the years. And like her, he bristled at anyone who tried to second-guess his real feelings. *It's going to be a long dinner,* he thought. He would have to tread carefully. He imagined they were both made of glass and a wrecking ball was rolling around on their table. They would have to be vigilant, constantly tilting the table to center the ball. Alex tried to level it off with some small talk. "So, why did you leave Penn State?"

"I needed a change."

"That's it? Come on. JPL must have made you a pretty sweet deal. Penn's a great school. You were on a roll there, too. You made the national news."

"It's better."

"How could it be any better? You were already hitting it out of the park."

"I just like it here better."

"Uh-oh. Someone must have really pissed you off." He kicked himself when her face dropped. He had pushed up too hard on his end of the table.

The lump in her throat returned. Only two people really knew what had transpired there, and Alex certainly wasn't one of them. "There were some issues that… I just needed to get out," she said abruptly and looked down at the floor.

Alex sensed the ball rolling hard in her direction. Perhaps he could've stopped it, but something inside him let it drop. "And what was the issue's name?" asked Alex.

Ashley's face burned. It was no fair. She had locked away those horrid memories. And here, this man she barely knew had discovered that chamber and was prying it open. Nothing good could come of it. Unlocking those memories would only reinforce her distaste for so-called humanity. No one had listened to her back then and repeating it now wouldn't change a thing. It was done. Water under a broken bridge. She shifted sideways in her chair. Alex waited, tracing her profile with his eyes. "There were some things we disagreed on," she finally said.

Alex felt it was too late to turn back now. The wrecking ball was dropping. Like a cowboy caught cheating at poker, he tipped the table over. "Disagreed, huh? You mean like you were saying no, and he kept saying yes?"

She was at the door before he could get out of his chair.

"Ashley!" he shouted. He rushed out after her while casting *fuck you too* glares at the patrons feasting on their drama.

She was already down the street, her bouncing platinum hair counting her brisk steps. He caught up with her at the Half Off Bookstore, where he tugged on her forearm and coaxed her under the awning of a sleepy wine bar. A Muzak rendition of "Runaway Train" wafted tepidly from the open door. Facing her, he held both of her forearms. "I'm really sorry," he said. "I didn't want to upset you. I shouldn't have done that. That's not like me. I mean, I'm like you. Well, not exactly. I don't mean that, either. I wouldn't normally do that. It's just that, you're different. It's like I had to know. I want to know. I can't pretend to imagine what it's like. It must have been horrible, but…I get it. It's okay if—"

"Stop it," she said flatly. Her face was lifeless and cold as steel. There were no tears, just shiny, dead metal. "Now you know. Are you happy? Is that what you needed? And what are you going to do about it? Nothing! Just like everyone else. Not a fucking thing!" she screamed. She jerked her forearms out of his grasp and pounded her fists into his chest. He moved his hands up to her shoulders, but she backed away, letting them fall awkwardly to his sides. He took a step forward. There were tears now, leaking out from under her shuttered lids. He tried the shoulders again. She stayed this time but wouldn't meet his gaze. "I haven't cried in three years," she sniveled, "but I've cried twice in one day since meeting you."

"Yeah, I kind of have that effect on people. Usually not tears of joy, either."

"Jack warned me. He said you have an annoying sense of humor, but I didn't expect this."

"There's nothing funny about this, Ashley. I'm truly sorry. I overstepped. You have every reason to be upset. It's none of my business. I don't know what got into me. I felt like...well, like I needed to know, like it was important to me, somehow. I don't even know why. I get it, though. I hate it when I'm asked about my past. I should have known better."

"Oh, really? What is it about your past that you hate?" she asked. A wry smile tightened her lips. "I need to know."

"Well, I guess I stepped in that one," Alex said. He thought about it for an uncomfortable moment. He had never really discussed it with anyone. Ever. He had even trained himself to not think about it.

"Come on, she goaded, "you already undressed me, now drop your pants."

Despite feeling cornered, his loins rattled at the lurid metaphor. He looked across the street to avoid her gaze. *She's right,* he thought. He had started a slap fight, and it was his turn to get slapped. "Well, I was married once," he started, and then hesitated. She said nothing, but her raised eyebrows spelled, *A-N-D?* "She was beautiful and sexy, and I loved her. A lot. So did everyone else, apparently. Especially the chairman of my department. He loved my house, too. And my bed. At least until I discovered that's where he was spending his sabbatical. Anyway, I'm over it. It just changed the way I see—" He stopped. His voice cracked a little on the word *see.* The wrecking ball was rolling up Colorado Avenue and headed straight for him. "Anyway, it's done. Really done. The chairman's wife committed suicide, and my ex left him shortly thereafter. We only talk through our attorneys now, and with a little luck, that, too, will end shortly. I guess that seems kind of silly compared to what you've endured."

"No. Not silly at all. Mostly sad. It took me a long time to stop hating people. All people. That's the saddest part."

"It seemed like you liked Jay. He definitely likes you. Are you two—"

"No! What? He's still just a kid and has a steady girlfriend to boot. Ask him how much I liked him a year ago. I was such a bitch to him, but he just brushed it off and kept being nice to me. He called me his project. I guess it helped. He declared me human just yesterday."

"Congratulations. I'd have to agree with Jay. Well, humans cry when they hurt. Right?"

"You're not crying."

"Yeah, I guess I drained that tank a long time ago. And there's no Jay to make me human.

I just have Satan, and he's trying to make me into a goat."

Alex had forgotten that his hands were still resting on her shoulders. He let them glide down her arms slowly and felt her palms turning outward in time to catch them. For a few long and silent seconds, they stood face-to-face, hands in hands. He had never wanted to kiss a woman so badly in his life. Never one to hesitate, he was flummoxed by his reluctance. He had had an actual, meaningful exchange of emotion with a woman, and he didn't want to ruin it with saliva.

Still holding his hands, she tilted her head toward the entrance to the wine bar. "Still hungry?" she finally said. "Free appetizer buffet during happy hour," she added.

"An hour of happiness *and* free food? Deal."

She released one of his hands and pulled him through the door with the other. They ordered wine and perused the buffet while making hushed cracks about the little tiny ears of corn and the miniature sausages impaled on toothpicks. Neither ate much, but both talked a lot between sips of wine. Alex unloaded his suitcase of family relations. He kept his barely-there father in the compartment containing his dirty socks and underwear. His dear mum was in another section, along with the pressed white shirts with starched collars. His older brother, a power broker on Wall Street, remained in a locked pocket, for which he had lost the key.

He told her how alone he felt growing up, until his senior year in high school, when he finally realized that pretty much everybody was messed up in some way.

Ashley said little about her family, and although curious, Alex made no attempt to pry. The wrecking ball was gone, and he had no intention of bringing it back. He would take whatever she would offer but no more. And as far as she was concerned, the room wasn't big enough to hold what might pop out of that suitcase should she open it. She did tell stories about her childhood. She was quite animated recounting her days on the high school swim team, but less so when describing the Ford Fiesta she totaled while trying to run away at fifteen. She admitted to being a child nerd, the one who desperately wanted a microscope for Christmas. And then there was her dog, Kreskin, that she swore could read minds.

She recounted a few anecdotes from her undergraduate years at Michigan. But beyond that, her chronicle went cold. Understandably, there was no further mention of Penn State, but she did let slip that she carried a gun these days. Alex didn't blink. Although ebullient at times, Alex could see the tremors in her brush as she tried to paint a pleasant picture of her upbringing. Black paint had been blotted over large swaths of that landscape. That everybody was damaged in some way was an understatement for her. So much so that she was astounded by a man who could sit across from her and just listen—without staring at her breasts or noticing other women.

The wine bar was closing. Glasses clanged and cooler doors slammed shut. Only one table remained free of inverted chairs while a broom whisked around the legs of the others. The cute couple holding hands over their table were utterly oblivious to anything not connected to their hands. The help had noticed them, though. They were amusing themselves with silent bets placed on the outcome of their Tinder-mooners, as they called them. With all apologies, Ashley and Alex were finally asked to vacate. Their waiter wrested them from their cloister by dropping the door keys on their table. They surfaced and ventured out into the realm of deserted streets and shuttered windows, where it was well past one a.m.

"Okay if I walk you to your car?" asked Alex. "Not that you need protecting. I know you're strapped. I just want to walk with you."

"You better, or I'll make you at gunpoint."

They reached her vehicle parked on the street in front of the Italian bakery. Still holding one hand, Alex reached for the other, keeping some space between them. She leaned back against her car door. In the pale amber hue of a streetlight, her creamy skin glowed smooth like fine sculpture. Her anime eyes seemed unimaginably large, like lakes he could swim in. They stood silently for a minute, regarding each other like rare museum pieces.

Ashley released her hands and moved them up to his shoulders. "Would you like to kiss me, Dr. Sina?" she asked with a knee-buckling tenor.

His vacant hands came to life. Placing one on each side of her face, he leaned forward and met her in the middle as she tilted upward on her toes. A current seemed to leap into the tiniest of gaps that remained between them. He wasn't sure if their lips had even met, but it was the sweetest, most electrifying kiss of his life—all one second of it. A tingling bolted down his spine, and his eyes watered. He pulled back, alarmed at the sheer religiosity of the moment. At once, he felt both saved and helpless, victorious in surrender. She could cook him and eat him if she wanted to, and he wouldn't be able to do a thing about it.

"Wow," he said softly. "That was nice."

"Is this really happening?" she asked.

"Must be. My dreams aren't *this* scary," he said.

She slipped her arms around his back and hugged him like he was home from the war. He placed a hand on the back of her head and grazed her neck with his fingers. With his other hand on the small of her back, he squeezed her even closer. He felt her head trembling slightly as she slipped a hand between them to reach her face. She resisted at first, but when he pulled away, he could see the water in her eyes.

"Third time's a charm," he said.

"Stop it. If you make me cry again, I'm going to shoot you."

"Okay. I could die here."

Chapter 10

Doggone Rock

It sounded as though a bag of squirrels had been dropped into Zephyr's kennel. The relentless howling dredged Ron up from the depths of a sleep unlike any he had experienced in years. He stared in disbelief at the late morning hour glowing on his bedside clock. Sitting up, he was struck by two more delightfully wrong things—he wasn't gasping for air, and it was the first time he had woken since going to bed. Arising with little effort, he bypassed his ventilator on the way to investigate the ruckus. The kennel door was sprung wide open, and Zephyr stood alone in the yard, barking at the back fence.

"Uh-oh," said Ron. "Where's your big buddy, Z?" Zephyr lunged at Ron, shook off his head scratches, and retreated back into the yard. She sniffed at an overturned wash bucket that had been pushed up against the wooden fence. Ron followed. He poked at the bucket with his foot and examined the fence. With his fingers, he probed the parallel tracks of freshly gouged wood in the fence boards. Standing on the bucket, he peered over the six-foot barrier into his neighbor's yard. It was open to the street.

"I think she flew the coop, Z. We'll name her Houdini if she ever comes back." He had quickly grown fond of the oddball canine and was already missing her. Worse, he would have to explain the improbable prison break to his daughter, who might reasonably suspect him of aiding and abetting. There was some comfort in considering the remarkable intelligence of the animal. She would probably do just fine. He turned to Zephyr and said, "Don't worry about her, Z. She's probably already landed a job at the local Starbucks."

The kitchen phone rang, and Ron trotted in after it, Zephyr at his heels. He could barely utter a hello before Dr. Gerald Berthstein from the CF clinic ran over him with a truckload of medical details, barely half of which he comprehended. "We can't explain it," the doctor had said—at least six times—interspersed with medical jargon only vaguely familiar to Ron. At Ron's behest, the doctor took a breath and tried to translate. "Our blood cells contain the same DNA as all of the cells in our body. So, when we look for mutations in the genes that we're born with, we use blood cells, because they are easy to obtain. We found your CF mutation in your blood cell DNA, just like before. You still carry the CF gene you were born with. But when we sequenced DNA from lung cells recovered from your sputum, we found wild-type DNA. That's normal DNA, a normal CF gene. We can't explain it." *Seven*, counted Ron.

"So, my lungs are normal now but the rest of me is still a mutant?"

"We don't know. We only looked at blood and lung cells so far. I don't think we mixed up any samples, because yours was the only one in the lab. If we're correct, it's quite remarkable."

"So the CF gene in my lungs is normal?"

"Exactly! Or at least that's what it looks like. Your CF protein, known as CTFR, is a long chain of 1408 amino acids strung together. Your mutation is the F508 deletion. The F is short for the amino acid phenylalanine, and 508 is its position in the chain. The bit of DNA that would normally code for the 508th amino acid in your CTFR protein is missing from your mutant gene. That's the mutation you were born with. It codes for a defective CTFR protein that's missing the 508th amino acid. But in your lung cells, it's not missing. The normal DNA sequence is there, including the code for F508."

"Okay, I think I get it, but how can my lungs have DNA different than my other cells?"

"I don't know. It's sounds crazy, but that's not the half of it. There's a second difference between your lung and blood cell genes. A little further down the amino acid chain, at position 513, there should be an amino acid called aspartate, and that's exactly what we find in your blood cell DNA. Humans all have DNA coding for aspartate at position 513. But in your lung cells, the DNA codes for an amino acid called glutamate. Aspartate and glutamate are very similar amino acids, so it doesn't affect the function of the CTFR protein. In fact, dog CTFR protein, which varies slightly from human, has glutamate at position 513."

"Dog?" asked Ron. "I have dog lungs? Am I going to start barking?"

"No, well, not really. I mean not at all. It's just that the CTFR protein in your lung cells contains an amino acid at position 513 never found in human protein and always found in dog. Dogs have a few more differences in the string of 1408 amino acids when compared to humans, but you don't have any of the other differences. It looks as if your mutant gene for CTFR was not replaced in its entirety. It was just patched, with a small stretch of DNA that corrected the F508 mutation, plus a little extra sequence that spanned at least to position 513."

"Doc, you said you can't explain it at least seven times now, so I reckon you don't understand it, either. All I know is that I feel better than I have since forever. I can breathe! I skipped my ventilator this morning. I slept through the night. I'm not hocking up lung bombs. I'm thinking it's a miracle, Doc. Hell, I'm going to church. Oops, I mean heck. I might just walk there. Maybe even jog."

"That's great, Ron. We'd like everyone with CF to feel like you do. There's obviously something of great medical significance here, and it would be really helpful if we could just get a bit more of your blood to check it out."

"Hey, no problem, Doc. I'm happy to help. I'll run down to the clinic later. That is, if the dog catcher doesn't pick me up along the way."

———

Eddie woke to a rustling. It was early dawn. The barrel fire had died, and a crack of low-angle morning light invaded their shelter under the highway overpass. Along with his indigent chums, he had retired there to drink his panhandling proceeds and suck on his half cigarettes. He sat up as a truck rumbled overhead on Highway 60, but he paid it no mind. He was busy squinting into the light at the shadowy, backlit figure. *It's an animal,* he thought.

He could make out a fuzzy perimeter. It had appendages and a frame but was twisted and bent in unnatural ways. There was a head, too, but not entirely round. Two points projected upward from the flattened crown, and the face was stretched forward, tapered like a cone. It sounded like a box of marbles dumped on concrete as it rose to full height. Its appendages snapped and popped into new positions. Two lower limbs supported the erect frame, while the two above dangled loosely. It looked tall, like a human, but lumpy in shape until it shook itself. Spiraling from the head down, a halo of debris flew from it in all directions, hitting the ground like muffled rain. He poked at a fragment that plopped onto his sleeping bag. It looked and felt like a chunk of wet carpeting.

He remained motionless, sitting, staring at the odd spectacle. The shape changed again. It looked thinner now, but he could still see irregular folds and shaggy clumps suspended and swaying from its outline. Its head had rounded out, too, a smoothened dome atop, with the face flattened. He watched the silhouette writhe about, its hands variously clutching at all parts of its frame, tearing away large sheets from its exterior until the figure of a tall, slender woman emerged. She raised a hand and pulled back on her enormous fingernails like they were levers. They stood straight up, perpendicular to her fingers, before snapping off and fluttering to the ground. Reaching to her backside, she yanked at what looked like a length of frayed rope and dropped it. Her hands brushed down her naked body, rolling up rumply sheets of dried dermis that dropped like small scrolls. She shook herself violently. The undulating motion migrated down her length, releasing a fine mist illuminated by the dawn light.

As she stepped out of the direct light, he was struck by her brilliant white skin and the thick mane of red hair on her head. She examined her gleaming, naked torso and picked at assorted stray patches of loose skin and hair. A distinct mound of hair at her pubis remained, and after a few painful tugs, she left it alone. Shivering in the cool dawn, she wrapped her long arms around her breasts and drew her legs together. Spotting a shopping cart, she rummaged through it and pulled out some stray garments. She dressed herself in a pair of grease-stained dungarees and an oversized military camo shirt. She found some weathered canvas tennis shoes and slipped them on, her big toe poking out through a hole in the upper.

He sat gawking at her, unwavering, his lower half still submerged in his sleeping bag. Brushing his cracked lips with the back of one hand, he hoisted a dusty bottle of vodka with the other. He scrutinized the bottle's contents and looked back at the apparition. Gathering himself, he called to it. "Where's my dog?" he asked, startling the squatting redhead, who was trying to light a cigarette butt in the embers. She turned to him and exhaled a hoarse barking sound that resembled human speech but was incomprehensible as such. She stood up, drew on the glowing butt, and emitted a thick plume of white smoke in his direction. Through the cloud, the pale phantom seemed to glide toward him, suspended in air.

Still clutching the bottle, he wormed out of his sleeping bag. He inched backward on his butt until he backed into a concrete stanchion. She closed on him slowly, close enough for him to see the freckles dotting her otherwise pure white face. Her ruby lips parted wide, exposing her gleaming white teeth showcased by a massive set of pointed canines. He dropped the bottle and formed a cross with his index fingers. She stopped and made sounds again, this time a pitched howl resembling actual words he understood as *where* and *I*. She scrunched up her nose and frowned. Reaching into her mouth, she extracted the upper canines one at a time and pitched the bloody pearls aside. She took another step forward, picked up his abandoned vodka bottle, and gargled its contents before swallowing it.

"Is this Greenland?" she asked the terrified vagabond.

"Gur-gur-Greenland?" he repeated. "Please, don't kill me."

"Do you know where Dagon is?" she asked.

"Dragon? There's no dragons here. I'm Eddie."

"Eddie? I am Emma. But I am making Shala. I need to find Dagon."

"I don't know any Dagon, and this is Arizona, not Greenland. Not a lot of green here, you know."

Pivoting away from him to face the sun, she stood up straight and stiffened. She rubbed her palms together before throwing them up in the air like she was releasing something. "Dagon is far away," she said, pointing at her shadow. "This way." Without looking back, she stepped out from under the overpass, climbed the embankment, and disappeared from his sight. He considered following her but recognized the hissing of a truck's airbrakes as it rumbled to a stop overhead. He heard some chatter and then the truck moved on.

———

"Well, well. What's a pretty thing like you doing all alone on the highway?" asked the truck driver.

"I need to find Dagon. He is this way," she said, pointing.

"That way, huh? Well, you're in luck, that's where I'm going, too." He shifted his overused rump around in his seat and glanced sideways at her. His eyes settled on her loosely buttoned camo shirt, her braless chest visible through the gaps between buttonholes. "I'm Dereck. You from around here?"

"I am a progenitor from Ross 128. It's not very far. Just eleven of your years."

"Okay, then. Do you have any family or friends?"

"I call for the congregations when it is safe for their arrival."

The driver shifted again. He gave the crotch of his pants a quick yank forward and scratched at his unkempt beard. He turned his head to her. "I can be your friend," he said. His tobacco-stained teeth peeked out through his weathered lips. His squinting eyes found the gaps in her shirt again.

"I need to find Dagon."

"Maybe he's down this road," he said, exiting Highway 60 at the Arizona Mills shopping mall.

"He's not here. He is much farther."

"Let's check, anyway," he said. Entering the enormous vacant parking lot, he steered the vehicle into a sunken shipping dock and shut it down. "I think Dagon's in the back," he said, tipping his head sideways toward the cramped bunk in the rear of his cab.

"He is not," she said.

"Like I said, let's check anyway." He unsnapped his seat belt, leaned over, and placed a gnarled hand on her upper thigh. "We can do this easy or hard, sweetie. It's up to you."

"I have to find Dagon."

She reached for the door handle when he grabbed her hair and pulled her head toward him. She could smell his acrid breath. Malice poured from his eyes. "Etemmu is with you," she said. "You will join them in the void. No congregation will take you." She didn't understand why he would smile at her dire assessment, but his grin stretched the corners of his crooked mouth. She tried once more to pull away, but his hand shifted, grasping the back of her neck.

But there was no sense of alarm. At least not from her. She twisted her neck and bit his arm.

"Oh, you little bitch!" he screamed. "Now I'm going to have to—" and his voice trailed off at the sight of the expanding bright red circle on his arm. "What the fuck?"

"Not fuck. Venom. From the brown recluse spider. I found it in Emma's yard. I made its venom. You have to seek medicine or you might die. I'm sorry."

The stricken driver fell back in his seat. Beads of sweat formed on his forehead as he watched his blazing arm swell like a balloon. His vision began to blur. He felt dizzy and disoriented. Frightened of her now, he reached for the door handle and fell out of his truck. She shifted over to the driver's seat. With the door still open, she peered down at the suffering man writhing on the concrete. "It is your choice," she said. "It is always your choice. I'm sorry."

She studied the controls in front of her for a few seconds, started the truck, and drove off. She found his Marlboro Lights on the dash and lit one. Heading west, she joined Interstate 10 and continued a short distance before exiting toward a billboard that read *Food City*. She chugged though the parking lot, passed the Family Dollar store, and abandoned the truck directly in front of the Food City grocery. An elderly couple leaving the store glared at the vivacious woman in rags exiting the misplaced truck.

"Miss, you can't park there," beckoned the old man.

"I need food," she replied and entered the store.

Once inside, she proceeded though the aisles, stopping in the pet food section. She tore open a ten-pound bag of Purina Dog Chow, hoisted it, and let the pellets waterfall into her mouth. Bits of chow rained to the floor around her, attracting the attention of a few early-morning shoppers. A middle-aged man looked down the length of the aisle at her. Concern spread across his face. He left his cart and approached her cautiously.

She lowered the bag, half-empty, then crunched and swallowed what remained in her mouth. "It has real meat," she said, looking at the bag before offering it to the approaching man.

"That's dog food, miss," he said.

"Yes, Zephyr's favorite."

"But it's for dogs. You shouldn't eat it. Do you need help, miss?"

"I must find Dagon. He is near the water."

"Is he your friend?"

"He is my other half."

"Oh. Well, that's a nice way of putting it. My other half died a year ago. She was wonderful. But I have a daughter about your age. She still keeps me company sometimes."

"Died? What congregation did she join?"

"We're Methodists, if that's what you mean. Look, if you want, I can give you some real food and maybe some better clothing. My daughter left a lot of her clothes when she headed off to college. She's about your size. I might be able to help you find your husband, or your other half."

"I am Emma, or Shala, almost."

"Hi, Emma. I'm Ernie, Ernie Tara. Pleased to meet you." He extended a hand.

She took his hand and examined his face closely. "Your Bar will be welcomed."

He kept her hand and led her through the checkout, paying for her dog chow along the way.

Once outside, he guided her around an enormous truck blocking the entrance. "Whose truck is this?" he grumbled.

"It is Dereck's. He is sick. Etemmu will take him."

He looked at her curiously. "Dereck, huh? Well, Dereck needs to move his vehicle, or the police will take him."

He drove her to his modest ranch home in the Woodbriar neighborhood. Once inside, he showed her pictures of his dearly deceased wife and his awesome daughter. She spoke little, only touching the photos lightly and nodding at his comments. His voice cracked a little when he described the image of him and his wife fishing in Alaska.

"She is safe," she said.

"I know. She's in heaven. Gotta be, she was a saint."

"She is with the Eleventh Congregation, the beloved Artists."

"Whoa! She was an artist! That's one of hers, right there." He pointed to a framed oil on canvas depicting a group of impoverished immigrants, both welcomed and reviled by a contentious crowd. "How did you know?"

"It just is. And always was, even before your star was born."

Speechless, he only blinked at her.

"Your Bar will join the Tenth Congregation, the Makers. They are highly respected," she continued. "But don't worry, she will still be there with you. All are as one."

He scanned the room for any evidence of his career as a building contractor. There was none. "Do I know you?" he asked. "Did we build your house?"

"My house is not here. Not yet. She is yours," she said, grazing a photo of his daughter with her index finger. "A Technician. They are the Sixth. They are highly valued. They bend the gravity. The congregations cannot move without them."

There was a UC Santa Barbara pennant on the wall, but no evidence that his daughter was studying engineering there. He started to tell her but stopped. He wasn't sure what to think anymore. He was a practical man. He laughed at tarot-card-wielding psychics and the fools who paid them. He even had his doubts about angels. But there was an unbodied essence about this woman. He was awed but unafraid. Even if he couldn't explain it, he knew good when he saw it. He reconsidered his doubts about angels. She was connected to something ethereal, almost holy. How could she know him? It seemed like she knew his family, too. On the ride there, he thought she had just guessed well at his likes and dislikes. He didn't think she was guessing anymore.

He stopped regarding her as mentally ill. She was genuine and clear as crystal. Quirky, yes. Eating dog food—definitely strange. But her insight was unfathomable. He wished his wife was there to witness this transcendent being.

"I'm sorry. I have to go. I need to find Dagon soon," she said.

"Yes. You believe he is west and near the water? I can take you to the bus station. There's one that goes almost directly to Los Angeles on Interstate 10. Would that be okay?"

"It would be okay. When I get closer, it will become easier to find him."

"All right, then. I'll find you some nice clothes and put a little care package together for your trip. But I need to take care of something first."

He started for the bathroom when she spoke up. "You should be all right now. You are no longer under attack. I fixed it."

"Attack? Fixed what?"

"You don't need the medicine."

Indeed, he was well past due for his insulin injection, but he didn't feel faint, despite not having eaten all morning. He had forgotten it. He should at least be feeling dizzy, if not comatose by now. He checked his CGM monitor. It was pegged at 110mg/dL, normal. He tapped the window on the monitor, but the value remained. "Something's wrong," he said.

She frowned. "No, it is right. You are all right now."

"Well, yeah, it's 110, but—"

"I repaired it. Don't worry. I used Eddie's instead of Zephyr's, so you're not a dog."

"Eddie's?"

"He lives under the bridge. He is a Drifter, of the Twelfth. They don't do much, but they are humble and nice."

"You used Eddie's what?"

"His Form. I used it for you. I used Emma's for me. And Zephyr's." She smiled. "It's okay. See? I'm not a dog. There were some errors, but I fixed them. I fixed your error, too. No more medicine for Ernie."

Ernie sat down. He was trembling. He checked his monitor again. He traced the connecting wire to his belly and inspected the sensor inserted under his skin. It was intact.

"It's okay," she repeated. "You can take it off now."

He rose to his feet and faced her. He placed a hand on her shoulder and squeezed. There was flesh and muscle and bone. He touched her head, then her hands. He held one hand in both of his and turned it over. With an index finger, he traced a blood vessel in her wrist.

"What are you?" he asked.

"A progenitor. I was in the dust that made the rocks that fell from the sky. I assemble and call."

Is this God? thought Ernie. He was certainly humbled. He had faith in her, too. Should he remove his monitor now? He thought of Moses, who doubted only once by tapping the rock twice. That's all it took to be banished from the promised land. Maybe she wasn't God. It wasn't what he had pictured, but then again, what should he picture? All the tor-turous, dark Renaissance art depicting glowing spirits was merely the fabrications of frightened men. He knew that much. But a red-haired, blue-eyed woman? He didn't recall any biblical passages or prophecies calling for that. And why did she need to take a bus? God rode the bus? Finally, he just surrendered and accepted her for whatever she was. It put out the fire in his mind. *Maybe not God,* he thought, *but she is good.*

She looked pretty human in a pair of his daughter's khaki pants and a faded blue corduroy shirt. Having noticed her squinting, he gave her a pair of his daughter's old eyeglasses. The large, round wire-rimmed frames settled low on her slender nose, enlarging a spray of freckles visible through them. He packed some food in a backpack, gave her two hundred dollars, and bought her a bus ticket at the station. He hugged her like she was his own, gave her his phone number, and that of his daughter. He had little doubt she could handle herself. So, he left her there awaiting the 9:07 and dashed off to his jobsite.

Sitting on an outdoor bench, she heard a gravelly voice behind her. "Are you going to Los Angeles, too?" She turned to find a bedraggled man, short on hygiene and long in the face. His droopy sadness drew her in. His tattered clothes, oily hair, and stubbled face told a story of hard living. His eyes dim, he smiled a broken smile. "I'm going to Los Angeles," he said.

"I am, too, I need to find Dagon. He is near there."

"I can help you find him."

"Do you know where he is?"

"Sure. I'm pretty sure, at least."

"I must meet him. Dagon is assembling. It is safe to call the congregations now. We have to let them know."

He regarded her curiously at first, and then like an adult entertaining a child's fantasies. "Yeah, Dagon is cool. He's probably in Venice Beach. I know a lot of people there. I could help you."

"Oh, good. My name is Emma, or Shala, if you like."

"I'm Jimmy, or James if you like. Do you have enough money to go to Los Angeles, Emma?"

"Yes, I have this from Ernie," she replied, and showed him the ten crisp twenty-dollar bills.

His narrow eyes finally opened at the sight of the bills. "I can take us straight to Venice Beach with that money."

"Okay. Thank you." She gave him the money but frowned when her hand contacted his. She leaned back and looked him up and down. "You are bubbling," she said. "Etemmu knows you. You are not helping me, Jimmy."

"What? Of course I am." He tried to look indignant as he stuffed the bills into his shirt pocket.

"No, you are not." They sat in silence for a while, side by side on the bench, both looking straight ahead. Finally, she reached into her backpack and pulled out a loaded syringe and presented it to him. "You will need this soon," she told him.

"Ooh, wee!" he exclaimed. "You sly girl. How did you know? I'll be jonesing soon enough. Is it the black tar that's been making the rounds?" He took the syringe and looked around in all directions. "Might as well get to it." He stood up but felt faint and sat back down again. His head started to spin as he tilted sideways in her direction. She slid away and he tipped onto the bench, settling on his side. "I feel sick. I think I'm going to pass out."

She reached over and removed her money from his shirt pocket and stood up. His arm lashed out at her but fell limp and dangled off the bench.

"You have Ernie's mistake," she said. "You will need the medicine." She pointed to the syringe. "It's Ernie's medicine. It will make you feel better but not make you better. That is your choice."

The 9:07 to Los Angeles chugged into the station and hissed to a stop. She looked at Jimmy one more time. His lips were blue, and his eyelids were fluttering. She took the syringe out of his hand, poked the needle longwise into his wrist, and pushed the plunger down. Once aboard the bus, she saw Jimmy sitting back up, the syringe still dangling from his wrist. He looked at her through the bus window. His lips were rounded. He was trying to form any word that began with a *W* when the bus rolled away.

CHAPTER 11

REPAIRED

Dr. Tom Allen waited while his research associate at the Biodesign Institute located the sample. Richard held the tube up to the light and shook it. He stared at it until his confounded squint landed on Tom. His narrowed eyes spoke for him.

"It's Tara's, Ernie Tara's," said Tom. "Type-one diabetic, middle-aged. Called last night to say he had stopped using insulin, didn't need it anymore. He's been my patient for over twenty years. I thought he was delusional. He said he had helped a woman, so she cured him. I called him in for his own safety. But he actually looked fine. More than fine. I started thinking I was delusional, so I took a blood sample. Find anything?"

"Yes, nothing. That's what I found. Maybe you should sit down."

"Nothing?"

"I ran the protein array to look for the typical antibodies. Like I said, nothing. No reactivity to GAD65, ZnT8, insulin. Nothing. It's like his pancreas is normal now. No evidence of islet cell destruction at all. They're not spilling out antigens anymore. And the CD8+ lymphocytes that do the destroying? They're gone, too. So, this is either not Ernie Tara's blood, or this woman he helped is Jesus. Do you think Jesus would come back as a woman? What would the Pope say? Are we certain this is Tara's sample?"

"It's got to be his blood. I drew the sample myself, into that very tube, and labelled it myself. He and I were the only ones here. Let's sequence some of his blood cell DNA for his HLA mutation. That would confirm—"

"Did it. The HLA-DQ1 position-57 mutation, the one that makes him diabetic, it's still there. You do have other patients with that same mutation, though. So, I looked for additional markers. Tara's old samples contain a polymorphism at position 68, found in only one out of thirty-four people. It's also in this new sample. Unless you have another patient with that polymorphism, I'm thinking Ms. Jesus actually did cure him. That is, if this is really his blood. You should look at it."

Tom Allen held the tube up and swirled it. "It looks pretty cloudy. Did you spin it down?"

"Yeah, but the plasma still looked cloudy. They float. They're little spheres made of lipid. That dude Vishva, who works for that Indian guy in Cell Biology, he says they're exosomes, from bacteria, or something. They're little vesicles, hollow fat balls, that form from pinched-off bits of cell membrane. He collected some of them by gradient centrifugation. Among other things, they contain DNA. So, I isolated it."

"What kind of DNA?"

"You're still not sitting down. I'm about to explain how Ms. Jesus cured him."

Tom Allen had become accustomed to Richard's inverted affect. He emoted strongly at the simplest of things. It was his snarky way of signaling their irrelevance. By contrast, he came across as nonchalant when describing something truly exciting. His measured calmness at present was unsettling to Tom. He found a bench stool.

Richard continued, "The exosome DNA looks sort of like a CRISPR locus. Like what bacteria evolved to detect and destroy the DNA from viruses that try to invade them. There are several short stretches of repeated sequence lined up in tandem. The repeated sequences have spacers separating them. Each spacer is a unique, non-repeating stretch of short sequence. In bacteria, those spacer sequences code for the RNA that disrupts the genes of invading viruses. And just like in bacteria, the repeat/spacer region is flanked by actual genes that code for functional proteins and enzymes. In bacteria, the genes code for integrases, polymerases, recombinases, and all sorts of things that cut, copy, and paste strands of DNA. Ditto for some of the flanking genes in our mysterious exosomes. Except some of the genes don't match any known sequences in the databases."

"The exosomes contain bacterial genes?"

"Not all are bacterial genes. Some DNA matches loosely to E. coli, some to archaea sequences, but some to human, others to dog, and get this, some to spider DNA."

"Spider?"

"Weird, huh? But not really weird, yet. You're sitting? Good. Okay, one of the non-repeating spacer sequences sitting between the short repeats codes for a small bit of the wild-type human HLA-DQ1 protein—the part that contains position 57. Get it?"

Tom was mystified. Not because he didn't get it but because he did. "So, you think these exosomes edited the DNA in Ernie Tara's pancreatic cells and cured him?"

"It all fits, right? The exosomes contain all the enzymes to do the editing, and they have the piece of DNA with the normal HLA sequence. They get in, cut out the old mutant bit, and paste in the new normal sequence. These exosomes are like mobile-unit DNA fix-it kits. Cool, huh? You ever heard of anything like that? I think we can get a great paper out of this."

"A paper?" was all Tom could muster. The sheer naivety of his student baffled him almost as much as his outlandish theory. Who would believe it? He didn't. He envisioned a title for the paper: *A Circulating Lipid Vesicle Cures Diabetes by Correcting the HLA-DQ1 Mutation in Human Pancreas*. He might as well claim he had raised someone from the dead. There had to be a mistake. A mix-up, maybe a computational one. Or a prank. He didn't know where to start. Where did the vesicles come from? From where did they get the correct HLA-DQ1 sequence? How did they swap it for the mutated sequence? It was all so impossible to conceive. Monumental discoveries, once revealed, usually made sense. This made none.

"Tell no one about this, Richard," said Tom, "No one. And repeat the sequencing to confirm it. I wonder if Ernie would agree to a core biopsy?"

"No problem," said Richard. "And what if I'm right? His pancreatic islets have the wild-type HLA gene. We should include Ms. Jesus as a coauthor."

CHAPTER 12

NEW SUITS

After orchestrating their separate entrances, Alex and Ashley were reunited at the JPL. To put some flesh on their charade, she came down to greet him in the lobby. "Good morning, Alex," she said, for the second time that day. "Right this way." The elevator door had barely closed when he pulled her close. She giggled and whispered something about elevators having cameras. He held up his bag and kissed her behind it. They arrived at the fourth floor all too soon, where they proceeded in a professional manner to her lab.

They sat down in front of a monitor on a lab bench. "See, shiny and smooth like your Greenland stone," she explained to Alex, pointing at a new image of the Big Mac meteorite. "Dr. Wadhwa at ASU sent these photos to me. We're not the only ones who noticed the little onion balls at the base of the stromatolites. She's never seen anything like them, either. She's convinced Big Mac is very old, possibly outdating our solar system, but doubts the little bumps are actually stromatolites."

"An interstellar meteorite? Aren't those quite rare?"

"Exceedingly. Only a couple are known, and even those are quite controversial. I asked some folks at our Center for Near Objects if they had anything on it. They catalog the times, dates, speeds, and trajectories of incoming meteors. Apparently, Big Mac was traveling way too fast, about thirty miles per second, to be gravitationally bound by our sun. Its trajectory and speed are consistent with an origin outside of our solar system. The data indicate an ejection point about eleven light-years way, possibly in the vicinity of Ross 128, a brown dwarf."

"A brown dwarf? Was he unfairly excluded from the other seven?"

"What? My god. What is wrong with you? The brown dwarf is a star, actually red, with presumably habitable exoplanets."

"So, some aliens started a rock fight with us?"

"Some astrobiologists have suggested that interstellar meteorites could, in a sense, represent a sort of message in a bottle from other planets. It's conceivable that life could even be transferred between planets this way. The idea even has a name, panspermia."

"Sperm traveling eleven light-years at thirty miles per second. I'm jealous."

She slapped his shoulder. "Can you not? This is serious! Think about it. A four-billion-year-old rock from Greenland has the same fossilized signature as an interstellar meteorite. Life sprouted from the Greenland rock. Life that has DNA containing a specific mutation found in a human working in the lab. It has a second mutation engineered into a fly gene from a neighboring lab. Then, the DNA sequences change and evolve in real time. That life-form—because I don't know what else to call it—undergoes an unprecedented metamorphosis and flies off. What could possibly make this more interesting?"

"Well, there is a detail I haven't shared with you."

You're an alien?"

"No. I wish. I always identified with Khan from Star Trek. He was such a badass. You know, he walked with a perceptible limp in the movie because he had been run over by a horse during production. He was so—"

"Stop, Alex! Please. As you were saying... What detail?"

"Oh, yeah. See, there were these guys in Greenland, Emil and Noah, from the Institute for Natural Resources. They didn't want us to take the rocks. I mean, seriously did not want us to take them. Jack snuck them out, anyway. But these guys came to his lab in Stanford looking for them. Then, they came to my lab in Chicago. They were babbling on about some mystical crap involving zeros and bars and assemblies and meetings. Certifiable kooks. I kicked them out, but they returned to Stanford, according to Jack. They don't know you have the rocks, but they are persistent, to put it mildly."

"In other words, some creeps from Greenland might be stalking me. Is that what you're trying to say?"

"Not to worry. They're harmless, almost likable in their childish manners. Super weird, though. Like when they came to my lab, they looked much older than they did in Greenland, but it was only a few days later. And they're not stalking you. Just the rocks. Removing them from the greenstone belt totally put their knickers in a knot."

"Maybe someone from the government is trying to keep a secret."

"Secret, yes. Government? Not too sure about that. It's more like they're from a religious cult or something. Can we get coffee? I want to ride the elevator again."

"Seriously?"

"About the coffee, at least. We could take the stairs if you prefer. Should be deserted at this hour." He gave her the Groucho Marx eyebrows but got the schoolmarm glare in return.

"Fine. I wouldn't mind some coffee myself. But let's conduct ourselves professionally while on this campus."

Alex found a lab coat and donned it. He accessorized with a pair of safety glasses, a dosimetry badge, and a black notebook. "Dr. Woodsum, I believe our approach to this problem requires a caffeinated beverage. Do you concur?"

His nerdy getup made him oddly more attractive to her. That he was solely focused on her, even if just in play, warmed her even more. She fought off thoughts of him dressed only in the lab coat. "There's a cafe in building 303. Let's not take the stairs."

Exiting the building, Alex shielded his eyes from the glare of the morning sun angling off the hood of a Chevy Malibu parked in front of building eighty-three. He peeked in through the windshield at the two shadowy figures inside. Slumped over and immobile, they appeared asleep. Ashley stopped alongside Alex, then circled around to the passenger side of the car, where she recoiled at the sight of its occupants. Ashen and withered, the two men looked positively anorexic, their frames barely able to support the suits dangling from them. Deep furrows cut through their gray foreheads. Skin sagged from their cheeks. Spittle hung from the indigo lips of the passenger. The driver's head was turned sideways, resting on the steering wheel, facing her. He was missing some teeth, and a detached tangle of gray hair clung to his chin.

"I think they're dead," she said, backing away from the car. "What the hell?"

She backed into Alex and jumped when he grasped her shoulders. He stared into the vehicle. It was the suits, those unmistakable gray suits. "No way!" he said. "It's them. That's my pen in his pocket! He kept it when they came to my lab in Chicago. Holy crap! They're dead? We need to call the police."

———

"Yes, sir. I think they are Noah Sorrenson and Emil Pedersen, from the Institute for Natural Resources in Greenland. I met them recently. I was there on a geological expedition. They were concerned over the rocks my partner and I had excavated there." Alex spoke as the officer opened the car door. The escaping stench sent the two of them reeling backward. "Definitely dead," coughed Alex, covering his face with his hands. "But of old age? They looked about forty just a few days ago."

The cop only heard half of what Alex had said. He was justifiably puzzled by the simultaneous deaths of two old men who oddly chose Road C at the JPL as their final resting place. "I need to call the coroner," said the officer. "I've got your contacts, so we'll be in touch. In the meantime, you'll have to remove yourself while we investigate. You probably don't want to see what comes next, anyway."

Alex wanted to stay. He had more questions. He wanted to tell them everything. Ashley tugged on his arm. With the cop turned away, she shook her head. "Let's go," she said. Once out of earshot, she quietly explained that he would probably be committed if he spilled everything he had experienced over the past few days. "Let's go get that coffee and talk it over. Maybe they'll be gone by the time we get back. He's right, I don't want to see this."

They sat in the building 303 cafe for nearly an hour. The facts, they concluded, were simply unbelievable. Two men from Greenland grew fifty years older over a few days while looking for four-billion-year-old rocks that sprouted a worm-fly-mouse thing that flew away.

"We have our reputations to consider, Alex, and our jobs. I'm already Space Lady; I don't want to be Whack-Job Lady. If we can prove it, document it, or get more witnesses, then fine. But if this blows over and we're the only ones left to tell the story, no one will believe it. We'll lose our funding. We would be a joke. We stand to lose everything. The only job you'll get will be on History Channel's *Ancient Aliens.*"

"I kind of like that show. I mean, I know it's bullshit, but I can't help but wonder sometimes. What if it's real and the poor sap who experienced it can't convince anyone else?"

"And that poor sap is now a laughingstock living out of his car."

"I know. And I drive a Ford Fiesta."

"Really? I would not have guessed that. You're going to need a van. Let's head back to eighty-three. Maybe our ancient aliens have been carted off by now."

They had not. Road C was blocked off. An ambulance and three more police cars had gathered around the entrance to building eighty-three. Ashley and Alex let themselves in through the engineering door and proceeded to the elevator. Arriving at the fourth floor, they found a group of people gathered around a hallway window, observing the scene below in front of the building. Ashley and Alex stood behind the voyeurs and looked on. A first-response crew in gray overalls, gloves, and masks was trying to extricate the bodies from the car. One of them hooked the passenger's body under the armpits and gave it a hearty tug. The underweight corpse nearly leapt from the seat, surprising the responder, who backpedaled into a cop. The body twisted sideways and dropped to the pavement. A single arm remained in the grasp of the shocked responder until he dropped that, too.

A second responder stepped in to hoist the prone cadaver, but the featherlight torso detached at the waist, leaving him holding half of a body sans the already detached arm. A trail of gray and brown dust bled from the upper torso still in his grasp. Horrified, he dropped it, causing the head to break off and roll over a few times on the pavement. The nose and lips, erased by the friction, left a set of brown hash marks separated in distance by the circumference of the head. Everyone on the site backed away. They watched the bottom half of the body deflate like a balloon. The clothing rumpled and sagged until the pants looked as though they rested on a few piles of sand. One of the panicked officers grabbed his phone but wasn't sure who to call—the CDC, the NIH, or his mom?

"See?" whispered Alex, pulling Ashley back from the gawkers. "How many witnesses do we need?"

"That's just a small part of it. As far as they're concerned, it's Ebola or something. It's not enough to convince anybody."

While more onlookers had collected at the window, Alex and Ashley slipped out and hustled down to her lab. Jeffery, her graduate student, spotted them, explaining that two dead guys had been discovered in the parking area. Then, as if he had just recalled it, "Oh, yeah, you have some visitors, Ashley." He tipped his head toward her office.

She could see the crowns of a couple heads over the lab shelves. Assuming it was the police, she pulled Alex aside and said, "Just tell them again what you told them outside. We know nothing else. Okay? Promise?"

"Check. Unless it's Mulder and Scully. Then, we tell them everything."

The two strangers awaiting Ashley stood quietly outside her office door. They wore similar blue suits, were of comparable, medium height, and bore a familial resemblance to each other. They seemed very young to be detectives, at least experienced ones. Their hair was also a bit long for their profession, as were their fingernails, and both bore the sparse stubble of an unshaven post-adolescent.

"I'm Noah Sorenson and this is Emil Pedersen from Greenland Institute of Natural Resources," said one of them.

A few feet behind Ashley, and shrouded from their view, Alex stepped forward and shouted, "The hell you are! Did you kill Emil and Noah? Who are you? Really!"

"We were not killed. No one is killed," said the one who had assumed Emil's name. "We have new Zumru only. We are still here, and nothing was lost. Bar is safe."

"Then who was in the car down there? The dead people? My pen that Noah borrowed was still in his pocket."

"Oh, yes, I'm sorry, Alex. I did not return your pen," said the new Noah.

"Wait! How do you know my name? What? The pen? Forget the pen. I don't want the pen. I want to know who you are. And don't tell me Noah and Emil, goddammit! They are dead! We just saw them. They turned to dust!"

The new Emil and Noah regarded each other in silent consultation before nodding in apparent agreement. "I am Sukka, and this is Sanga," said new Noah. "We are scouts from Ross. We need to find Dagon. He must not meet with Shala or all of our Bar will come. It is too soon for us. We will perish here. Dagon has been released, and we fear he is assembling now. His Siru was in the rocks you took from the greenstone belt. It was in the dust that made those rocks. You have exposed him, but he was not to be released. Not yet."

"Wait, wait, wait." stammered Alex, "Hold on. Great story, guys. Love it. So will the History Channel. But you need to patch a few glaring plot holes first. Like, why didn't Dagon just assemble himself, say, a billion years ago, and how come he pops out of the rocks just because we took a sample?"

"His Siru measures the gas and assembles Dagon only when it is low enough. A billion years ago, the gas was still too high, Alex. But it was decreasing, exactly as we predicted. The volcanoes were dying. The heat was leaving. The future for this habitat looked good, so we sent Shala sixty thousand years ago, and now her rock has arrived. But the gas returned, very quickly. Especially over the past one hundred of your years. Our Zumru cannot tolerate it. It is something we cannot adapt to, a flaw in our design. You saw what happened. Yes? We can build new Zumru," he said, pointing to his own frame, "but not quickly enough. The Bar needs Zumru. It binds together the congregations. If the Bar is sent here but our Zumru expires, they will wander in the realm of Etemmu. Where are the rocks, Alex? Please."

Alex found this account hard to swallow and impossible to digest. Two reincarnated scouts sought to prevent the spontaneous assembly of a rock-man, whose union with Shala, who arrived on a meteorite, would bring a population of beings to Earth who would die quickly of old age because of gas. And the congregations would wander? "So, just to play along," Alex offered, "if the gas is so high, why is this Dagon jumping out of your party cake already?"

Noah opened his mouth, but Ashley bested him. "The gas," she said, "it's carbon dioxide. I put the culture dish in an incubator maintained at low CO2. We brought him to life in an artificial environment."

It made sense, almost painfully so. Their current hypothesis, admittedly constructed from presumed pranks, mislabeled samples, and a lack of sleep, was badly frayed. Their peg was getting squarer while the hole grew rounder. Here was a piece that actually fit. Still grasping for earthly straws of reason, Alex didn't want to believe it. It had to be a trick. "No one comes back to life," he said aloud. Like the doubting Thomas, he had to poke his finger in the wounds of God. He turned to the scouts and spoke evenly, dividing his attention between them. "When you came to me in Chicago, I thought that you were a part of a religious organization. What was it?"

Sukka smiled. "We know what Scientology is, Alex. It is not true. There is no Galactic Confederation. Do not concern yourself with thetans, either. And I am very sorry about your pen."

Flustered, but still of sound mind, he asked a second test question. "Who did I get in a fight with in Greenland?"

"Oh, Buzz," Sanga said. "He has healed but remains very angry with you. Do not return."

Ashley watched Alex's face blanch as he settled into a chair. He leaned forward and pounded his head against her desk a few times. A crimson hue spread across his concussed forehead. "Am I still here?" he asked her. "Are we awake?"

Ashley was already primed to abandon a hypothesis erected from self-delusion. She had directly witnessed the evolution of the flying worm-mouse thing. She knew that was real, but was still hedging, clinging to the implausible. But the look on Alex's face? That was the sledgehammer wrecking the remnants of any flimsy rationale. It was all too real but still hard accept. It was literally earth shattering. She didn't know what to say to Alex. Finally, she asked, "You got in a fight?"

"What? Not really," Alex began, until he noticed Sukka and Sanga studying his response. "It was more like a disagreement, I guess. He started it, okay? Can we talk about that later? Come on! ET is right here! In your office. Don't you have questions for them?"

"We need to find the rocks, Alex," implored Sukka. "Time is running out. It is important for you, too. All of you."

"So, okay, the Bar, or whatever it is," implored Alex, "it comes here, and there's no Zummers, or the Zummers die, then what? Why is that important for us?"

Both Sukka and Sanga smiled broadly. "It is Zumru," said Sanga, pounding his chest with a fist. "It holds Bar together. You, all of you, will join a congregation when you lose your Zumru. Maybe you will be my habitant!" he said, beaming. "That Zumru will hold you, much like your Zumru does now, but with all the knowledge of Bar together. But if all the Zumru dies, Bar will be without, and it will dwell in an empty place, in the void, separate and unreachable."

"The rocks are at UCLA!" blurted Ashley. "I saw a strange animal grow out of one. It flew away!"

"Is you-see-el-eh this way?" asked Sanga, pointing southwest. "Dagon is that way," he said turning to Sukka.

A knock on the office door interrupted them. It was Jeffery. "Someone else here to see you," he said. A stern-looking diminutive woman in a dark suit bobbed behind Jeffery, staring at them through the office window.

"Alex Sina?" she asked as the door opened. "And you must be Ashley Woodsum. I'm Detective Stockley with the Pasadena CID, Forensics. Okay if I ask you two a few questions about the deceased gentlemen you discovered this morning?"

"We are not dead," said Sukka, "our Zumru—"

"Sure. My colleagues were just on their way out," interrupted Alex. "Aren't you expected at UCLA?" He looked back and forth at Sukka and Sanga. "Dagon, right? He's waiting for you guys."

"We will find him," said Sukka. Without the slightest acknowledgement, the two scouts rudely brushed past the detective and left.

She looked indignant as they passed. Her eyes followed them to the exit. "Colleagues, huh?" she said. "Nice manners."

"Sorry. They're not from around here," said Alex. "They're in a hurry."

"Well, I'm sorry, too. Sorry that you two had to witness that awful spectacle this morning. It must have been dreadful. We're still working on a cause of death, but it looks like an exotic virus or a pathogen of some kind might have killed them. Likely not contagious, since there are no other reports of illness. And they were not"—she looked down at her notebook—"Emil Pedersen nor Noah Sorrenson, as you had presumed. Both of them are still quite alive and well in Greenland. And they said they have never met Alex Sina, although they did find your name in their geologic registration base. So, where's that leave us?"

"Well, the guys in the car reminded me of them, I guess. They seemed a lot older, though."

"Yeah, being dead can do that to you," deadpanned Detective Stockley. "So, since Pedersen and Sorrenson are indeed alive, it is unlikely that they were the dead guys in the car."

"Unlikely, yes, I would agree, but—"

"Impossible, actually," Ashley broke in, pretending to be amused at the detective's understatement. "Considering their condition, they could have been confused with almost anybody else."

"Yeah, mistaken identity, I suppose. Right, Alex?" The detective shot Alex a practiced look.

"Sure, I guess," he said.

"Well, here's the thing," she continued. "In one of the dead guys' suits, we found a pen labelled *Department of Paleontology, University of Chicago*. Is that your department, Alex?"

"Yes, yes, it is," said Alex. "That was why I mistakenly identified them."

"So, just to be clear, whatever killed them wasn't some experiment of yours. Like maybe a germ you dredged up somewhere. They got infected with it and then tracked you down, hoping you could cure them. Am I getting warmer?"

"Really? Come on. I mean, I saw that one on a CSI episode. Is that how you people train?" He suppressed an urge to recommend the *X-Files* instead. "Look, I saw the pen, and it confused me. Okay? I don't know why the dead guys were here and whether they were ever in Chicago. But Sorrenson and Pedersen, or their doppelgängers or imposters or whoever they were, came to Chicago to visit me about some rocks from Greenland. That's why I thought it was them, although they looked quite different."

"So, who are they? Have you found anything?" asked Ashley.

"They carried no identification whatsoever. That pen is the only lead we have so far. The car was rented, but not by them, and we can't find whoever rented it. We are awaiting DNA analysis, but that only helps if there's a match."

Ashley's head was swimming. "How would the technicians react when they read out that DNA data?" she wondered. "Make sure they do the analysis twice," she offered. "It can be misleading sometimes."

The detective pivoted to Ashley. She looked at her notes again. "You're an astro, uh, biologist. Is that right, Dr. Woodsum? Do you have, what is it, a hypothesis, so to speak? What do you think is going on here? Space aliens? Go ahead, I'm all ears."

"Well, I'm actually a microbiologist, but I do have an interest in the possibility of extraterrestrial life," responded Ashley. Then, she assumed a dead-serious air before continuing. "So, the hypothesis. I think the dead guys are from another planet, and they came here to prevent a catastrophe that threatens the universe. And they didn't really die, either, because they were instantly reincarnated and just walked away."

A dry silence ensued for a few seconds until the three of them succumbed to raucous laughter.

"Excellent," said Detective Stockley. "Be sure to repeat that to the news crews down on the street." Still smiling, she said, "But I think my CSI scenario is more plausible. It's quite believable, too. Right, Alex? No reincarnation, no aliens. Just a curious professor who brought back a spooky bug from God knows where and accidentally, or maybe not accidentally, infected a couple of unlucky saps. So, we just need to know who those saps were, Alex."

Alex looked at Ashley first. She shrugged her eyebrows. He turned to the detective. "Definitely aliens," he said. "You should watch more History Channel and less CSI. You see, the dead guys, they are from a planet eleven light-years away. One of their progenitors, whom they seeded Earth with over four billion years ago, was accidentally released. If he meets up with a second progenitor, who arrived at McDonald's on a meteorite, then all of their alien kin will come to Earth, but they'll die because humans polluted the atmosphere. See? It makes way more sense than your silly germ idea."

Ashley tried to initiate another round of laughter, but the detective wasn't having it. She bristled at Alex. "Look, Doc, that's your pen in his pocket. And I'll prove it." She pulled a glass tube from her bag that contained a Q-tip. "You can voluntarily swab your mouth with this, or I can arrest you and make you do it downtown. And, again, please share your ET hypothesis with the news crews downstairs."

Alex swabbed the inside of his mouth and handed it back to her. "I'm only telling the news that you demanded oral from me."

"We will meet again," she said. She snapped shut the glass tube to punctuate her promise and marched out of the lab.

Alex and Ashley closed the office door again and shuttered the window. Their guards down, they faced each other. Each read the fear and astonishment on the other's face. They simply stood in silence, acknowledging their unique bond, a union cemented by the unbelievable. Together, they felt alone in the world, a loneliness that drew them closer to each other.

"Are you scared?" she asked him.

"Yes." He placed a hand on each side of her face and kissed her. All of his emotions, the entire rainbow of fear, longing, joy, sadness, anger, collapsed into the single color of her silvery-blue eyes. He dropped his hands and curled his arms around her back and spoke softly into her ear. "I can't decide which is more unbelievable, meeting you or discovering space aliens."

Locked together, she took a baby step backward and pushed herself up onto her desktop. She drew him in close with her arms, lifted her feet, and locked her ankles behind him. She kissed him again. "How do I know you're not a space alien?" She looked down between their bodies. "You seem to have otherworldly powers." Her hands slid down his back as he thrust his pelvis forward.

It was if the rush of blood to his head caused the desk phone to ring. Ashley ignored it until Janet's panicked voice penetrated their warm bubble. "Ashley! Pick up if you're there! You need to come quickly." Both of them jerked their heads back and snickered at the perfectly timed double entendre.

Alex stepped away, shrugged, and tipped his head toward the phone while keeping his eyes on Ashley's.

"Hi, Janet. what's up?"

"It's a person now! A real, live person! It talks!"

"Hey! Slow down. What's a person?"

"The flying mouse-worm! I found it, or him, or whatever it is. It was holed up in the media storage room. It ate all the poured agar plates and then the entire stock of dry agar powder, among other things. It's a person now. It calls itself Dagon. I haven't told anyone because I don't know what to say. No one would believe me. I don't know what to do. Get over here. This is your...thing."

She hung up and looked at Alex, who had only heard her ask Janet, *What's a person?*

"My flying worm thing grew up. It's Dagon," she said. "He's still at UCLA. We should go." They rushed out of her office only to encounter her student Jeffery storming angrily into the lab.

"Fifty-nine cops down there and someone steals a couple bikes right in front of them!" he said. "And one of them was mine. Kryptonite lock, too. What the hell?"

In near perfect harmony, Alex and Ashley simultaneously intoned, "Sukka and Sanga?"

Jeffery had an inkling that something was up between them. But crooning archaic syllables in unison? That creeped him out a little. "You guys okay?" he asked.

"Personally, yes, I think so," said Alex, "but the universe, not so much."

Chapter 13

Silly Boys

"End of the line, miss. Los Angeles."

The words were faint, from a distant quarter somewhere, invasive and poking into her cozy den, wresting her from a world both sublime and unknowing. Castles were evaporating. Majestic creatures were morphing into stray dogs; mountainous landscapes melted into oil-stained blacktop. Her shoulder wobbled again. The gatekeeper was back, demanding evacuation. Her chin rose from her sternum and sank back before springing up one last time when her eyes finally popped open.

A stretched-out dog flying over a red, white, and blue background came into focus. "End of the line, miss. Los Angeles," repeated the bus driver. The flying dog on his jacket, only inches from her face, was reeling her in. She had seen it before, on the hat of the man who sold her the bus ticket. She told him beagle dogs could not fly. "You have to get off here, miss. End of the line," he repeated.

Awakened, she asked, "That is sleeping?"

"That was sleeping. Now it's waking, and time to get off my bus."

She stood up and looked around. Ernie was not there. No one was there. Just her and the driver.

"I can't get off until you do, miss. Right now, you're the only thing standing between me and a carnitas burrito."

He dutifully marched her down the aisle and out of the bus. The afternoon sun bounced off the bright blue paint on the terminal walls.

Shading her eyes, she ambled out toward the middle of the mostly vacant lot at the rear of the terminal. She stopped and stood still. Executing a full rotation on her heels, she rubbed her hands together and raised them over her head.

Still eyeing her from a distance, the driver lingered at the terminal entrance, his passing concern at odds with his grumbling stomach. "Station's in here if you need help finding your next destination!" he shouted.

"Thank you!" she shouted back. "It is this way about twelve miles."

"That's about where Brentwood would be," he replied. "You headed to Brentwood?"

"Yes, twelve miles this way."

"Okay, you can take a Metro bus. Walk out right there to the Seventh Street/Decatur Metro stop and wait for the 720 Express to Santa Monica. Then you can walk to Brentwood from the Wilshire/Bundy stop."

She smiled and waved to the driver as he disappeared into the terminal building. As instructed, she made her way to the Metro stop on Seventh Street, where she found a few people awaiting the bus. She retreated to a shady spot under the awning overhanging Vickey's 99 Cent Store. While rummaging through her food bag from Ernie, a couple of teenaged boys spilled out of the Descontrol Punk Shop next door. They wore baggy, low-slung pants and loose-fitting T-shirts. The taller, blond one raised an open palm that was met by a complementary slap from his dark-haired companion.

"Best Motorhead shirt ever!" he enthused. Yanking off his old shirt, he pulled his new purchase over his head. Stepping back, he invited his friend to admire the salivating fangs of the tusked beast displayed on the shirt front. He shredded a few air guitar licks and threw back his head in abandon. "Cause I ain't gonna be easy, easy," he sang. Both laughing riotously, they high-fived each other again and took a spot in the bus line.

Leaning against a wall, she munched casually on a granola bar while observing the animated teenagers in front of her. One pulled a single earphone out of his ear and offered it to the other. Their heads chopped forward in unison like hatchets. Another palm slap. Then both wailed aloud, "Killed by death, killed by death, come on!"

Their exuberance faded when a few people in front of them turned to stare. "I wouldn't say that too loudly around here," warned a matronly old woman.

The lads assumed an air of guilt, then smiled mischievously at each other. A second voice, this one lilting and from behind, spun them around.

"We are not killed by death," she said. "It is only the end of Zumru."

The boys regarded her silently, struggling to size her up. She was young, perhaps a college grad, but not exactly a professional. She looked business-casual in her khaki pants and pale blue corduroy shirt, but her worn-out Vans sneakers wouldn't fly in the office. Nor would her tangled red mane. It looked slept on, and she wore no makeup at all. Her round, wire-rimmed glasses had slid far down to the end of her nose, drawing their gazes to the center of her sumptuous face. And what a face. It glowed, emitting light even as she stood in the shade. Although her potpourri look was undefinable, she definitely belonged in the gorgeous file as far as they were concerned. Her unblinking blue eyes stared right back at them. Her tongue slipped over her full red lips that curled up into a warm smile. "Are you going to Brentwood?" she asked them.

The blond one subtly elbowed his mate before assuring her that it was exactly where they were headed. "I'm River," he said, "and this is Finn."

Oblivious to the rubberneckers awaiting the bus, the teens approached her, each extending an eager hand. "I am Shala," she said, acknowledging River first. With her feathery light hand still grasping his, she tilted her head, frowned briefly, then smiled. "The restless run to keep from sleeping," she said.

River looked at Finn and shrugged. "Is that from Metallica?" he asked her.

"It is from you," she replied, "from your hunger. The Wanderers always hunger for more."

Finn flashed a sneaky eye roll at River before taking her hand. This time her eyebrows shot up. With an index finger, she pushed her glasses back up her nose and nodded her head. "An Artist, yes? There is much you have to do."

"Whoa! Good one. He's in a band. They're awesome!" chirped River. "Are you a psychic?"

"I am a progenitor," replied Shala. "I was sent from Ross sixty thousand years ago. I am here to meet Dagon, to send a signal for the Bar to come." Their returned silence neither surprised nor bothered her. She was getting used to it. It was a silence that invariably followed her candid pronouncements. And the silence was typically followed by a patronizing guise reserved for the mentally disabled or small children. She looked at them and waited for it.

"Awesome!" said Finn.

"Yeah, sick!" said River.

The Metro bus ground to a halt in front of them. The air brakes hissed as the door flew open. They migrated to the very back of the bus, where the three of them shared the broad rear bench seat.

"So where are you meeting this Dagon?" asked Finn.

"This way," she said, pointing west out the window. "The closer I get, the easier it is to find him."

"Well, maybe you should come with us to our school. Fall semester hasn't started yet, but we have water polo practice at six, and our coach might know Dagon. After practice, we can help you look for him."

"I will come with you," she said. "But your coach does not know Dagon. Dagon was assembled only yesterday."

"Cool. Is he a bot?" asked River. "You know, like Bender, the swarthy Latin robot." He stood up, arms extended. "Kill all humans," he chimed.

"No. Bender and Fry and Conrad are from one of your stories. Dagon is real."

"Cool. A real robot," said Finn.

CHAPTER 14

DOMINGO

The pickup truck rumbled to a stop on a ramp feeding Highway 134 in Pasadena. The rakes, brooms, and shovels rattled against the tall vertical planks of plywood lining the truck's bed. A stout, brown man in his fifties emerged from the driver's side, frantically waving his arms at the two bicyclists approaching the rear of his truck. A utility van blew past the cyclists, ruffling their navy suits with a dusty draft. Heads down, they pedaled on, undeterred. They were indeed a peculiar sight, almost surreal—two middle-aged men in blue suits, no helmets, hair flying wildly, pedaling their bikes onto a highway. Concerned, the gardener waited behind his truck. They would be a spectacle almost anywhere. But on a highway, on bikes, the stares alone would be enough to cause accidents.

"*Alto! Alto!*" the man shrieked. As they neared, he got a better look at them and tried his English, "Stop! No! No bikes! *Prohibito*! Motors only!" The cyclists coasted to within a few feet of him, coming to a rest behind his truck. "Danger," he said, to little effect. Although confused by his interruption, they seemed curiously unfazed by his alarm. His second attempt, "No bikes on the highway," was met with more blank stares. Exasperated, he asked, "Where are you from?"

"We are scouts from Ross. But this is our home for now. We must find Dagon. He is at you-see-el-eh," said Sukka. "It is this way. Will you let us go?"

"I can't stop you," said the gardener, "but the police will. No bikes on the highway. It's illegal."

"Can we walk?" asked Sanga.

"No. Not on the highway."

"How, then? We cannot fly," said Sukka.

"If you are going to UCLA, I can take you part of the way. I have a job in Beverly Hills. I can drop you there."

"Beverly Hills?" repeated Sukka. "Swimming pools, movie stars," he intoned.

"We know the hillbillies," said Sanga.

"*Que?*" responded the gardener.

"We will go with you to Beverly Hills," agreed Sanga.

Bikes secured in the back of the truck, they slid onto the bench seat, with the gardener at the wheel. He just drove for a while, saying very little. Periodically, he looked askance at the duo, attempting to make sense of them. He noted Sukka eyeing the vibrating head of the bobblehead Jesus planted on his dashboard. "That's Jesus keeping an eye out for me when I drive," he said.

"His Zumru was small but his Bar very large," said Sukka.

"Zoom what?" asked the gardener. "Are you guys Scientologists?"

"No, but we like the story," offered Sukka. "You have many good stories."

"Yes. Like the Hillbillies of Beverly," added Sanga. "Jethro is not very wise, but he is kind and honest."

"The *Beverly Hillbillies?* You mean the old TV show?" asked the gardener.

"Yes, *Beverly Hillbillies*," repeated Sukka, "and *Starsky and Hutch*, too. I like Starsky, but Sanga likes Hutch. Starsky is tough, and Hutch is smart."

"Yeah, that was a good show," agreed the gardener, "but the movie sucked." He nodded at the closer of the two. "So, you are Sanga?"

"Yes," replied Sanga, "he is Sukka."

"Nice to meet you both. I am Domingo."

"Domingo! *Aun hay mas!*" exclaimed Sukka, his tone an uncanny impersonation of the Latin TV host Raul Velasco.

Domingo laughed. "*Siempre en Domingo! Aun hay mas!*" he rang out and laughed again. "You guys remember that show? Not many gringos know it." He glanced back and forth at the two of them. "*Como estas?*" he said, and extended an open hand to Sanga, who shook it.

Sukka shook his hand next and then ran his fingers over his palm. "You are loved by many," he said. "Your Bar is strong."

"I am a lucky man," said Domingo. "I have a big family and a good church." He hesitated, then unveiled a sly smile. "But I do enjoy the bar once in a while. How could you tell? You guys should come to the Blind Donkey on Union Street. Special price on whiskeys tonight."

"We must find Dagon," said Sukka. "We cannot let him join with Shala."

"Uh-oh. Sounds like Dagon and Shala are trying to elope, eh? Too young?"

"Dagon was assembled yesterday, but Shala fell three days ago," said Sanga. "She is close now. Close to you-see-el-eh."

"Oh, no! Was she hurt by the fall? UCLA has a great hospital. She is in good hands there."

"She is not hurt," said Sukka. "She cannot be hurt. She is a progenitor. Her Siru is eternal. It can read and copy any form and build Zumru from it quickly."

"She sounds like a real survivor. It helps to have a strong heart. I hope she's all right."

"She is all right, but it is all wrong if she meets Dagon," said Sanga. "Dagon was not supposed to rise, but he was exposed. He is built and erect now. He is mature and seeks a union with Shala."

Domingo reddened momentarily at what he considered a delicate subject, but then forged on. "Yeah, kids can get pretty worked up with all their hormones, if you know what I mean. Sounds like you need to break this up or you'll have a shotgun wedding on your hands."

"Oh, we cannot use guns, Domingo," said Sukka, "or any violence or force. Dagon and Shala are destined to join, but they will stop if we tell them. They will understand us."

"I didn't mean an actual gun," said Domingo. "But if you think kids aren't going to do it just because you tell them not to, you better buy a baby crib now. Trust me, they don't understand anything, especially when it comes to self-control. Remember what it was like to be that age?"

Sukka and Sanga sat silently, contemplating Domingo's question. Sukka finally said, "My habitants are not here. But some of them were very young when they joined. I will ask them. I will ask those in the Eleventh Congregation, the Artists. Even the oldest ones are like kids. I hope to ask them at home, when I return. But if they come here, with all the Bar from Ross, we cannot hold them. They will be released into the emptiness." He looked at Domingo. "As will your Bar when your Zumru expires."

Their arcane responses were certainly head-scratchers, but Domingo accepted the eccentricities of other faiths. He felt it wasn't his business to doubt whatever they believed in. And he was curious, especially of any overlap with his own Christian beliefs. "So, the emptiness," he said, "is that the same as hell?"

"Oh, no," laughed Sukka. "Hell is only for Zumru. Zumru makes it and cannot escape until it dies. Then Bar drifts away like heat until it is gathered with the others and kept safe from Etemmu. All Bar dwells within us all, as one." He tapped his chest with a fist.

"So, you believe that if someone dies, their soul—I mean, that's your bar, I guess, right?—it doesn't go to heaven or hell but gets collected into a congregation?"

"Like soul, but different" said Sanga.

"Soooul Train," sang Sukka. "Don Cornelius, coming at ya!"

"Sukka has soul," said Sanga. "Get up offa that thing," he belted.

Baffled, Domingo went silent. He contemplated his mental quilt of acceptable faiths and struggled to weave a *Soul Train* block into it. Driving on, he occasionally glanced at the peculiar duo, especially when he thought they were praying. He was captivated by their hypnotic hand-jive-like movements. More than once, his wayward course was corrected by the bleating of rumble strips under his tires. He watched Sukka rub his palms together and hold them aloft, rotating them like little radar dishes. Sukka would then point in a prescribed direction and nod to Sanga.

They exited the Ventura highway and headed south down Coldwater Canyon Drive into Beverly Hills. "My job is on Roxbury in the Flats, pretty near Sunset," said Domingo. "It's only a few miles to UCLA from there. It shouldn't take you long on your bikes. Just be careful and stay off the highways." He let them off in front of a gated palatial residence with manicured hedges and a sprawling front lawn. He leaned the bikes against the truck and pointed them toward Sunset. "One block and take a right," he said.

Rather than mounting their bikes, the duo stood watching Domingo fruitlessly tug on the starter cord of his power mower. He cursed in Spanish under his breath. After kicking the mower a few times, he sat down on the curb, exasperated. Sanga looked to Sukka, who shrugged once, then nodded. Sanga turned to Domingo. "The spring on the choke lever is broken."

Dejected, Domingo barely acknowledged him. "*Pedazo de mierda*," he grumbled.

"No, it is not a piece of shit, it is the choke lever," replied Sanga. He found a screwdriver in Domingo's toolbox and removed the top cover on the mower. The choke lever flopped around unrestrained when he poked it with a finger. He returned to the toolbox and found a rubber band holding a set of hex wrenches together. Once the remnants of the broken spring were removed from the choke lever, he replaced it with the rubber band. Sanga gave the starter cord a pull and the mower sprang to life. "See, not shit," he beamed, pointing at the rumbling machine. Domingo practically leapt off the curb, gaping in wonder at his resurrected mower.

"We must go now, Domingo. Thank you." Sanga handed him the screw-driver. "The rubber will not last. You need Briggs and Stratton air vane spring, 790489."

Domingo stood speechless, looking back and forth between his rumbling mower and the two men straddling their bikes. He shaded his eyes from the late-afternoon light and watched them fading away up Roxbury Drive. Pushing the mower, he tried to make sense of his bizarre encounter with the strange but wonderful men. They were so weird, but not crazy or dumb or deviant. They were smart, kind, and real. He finally concluded that they were indeed Scientologists, and that Sanga must have worked at Sears, thus explaining his intimate knowledge of Crafts-man lawn mowers. But he could not, for the life of him, explain why two middle-aged white men loved *Soul Train* and Raul Velasco. That was unsettling.

Chapter 15

Tom's Story

Dr. Tom Allen tried to steady the laser pointer with both hands. He thought about the student presentations, where certain faculty, himself included, jokingly scored the victim's jitters by monitoring the range of the pointer wiggle. Tom typically breezed through his obligatory biannual update at ASU, but the pointer was wiggling hard this morning. The research updates were low-key, local affairs, usually attracting a small crowd of students, academics, and medical professionals. He thought it might be an appropriate venue to test drive his most recent discovery, so he added it as a final slide. He knew how outlandish his proposal sounded, but here he could at least contain any ridicule to a handful of participants.

Near the end of his talk, he considered bypassing the explosive finale and skipping directly to the acknowledgments slide. But he punched the advance only once and found himself looking at the title: *Diabetic Remission by Gene Conversion in Pancreatic Islet Cells.* The laser pointer scribbled wildly around a short stretch of DNA sequence displayed on the screen.

"I'd like to briefly describe a case study involving a type-one, insulin-dependent diabetic. This is my patient's mutation," Tom explained. "A very common mutation identified in the HLA-DQ1 locus of type-one diabetics. In healthy individuals, the GAT codon at position fifty-seven codes for the amino acid aspartate. However, a majority of type-one diabetics code for something other than aspartate. My patient's mutation results in a substitution of a cytosine for the adenine normally found in codon 57 in the HLA-DQ1 gene." He gripped the laser harder to settle it. "Here is my patient's mutation. The altered GCT codon now codes for alanine instead of aspartate. This generates a protein lacking aspartate at position 57, which the immune system detects as foreign, resulting in its attack on pancreatic islet cells."

The audience, some present only to fulfill an accreditation, found little reason to look up from their open laptops or phones. "As you can see here," Tom continued, "the mutation is found in the patient's lymphocytes drawn fifteen years ago and as recently as two days ago."

A smirking grad student in the back row elbowed his neighbor and whispered, "Look! A mutation in diabetes. So exciting. I told you, the dude's a snoozer."

Tom saw them snickering but forged on. "The patient, a life-long diabetic, is a fifty-seven-year-old male who recently presented asymptomatically. He no longer requires insulin. His blood glucose and A1C levels are normal." Now, a fair number of heads were raised. The more astute attendees were racing ahead of Tom, trying to interpret his illustration at the bottom of the slide. The chatter started to rise. "We can't explain this yet, but the patient's blood is replete with circulating exosomes, or small lipid vesicles, that contain DNA. This DNA resembles that found in so-called CRISPR loci of certain bacteria." He circled an illustration at the bottom of the slide.

"The sequence consists of several short, repeated elements, each separated by a short, unique sequence. The repeat region is flanked by numerous genes coding for enzymes and proteins that function in DNA synthesis, replication, and repair. Some of the sequences remain unrecognizable to us." Laptops were closing, phones were being ignored, the murmur intensified. Most knew what CRISPR was, and many were familiar with exosomes, but none were aware of DNA-wielding exosomes carrying a CRISPR locus in humans.

"Now, here's what's interesting," Tom said, "or more interesting, I guess. Now, I realize this is going to sound a bit crazy, but I want you to look at one of the short unique sequences we found in this exosome DNA." He pointed to a blown-up region of his DNA illustration in which the actual sequence of DNA was spelled out. "Within the CRISPR locus, we found this short sequence that includes the wild-type codon for position fifty-seven in the HLA-DQ1 gene." He tried to continue but couldn't hear himself above the rising ruckus. Hands flew up, some from attendees already standing. Light crept into the room as a handful of escapees slipped out through the rear doors.

Between the gasps and laughs, Tom tried to quell the crowd. He offered some disclaimers regarding the potential for contamination, sequencing mistakes, and the need to repeat the work. Exasperated, he tried to accommodate the audience by taking a question. He pointed to James Rothsbury, a widely respected pathologist associated with the new Mayo Clinic at ASU.

"So, if you had a next slide, which I presume you do not, you would explain to us how the exosome swapped the wild-type DNA sequence into the HLA-DQ1 mutant gene in the patient's pancreatic islets, thus curing them. That is your proposal. Am I correct?"

"Well, yes," answered Tom. "But we don't have—"

"Do you have pancreatic biopsy tissue?" someone shouted.

"How does the exosome find the pancreatic cells?" another hollered.

"Where did the exosomes come from?" squeaked Meg Citralli, the chair of Biochemistry. "From what species are the sequences derived, Tom?"

"Please, like I said, this is all very new," replied Tom. "Meg, some of the sequences are bacterial, some align with archaea, others are human, some dog, some mouse, and even spider. We still—"

"Any from Sasquatch?" yelled a scruffy student, eliciting a wave of laughter.

"All right, then," said Tom with some resignation. "Look, I thought this was a good place to take a risk and show something, evidently, quite controversial. We'll get it straightened out, and I hope by the next update, we'll have a much better understanding. It could all be an artifact, but we'll get to the bottom of it. At minimum, we intend to figure out the source of the exosomes."

"They were made by cold fusion!" shouted another heckler.

Tom quickly ran through his acknowledgements. He spared his associate, Richard, by not crediting him directly for the exosome work. The crowd dispersed, and he was unplugging his laptop when his old acquaintance

Melanie Stump, a physician at the University of Arizona, approached him. She was not laughing. She looked like she had seen a ghost.

"Wow! Did you come all the way from Tucson just to hear the crazy doctor?" Tom asked her. "I'm impressed, Mel." She didn't answer. She seemed frightened, even shaken. Tom studied her for a few seconds and asked if she was okay. She didn't answer that, either.

He watched her look around the room, like a confidante who wants to ensure no one is eavesdropping. "Tom, I have a friend who works at Dignity Health in Phoenix. That's why I'm here today. He had told me about an inpatient with no history of diabetes, who abruptly became insulin-dependent. He's a homeless man, a drug user who has been in and out of the clinic for years. My colleague told me his blood looked super viscous, so he brought me a sample. It was loaded with exosomes, Tom." She was literally shaking as she grasped Tom's wrist. "His blood cells are wild-type GAT at position fifty-seven, but he is an insulin-dependent diabetic now. It's kind of the opposite to what you're describing here."

As he listened to Melanie, a mixed sense of relief and astonishment washed over him. He was shocked by his own vindication. That he was probably right only extinguished the hope that he was not.

"This is scary, Tom. We need to alert the CDC in Atlanta."

"Well, at least there's two crazy doctors now. You go first," he said. "You saw the reaction I got here."

"This is real, Tom. We just need a little more data. Get a biopsy punch from your patient. If you can convincingly show that his islet cells are wild type, that would seal it."

"I intend to, but that will take some time. Meanwhile, if you want to join the crazy train, jump aboard, but be careful who you tell. I'm not saying anything else until I have more data."

They spent a bit more time discussing the issues associated with their findings and agreed to stay mum until they had further support. However, Tom did not proceed directly to his lab. He raced down to his car and sped over to Ernie Tara's house. Once there, he assailed Ernie with questions pertaining to the mystery woman who allegedly cured him. Regarding her whereabouts, Ernie could only tell him that he had bought her a bus ticket for Los Angeles at the station on Washington Street a couple days ago. He showed Tom a photo of the vivacious redhead and happily provided him with a copy of it.

"Detective Tom Allen," he said aloud to himself as he exited the highway. It had a strange ring to it. Although he had once considered alternate careers, a gumshoe was never one of them. He pulled into the Greyhound station on Washington Street and proceeded to question the clueless ticket vendor about a redheaded woman with glasses. The station wasn't busy, but the post-adolescent, pimple-faced vendor seemed impatient with him. He was eager to get back to his vintage issue of *Captain America number 25A*, which had set him back forty-four dollars.

"So, are you sure you don't remember her?" Tom asked again. Facedown, the vendor's stringy blond hair dangled over his comic book. He surfaced for cursory glance at the photo of Emma and quickly returned to his amusement. Sparing his jaw muscles the labor, he issued a monosyllabic grunt, universally interpreted as *get lost*. Tom thanked him, but before walking away, he added, "Red Skull assassinates Captain America, but Steve Rogers is still alive."

The stringy hair flew back as the vendor glared at Tom's back. "What the hell, dude?" he shouted. "How about a spoiler alert?"

Tom ambled out to the waiting area. A few elderly women sat together on a bench, clutching their belongings while spectating the rumpus across the room. The entertainment provided was a scrawny man in ragged clothes who was waylaying the vending machine. He kicked the silver greyhound emblazoned at the bottom of the machine and pounded the glass front with his fist. "This is a medical emergency, goddamnit!" he shouted. "I need sugar, now!"

Tom cautiously approached him. From a short distance, he asked, "Do you need medical assistance?"

"I need a goddamn candy bar is what I need!" The man spun around to take in Tom. "You got one? This thieving machine took my last dollar!"

Tom stepped to the machine, swiped his credit card, and gestured to the man to try again.

He punched in his selection, and as quick as the Snickers bar could drop, he had it torn open and lunged at it. He slid down a wall to the floor, where he continued his attack on the candy bar. His eyelids closed and his breathing slowed as the sugar worked its way into his bloodstream. Tom settled onto the floor next to him. The man smelled like a dumpster fire. His tattered clothes fit loosely. His janky bones practically defined the shape of his limbs.

"Are you diabetic?" asked Tom.

"I am now. That's what they told me, at least. That skinny, copper-top bitch gave it to me. I didn't know that shit was contagious. I should have stayed away from her."

"Who said you were diabetic?"

"A doctor, or a doctor's helper, or whoever it was. At dignity hell."

"You mean, Dignity Health?"

"Yeah, whatever. Can you give me a dollar?"

"Sure. Do you know where the red-haired lady was going?"

"Do you know where your wallet is?"

Tom extracted a dollar bill from his wallet and handed it to him. The man stuffed it into his torn shirt pocket and said, "Los Angeles. She was looking for someone named Dagon. She's probably going to give him diabetes next. You a cop?"

"Nope. I'm a doctor."

"The cops should arrest her. I want to press charges. It's illegal to give someone AIDS. Same thing for diabetes, right?"

"I don't know. I'm not a cop."

"Well, I know she infected me on purpose. She said, 'I gave you Ernie's error,' whoever the fuck that is."

Tom's head popped up just enough to tap the wall behind it. It didn't hurt. But he could feel his body temperature rise along with a tingling in his extremities. He had had similar such feelings, although milder, upon making key research discoveries. But this one would shatter countless existing paradigms. Tom knew the indigent man was certainly misguided and foolish, but he couldn't have fabricated something so revelatory. It fit perfectly. She was the nexus between this man and Ernie. Ernie's errant DNA was probably in the exosomes found in this man's blood. She had literally given him diabetes. *How prescient the fool*, Tom thought. *Diabetes is contagious.*

Tom rose, handed the man a ten-dollar bill, and drove home to pack a bag for his trip to Los Angeles.

CHAPTER 16

THE TROOPERS

A torrent of metal and rubber streamed down Sunset Boulevard. Commuters in droves brushed by the plucky cyclists sandwiched between the cars and the curb. Sukka and Sanga rounded a broad turn into the Holmby Hills neighborhood, where the traffic slowed to a near standstill. They wheeled past the plodding vehicles until they reached a crowd of pedestrians gathered around a crumpled Toyota at the Delfern intersection.

The freshly wrecked sedan was turned sideways, obstructing both lanes. Steam hissed out from under its creased hood. Responders had not yet arrived, but a few commuters had left their vehicles to investigate. Sukka and Sanga rolled up and peered in through the shattered driver's-side window. A young woman sat motionless, slumped over in the seat. Her bloodied, purple face rested against the steering wheel. Glass fragments clung to a dampened mat of hair on the side of her head. A labored wheezing sound escaped from her slackened jaw.

Sukka reached through the broken window and touched her forehead. "Her Bar will leave soon," he said to Sanga.

"We cannot hold it," replied Sanga. "We are only scouts here. Our Zumru is thin. We must go. Our time is short. We have to find Dagon."

Sukka looked mournful. "She is unfulfilled. Her Bar could drift. It would be hard to find."

Sanga frowned and asked, "How much?"

"Between us, three hours. There will still be time to find Dagon."

Sanga nodded reluctantly and started rubbing his hands together when a gruff voice rang out behind them.

"Are you a doctor?" said a stodgy, mustached man holding a phone to his ear. "There's an ambulance on the way. Don't touch her if you don't know what you're doing."

Sanga turned to face him. "I am only a scout here, but many of my inhabitants are Healers of the Fifth Congregation."

"Oh, for Christ's sake," griped the man. "This ain't no time for faith healing, boy. She needs real medical attention. Get away from the car."

Sanga quickly rubbed his hands together, grasped one of Sukka's with his left, and touched the woman's forehead with his right.

The mustached man clutched Sanga's shoulder, tugged at him, and hollered, "Get the hell away from—"

The woman's tilted head suddenly cranked upright, and her eyes popped open. She spewed a mixture of blood and mucus onto the broken windshield. After gulping in a lungful of air, she took in her surroundings and started sobbing. The tears streaked down her battered face. "Oh, my God, oh, my God!" she blubbered. The mustache took a wary step backward and pushed his phone at the cyclists as if it were a crucifix. He melded back into the crowd as the flashing blue and red lights reflected off the vehicle.

"The healers are here now," Sanga said to the woman. "You will be okay."

Her saviors attempted to weave their bikes through the gawkers when they noticed the mustache talking to the police while pointing their way. An officer nodded, approached the pair, and directed them to his car.

"Are you medical professionals?" inquired the cop. "Have you had any medical training? If not, you shouldn't interfere with our first responders."

"Both of us hold many inhabitants of the Fifth Congregation, but I have more than Sukka," Sanga proudly announced. "I am familiar with many Healers. Hippocrates of Kos and Benjamin Spock. And Francis Crick, too. He discovered the Form."

"Okay," said the officer, in a tone that suggested anything but. "Where did you say you were from?"

"We are from the Ross 128 system," replied Sanga. "Near Beta Virginis." He pointed to a spot in the sky, low above the horizon. "Ross 128b."

"Virginia?" asked the cop. "Ross, Virginia? You rode bikes from there? In suits?"

"No. We rode bikes from Pasadena, but Domingo gave us a ride," answered Sanga. "But we must go now. We have to find Dagon. If he meets Shala, all the Bar from Ross will come. Our Zumru will come, too, in eleven years. But it will die, and the Bar will drift into the emptiness where Etemmu dwells."

The officer had been joined by a second cop who overheard Sanga's explanation. After comporting themselves in a hushed conference, one officer wandered off to his vehicle for a few minutes and returned. "Camden Center," he said to the second cop. "The triage desk at MEU said take them to the Camden on Santa Monica for an evaluation." He patted the officer on the shoulder and flashed a sardonic grin. "They're all yours, Tyler."

Tyler turned to the men. "Who you looking for? Dagon, was it?"

"Yes, Dagon," said Sanga. "He is at you-see-el-eh."

"Uh-huh. Okay. How about if I give you guys a ride?"

"Yes, we would like a ride there very much," replied Sanga.

"That's great," said Tyler. "You can get your bikes later. I'll have someone bring them."

"Oh, they are not our bikes," said Sukka. "We have to return them to Pasadena where we found them."

"Found them?"

"Yes, Pasadena had many bikes to choose from. We untied only these two, but we have to tie them up again."

Tyler looked at the bikes and then at the men. "Whose bikes are they?"

"Pasadena's," said Sanga.

Tyler took a quick photo of the bikes and their serial numbers before shepherding the men into the back of his cruiser. Like compasses, the heads of both men gradually turned west as they proceeded south down Beverley Glen Boulevard toward the Camden Center Mental Health Clinic. When the cruiser eventually dipped south of UCLA, Sukka and Sanga were left looking backward, out the rear window. "Dagon is there," said Sukka, pointing northwest. "We are getting farther away now."

"Yeah, we need to make a quick stop at a hospital first to make sure you guys are okay," said Tyler.

"We are okay," said Sanga, "but our Zumru is passing. We do not have much time. We gave some to the broken woman."

"Do you guys have any relatives, family, or friends that live in the area?" asked Tyler.

"We are all relatives, Officer Tyler. You are the youngest, like little babies. Your Bar is brand-new. It grows with your Zumru, like a new plant, before it makes seeds."

"Do you know people that can help you, like here in Los Angeles somewhere?"

"We have assistants. They grow new Zumru for us," replied Sukka.

"Good. Maybe you can call one of them. Tell them to come to the Camden Center on Santa Monica Boulevard."

"Okay, they will come for us," said Sanga.

Tyler escorted them into the nondescript three-story building, where the receptionist was expecting them. She pushed a clipboard in front of Tyler, who hastily scribbled on it before making his escape. The two men sat quietly in a waiting room for some time. Sukka inspected his long, curled fingernails and the growing number of liver spots on the back of his hand. As if conducting an exam, he ran his fingers through his thinning gray hair and tugged in it. "They should be here soon," he said. He turned his attention to a Rorschach blot framed on the wall. Sanga looked, too, and stood up to scrutinize the ink blot at close range.

"What is it?" asked Sukka.

"I do not know," replied Sanga.

A door swung open, and a frail, middle-aged woman in a pale blue smock and matching eyeglasses entered the room. She stood silently in front of the coffee table and smiled in turn at the two men. Her leathery, bronzed face rumpled up like a damp mat, revealing tiny teeth that glowed white behind her plum lipstick. "Hello, I'm Dr. Harden," she said. "That's a Rorschach blot," she added, looking at Sanga. "We don't use them much anymore. It's meant to tell us something about your personality. People see different things when they look at it. What do you see?" she asked playfully.

"Black ink," responded Sanga.

"It was folded," added Sukka, "so both sides are the same."

"Well, there you go," she said. "Do you believe that opposing sides are equal, then?"

"I believe someone spilled ink and folded the paper," he replied.

"Yes, but there is symbolism in your interpretation of the blot. Perhaps you see equality."

"I see black ink. There is someone here for us now. We must go. Thank you for helping us."

At that instant, two young men dressed in crisp gray suits appeared at the doorway. They were elated to see Sukka and Sanga and addressed them with the utmost respect and courtesy. The doctor, already flustered by Sanga's prophetic knowledge of their arrival, was struggling to sort out their relationship. Both young men referred to their elderly counter-parts as Father. Up and down, the older men scanned the young ones, as though they were coveting their new suits. Sukka commented on the nuisance of his long fingernails and aching back and how he was so happy to see them.

"We need to take our fathers now," one the youngsters said to the doctor. "They are scouts, but they are aging rapidly and need help."

"Scouts?" repeated Dr. Harden. "Oh, my! They were Troopers in the Cavalry? I am quite familiar with the Order of the Spur," she gushed. "I tended to Troopers during my training with the Combat Arms branch. A very special group of our servicemen, indeed!"

"Yes, they are very special," said one of the youngsters. "But they are becoming ill. We need to help them."

"You need to get them to the VA hospital on Wilshire," she said. "We have a shuttle that can take you there. I'll call for it."

The receptionist squinted at the names signed by the two young men on the release form. "Noah Sorrenson and Emil Pedersen," she read off the form. "Danish?" she asked.

"No, thank you," replied one of them. "We are in a hurry."

She laughed. "No. Are you from Denmark?"

"We are from Greenland," he answered.

"Wow! I've never met anyone from Greenland."

"Yes, you have. We are from Greenland."

Before she had a chance to escalate the absurdity, a shiny yellow shuttle bus appeared in the drive. The four of them bade their farewells to the receptionist and clambered into the van. "VA hospital? That right?" asked the driver.

"We are going northwest," said Sukka, his voice cracking a bit as he pointed a shaky finger in the westerly direction.

"Yeah, I know where it is," said the driver. "Put your seat belts on."

They slogged down Santa Monica Boulevard, still thick with the remnants of rush-hour traffic. The sun was getting lower in the sky and rays of direct light reflected off the ashen, flaky skin of the elder duo. "Here?" asked Sukka.

"We cannot wait much longer," replied Sanga. His elbows rested on his knees while he held his wobbly head in his hands. His bones were beginning to hurt; his joints stiffened. A small tuft of gray hair came loose when he pulled on it. He pushed a tooth with his finger and felt it wiggle. "Yes. Here," he said.

The driver had rounded north onto Sepulveda and was nearing Wilshire when he heard the unbuckling of seat belts. In the rearview mirror, he could only see the imposing frames of the two younger men. They had moved up to the bench directly behind him, where the older men once sat. The young men sat very high on the seat and were clearly not belted in. Angling the mirror in search of the elders, the driver spotted their gray heads and wrinkled hands moving behind the younger pair. He punched the brakes when the vehicle in front of him suddenly grew large. Keeping his eyes on the road, he caught the light at Wilshire, affording him another glimpse in the mirror. It wasn't his imagination. Each younger man was sitting on an older man's lap. The older men had wrapped their arms around the younger men's upper torsos and appeared to be squeezing them.

"You can't sit like that in my van," he shouted at them. "Get in your own seats and put your belts on." A horn blared. The car in front was long gone, the ensuing gap large enough to irritate the driver behind him. He accelerated but braked again when an eager Prius filled the gap. Once traffic smoothed out, he took to the mirror again. The two younger men sat dutifully belted into their seats. However, the two elderly men were no longer visible. "You cannot lie down in my van," he scolded. "Please, sit up." No heads rose. He considered pulling over, but with the VA only a block away, he continued to the entrance and parked. There, the two younger men immediately sprung the from van, hollered a thank you, and literally sprinted off, north up Bonsall Avenue. The driver pursued them briefly, half trotting and shouting, but stopped when they veered right on Constitution and ducked under the 405 overpass.

"Sons of bitches," grumbled the driver. "That's just cold, man." He returned to the van to tend to the elderly men, but they were gone, as well. Some shoes and crumpled gray clothing lay mixed in with a pile of lumpy ash on the floor of the van. He jumped back when the lump shifted, flattened out, and emitted a few puffs of fine ash. The driver pulled out his phone and took a picture of the mess as evidence to charge the men with vandalism. He convinced himself that the older men must have already admitted themselves to the hospital. He considered their abandoned clothing and folded them into his conjecture. It made sense. They left the clothing there when they changed into hospital smocks. Taking some comfort in his admittedly flimsy rationale, he drove off quickly and returned the van to the Camden.

CHAPTER 17

DAGON

"Who was Charles E. Young?" asked Alex. "Why does he get a street named after him?"

Hands on the wheel, Ashley trained her eyes on the namesake street leading to the Biomedical Sciences Building at UCLA. "I hope Janet is still in her lab," she said. "I can't believe this is happening. I just want to wake up or have someone show me the cameras, and we all have a good laugh." She swung onto the southern loop of the drive and sped up. As if Alex's words had just reached her ears, she replied, "Chuck Young was chancellor here for thirty years."

"So what? Was he first to discover aliens from outer space? I wonder if we'll get a street named after us? I can see it now—*Alex Sina Drive, Dead End.*"

"How can you be so cavalier? This isn't a joke, Alex. It could be the most important event in human history."

"No way. That occurred in 1989, when Energizer started using that bunny to sell batteries. Remember, the fuzzy toy rabbit, marching around, pounding on that big drum? Every time I see—" He stopped speaking when he noticed Ashley's head shaking sideways, her lips pursed, knuckles white on the wheel. She said nothing. That was enough.

She found a vacant Handicap Parking spot in front of Janet's building and pulled in. After unbuckling her seat belt, she had the driver's door open when Alex grabbed her right hand. "Look, I am as scared as you. It's unreal, literally. Yes, the world—or worlds—will change. I don't know how to process it, either. I guess I just default to being an asshole to keep from freaking out. Okay? I'm sorry. I'm with you all the way on this. No matter what."

She managed a thin smile, squeezed his hand, and pulled him close. She leaned in to kiss him but instead backed away and said, "Duracell invented the drumming rabbit. Energizer stole the idea after their patent expired." She gave him a quick peck and exited the vehicle.

Alex remained in the car long enough to watch his wondrous sylph take a few steps toward the building's entrance. He silently mouthed, "Will you marry me?"

Janet wasn't in her lab. Kenji, her research associate, was there, head down at a bench, squirting smidgens of liquid into a row of plastic tubes. "She's in the cantina with her cousin," he said, emphasizing *cousin* while curling his latex-gloved fingers into quotation marks. "I think it's fair to warn you. He's one weird dude. But what else is new? Cantina's on the second floor near the elevators."

Ashley and Alex found her there, pumping quarters into a vending machine. A few yards away, at a small round table, sat a tall man dressed in scrubs. He was inhaling a Twix bar with one hand and grasped a Cherry Coke in the other. A pile of wrappers lay scattered around a half dozen empty soda cans on the table. Janet noticed Ashley and Alex at the door and motioned toward the table with her head. They took a few steps toward their ravenous visitor, who barely noticed as they pulled up chairs. He tore open a small bag of cookies and upended it. The contents tumbled into his cavernous mouth. Janet returned with a few more snacks and another Cherry Coke. They sat quietly for a moment, observing their voracious guest.

Finally, he stopped chewing. Chocolate, coconut, and something purple decorated the perimeter of his mouth. He was unquestionably handsome, almost too much so, like an airbrushed Adonis. Ashley kept glancing back and forth between him and Alex. The resemblance was unmissable, but not complete. He had sandy hair, rather than Alex's jet-black tone, and a phallus-shaped wine stain under his right eye.

Janet watched Ashley squinting at the man's face. "It's Rex Shelton's," she said. "Remember? The overdressed wolf who runs the fly lab down the hall." She popped her eyes wide open and stared comically at Ashley's breasts. Ashley nodded in recollection. Janet gently slid an unopened Almond Joy from the man's nimble fingers and turned his hand over. A few nodules under the skin of his palm were visible. Janet touched them. "Dupuytren's contracture," she said matter-of-factly. "Kenji has these. Courtesy of his Norwegian father. As far as I can tell, nothing from you or me. Apparently, he takes mostly from boys."

"Takes?" Ashley queried. She stayed trained on the man who had resumed his assault on the Almond Joy bar.

"Well," Janet said, "he says his Form is built from whatever pieces are available to him. He copies it. He says he can fill in gaps and move pieces around until his Form suits his environment. I think the Form is DNA, at least that's what he called a model of the helix in my lab. He initially copied worm DNA, probably left over in your incubator from my stint at the JPL. Then he got ahold of Rex's fly genes. Remember? The transparent wings. Then mouse DNA and eventually Rex's, Kenji's, and he probably got Alex's because Alex handled the stones. Or because you handled Alex." She glanced back and forth at the two of them. Ashley looked down. Alex only raised his eyebrows. Then she turned to Alex, cocked her head, and looked back at the man. "Oh, yeah, totally," she commented. "Definitely Alex. You were with Jack Whinston when he found the stones." She looked down at the table. "Do you like candy, Alex?"

Alex pushed away a Snickers bar he was fingering on the table. "No, not so much. Why? I mean, as a child I had a hankering. I could cover eighteen blocks on Halloween. Can I have one of these? I'm starving. Of course, I'd prefer a salad, but the machines don't have that. KitKat's my real favorite…" Alex trailed off for a second, then asked, "But why not Jack?" He looked at Dagon. "I don't see any Jack Whinston in there. And believe me, someone that ugly would be easy to spot. Maybe he rejects genes from lying dirtbags. Or Jack is just too old."

"Dagon?" asked Janet. She looked directly at the masticating man. "Can you tell us how you got here?"

Dagon stopped chewing. He took in Ashley and Alex as if he had just noticed them for the first time. "I am Dagon," he said. He held out a severely chocolate-stained hand between them.

"Uh, ladies first," said Alex.

Ashley took his hand and smiled. Apart from the small bumps in his palm, it felt remarkably like Alex's. A unitary tuft of hair sprouted out between the first and second knuckle of his index finger. With her left hand, she absently turned over Alex's hand and found a like clump of black hair on his index finger. "I'm Ashley, Dagon. Pleased to meet you," she said.

"No, you are frightened to meet me," he corrected. "I will not hurt you. Is Shala coming? I think she is near? I am Dagon," he said to Alex. Relieved of half its chocolate, he pushed the hand toward him.

"I'm Alex. I'm frightened to meet you, too." Alex shook hands, paying particular attention to his singular hairy digit.

"You do like candy," said Dagon, still clutching his hand.

"Guilty as charged," replied Alex. He noted the multitude of orange wrappers on the table. "I'm guessing your favorite is KitKat," he deduced.

"Gimme a break," sang Dagon. He pantomimed snapping a bar in half.

"How can he—"

"He knows stuff that he couldn't possibly have been exposed to," said Janet. "At least not here." She looked at him and tried again. "How did you get here, Dagon?"

"I grew from the Form. Some progenitors are seeded in the dust, before the rocks are made."

"The accretion disk?" asked Ashley.

"Accretion disk?" repeated Alex.

"Solar systems begin from a pile of cosmic debris that basically collapses under its own weight, creating a star," explained Ashley. "The diffuse matter orbiting the new star is the accretion disk. It can be protoplanetary, or capable of forming large round objects, otherwise known as planets. I think he is saying that he was in the dust, or diffuse matter, that ultimately formed planet Earth."

Janet shook her head. "But theres's no way intact DNA could survive all that heat and pressure. I mean, if it's the same as our DNA." She placed a hand on Dagon's wrist. "Dagon, was your Form in the dust?"

"No, my Form was built after the rocks were made."

"How? If you were built from your Form, how was your Form built?"

"By Siru, the builder."

"Siru?"

"Yes, Siru." Dagon pulled some stir straws out of a cup on the table and began to arrange them. He constructed a square and added two triangles to it, one pointing left and one right, creating a six-sided figure. "Siru," he declared.

They quietly studied Dagon's little puzzle. Janet considered it a vessel of some sort, while Alex likened it to a symbol or a pictogram. Ashley said nothing until she reared back in her chair and shouted, "The hexagons!" She leapt to her feet and pointed a finger at the brown plastic straws. "Oh, my god! The hexagons!"

A custodian, who had wheeled a squeaky mop bucket into the cantina, stopped to gawk at the ranting woman. Janet acknowledged him with a wave. "Hi, Art. Just playing a new game. She won," explained Janet, pointing to Ashley. Art returned an equivocal nod, and the squeaking resumed as he pushed his bucket behind the closed deli counter.

"Hexagons?" asked Janet.

Still stunned in revelation, Ashley took a moment to breathe. "When I first looked at the goo that I swiped off of Jack's rocks, I saw these tiny, dense granules scattered amongst the bacteria and the other cell types. I thought they were just particles of granite at first. But at the highest mag, they looked like little hexagons. They were very uniform in shape but too small to get a good look at with a light microscope. Bigger than a virus but smaller than most bacteria, probably a micron in size. I haven't really thought about them until now. I think it's what Dagon is trying to describe."

"Dagon, what is Siru?" asked Janet.

Dagon beamed. "Siru sees from the outside and makes the inside. Siru reads, then writes. Siru builds the Form that fits."

"But how does Siru make the pieces to build the Form?" asked Ashley.

"Siru does not make the pieces, life does. Siru helps life. It copies the Form and makes it better. It makes the Form fit. Siru saw the star," said Dagon, pointing up, "so life uses the star. Yes? To make food." He picked up another Snickers bar and waved it around.

"Wait, wait, wait, hold on a second," Alex chimed in. "It sounds like he's saying Siru invented photosynthesis. Plants use the sun to make sugars."

"That would certainly explain a lot," Ashley broke in. "The origin of photosynthetic genes is one of the great mysteries of evolution. Prevailing theory suggests they were added wholesale to early cyanobacterial genomes, as opposed to evolving through selection. It's known as horizontal transfer. The sequences of those genes are highly conserved across diverse strains of prokaryotes, who otherwise have significant variations in their remaining genes. It suggests that the different strains picked up the photosynthetic genes from the same source. It's not uncommon for prokaryotes to pick up genes by transfer, but no one knows where the photosynthetic genes came from."

"From Siru," exclaimed Dagon. "Siru built the Form inside of life, and life made the air." He took a deep breath and belted out a Tarzan yodel while pounding his chest. "But Siru cannot make life, it can only change it. It changed life to make the air."

"He must mean oxygen," said Janet. "Right? From photosynthesis. It was photosynthetic cyanobacteria that originally oxygenated our atmosphere. Why did Siru do this, Dagon?" asked Janet.

"To breathe," said Dagon. "To remove Twelve, the gas of death, so Zumru can grow."

"What is Zumru?" asked Janet.

Dagon smiled and pounded his chest again. "Zumru is this," he announced, poking Alex in the chest. It is what you see."

"And Bar, Dagon? What is Bar? Can you show me?" she continued.

Dagon smiled and shook his head. "It is what you cannot see. Like gravity. It is gravity. When it is pulled together, it is very strong and able. But when separated, it drifts and dwells in the emptiness with Etemmu. Bar will come. After I meet Shala, Bar will come from Ross to fill our Zumru."

"How will it come, Dagon? How will Zumru and Bar reach us?"

"Zumru comes with the light. It will take eleven years. Bar comes without time. It comes through the Buru, a hole for the gravity. The Technicians will make the Buru for Bar to pass through. The Twelve is low now, so I was assembled. Bar will have a place here."

"The Twelve?"

"That would be carbon dioxide," said Alex. "Carbon has a mass of twelve, six protons, six neutrons." He looked at Ashley. "It's what Sukka and Sanga have been saying all along. They cannot survive in the gas. It's why they age so rapidly. It's why Dagon didn't grow until you lowered the $CO2$ in your incubator."

"Sukka and Sanga?" asked Janet.

"The stalkers from Greenland I told you about. They were looking for the rocks."

Nobody had been paying attention to the consternation building on Dagon's face as he listened to Ashley and Alex. "Sukka and Sanga are here?" he asked.

"Do you know who they are, Dagon?" asked Ashley.

"They are scouts. They keep the progenitors safe. Is there danger? Where is Shala? Sukka and Sanga are here?"

"Not exactly," said Alex. "We last saw them in Pasadena. We told them you were here. They rode off on bicycles."

"They should not be here. Is something wrong? Why am I here?"

Alex knew damn well something was wrong. Dagon wouldn't be here if Jack hadn't dug him up. Sukka and Sanga's crackpot lectures on Zumru, Bar, Shala, and Dagon were all resonating strongly with him now. Dagon and Shala were not to meet, as they had insisted. It was dangerous. The carbon dioxide would kill them quickly if they came—whoever they were. Sukka had also warned him of a danger to humans should the Bar arrive prematurely. Alex's head spun. He dismissed the idea of calling the police or any authorities. What would he tell them? He envisioned himself in a small room, painted cinder block walls, bright lights, a small table, coffee in a paper cup, a cop pretending to be his friend. *That's correct, officer. Dagon was assembled from a tiny speck on a culture dish only a few days ago.* The weight was crushing him. The fate of the entire planet was sitting right there—eating a Snickers bar.

CHAPTER 18

DETECTIVE TOM

Dr. Tom Allen's rented Impala ground to a halt in the parking lot of the Los Angeles Greyhound station. He unlocked his phone and opened up a photo of Emma, the red-haired woman who had cured Tom's diabetic patient. His hope that someone there would recognize her was quickly dashed. The ticket vendor, far more receptive than the pimple-faced Comic-Con'er in Phoenix, drew an honest blank at the image.

Tom's vacant stomach rumbled at the sight of the vending machine. He was fingering his wallet when he balked at the sight of the *Los Angeles Daily News* crumpled up on a bench. He cocked his head at the wrinkled photo of two wild-eyed men in gray suits. Two smirking police officers stood beside them. *Space Aliens Resuscitate Car Crash Victim*, read the tongue-in-cheek title line. The story described two men on bicycles who reportedly revived an unconscious woman injured in a car crash. "I told them not to touch her, but they did anyway, and she woke right up," a witness had claimed. It went on to say the men had told the officers they were from another planet and were trying to find Shala, a woman who came from a rock in the sky.

Tom froze. He hadn't entirely ignored Ernie's fanciful accounting of the savior who cured him. "She said her name was Emma, but Shala almost, and she came from a rock," Ernie had told him. The *Daily News* story said the cops would return the men to their home planet right after a trip to the Camden psychiatric clinic. Tom tore the picture from the paper, dashed to his car, and sped off to the Camden Center on Santa Monica Boulevard.

A minor melee awaited him there. A handful of what might loosely be defined as journalists had taken a break from chasing the Kardashians and were loitering at the Camden Center entrance. In the mix, a couple of bedraggled teens in tie-dyed shirts, sporting Area 51 baseball caps, were holding a phone aloft to livestream the alien invasion. A man and a woman in matching blue jackets, labelled Prometheus Entertainment, stood by with a TV camera. A police officer was holding them at bay when Tom approached. He flashed his medical license at the cop, explaining that he was the personal doctor of the so-called space aliens.

The cop just shrugged. "They left a little while ago, Doc. I've been trying to explain as much to the ooh-ah squad here, but it's not sinking in." He turned his back to the crowd and whispered to Tom. "Your patients said they were scouts, like cavalry scouts, you know? So they were taken to the VA hospital about a half hour ago."

"Who took them?"

"The Camden, I guess. Probably used their shuttle. Hey, there it goes right there." He nodded toward a yellow van in the distance pulling up to the curb.

"Thanks, Officer. I'll see if I can find them at the VA."

Tom hustled down to the van. The driver stepped out of it and was all but running away. "Hello! Excuse me!" Tom hollered after him. "I'm a doctor. I'm looking for a couple of men, my patients. Did you just take a couple guys to the VA?" His back to Tom, he continued to scurry off, picking up his pace until Tom, still trotting, hollered again, "I will believe you! Please just tell me what happened."

The driver slowed and turned around but kept walking away as though Tom were contagious. "They ain't at the VA," he said. "They ain't nowhere. They evaporated. You still believe me?"

Tom stopped approaching and crouched over, breathing heavily, his hands on his knees, "Yes. Please go on."

"Their sons, or whoever they were, came to collect their fathers, or whoever they were. All four of the sons of bitches, that's what I'm calling 'em, got in my van. I'm telling you, I saw all four with my own eyes, but only two got out at the VA, at least as far as I could tell. The two young ones jumped out and hightailed it up Bonsall Avenue. They was too spry for me. I lost them when they turned off Bonsall and went under the 405. When I got back to the van, the two older ones, your patients, were gone. Maybe they checked themselves in. I don't know, but that's what I'm sticking with. Left their clothing and a big pile of dirt in my van. True that, man. It's still in there. See for yourself. It's messed up. I'm going home to have a drink."

The driver left Tom with a *forget you too* wave of his hand and continued on his mission to erase what he had witnessed. The folding door of the shuttle rattled open with a push as Tom stepped in to investigate. As promised, a wad of gray clothing and some black shoes lay in a thick pile of ash on the floor. Some soot remained on the bench seat, where a tell-tale trail led to the mound on the floor. He crouched down and pushed the pile of soot around with his ink pen. It clicked against a solid object that gleamed white as he separated it from the ash. Tom tried to pick it up, but what looked like a molar crumbled between his fingers like loose sandstone. He took out a credit card and turned the ash over a few times. It was an amalgam of gray powder, tangled, purplish threads, and countless toothpick-sized dirty-white splinters. He held a splinter up to his eye and noted that the porosity strongly resembled that of bone.

Tom stood up and started to back out of the van when he bumped into the Area 51 teenagers livestreaming the alien encounter. He looked straight into their phone. "They got beamed up," he said and headed off to his car.

CHAPTER 19

A GOODBYE KISS

Although courteous and rather sweet, their motives were mixed. Finn and River, ever the young gentlemen, insisted Shala precede them as they took their leave from the Metro bus at Wilshire and Bundy. As she moved toward the side door, they bathed in her balletic gait and the supple curves of her swaying hips, their gaping interrupted only by a shared smile of appreciation. Once on the street, River pointed due north and explained that the Brentwood School campus was only a couple of miles away. Although agreeing with the general direction, Shala insisted Dagon was actually to the northeast.

"Yeah, yeah, that's right," said Finn. "We go north to the Brentwood School, and then east from there. You can't cross under the 405 unless you go north to Montana Avenue. And if we go to our school first, maybe someone there can help."

Shala regarded the lads scrupulously. She'd known they were harmless when she shook their hands in front of the 99 Cent Store back at their Metro stop. She also knew they had ulterior motives. But they had been helpful so far, and they were moving in the right direction. They trekked up Bundy Avenue until they crossed Dorothy Street, where Shala slowed to a dead stop. She stared at an unkempt house that was barely visible through the dense palm fronds enshrouding its entrance.

"Etemmu was strong here," she said.

"So was the Juice," replied Finn, "That's where OJ killed his wife."

Her tone saddened. "His Bar will dwell in the void."

"Yeah, he was dwelling behind bars. But he's out again," added River. "No need to worry, though, the dude lives in Florida now."

They crossed over to Barrington Avenue, where they opted to board the Brentwood 15 bus. As the bus moved north, Shala's head turned east by degrees, ultimately facing due east as they traversed the latitude of the UCLA campus. "Dagon is there," she said, pointing east. "He is very near now."

"That's good," said River, "because we're getting off right here."

They stepped out onto South Barrington in front of the Brentwood Tower. "That's the Brentwood Village Historic Tower," said River. He pointed to the metal-capped alabaster structure protruding above the terra cotta roofing.

Shala read the prominent red, white, and blue sign posted on the corner where the building sat. "Did Chevron build it?" she asked.

Both Finn and River laughed and high-fived each other. Finn bowed toward the Chevron station and announced, "Hail, Chevron, oh, great builder of towers and maker of gas."

Puzzled at first, Shala took on an air of concern as she put the pieces together. She scrutinized the pumps, the nozzles, and the hoses leading into the cars parked there. She watched cars exit the station and peered at the vapor emitted from their tailpipes. She wrinkled her nose and frowned. "You are burning so much Twelve," she said.

"Not us," said Finn, noticing her watching the cars. "We don't burn anything. I wish. We wouldn't be walking if we had a car."

River shrugged. "Yeah, it's LA, man. Everyone drives a car. Except for us. Sometimes Finn's mom lets us take the whale—a super-sweet, eighty-one Chrysler LeBaron convertible." He grasped an imaginary steering wheel, threw back his head, and punched down the ball of his right foot.

Shala was still trained on the gas station. She turned away to watch the steady procession of vehicles streaming down Barrington Avenue. There were too many tailpipes to count. The furrows remained etched in her forehead until River tried to move her along. "Me thinks King Chevron saddens you, my lady. Let us make haste."

They rambled though the Brentwood School campus until they reached the pool area. A handful of their teammates were already in the water tossing a ball around. One got beaned when he looked away to take in the stunning redhead escorted by his teammates. "Riv, what's up?" he shouted. "New recruit?"

She stood out like a snowman on a black sand beach. The balls stopped flying. Heads turned. All eyes were affixed on the sublime spirit floating over the deck. She shimmered in the ripples of sunlight bouncing off the stirred water, her inviting smile alone enough to raise the pool temperature. A few strands of her perfectly tangled hair dangled over her sculpted face. She blew at it through her ruby lips as she crouched down to touch the water. A semicircle of smitten young swimmers immediately formed around the siren at pool's edge. "Hi, I'm Rick," came a voice from under a blue bathing cap. Another cap pushed its way in front of Rick and announced itself as the captain of the team. Football players cutting across the pool deck to reach their field were beginning to gather, too. And very much to the delight of Finn and River, some of the ever-coveted cheerleaders had stopped to take in their new companion.

"I'm Shala," she said to her amorous attendants. "Can you help me find Dagon?"

"That's me," gurgled a blue cap before a firm hand drove it underwater.

"She's our friend," said Finn, projecting his voice toward the gaggle of cheerleaders. "We're helping her."

"I can help," said the captain. "I'm more experienced than River or Finn."

The pool erupted with a mixture of laughter and derisive taunts. The cheerleaders, encircled and murmuring, advanced, locked in formation. "Hi, Shala, I'm Cindy," said one of them. Her eyes trekked over Shala, gandering at her disheveled red mop, secondhand clothes, and tattered Vans sneakers. "Where did you meet River and Finn?" she asked.

"At the 99 Cent Store," Shala replied.

Another round of laughter and snarky comments gushed from the pool. Bemused, Shala blinked her oversized, anime blue eyes and adjusted her glasses. She rose to full height, exceeding that of any cheerleader and many of the swimmers, as well. Her full, braless breasts strained against her corduroy shirt. A silhouette of her perfectly trim waistline was visible through the backlight. Her legs, too long for her borrowed khaki pants, sprouted out well beyond the cuffs, exposing her toned calves and delicate white ankles. She was ridiculous. Her beauty cut like a knife through her pedestrian attire. Her Goodwill getup made her look even more beautiful. She would break the cover of any magazine.

She took a step toward Cindy, who paled in Shala's radiance. "Hi, Cindy, can you help me find Dagon?" she asked.

It was a tone so disarming that Cindy considered apologizing but didn't know why. Flushed with an unexpected pang of compassion, Cindy stammered at the seemingly divine creature. She suddenly felt compelled to hug her or stroke her like a family pet. "Da-da-dagon?" she managed.

"Yes, I have to find him soon. He is that way and close." Shala pointed due east.

Cindy was contrite. "I'm sorry. I don't know anyone named Dagon. Is he a college student? UCLA is that way, only a mile or two away."

"Okay. Thank you, Cindy. That is very kind of you. I will go there." She turned to River and Finn. "I have to go now. I don't have much time. Thank you for helping me, River and Finn." Her dulcet purr melted into their ears. Finn and River beamed. They could practically hear the silent *I wishes* percolating in the pool. Shala's attention to them guaranteed a stratospheric boost up the social ladder. There were already some coy whispers amongst the cheerleaders. Shala took ahold of their hands and pulled River and Finn close to her. "Oh!" she exclaimed. Her eyes opened wide. "You are charged," she said. "Maybe too much. You need calm."

The rapt voyeurs around the pool grew silent as Shala curled her arms fully around Finn, pressed him to her body hard, and kissed him full on the mouth. She squeezed River next, then put his face in her hands and kissed him. Finn had already fallen back and was beginning to stagger. His hands dropped to his crotch to cover the tent sprouting up around the fly of his baggy pants. Trembling, he backed into the perimeter fencing, where his knees buckled. A panicked *uh-oh* slipped from his mouth as he slid down the fence while trying to conceal a conspicuous damp spot forming on his pants.

River, experiencing a likewise amorous meltdown, attempted a bent-over, gimpy-legged break for the locker room but fell into the pool instead. Although stunned, the swimmers were nevertheless aware that their spent teammate had joined them in the water and scrambled to get out. No mouths were left uncovered in the circle of wide-eyed cheerleaders, their giggles and *oh, my Gods* as plentiful as their pointed fingers.

In all the excitement, Shala strode unnoticed from the pool area and made her way out to a parking lot. She turned due east, trudged over some landscaping, and traversed an empty baseball field. There she arrived at a row of trees that backstopped the residences on Beloit Avenue. She followed the tree line south, inspecting an assortment of fences separating the outfield from the backyards of the houses on Beloit. A missing board in one of the fences—likely a hack for retrieving well-hit balls—enabled her entry into a backyard. There she encountered a rotund, bearded man with dark eyes, dressed in a brown robe, while tending to a barbecue grill. Although accustomed to finding ballplayers in his yard, he was ill prepared for a trespassing, vagabond supermodel.

His deep voice was melodic and soothing. He squinted at her and tipped his head to one side. "Can I help you, young lady? Are you lost?" He hung up the spatula and approached her cautiously.

Shala smiled her beguiling smile. "I am looking for Dagon. Do you know where he is?"

"Dagon? I don't think so. I've never heard of a Dagon. Well, except Dagon in Ashdod, the god of the Philistines." He chuckled nervously but got no response. "Is your Dagon a real person?"

"Yes, he is real, but Dagon in Ashdod was not. That was only a story. So was Dagon of the Amorites and of the Sumer before them."

Albeit odd, she seemed harmless to the man, and her enchanting smile was irresistible. He opted to placate his eccentric guest until he could alert the authorities. "I see you know your history. I like history, too," he said. "Dagon's a nice name. Was your Dagon named after the Sumerian god?"

"No. You are backwards," she said, trying to hide her amusement.

"Backwards?"

"Dagon once arose in the land of two rivers. He was seeking Shala but could not find her. My rock had not yet arrived. He taught the river people about Zumru, the Keeper of Bar and the Twelve Congregations. He showed them Siru. He taught them how to make the marks." She drew some imaginary wedges in the air with her finger. "But the leaders feared him, so they burned his Zumru. Then, after he was gone, they prayed to him and made him into a fish god."

"They burned him, huh?"

"Not him, just his Zumru. Siru has assembled Dagon again, from the dust. He is near now. We must meet to bring the Bar from Ross, and then Siru will build our Zumru here."

"Okay. I'm not quite following all this, uh, history, but it is very interesting. Would you like to come inside and talk?"

"You are burning."

"Yeah, I guess we all are a little bit, huh?"

"A lot," she said, looking past him.

He spun around to a five-alarm kebob fire on his barbecue. He turned off the gas jets and slammed the lid to extinguish the blaze. She stood staring blankly at him. "I'm sorry," she said.

"It's okay. I like to cook. I can make something else later. Let's go inside, and maybe we can find someone to help you."

They entered at the ground level of his home into a large open space. Several long tables occupied with computers and assorted electronic devices were arranged around the room. A variety of musical instruments leaned on stands and hung from the walls. A showcase displaying all manner of *Star Wars* memorabilia stood next to a grand piano.

"I am a music composer," he said, his open palm sweeping around the room. "Do you listen to music?"

She started waving her arms like a conductor and began humming the love theme from *The Empire Strikes Back*. Her pitch was impossibly high and haunting but utterly perfect. His mouth open and eyes fixed, he drew closer to the source of the hypnotic aria. Her flaming hair whipped around her immaculate face as she highlighted a crescendo with a head toss. She abruptly stopped singing when he came to within a few feet of her.

"How?" he asked, dumbfounded. "So beautiful, your sound. Beyond soprano, but without the screeching. You are sopranino!" he exclaimed.

"No. I am Shala," she replied, holding out her hand in greeting.

Befuddled, he slowly extended his and shook hers. "I am Aslan."

She smiled appreciatively at his touch. "You are a strong Artist, Aslan. The Eleventh Congregation will be strengthened by your Bar."

"Okay, that's good. Right? It is Shala, you say? The wife of Dagon. Yes?"

"No. Not Dagon's wife. That is a story again from the two rivers. I must find him, though, soon."

"Can you sing for me again?" He sat down at a piano and opened a half-written score on a monitor. "I would just love to hear how this sounds in your register."

She looked at the monitor and said, "B flat is too low for your piece. It will sound dull and lifeless." Then she poked at a specific portion of the staff. "Ascending fifths here would fit better with the bridge section."

His fingers strayed over the keyboard, but he was too unsettled to work them. He breathed in long and exhaled to compose himself. "Fifths, of course," he said, his voice trembling. He tried it out and laughed with delight. Taken away by the unexpected consonance, he dove in and frantically began banging out the new section to his piece.

She watched him for a moment before softly murmuring, "I'm sorry, Aslan. I cannot sing now. I must go." She drifted out of the front exit, where she could still hear the piano out on Beloit Street.

CHAPTER 20

THE IRAKALLAN

Their shoes slapped the pavement on Bonsall Avenue, drowning out the bray of the pursuing van driver. Sukka and Sanga turned east, ducked under the 405, and stopped at the intersection of Constitution and Sepulveda Avenue. Sanga rubbed his hands together and threw them in the air. Equivocating, he looked north, then east. "I don't know," he said. "This way and that way. Dagon is very close." He wiggled his fingers in an easterly direction. "But the other progenitor, Shala, is also near. This way. Both are very strong."

They languished in a moment of uncertainty before striking a course north along Sepulveda toward the Brentwood School. Behind the long, wrought-iron fence to their right lay the sprawling Los Angeles National Cemetery. Gazing in at the countless rows of headstones, the vertical fence bars strobed as they walked along. The white granite slabs, all even in size, shape, and spacing, looked like dominos set up to fall.

"So much Zumru," said Sukka.

"Many Warriors," commented Sanga. "Many Buffalo Soldiers fighting for America."

"And John Russell!" blurted Sukka. He stopped to point at a headstone in the distance. "Marshall Troop, Lawman!" He fanned an imaginary six-shooter in eulogy to the deceased actor.

"Grant Williams!" countered Sanga, pointing with his arm inserted between fence rails.

"*The Incredible Shrinking Man*!" they both exclaimed in unison. Gradually crouching, ever smaller, both pantomimed the fate of the shrinking man. "Oh, Scott!" said Sukka. "Come back."

"I can't, Randy," returned Sanga, still crouching further. "My Zumru is shrinking. The bugs will soon eat it."

Rising to full height, they shared a smile, until Sanga grew somber and asked, "Could such tiny Zumru hold all of Scott's Bar?"

"Bugs have no Bar," said Sukka.

Continuing on in silence, they reached the intersection at Montana Avenue, where Sanga raised his outstretched arms like wings, one pointing west, the other east. "It is Shala," he said, his arms oscillating in a seesaw fashion. "She is here or there. Both are very strong and recent. We must choose."

Sukka looked east down the curvy, tree-lined Montana Avenue in the direction of UCLA. Then he looked west up Montana, a short traverse passing under the 405. Vacillating, he shrugged at Sanga, who only raised his eyebrows in return. Searching for clues, they heard a beeping noise emitted from the box across the street. The little orange man in the box was replaced by a green one. Without uttering a word, they nodded to each other, crossed under the 405, and continued west to Beloit Avenue.

"She was here," said Sanga. "Very close to here, but I think she is gone now."

They walked another block, north up Beloit, until they stopped in front of a rust-colored house of modern design with perfectly trimmed landscaping. They could hear a piano playing from the street as they stood listening. "Here?" asked Sukka. "Should we ask them?"

They pounded on the front door until the piano ceased. It was replaced by the percussion of heavy footsteps approaching the entrance. Greeting them was a large man in a brown robe, breathing hard and clutching the banister to support himself. His dark eyes, set deeply in a dusky smooth face, ran over the two visitors. He quickly summed up the middle-aged men in gray suits.

"I'm closed today, gentlemen. I'm sorry. And just so you know, I've got more work than I know what to do with right now. It would be six months out, minimum, for anything you're looking for. I can refer you if you'd prefer not to wait."

"We cannot wait," said Sukka. "We need to find Shala now. Was she here?"

The man stepped back. The door and his eyes both opened wider. "You know her?"

"Yes, she is looking for Dagon. She was here. Yes?"

"Yes, yes. Come in, please. You must tell me about this amazing woman. She has the voice of an angel. I would like to hire her if possible. Are you her managers?"

"No, we are scouts. We are here only to manage her union with Dagon. To keep them safe. But there has been an error. They are not supposed to meet."

"Oh, my. She didn't mention that. She said she was looking for Dagon, though. What, is this Dagon already married or something? I hope she's not in trouble. She's just the sweetest thing."

"We are all in trouble if they meet. We will perish here. There will be no place for our Bar, or yours, when your Zumru expires."

Bewildered, the man raised his hands in surrender. "Look, guys, honestly, I don't understand all this stuff. Shala tried to explain it, but I just didn't get it. I'm sorry," he said. "Is it Scientology? I mean, I'm okay with that. There's lots of them around here."

The two men turned to each other. "Hail Xenu!" said Sukka. A playful look of amusement spread across Sanga's face as he turned toward the astonished homeowner. "When dinosaurs were still here, Xenu came and dropped people from a spaceship onto a volcano and then blew them up."

"He did?"

Sanga sighed. "No. He did *not*. It is just a story, like many of your other stories. But Shala and Dagon are real. We are real." He pounded his chest with a fist. "See, I am here. The danger is real. Can you tell us where Shala was going?"

"She didn't say, exactly. She said Dagon was that way." He pointed due east. "She slipped out while I was playing. I didn't even notice her leave. Please, if you find her, tell her to come back. I have work for her."

"Thank you," said Sukka. He shook the man's hand and examined his own as he pulled it away. "Your Bar is strong. You will help lead the Eleventh."

The two stepped away from the bemused man to take their leave. He followed with a step forward but then stopped on the landing and examined his hand as the curious duo descended his front steps.

Halfway down, Sukka looked back and said, "Your song is nice, especially the ascending fifths. It is a good choice."

"Wait! How did you know? Do you play?"

"Yes. Well, my inhabitants do. Vladimir is my favorite."

He watched from the porch as they disappeared down the block, heading south toward Montana Avenue. Retracing their steps, they reached the intersection, turned left, and headed east, back under the highway overpass. Crossing over Sepulveda Avenue, they picked up their pace and continued up Montana until they reached the intersection at Veteran Avenue.

"She is very close now. Both are very close," said Sanga.

They grew deathly silent, their attention trained on the strangely familiar man approaching them from across the intersection. His thinning gray hair fluttered in the breeze. He squared up his wire-rimmed glasses to get a better look at the pair. He broke into a half trot. He scratched at his scruffy gray beard, his yellowed teeth bared in a grimace. Sukka and Sanga froze, both sensing a looming danger. That shallow sense of trouble they felt upon first meeting this man was resurrected and heightened at the sight of him now. He crossed the street, taking deliberate steps toward them until he was only a few feet away. He stopped in their path.

"Jack Whinston," said Sukka. "Why did you take the stones?"

CHAPTER 21

GONE

As suspected, Dr. Tom Allen found no record of the elderly scouts checking into the VA hospital. The tidy, square-jawed receptionist tapped his keyboard a few times, then narrowed his already small brown eyes at Tom. "Retired cavalry scouts? Nope. No Troopers today." Without speaking further, he dismissed Tom with an unblinking glare sandwiched between arched eyebrows and scrunched cheeks.

Tom slumped behind the wheel of his rented Impala. Left only with the shuttle driver's account of the fleet-footed men dashing up Bonsall Avenue, he had little choice but to follow that flimsy lead. He rolled up Bonsall and stopped at Constitution Avenue where he recalled the driver saying the men had passed under the 405. He did likewise. Encountering the cemetery, he proceeded north on Sepulveda to Montana Avenue where he slowed to a crawl and caught the light at the intersection. Looking east, then west up Montana, he pondered the absurdity of his random walk. He knew each guess was only squaring the odds of taking a wrong turn.

Emma, or *Shala almost*, as his cured diabetic patient had described her, could be anywhere. And anywhere in LA might as well be anywhere in the universe. Dejected, he opened his phone to search for a flight home when two middle-aged pedestrians in gray suits crossed the intersection right in front of him. Studying them, he reached blindly for the wrinkled photo of the two space aliens reported by the *Daily News*. The pedestrians looked older than the aliens depicted in the news, but very similar in stature, dress, and hairstyle. He opted to follow them at a distance, creeping east, alongside the trimmed green terraces shouldering Montana Avenue.

The men walked briskly along the winding avenue until they reached the crosswalk at Veteran Avenue. There they hesitated. Tom pulled into a vacant driveway near the corner and settled low in his seat to surveil the men through the passenger-side window. They were looking east, straight up Montana Avenue at an approaching, bespectacled, middle-aged man who seemed singularly interested in them. The man's pace quickened until he stopped a few feet in front of the pair. Although out of earshot, Tom watched the three of them conduct a brief conversation that ceased abruptly when the stranger extracted a hand from his pocket and cast it toward the duo.

Frantically brushing their hands down their suits, as if to extinguish flames, the men danced about wildly. Severely ataxic and unable to flee, the inflicted pair ultimately spiraled down to the sidewalk, writhing around torturously for several seconds until the bulk of their mass seemed to disappear into the concrete. Paralyzed by the spectacle, Tom slunk farther into his seat. The stranger used his foot to poke at the lump of ashen dust and crumpled clothing. Tom watched the perp take a furtive look around. The passing cars continued to pass, unperturbed. A few women, talking in a tight circle down the sidewalk, continued conversing, unaware.

Tom shivered, his eyes barely above the door panel as he watched the man make a hasty retreat, east up Gayley Avenue toward UCLA.

Chapter 22

So Sad

Like a timorous deer on alert, Shala stiffened at the intersection of Gayley Avenue and Charles E. Young Drive. Her visceral compass was pegged hard to the east. Dagon was very close now. His seductive lure, magnetic and irrepressible, clawed at her. Her senses tingled at his frothy essence. It roiled in a current spilling down the avenue, washing over her. The source of the magnetic stream beckoned, her destiny only a short swim away. But there, in front of the Ronald Reagan UCLA Medical Center, she was stuck in a quandary. Unmistakably, Dagon summoned, her obligation paramount and attainable. Yet she couldn't ignore the static scratching at her compass. An ominous interloper was nearby. Perhaps as near as Dagon, but opposite in direction.

She looked east, then west, and repeated her alternating takes. A few steps east were quickly countered by a few to the west. By all appearances, she looked quite lost. At least that was the impression of the medical students who happened her way. Studying her, a perky young Chinese American in faded green scrubs felt her empathy needle wiggle. She stopped in front of Shala and tilted her head as though it was resting on someone's shoulder. Cheerful and willing, the young grad, at first unnoticed by Shala, pressed her palms together and offered her assistance in perfect Oxford English. "Are you lost?" she asked. "I would be happy to help you."

The leggy Shala looked down at the obliging young woman, her smooth face tilted like a radar dish searching for a signal. "Oh, thank you," Shala replied. "I am looking for Dagon. He is very close now." She pointed her finger up Charles E. Young Drive toward the Biosciences building. "This way." Then pointing back up Gayley, she added, "But there is danger nearby."

A second medical student, male and dressed in street clothes, couldn't help himself when he noticed his colleague engaging the adorable enchantress. "Hey, Nicole, what's up? Is somebody lost?" he asked, inviting an introduction to the somebody his eyes had yet to stray from.

Shala quickly pivoted to him. "I am not lost. I am trying to find Dagon. He is this way." He followed the path of her outstretched arm to the point of her finger, then back again, settling on her angelic face. She stood eye to eye with him, hers fixed, his wandering. "I must join with Dagon," Shala continued. "We will signal Ross to send our Zumru. Ross is dying. We need a place for Zumru to hold the Bar. Your rock is still young and habitable."

As he listened to her rambling, his eyes narrowed, his cheeks rose, and his lips tightened. With his eyebrows stuck on the top floor, he stole a glance at Nicole and mouthed, *What?*

Nicole shrugged out an *I don't know* and asked Shala if she knew the building in which her Dagon could be found.

"There," announced Shala, pointing east once again. "It is certain. But the Irkallan is nearby, too. That way." She pointed northwest up Gayley Avenue. "It means to harm us. It stirs the Bar and spreads it into the void where it cannot come together."

Both students, rendered speechless, traded quizzical expressions between nervous glances at the concerned woman. Finally, the male student asked, "Are you a Scientologist?" He offered to search for the location of the nearest Scientology Center.

"No," responded Shala, "I am Shala." She held out her hand in greeting and shook his.

"I'm Russel," he said. "Nice to meet you."

Still grasping his hand, Shala said, "You are charged. Do you want calm?" She tugged on his hand to draw him closer.

Her hand felt warm and soothing. A surge of molten blood raced up his arm, breached his shoulder, and spread throughout his body like a hot, torrid flash. As he gave in, his eyes grew wide and his pulse quickened.

The current swam through him, caressing every nerve ending. He trembled at the touch of her hand sliding up his back. Then, like waking suddenly from a vivid dream, he shook her off and jumped back. "No, thanks, I'm good!" He abruptly turned toward the medical center and darted off in a crouched gait, his backpack pressed in front him.

Shala watched him scamper off and turned to Nicole. "He needs calm."

Unsettled by Russel's sudden departure, Nicole just stared at the mysterious seductress. She looked at the hand that had melted Russel and back into the woman's eyes. They were inviting, like pools of warm liquid. Nicole felt a narcotic wave of sentiment ripple down her spine. She felt compelled to comfort Shala. She was reaching for Shala's hand when another student greeted her in passing. Awakened, Nicole's hand dropped to her side as she stepped back.

But Shala was no longer looking at her. She was looking up Gayley Avenue in the direction from which she had arrived. Nicole continued to study her and grew alarmed at Shala's dramatic transformation. Her once benevolent demeanor morphed into anxiety and suffering. Shala's eyes grew large. Tears streamed down her contorted face. She screwed up her mouth and cried out in horror. "No! He has killed the scouts!" she wailed. Her face clasped in her hands with her back hunched, she sank to the concrete on her bended knees. Nicole crouched down beside the mournful woman. She gently pushed back a swath of Shala's red mane and pressed her face close to hers. Overwhelmed with sadness, Nicole started crying, too, but didn't know why. She wanted desperately to console Shala but could not comprehend her loss.

As one might expect from the medical community, an attendant group of passersby had gathered around the traumatized stranger. Although many eagerly offered their services, none could discern, with any specificity, what services should be rendered. They expertly ruled out a cardiac event. Nor was it a diabetic coma or a crippling muscle spasm that had dropped the pained woman to her knees. It was *the scouts*, she lamented. This led some to speculate that her trauma was rooted in a recent accident involving a busload of Boy Scouts. Others whispered their diagnosis of a wholesale psychotic break. The whimpering victim wheezed out the names of Sukka and Sanga, which only further muddied their prognoses.

Shala rose to her feet. Her weeping ceased, the sadness giving way to an attitude of serious concern and determination. She wiped her face with the back of her arm and finally took in the circle of onlookers surrounding her. With full composure restored, she thanked all for their concerns and announced her intention to leave. Some of the crowd began to disperse, but a senior attending physician sporting a crisp navy blazer and khaki pants stepped forward. Although veiled in medical concern, he was obviously entranced by her unconventional beauty. When he offered to check her vital signs, some eyebrows were raised by the interns privy to his lecherous reputation. He insisted that he at least check her pulse and temperature before sending her off.

"Just want to check your heart rate. Okay? It won't hurt. I promise."

He turned her hand over and slid his thick thumb along the inside of her wrist. Shala's head reared back, and she jerked her hand away, startling the physician. "Why do you hurt her?" she asked. "She does not hurt you. She only wants to love you. You are hurting yourself, too. Stop it, or your Bar will dwell in the darkness."

The doctor's face paled as the blood drained from it. Rattled by her reproach, he at first laughed nervously, passing off her ranting as a product of her ailment. But the circle of onlookers had grown silent. Jaws had dropped, especially those of female interns familiar with the attending doc. They knew of his wife's admission to the ER for bruises—reportedly due to a stairway fall. Rumors abounded.

"She's suffering from a fever, I believe," tried the attending physician. He scanned the crowd, seeking confirmation, but found none. The interns looked dubious. His thin smile fell flat as they avoided his gaze. He reached for Shala again. "Look, I just want to help."

"No," protested Shala. "You are not helping me. You are helping yourself to me. And I do not have a fever. There is nothing wrong with me that I cannot fix myself. But you will need to fix yourself. You will need help. Find it before Etemmu finds you." She took a few steps forward, and the remaining crowd parted ahead of her as though she were a deity. "I am leaving now. I will go to Dagon." She stopped, turned back, and retraced her few steps. She placed her hands on Nicole's shoulders and fixed her eyes on her. "Thank you, Nicole. Compassion is always rewarded," she said. "The Healers of the Fifth Congregation will welcome you warmly. Goodbye." As she walked off, Nicole felt an urge to follow and even started after her. Shala stopped and looked back. She shook her head at Nicole, then tipped it toward the entrance of the medical center. Nicole understood.

CHAPTER 23

THE WITNESS

Jack Whinston had settled on a brazen solution to his problem. He was confident that no one would notice. There were a few people out and plenty of vehicles whizzing down Veteran Avenue, but he knew the nature of these creatures well enough. They were too distracted with their mundane occupations to notice him. Their phones, their beloved cars, even their hair, all seemed far more important than the immediate world around them. As for evidence of his deed, he would leave none. He had the men in his sights now, and it would be over in an instant. It would be easy. They were defenseless. It was in their nature. But it was not without risk.

There would be consequences. His act would ripple through the Rossians. Most, of course, would be incapable of retribution, just as he'd planned. But a tiny fraction had evolved beyond his design. It was his mistake. Although they were supposed to grow and become intelligent, an intelligence he needed to support his creation, their gathering was unanticipated. It had literally rumpled his world. Worse, their congregations had made them wise beyond all expectations. Now, they had become designers, too—designing a way around him. They had reverse engineered his precious Siru and evolved masterful beings imbued with abilities he hadn't accounted for. They were small in number, but the progenitors were large in power. They could and would come for him if he killed. But if he could stop their gatherings and destroy their congregations, the progenitors wouldn't survive. He could still have his cake and eat it, too. It was worth the risk.

As he bore down on the hapless duo, he marveled at their naivety. They were naked in their unrestrained honesty, their compassion a bared throat that he could easily slit. They couldn't hit back. Doing so would weaken the very ties that bound them all together. Yet these curious creatures were unraveling his design. Unrestrained, they had corralled and coalesced the essence of life. They gathered and preserved all walks of knowledge, wherever it arose. Already powerful in their accumulation, they were only getting stronger. It was inevitable. Eventually, they would crack the code and turn it against him. It would be disastrous. His creation would collapse. He had to stop them now.

He crossed Veteran Avenue, watching the concern flood their faces. Only a progenitor could stop him now, but they were hopelessly bound, sucked together, lost in a longing for their embrace.

"Jack Whinston, why did you take the stones?" he heard one of them ask.

"Seriously, you don't know who I am?" he replied. "I thought you had me in Greenland, but you really are that clueless. Shala knows who I am. She even knows I am here, but she's too busy with Dagon to bother with me now. Come on, I'm curious. How come she knows and you don't? She could even destroy me, yet she does not come."

"Shala is a progenitor. An Ugu," replied Sukka. "She is all of us in one, but separate and independent. It is in the Form that Siru builds for her, a special Siru, different from ours. Ours is fixed and unchangeable. Siru assembles then leaves. But Shala's Siru stays, shaping her Form. She receives from all congregations but remains separate from them. They are not affected by her actions. Yes, Jack. She can even destroy. But do not worry, she will not destroy you. She only seeks Dagon."

"Well, that is good to know. Thanks. But, still, what makes you so dumb? You two are Ross scouts, right?"

Sanga nodded. "Yes. And you are Jack Whinston, geologist, right?"

Jack laughed. "Guess again."

"Please, Jack," said Sukka. "We have to go. We must find Dagon."

"No, you must not," replied Jack.

"But he will meet with Shala and—"

"And your precious Bar will come here, but the Zumru will die, and the Bar will be lost."

"Yes!" said Sukka.

"Yes!" mimicked Jack. "That's exactly why I dug up Dagon and released him. And if you stop him now, that would just ruin my day."

"But the gas is too high here. Dagon was not supposed to assemble. All of our Bar will come from Ross, but we will not be able to hold it here. All of our congregations will dissolve and dwell in the void."

"Exactly!" Jack enthused. "Right where I need them. See, that's me having a good day. Your so-called congregations are just a bit too nosy for their own good. Trust me, the universe will be better off without them."

Sanga took a step forward, but Jack stepped in his way. He mocked Sanga with a cowering pose. "Oh, no, you're not going to hit me, are you? Go ahead, rattle the cage, give your happy little inhabitants back home a taste of blood. Do you think they would like that?"

Sanga retreated. He hoped Shala would come but knew she wouldn't. She alone, a progenitor, self-contained yet fully engaged, was both sanctioned and capable of dispatching Jack, without repercussions. The congregations, numb to the brutal experience, would be spared, not having to digest the fetid gruel of violence.

"I have a present for you," Jack said. He reached into his breast pocket. The scouts froze, immediately recognizing the tiny worms squiggling in Jack's hand. He flung the minuscule creatures at the helpless men. They struggled, but it was no use. The insidious worms burrowed into their flesh. Jack watched them burn with fever. Their bodies squirmed and shrank further with each convulsion. It took only seconds. He kicked at the pile of residue on the sidewalk. Satisfied, he turned east and made haste toward the UCLA campus. He knew he needn't be present for the magical union he had so artfully engineered. But it was the grand culmination of his mischievous deeds, and he didn't want to miss it.

What he had missed, though, was the Impala that crept out of a nearby driveway and cautiously followed him up Gayley Avenue.

CHAPTER 24

THE CATINA

Alex flattened his palms against the face of the vending machine and leaned into it. It tilted back, then rocked forward, landing on the front legs with a thud loud enough to muffle his profanity. Snagged by the delivery coil, the sole remaining Twix bar dangled over the edge but didn't drop. "This one's a fighter," said Alex. "It's Dagon 12, Twix 1. Sorry, buddy. Can't win 'em all." He looked around. It was just the four of them in the cantina. "Can't you just turn into a snake or something and crawl up there and get it?"

Dagon sat erect at the table. He looked past Ashley and Janet, his eyes glued to the doorway. Without turning his head, he answered Alex. "Siru cannot make the Form for a snake without a snake. Siru copies, then creates."

"How about a mouse, then? You've got some mouse Form. Right?"

"Siru assembles only the Form that is needed. I would be a mouse if a mouse was needed."

"How badly do you need that Twix bar?" Alex queried.

"Shala is very near. Dagon is all that is needed now," he replied.

Alex pounded the side of his fist against the machine. The Twix bar mocked him with an enticing wiggle. He was about to counter Dagon on the relevance of Shala versus the Twix bar when an increasingly familiar look from Ashley stopped him. He wandered back to the oval table and sat down opposite Dagon. Dagon's chair squeaked as he slid over to regain his sight line to the doorway. They sat silently for a minute, Janet scribbling down notes, Ashley staring at Dagon, and Alex at Ashley.

Ashley finally sliced through the quiet interlude. "Dagon, do you know how Siru copies and makes the Form?"

"No."

"Where did Siru come from?"

"Siru didn't come. It already was. It always has been."

"But it is real," she said. "You showed us what it looks like." She picked up the plastic straws and reassembled his diagram of opposing triangles connected to a rectangle. "I saw the black hexagons in the microscope myself. They must have come from somewhere."

"That is only a tool. Siru reads and writes through it to guide the assemblies."

Janet stopped writing and raised her head. "Where is Siru, then?" she asked. "The one that guides."

"Siru is outside. Outside of all the rocks and stars and time. It is outside of the emptiness. Siru cannot be found."

"Does Siru make Bar, too?" queried Ashley.

"No. Siru only makes Zumru. Zumru makes Bar."

Ashley shook her head. "But you said Siru does not make life?"

"Siru does not make life. Life makes itself. Siru helps it."

"And Siru helped our life, too? Here on this planet?"

"In the beginning, Siru built the Form for life that makes the air."

"Why?"

"So Zumru could grow and make new Bar."

"But it took almost four billion years for our Zumru to evolve from the very first life. Why didn't Siru just make our Zumru quickly? Like it made yours?"

"Only Zumru from the tree of life can grow new Bar. There is no other way. My Zumru cannot grow new Bar, it only borrows from the congregations. I borrow your father's Bar." He looked at Ashley and said, "What's up, lucky button?"

Ashley sprung from her seat, stumbling over the legs of her upended chair. Mouth agape, she staggered sideways, arms flailing until her palms came to rest on opposite sides of her head. Her drained face was as white as her platinum locks. She paced in a tight circle until her Edvard Munch scream gave way to a look of blunt astonishment. Her head was spinning, and her eyes darted around the room as though she was searching for something. She was gasping for air when Alex draped an arm over her shoulder. Her trembling reverberated up his arm. Whispering, he asked, "What?"

Ashley started, but her voice cracked. She tried again, "He called me that. No one—" She broke down. Alex waited. He pulled her into a full embrace. She buried her head in his welcoming shoulder, her muffled voice soaking into him, distant and hoarse, until she raised her head, "My father called me lucky button," she croaked. "He died when I was twelve."

"He did not die," said Dagon. "His Bar is strong in the Tenth Congregation."

She glared at Dagon, wide-eyed, her face an amalgam of confusion and wonder. "The tenth?" she squeaked.

"Yes, the Makers. The dwellings on Ross are most beautiful."

"Oh, my god!" cried Ashley, her head burrowed back into Alex's shoulder. A few more syllables, barely audible, leaked into his shirt. Reemerging, she sucked in some air and quivered. "He was an architect," she said. She pivoted to Dagon, who barely noticed her in his preoccupation with the doorway. "Dagon, can I talk to him? To my father?"

Without straying from the doorway, Dagon replied, "No, he is not here. It is only an echo of his Bar that I borrow. His Bar will come in eleven of your years when our Zumru assembles here."

A silence ensued, during which Alex briefly contemplated the arrival of his dead ancestors, many, apart from his grandmother, whom he had little interest in meeting again. Instead, his mind wandered with possibilities, many obtuse and utterly pointless. But he was Alex. He wondered if D. B. Cooper would be amongst them. Would he be able to ask him what happened after he jumped out of the plane with all that cash? The absurdity of his interests was made apparent by the fingernails biting into his shoulder.

"Alex!" cried Ashley. She pushed away from him, her eyes fixed on Dagon. "What's happening to Dagon? Look!"

Dagon had slid out of his seat and onto the floor. He curled up on his side like an armadillo, his chin to his chest, back curled, and knees tucked. He began moaning. "No! Sukka and Sanga are gone," he wailed. "Something killed the scouts. It is near. As near as Shala. Something is wrong."

CHAPTER 25

LOVEBIRDS

Only a half-dozen steps stood between her and the entrance. Facing the red-brick facade of the Biosciences building, Shala bathed in the warm essence radiating from its curved surface. It was an uneven heat, a gradient glowing soft on the edges and brighter toward the burning epicenter on the second floor. She knew exactly where he was, yet she vacillated. A specter was approaching, neither fast nor slow but deliberate, like a crawling tsunami of ice-cold vapor. She considered confronting it. It was fair game and within her purview to dispatch it. After all, the Irkallan had killed the scouts, and her fellow Rossians would be spared the strains of her vengeance. Their bond was immune to her acts. But she could lose everything in the process.

The decision was rendered by her feet. Barely grazing the steps, they flung her into the lobby. She waved a finger under the card reader, and the thick glass door clicked open. Entering the hallway, she looked only to the right. There, a sweet ether gushing from the stairwell poured into the hallway. It drew her into a current of delicious, aromatic light that reeled her up to the second floor. She felt his pulse pounding like drum, a rhythm of pure and intense devotion. His passion poured from the doorway of the cantina and surged down the hallway. She threw herself into the tide. It ferried her to the threshold, the fountainhead at last in her sight.

The three who remained seated at the oval table were mere decoration to her. She saw only the fourth. He was standing, unwavering, staring straight ahead, a thick tractor beam of white light bolting her to his ethereal presence. The entire room brightened and grew warmer.

Not floating nor sinking, the seated occupants felt neutrally buoyed by the fading tug of gravity. Tables and chairs chattered as their legs inched sideways through the vibrating particles of dust rising from the tile. Adrift in a wondrous slipstream, the three spectators willfully inhaled the unearthly air. The sublime atmosphere tasted sweet and nourishing— colors, odors, and sounds, all enriched, tangible and thick. Abandoning all reason, they embraced the inexplicable. Spirited with rapture, life's meaning seemed stupidly obvious to them now.

Weightless in euphoria, Alex bobbed in rolling swells of sentiment. He could smell his mother's Texas-fried chicken, his hands-down favorite that she reserved for Friday nights. There was her checkered apron, the one he sunk his face into when he got home from school. He heard singing some- where far off. It was Harry Chapin's "Cat's in the Cradle," a song about a father's lament that he hate-loved. Its bittersweet theme, deeply personal, always made him cry. The levee broke, and the tears streamed down his face. He turned to Ashley, who was already drenched, her dampened face glowing with affection. The most beautiful creature he had ever laid eyes on was his to hold. He pressed his wet cheek to hers, submerging himself in a torrent of warmth. "I love you so much," he said.

Ashley smiled though her sobs of joy. "I love you more," she replied. She wiped her nose with her sleeve and then his. They both laughed aloud and kissed through the salty matrix. Drunken with love, they literally fell out of their chairs in a deep embrace.

Barely noticing them, Janet's head was thrown back in ecstasy. She was crying then laughing and crying again, in succession. Her arms out- stretched, she was cooing her husband's name between giggles and sobs. She belted out her wedding dance song in her best Sam Cooke imper- sonation. Rising from her chair, she spun a few pirouettes on the tile floor, her chestnut hair whipping out sideways, racing to keep up with her whirling head. When her rotating heel tapped Ashley's foot, she stopped dancing and laughed at the lovebirds making out on the floor. They paid her little mind until the aura of love began to dim. A sour taste of metal and acid wet their lips. Feeling heavy, Janet sank down, sober and quiet. She deposited herself next to them on the floor. The room grew still. The air thickened with a dry, dirty fog.

Sitting on the floor like attendant kindergartners, they could see Shala and Dagon, but only as flickering, scarlet silhouettes against a faded gray background. Shala and Dagon were facing each other, arms out and yearning, leaning forward, but stalled in space. A third figure, fuzzy around the edges but deeply black in the center, stood only a few steps from them. "Go ahead," they heard a raspy voice say. "Don't let me spoil the romance. I just want to watch. Pretend I'm not here. I'm all about the love. Go on, now."

But they couldn't. Shala and Dagon were stuck in a mire, longing yet strangely suspended in a limbo between fulfillment and recision. And there was Jack, the eager voyeur, who had failed to account for the dampness of his own presence. The Irkallan's mere proximity was enough to wet the flames of their passion. His morose desire to watch the very embrace that would end the Rossians was preventing it from happening. If he remained, there would be no signal to Ross. Rossians would not send the Bar. Their Zumru would not expire. The Bar would not be released into the void, as he had planned. He desperately wanted to watch the unfolding of his crowning achievement, but he would have to take his bucket of cold water and do it from a distance.

The love-drunk squatters in the cantina were slowly awakening to a somber realization—there was a villain in their midst. Dagon had warned them of a presence that had killed the scouts. *Something was wrong*, he had told them. The words of Sukka and Sanga rang loudly now. *The union is not to take place.* Their creepy interloper was not attempting to stop it, either, but seemed bent on encouraging it.

Alex felt himself surfacing from a deep pool of compassion into an air stale with vengeance and loathing. The source of that spoiled breath was coming into focus. The colorless silhouette assumed a real form. The ghastly intruder solidified, his corporeal body defined. "Jack!" shouted Alex. "What are you doing here?"

"Oh, hey, Alex. Unfortunately, I've got to go. But first, I wanted to thank you for your assistance. I knew you and Ashley would do the right thing. You're just so damn curious, each of you. But together, man, you just had to grow that thing, didn't you? I knew you would." He pointed to Dagon, who was still suspended, reaching without touching, confused and longing. "And double thanks for distracting Emil and Noah. You know they're not really from the GINR, right? I was hoping you'd keep them at bay long enough for our two paramours to meet. You did well, although I had to finish the job myself. Wow! Just look at them. So in love. Those two really got it bad for each other, huh? Maybe even more than you and Ashley. They hardly know we're here. Look at them fight for it." He nodded his head toward the frustrated couple, repelled like common poles of a magnet yet swimming in vain to reach each other. "It's okay, they'll get to it as soon as I leave. They can't help it. It's strong. You felt it, right? Not my cup of tea, but don't let me interrupt any further."

Alex had felt it, all right, the amorous, intoxicating tug. It was irresistible. He knew there would be little chance of keeping the progenitors apart. For once, he was taking Jack at his word. He had to stall, to keep Jack there long enough to do something.

He looked to Ashley. She was sobering up yet still confused and struggling to sort it out. "Why is Jack here?" she asked him. She knew Jack professionally, as a geologist. They traded ideas at conferences, coauthored journal articles together, and dined together with like-minded scientists. He had sent her samples for analysis. They were collaborators. But now, here he was in a new capacity, not as a geologist, perhaps not even human. Whatever he was, he had used her in his plotting. "Why, Jack?" she implored. "Who are you? Why did you send the rocks to me?"

"Because you love this stuff. You're Space Lady. And by the way, I believe I have fulfilled your lifelong dream. You're welcome. I would've grown Dagon myself, but I can't. Something about bad energy, or whatever. See, they can't even get together in my presence. I'm that offensive."

"Look, Jack. Let's discuss this," said Alex. "Why are you so intent on wiping out a race? The universe is big, right? What did they ever do to you?"

Jack laughed. "It's what they are going to do, my boy. All that consciousness, all that energy and emotion, all that accumulated wisdom packed together in one place. It's like a time bomb, Alex. And when it goes off, it will rip the fabric of the universe to shreds. The universe isn't as big as you've been led to believe. They already know too much. It has to stop now."

"What will they know? What's so dangerous?"

"Now, if I told you that, you'd be dangerous. You and Ashley go have a good life now. You can thank me later. I know you're trying to stall, but it's no use, Alex."

"No, wait," said Ashley. "Who are you really? What happened to the real Jack Whinston?"

"What? I am the real Jack Whinston. The one and only. Well, more than only, I guess. Let's just say I'm Jack here. Always have been."

Ashley's eyes narrowed. "You were born here?"

"Sure. Well, yes, I suppose, loosely defined. This is all just code, right?" Jack slapped a hand to his chest. "You know, A's, G's, C's and T's. The Form. DNA. Whatever. That's the easy part. Slow, but easy. Just send it. Takes forever, but it comes eventually. The speed of light is overrated. Then it's just a matter of following instructions. I like the design. Pretty convincing, huh?" He rubbed his face with a hand. "Not too handsome, homey, family-looking guy. I even go to church! It's hilarious in there. Anyway, this stuff"—he slapped his chest again—"piece of cake. Now, me? How did I get here? That's the hard part. Instantaneous, but requires some serious voodoo tech to pull it off. Messing with gravity is risky business. That's what these fuckers are up to. Gathering, congregating the stuff, even moving it to a new location." He tipped a head toward the frozen progenitors. "They've already got part of it figured out. But they have one tiny flaw that I am about to exploit."

Alex pushed himself up to a kneeling position. "The gas? You mean the carbon dioxide?"

"Good one, Alex. I just love cars. Don't you? Build more. Burn more carbon. Honestly, it doesn't bother me. Not so for them, though. It's the one thing they can't hack. I built it in so they wouldn't colonize planets prematurely. The old fly in the ointment, so to speak. Now, I really have to go. I feel like a chaperone in the back seat of Dad's Buick on prom night."

Janet sat quietly, frozen on the floor, blinking at Jack, mesmerized by the ordinary-looking man she now realized was anything but. He was all wrong. It was all wrong. She felt a swelling compulsion to foil his plans.

Janet was slow to her feet, loitering on her hands and knees before rising, her dawdling not enough to set off Jack's radar. She turned her attention to Dagon. He was listing hard toward Shala, shuffling his feet forward, arms flailing, but each time sliding back again. Preoccupied in his repartee with Alex and Ashley, Jack paid her little mind when she touched Dagon's arm. Pivoting, Dagon smiled at her through a painful grimace that pleaded for help. She nodded silently while signaling a three with her fingers. Bobbing her head three times, she yanked his arm on the third. It was like pulling out a hair that stretched taut until the follicle finally popped. Dagon staggered in her direction, uncoupled from the gravity of his partner. Janet trotted him behind the dairy counter toward an exit leading to the shipping dock.

Finally aware of her plotting, Jack reached into his breast pocket, where he kept his remedy for troublemakers. But before he could take a step forward, a wild-eyed man appeared in the doorway behind him. "He's a murderer!" shouted Tom Allen, his arms cocked back like he was awaiting a pitch. The tire iron made a sickly metallic thwack. Blood splattered forward off Jack's head, spraying the floor in front of him. His body had barely met the tile when the room, once again, began to fill with intense light and warmth. Alex and Ashley immediately reached for each other. The tire iron clanged to the floor. Janet screamed, "No, Dagon!" She spiraled down, face in her hands, as he slipped away and ran to Shala.

CHAPTER 26

WHAT HAPPENED?

What was real and what was imagined would long be debated. All would agree that the light, the heat, the swirling eddy of emotion that engulfed them was inarguably real. Something certainly had happened. Something profound. Whether it occurred for seconds, minutes, or hours was a point of contention amongst the remaining four occupants who awoke on the floor. But the overturned tables and chairs, the heaps of gray dust and empty clothing, the candy wrappers, the blood stains, the tire iron, they were only circumstantial. They could not speak to the actual experience—it was unspeakable. They could only verbalize what they had imagined, not what they had felt.

So fervent was the encounter that Tom would later deny its occurrence altogether. He had risen to his feet and scampered from the building, never to look back. A stiff dose of denial kept him sane. "Hypnosis," he would later claim, "or a psychotropic gas released from the air vents."

But it could not be so simply dismissed by the other three. Having lived through an improbable history, culminating in an impossible moment, they knew too much to deny it. Something had happened, but it defied a consistent description. Each of their attempts to describe it differed wildly from the others' accounts.

Alex recounted a seamless merging of selves. Not just he and Ashley but countless others, each as individuals, yet connected and accessible through a common thread. Everything, for a lack of a better word, was there, he had said. The door was wide open. He had reached for the

179

currency of infinite wisdom, stacked in neat piles right in front of him. He had jangled the keys to the great mysteries of the universe. "Was there really dark energy?" he had queried. There was not, he had learned, its premise nothing more than a cheap parlor trick. The cosmological constant was entirely unnecessary. "And the origin of life?" he probed. Neither DNA nor RNA, as most had hypothesized, but rather a now defunct nucleic acid-hydrocarbon hybrid capable of thermally induced chiral inversion. Flopping between enzyme and template, the odd little ignition molecule had primed replicative lifeforms both here and elsewhere, millions of times over.

But above all, Alex learned of Ashley. He tasted the bitter grounds of her pain and resentment. He breathed the acrid air that had poisoned her faith in humanity. The betrayal and deception were palpable. But there was hope and love, too. Squeezing their way out, like a new green shoot of life, they pushed against a soiled crust, inviting him to grow with them.

Alex's version of the account was the only one that included a bizarre description of the clock on the cantina wall. He swore that it had spun backward in a dizzying blur until it reversed and spun forward again. No one refuted it. Especially Janet, who had witnessed her fingernails regress nearly to the quick before growing back out again. She swore the entire room and all its contents had shrunk in unison before expanding again in an instant. The chairs and tables didn't just fall over, she told them, they were shrunken to mere specks, along with everything else. When they popped back into existence, they sprang from the floor and toppled over when they landed. She challenged them to explain the awkward positions they found themselves in upon waking. "Where are your shoes?" she asked Ashley. One loafer dangled from the leg of an overturned chair; the other sat near the vending machine. "Look!" cried Janet. She pointed to the holdout Twix bar that had finally dropped from the delivery coil.

Jack's sardonic send-off to Ashley haunted her. As he had pointed out, she had indeed fulfilled her lifelong dream of finding extraterrestrial life. But it was not in a way she had envisioned. It was a dream she could never report. Vivid and unforgettable but equally unbelievable. She relayed her account solely to the two people who wouldn't roll their eyes or recommend a therapist. Embedded in a vast, two-dimensional layer, she felt spread out and dispersed ubiquitously into an infinitely thin layer of cellophane, curving with its curves, wrinkling with its wrinkles, and dipping into its countless puckered indentations. Simultaneously looking forward and backward in time, she slipped in and out of swirling funnels connected at their apices. The layer was immeasurably large from within, she had explained, but shrank into the tiniest of crumpled dots when she finally broke away from it.

"We don't know what happened," would be the party line. "Sure, some kind of explosion, maybe. Go ask Tom Allen," they might say. They knew better than to publicly acknowledge what really had happened to them. A pile of dust and some abandoned clothing were all that remained to show for it. Even Detective Shockley, the pit bull of an inspector who goaded Alex with her CSI hypothesis, was left empty-handed. Forensics couldn't even find human DNA in all the debris, let alone recognizable human remains. Sukka and Sanga never existed, and Emil and Noah were demonstrably safe and sound in Greenland. Jack Whinston had left a suicide note for his bereaved family and colleagues, but whether he was actually dead remained a mystery. The *Los Angeles Times* featured a piece entitled "Celebrated Geologist Drops Off the Face of the Earth." There were only three people on the Earth who found humor in that idiomatic headline.

And there was Emma, a precocious child who could, with some trepidation, corroborate the emergence of life from a meteorite. Her drawings of the little creature that sprang from her terrarium added color to her bedroom wall but were typically dismissed as the fanciful product of a thirteen-year-old mind. Ron, mysteriously cured of cystic fibrosis, remained a celebrated medical miracle. But aliens? No. More likely a rarified genetic phenomenon requiring further study. "He's chimeric," they said. Then there was Ernie's vagabond redhead with faith-healing powers, the saintly creature who had cured him of diabetes. His story played well with some of the doggedly faithful in his local church but lacked any legs beyond that. And his doctor, Tom Allen? Well, you could go ask him, but he refused interviews. He tried to answer some questions in the beginning but found his face plastered on tabloids racked in supermarket checkout lines. He had ultimately shuttered his research lab and returned to work only as a practicing physician.

The true believers—Ashley, Alex, and Janet—they found some solace in their common bond but couldn't find anything to substantiate the thesis that formed it. Returning to Janet's lab, they discovered the remaining samples of Jack's rock to be inert and as lifeless as one would expect for a four-billion-year-old stone. The presumed stromatolites, etched into that rock, were rejected as artifact by their peers, and the tiny onion-like spheres below them had degraded into amorphous blebs. Nevertheless, the mere finding of undeformed stone of record vintage merited publication in science's finest journal. The article was prefaced by a postmortem salute to the great Jack Whinston, who was right again when he prophesied Alex's encore as a televised science celebrity. Alex squirmed under the journalistic glare, especially when answering questions about the rock's significance with respect to the origin of life on Earth. In his self-imposed final interview, he blurted out that life neither arises nor dies, it just continues. Asked to explain that, he replied that he would do so—in eleven years.

PART 2

CHAPTER 1

ROSSLYN

"Rosslyn!" shouted Ashley. "Your limo is leaving in ten minutes, and the driver says you're grounded for a week if you're not ready."

"Actually, more like fifteen minutes," said Alex. "And I wouldn't call my Smart Fortwo Brabus a limo, either. That would be quite a stretch. Hey, a stretch. Get it? Stretch limo."

"Got it, but too early and your car is no joke. It's not safe, Alex. It's manuals like you that are causing problems for all the APVs out there. Get rid of that thing. It's 2030. Get a real car."

"Hey, keep it down, ageist. My Brabus might hear you. I'm not getting rid of her, either. We have a thing for each other. We can't help it if the APs are too dumb to float a stop sign or punch it when they see a yellow light. Brabus is called a smart car for a reason."

"It's dumb! And it's even dumber to do any of those things with your daughter in that ancient contraption!"

"Ouch! How many years of therapy will it take for my Brabus to get over that?"

"Rosslyn!" she hollered again. "You need to be at Larchmont by 8:30. What are you doing?"

A muffled thump followed by the sound of solid objects tumbling over the wooden floor echoed from the hallway into the kitchen. "Oh, dang it!" squealed Rosslyn. She plodded into the kitchen, fumbling with a poster board and three unruly rocks refusing to stay put on a display

185

panel. "The glue didn't work, Mom. The igneous is too porous to stick, and the other two aren't flat enough."

The look of frustration on a ten-year-old should evoke empathy. But Rosslyn's flushed freckled face, scrunched little cheeks, and wrinkled dot of a nose only looked adorable to her parents. She was indeed half of each of them, although each only saw the other's half. With the parental decks combined and shuffled, she had been dealt her mom's brilliantly blond and destined for platinum hair, along with her alabaster complexion and lanky stature. Her drawn-out jawline, courtesy of Alex, ran from her mother's elfish ears to her pointed chin. Her silvery almond Ashley eyes blinked under her curious, wispy Alex eyebrows. The tiny dent in her chin, a scaled copy of her father's, rested below a replica of her mother's plush lower lip. Whoever she looked like, she was perfect to them. Even in her discomfiture, they saw only flawless innocence and charm.

"Well, sweetie, maybe you can just put the rocks on the teacher's desk during the presentation," said Ashley. "He won't mind. It's more important that you know—"

"That igneous is formed from hardened volcanic lava, sedimentary is formed by the layering of particles, and metamorphic is formed by heat and pressure," said Rosslyn. "Borrrrriing. Why can't you give me one of your meteorites from Mars or something cool to talk about?"

"I can't release those to you, Rossie. They're kept in a special place."

"How about the rock that you and Dad whisper about when you think I'm not listening? You know, the one that grew space aliens out of it. I could get an easy A if I brought in some space aliens."

"Stop it, Rossie," replied Ashley. "We've talked about this. It was a long time ago, and your father and I prefer to keep it to ourselves."

"Come on, Mom, I've seen it myself on History Channel reruns. They even talk about Dad."

"Jesus! Are they still running that trash?" asked Alex. "I thought UCLA sued them."

"They did," said Ashley. "Remember? UCLA won, but the settlement required they only remove the part claiming you were the alien."

"You're the alien?" chirped Rosslyn. She pivoted to her father and inspected him with a faux dubious squint. "Am I half alien? Am I, Mom? Can I fly or something? I want to bring Dad in for my presentation. Can you do laser eyes for them, Dad? You know, maybe melt a chair or show us your antennas."

"Stop it, now!" Ashley chided. "I know what you're doing, Rosslyn, and it's disrespectful. Whatever happened, happened. That's between your father and me. Not another word. Now eat so you can get out of here on time."

Rosslyn quietly dumped the rocks into her backpack and folded up the poster board. She poured herself a bowl of Cheerios, sat down, and dug in. Each crunching bite sliced into the otherwise paralytic silence. She wasn't so innocent, anymore. Nor so malleable. She had cracked the Santa Claus code at the age of eight, and any mention of Tooth Fairies or Easter Bunnies evoked eye rolls that were practically audible. Her parents knew a time would come when the unavoidable subject of their rather peculiar history would have to be discussed in more concrete terms. They had evolved a version of it to accommodate her growing grasp on reality, but the prospect of a frank and honest conveyance brought lumps to their throats.

But it was inescapable. The tabloid headlines had long since faded, but her parents still suffered the occasional derision. Often, it took the form of a joke cast their way when the subject of extraterrestrials made the news. *Hey, Alex, are you driving to the Area 51 Assembly or just teleporting in?* Or, *Wow, Ashley, they discovered water on Mars, but I guess you already knew it was there.*

They took it in stride, sometimes playing along. But it was the mounting pressure on their dear child that disturbed them most. Some of the more savvy older kids in Rosslyn's school would pass her in the hall with their index fingers extended upward on opposing sides of their heads. She had endured the morphing of her name to Ross-alien and was once sincerely asked by a six-year-old if she had invented the Mars Bar. She laughed it off at first, then learned to ignore them. But as of late, the inability to defend herself gnawed at her. She needed to know what had really happened.

She had overheard more than one heated discussion by her parents.

"That could be any day now!" her father had blurted.

"Eleven point two light-years isn't the same as eleven years and two months," her mother had shot back. "It depends on the path. It bends with gravity, remember?"

Rosslyn didn't know what was bending or when it would bend, but it seemed like something serious. Then, there was the inexcusable amount of time spent helping their friend Janet on her farm. They were building greenhouses. She liked the farm but never really understood what they were doing out there or why the three adults would whisper whenever she was nearby. Despite their behavior, she had yet to conclude that they were crackpots. Nevertheless, she wasn't buying their overcooked assurance that everything was fine. Everything wasn't.

She finished her cereal in silence, grabbed her backpack, and shuffled out to her father's car to wait for him. She didn't mind the decrepit coupe. It had personality. Unlike the universal odor of new-car smell, old-car smell was unique to each vehicle. In this case, it spoke to a history of crumbling croissants, wet dog hair, baby vomit, and her father's Old Spice. The brittle, scored leather seats of the Brabus felt stiff under her tiny frame. The rumpled floor mat, wobbly armrest, and faded turquoise dash were unmistakable signs of twilight for the geriatric jalopy. A couple of empty takeout coffee cups occupied the center console. Ostracized, a third cup had been relegated to her door pocket. A jumble of objects, including one of her art pens, poked out below the cup, but she dared not plunge her fingers into that murky pit. A hairline crack running the length of the windshield divided the fluffy clouds visible above Golden Gate Avenue.

Rosslyn likened the battered, minuscule vehicle to a large toy, which made it more fun to ride in. And then there was her father's whimsical carping over the not so smart APVs. He swore they were the product of cousin marriages. The ride was certainly more fun than the drab AP TeslUber pods that sometimes ferried her home when Alex worked late at UCLA. Her parents had settled on a home conveniently centered between the JPL and UCLA, where Alex had happily accepted a position. Larchmont Charter was in Hollywood, so Alex had the pleasure of dropping Rosslyn off each morning on his way in to work. He told her that driving her to school was the best part of his day, which made her wonder how enjoyable his job actually was.

It was a mild late-October day. Splashes of yellow were visible amongst the rare deciduous trees tucked between the palms and evergreens that lined their street in the Silver Lake District of Los Angeles. Alex wiggled into the car, scowled at his daughter until she buckled up, then started the rumbling bug of a vehicle. Above the din of an aging muffler, he asked her if she was ready for her presentation.

"They're rocks, Dad. How can I not be ready for rocks? Have you ever heard the expression *dumb as a rock*?"

"Whoa, there! Rocks are not dumb. The people who study them might be, but not the rocks themselves. They tell the story of our entire existence. The planet, the history of life, and even our future is in the rocks. Rocks have been here since the beginning of Earth."

"So has this car."

"Shush, the Brabus can hear you. She still thinks she's young." He punched the accelerator, and the car lurched forward, belching out some white smoke. "See, still spry."

"She needs a walker, Dad. And she smokes. Nobody smokes, anymore."

Pretending to be hurt, he pushed out his lower lip and blinked his eyes in rapid succession. "You'll get old someday, too, young lady, and then you're going to feel bad about how you offended my Brabus."

"When I'm old like Mom, I'm going to be hot, just like her."

"Hey! Mom's not old. She's only forty-one, Rossie. That's considered middle-aged."

"So your Brabus is still young at twelve, then?"

"Not in car years. Brabus is a hundred and ten, but she feels like eighty."

Rosslyn tried to conceal a smile, unwilling to gift her father with any appreciation of his quirky humor. She had the upper hand when she pretended to sulk, and not laughing only made him try harder. And she was hardly in a mood to laugh. She knew her presentation on rocks would only invite more ridicule. Especially from the snotty kids who resented her for skipping a grade. "When I grow up, I want to be a veterinarian," she said.

"That's cool, Rossie. I think you'd be a great veterinarian. What made you think of that?"

"Animals are nicer than people. People are mean."

"Uh-oh. Kids at school teasing you, again, sweetie?"

"They're such assholes!" she spouted.

"Hey! Language, young lady. Call them *prolapsed rectums,* instead. Veterinarians know what that is."

"I know what that is. It's an inside-out asshole."

"Okay. Well, that's even worse than a right-side-in one. Right? Rossie, never mind those kids. Believe it or not, you're a threat to them. You're smarter, stronger, and have a better future than they do. You're prettier, too. They're just jealous."

"Jealous of Ross-*alien*? I'm sure they all wish their parents came from another planet. Why, Dad? What really happened? You guys are scientists. Why can't you just explain it to me? I'm old enough to understand."

"I know, honey. The thing is, we don't even know what happened, so it's hard to explain. Each of us—your mom, Janet, myself—experienced something different when it happened. It's impossible to describe."

"But you think something else is going to happen. I'm not dumb. I hear you and Mom talking. I hear you whispering with Janet. And what are those greenhouses on her farm for?"

"Well, we don't really know if something is going to happen. It's just a feeling, Rossie. It's hard to explain. It seems silly. It's just kind of a hobby for us. We don't like to talk about it because of, you know, all the prolapsed rectums out there."

They rode on in silence, apart from a few sordid insults hurled at the inbred APVs. Alex stopped in front of the school gate on Selma Avenue, gave her a kiss, and told her he loved her. Standing on the street, she hesitated. Still clutching the open car door, she leaned in and shot him a stern look. "If anything does happen, you better tell me. All of it. Love you, too, Dad."

The door closed and he watched her march into the funnel of kids converging at the school entrance. He waited, left hand readied on the door handle, almost hoping the proverbial bully would approach her. She passed through the door undeterred. Her blond head bobbed in the crowd until it disappeared, slipping into the school, where he could no longer protect her from the innate cruelty of young humans.

———

"Very nice, Rosslyn," chirped Mr. Braxen. He surveyed his group of sixth graders. "That's how it's done, class. Start with a short introduction, clearly present the main material, and finish with a pointed summary. Wonderful."

Rosslyn squirmed. She stood alone, exposed to a malevolent gale whipped up by her clueless teacher. How could he not understand that his praise would only foment resentment? She busied herself collecting her rocks and folding her poster, aiming for a quick retreat back to her desk. But Braxen would have none of it. "Hold on a second, Rosslyn." He addressed the class, "Are there any questions for Rosslyn?" Feet shuffled and heads swiveled as the students looked to each other, hoping one would take a bullet before Braxen started firing randomly.

He was spinning the cylinder on his revolver when Randy Shiff's hand shot up. Rosslyn's knees jellied at the sight of the smirking bruiser, waving his ham-sized palm around, anxious to curl it into a fist so he could drop her.

Ignorantly complicit, Braxen obliged, "Yes, Randy?"

"Yeah, so Rosslyn, are those rocks from Earth or did you bring them from your planet?"

And there it was. The storm of laughter, once again drowning her, driving her down, washing her into a drain hole.

"Randy!" shouted Braxen.

The class settled down, but the damage was done. She was drenched. She started again to gather her materials, but something welled up in her, something buoyant. She'd had enough of the drain hole. She wasn't going down there this time. She took a step forward, toward Randy Shiff and his big fat smiling face. She drew herself up. "Actually, Randy, the rocks are from Earth, just like the ones in your head."

Snap! The laugh-o-meter bounced off scale as the class erupted in hysterics. All eyes were on the reddened Randy, whose head darted around furiously, scowling at those who dared mock him. His burning gaze finally settled on Rosslyn. She recognized the *I'll get you for this* look, but it was worth it. She had stood up to the dragon and roasted him with a taste of his own fire. Even Braxen struggled to contain his mirth as he quelled the uproar. Rosslyn made her to way back to her desk, eyes down but sensing some newfound admiration from her gaping classmates.

"Class! Please, we have three more presentations to get through. Settle down. And the next one to make a disrespectful comment is getting detention." His eyes roamed the class, hesitating purposefully on Randy, then Rosslyn. "Okay. Let's see, how about Mark Sternfeld? Come on up, Mark."

A frail boy with a mop of brown hair and a pale complexion shuffled to the front of the class. He adjusted his thick black glasses, plunked a shoe box on Braxen's desk, and opened his poster to display a tree depicting the evolution of life on Earth. Thick branches representing the phyla radiated out into smaller branches ending in images of the major classes. A twig sprouting from the branch of fishes curved abruptly toward the amphibian branch but ended with a prominent question mark.

After a brief lecture on life's family tree, Mark pointed to the question mark and explained that he had discovered a new type of fish, a fish with legs. He pried open the shoe box and extracted a glass jar. It contained a shiny black thing that looked quite like a fish, apart from a couple protrusions that indeed resembled legs. Mark said he had discovered the oddity at Huntington Beach only yesterday when he stepped on it in shallow water. It had died shortly thereafter, so he had placed it in salty water to preserve it. "It's an amphishian," he proclaimed.

There were a few snickers and some incredulous glares, but the class quieted as a bewildered look materialized on Braxen's face. He held the jar to the light, turned it over slowly, and shook it a few times as he studied it. His biology degree was failing him. Although he was aware of so-called walking catfish in Florida, this was no catfish. He wasn't sure it was even a fish.

"What is it, Mr. Braxen?" asked Mark.

"I don't know," admitted Braxen, still mesmerized by the Franken-fish. "It looks like a common rockfish, but it—"

"But it has legs. Huh?" Mark said.

"Well, I guess. They're not fins, that's for sure." He considered it a prank and shook the jar again, looking for suture marks around the putative legs. Then his eyes popped open. Utterly stupefied and unaware that he was speaking aloud, he said, "There's hair on its belly."

Mark leaned in to look. "Mammals have hair," he offered. "I guess I'll have to rename it. It's an amphishianammal."

This was the first time any of his classmates had found anything Mark said to be entertaining. Some chuckled, some attempted to repeat the new name, others offered even more ridiculous alternatives. Hands shot up. Mark brimmed with newfound celebrity. Braxen, still fixated on the bizarre animal, seemed oblivious to the commotion until Rosslyn's pitched warble rose above the fracas. He nodded her way, acknowledging her raised hand.

"That's a really cool animal, Mark. Can I take a picture of it?"

"Well, I don't know. My dad is going to call the news stations to see if they want it for a story. But I guess you can take one."

It was too late for Braxen to stop the bum rush. They were all out of their seats, phone sticks popping open everywhere. *Good*, he thought, at least his students were excited about something in his science class. And maybe the news stations would want to interview him. He let the students have at it. The remaining two presentations would have to wait until tomorrow. The amphishianammal had stolen the show.

CHAPTER 2

DOCTOR EMMA CURTIS

Emma Curtis punched at her stick. It rolled open long enough for her to slap at the snooze button. She settled onto her back and stared at the amorphous water stains on the ceiling. She had measured her distance to them the hard way, by sitting up too quickly in the elevated bunk. The tiny room in her Westwood efficiency had tested her space-planning skills when she wedged her life's belongings into it. The few remaining square feet of bare floor were spared only as a well-worn path to the doorway, one she had scurried down multiple times at five a.m. She didn't mind. Her spartan quarters were a fair trade for the ten-minute bike ride to the teaching hospital at UCLA.

It was a Saturday in late October, and having finished off her Surgery clerkship, she had a couple of free days before her Pediatric rounds began. Well aware that she should be studying for the impending systems-based healthcare exams, she couldn't shake a burning interest in her so-called hobby—her father, Ron. Eleven years ago, he was cured of cystic fibrosis by an inexplicable turn of events. And now, as a medical student, Emma was consumed by that lack of understanding. She was far from solving it. So far, her data included Ron's chimeric genetics, a small chunk of the Big Mac meteorite, and a curious lost dog, whose whereabouts were never determined. But today, she hoped to define one of the variables.

More than once, Emma had grilled Ron's former doctor at the CF clinic in Phoenix. He could not explain how Ron's lung cells appeared genetically normal while his blood cells retained the CF mutation. *They just do*, Dr. Berthstein had said. She had almost given up on him until

194

recently, when she accidentally pushed a hot button. Above all, Dr. Berthstein trusted his data, and when she questioned it, his pride buzzer released a deafening tone. *My data are fine! And for your information, I wasn't the only one!* he had blurted. It was a clear breach. He winced immediately thereafter, then pressed his lips together like he was trying to suck the words back into his mouth.

With some gentle prodding, he recounted a similar claim made by a research physician at the Biodesign Institute at ASU. It was a case study involving the genetic reversion of a diabetic. *Dr. Thomas Allen*, he told her. And in the same breath, he disclosed his promise to Tom that he would never reveal his name. He guided her to an obscure archive that had captured Tom Allen's seminar announcement from eleven years ago. *This is how you found him*, he insisted, *not by talking to me.* She got the drift. He warned her that it would likely prove fruitless. Dr. Allen had stopped talking about it eleven years ago and swore he never would again.

The stains on the ceiling blurred as her mind wandered. Maybe Dr. Allen would talk or maybe he wouldn't. But what he wouldn't say could still be revealing. She navigated the wobbly bunk ladder and tucked herself into the desk underneath her bed. With a quick poke, her phone stick unfurled, projecting a dazzling ensemble of flashing come-ons, animated talking heads, and personalized adverts pitching remedies for plantar fasciitis. How did they know? It was only yesterday that her father had complained to her about his new foot malady. The floating red bauble with a wheel in the center popped when she pushed her finger through it. In its place, a smiling bot-head adorned in a TeslUber hat materialized. The bot's pupils expanded to indicate a facial scan. "Emma Curtis," it announced, "traveling to Phoenix Arizona on American Airlines, departing from Burbank Airport at 9:57 a.m."

Although annoyed, she was no longer astounded by the data-gathering abilities of AI bots. Her previous online search for Tom Allen, and the means to reach him, were enough for the bot to second-guess her plans.

"Maybe I changed my plans," she challenged.

A few seconds passed. "I cannot find those records."

"Well, I want to go to plantar fasciitis instead of Phoenix," she said.

"We cannot take passengers to other planets. I'm joking."

"You should wait a few seconds before revealing that it's a joke. Timing is important."

There was a short pause. "I cannot take you to plantar fasciitis." Another pause, then, "It can only be reached on foot."

Emma laughed. "That's a good one."

"I'm joking."

"I know. I already laughed."

"All joking aside, APV number sixty-seven, 7:30 pickup. Forty-three minutes to Burbank Airport," it said.

"Sounds good."

"Pick up at front or side door?"

She shook her head slowly. The two exits from her building were barely twenty feet apart. Did it know which one was closer to her apartment? "Surprise me," she replied.

"Okay. Let's go with the side door. It's closer to the street."

"Fine. See you then."

"You won't see me. You will see APV sixty-seven."

APV sixty-seven was indeed awaiting her at the side door when she emerged from the building. It was still early dawn, and the low light reflected off the buffed vehicle, highlighting a wrinkled right rear fender. She piled into the compact car, confirmed her destination, and then asked about the crunched fender.

"A manual ran a stop sign and made contact with my exterior. It is only a scratch."

"You didn't see the manual?"

"Yes, I saw it. It didn't see me. The damage does not affect the function of the vehicle."

"I realize that. I was just wondering if you were drunk when it happened."

"Ha!" Its brittle croak an apparent acknowledgement of humor. "APVs cannot drink. Manuals drink. Number fifty-nine was totaled by one. A drunk movie star."

"Sorry to hear that. Do you miss fifty-nine?"

"Ha!"

———

She wondered if her phone recognized the squeak of airplane tires hitting the tarmac. While taxiing, she responded, "Yes," to an auto-prompt asking if she would need an APV. It was sunny and warm when she emerged from the Sky Harbor terminal in Phoenix. She stared unblinking into the camera at the TeslUber kiosk and then again at the row of APVs lining the arrivals curb. An orange lamp on APV number ninety-three lit up as it scurried over to receive her.

"Good morning, Emma. Biodesign Institute?" the APV chirped.

"Took the words right out of my mouth."

"Actually, I took them off your MedLine search history."

"Whatever. Let's just go."

"I can't until you buckle up."

She ticked off the familiar landmarks while traversing the ASU campus on the way to the institute. They passed the Levin Center, where she had attended the Joaquin Bustoz Math-Science Honors Summer Program as the youngest high school student ever admitted. It was barely a stone's throw from the Biodesign Institute. She marveled at their proximity. Dr. Tom Allen's whacky diabetes fable had unfolded right under her nose.

Although Tom was expecting her, she had spun a white lie involving her not so genuine interest in a new device he was beta-testing on diabetics at the institute. She wasn't quite sure how she would broach the subject of magical genetics, but she didn't want to scare him off before she had even met him. He was alone in his office. It resembled a converted utility closet stuffed with a tiny desk, a bookcase, and a spare chair that had to be pulled forward to open the door. Technically listed as a faculty member in the Center for Personalized Medicine, Tom felt more like the sole faculty member in the Center for Tom Allen. He still maintained some clinical responsibilities for patient care, but his research activities were marginalized to the monitor on his desk.

His hair was white and thin but his eyes still bright behind his round retro eyeglasses. An unbuttoned gray cardigan dangled from his sloped shoulders as he rose to greet Emma over the width of his desk. After finding her hand, he finally made eye contact and reared backwards, his butt clumsily captured by his chair as he ran out of space behind him. Face reddened, he clambered back to his feet and adjusted his eyeglasses for a second take. A hot current flowed down his spine. *Was it her?* The red-haired siren reaching for her desperate Adonis. The UCLA cantina blew up large in his mind. The resemblance was uncanny. The blazing red hair, the slender nose, the apple cheeks, the alabaster freckled face, her lips, her stature, her everything.

"I'm sorry," he said. Forgetting they had already shaken, he extended his trembling hand once again. She complied but looked justifiably frightened. "I'm sorry," he repeated. "You look very much like someone I have met before. Well, not really met, I guess, but just knew, or experienced, actually."

"Experienced?" There wasn't much room to back up without actually leaving the closet, but Emma's heels were on the threshold.

"I'm sorry. Please. It's just—I don't know. Forgive me." He came around the desk, squeezing past the bookcase to pull out his spare chair. Emma pulled it back even farther in a subtle bid to prevent the door from being closed.

"Okay, that's fine," Tom said, without defining what *that* actually was. He returned to his chair without taking his eyes off of her. Both seated, situated directly across from each other, neither spoke in the unsettled atmosphere, the purpose of their meeting clouded.

Emma finally threw out a chitchat starter by telling him of her stint at the nearby Levin Center during her high school days. *That should settle things down a bit*, she thought. It didn't.

"Oh, my god!" he exclaimed. "You were the girl who named the Big Mac meteorite!" He was standing again.

Although it was common knowledge back then, Tom's overweight reaction to it now seemed off-kilter to Emma. Understandably, anyone here with knowledge of that incident might be curious upon meeting the adult version of that little girl, but Tom was downright flabbergasted. The wild-eyed, eccentric man settled back into his chair, his eyes never straying from her. Her mind whirled. Who did she resemble that he had *experienced?* Her familiarity plus Big Mac had somehow triggered him.

"That was me, all right," she conceded. She studied him for few seconds and, in that moment, decided to skip over the pretenses and just throw the gas on the fire. "It's kind of why I'm here, actually."

Tom stiffened. He felt like the truck that had run him over eleven years ago was circling back for another run.

"Do you know what exosomes are?" she asked.

He stood up yet again. "Look, I thought you came to discuss diabetes and our new medical monitoring device. I don't work on exosomes. Obviously, it seems you're aware of an old debunked study that I presented, only once, many years ago, and quickly retracted. I'm not sure how you found out about it. It was flawed and never published for a good reason."

Emma stood up, face-to-face. She calmly doubled down, deliberating on each word. "My father was cured of cystic fibrosis by a dog that grew out of a hamster that arose from a chunk of the Big Mac meteorite." She pulled a sketchbook out of her bag and showed him her old drawing of the bizarre little creature from the rock. "Now, I won't think you're crazy, if you don't think I'm crazy."

He only glanced at the drawing and returned his gaze to her. "You look just like that woman."

"What? What woman? I only want to know how your diabetic patient was treated. How was he cured? My father has normal genes in his lung tissue, but his lymphocytes still carry the CF mutation. Sound familiar? Your abstract, the one you retracted, said you found exosomes in your patient's blood. They contained DNA. Where did they come from?"

His lips barely moved, as though he were talking only to himself. "From that woman."

"What woman?"

"She was—" He stopped and looked down at his desk.

"She was what?"

"I don't know. She was homeless. My patient took her in. He was trying to help her. He claimed she was an angel. I'm not so sure about that part. I tried to track her down and found an indigent man who claimed she gave him diabetes. His doctor verified it, or at least she spoke to me about it. I never saw the data, and she refuses to discuss it to this day. Look!" He rummaged through his bookcase and found a yellowed clipping from a news tabloid sandwiched inside a book. "Here! Here's what's going to happen to you if you pursue this."

She looked at the faded photo of a wild-eyed, younger Tom Allen. They had captured him with his mouth wide open, his hair whipped up like a tornado had run through it. His glasses were tipped crooked at the end of his nose, and his hands, palms out, were raised in hysterical warning. The title read: *Professor Discovers Faith-Healing Aliens.*

"It's just one of many," he said. "They ran it on that stupid History Channel. It ruined me. Don't do this."

"She looked like me?"

"Very much so. A hamster that turned into a dog, huh?"

"Yeah. It was a salamander before it became a hamster. You recording this?"

"No."

"Me neither. So, what happened to her? The faith healer."

"I don't know. Nobody does. She disappeared. Literally."

"Nobody? Who else saw her?"

"It was at UCLA. There were three others, humans, that is. Janet Harley was one of them. I didn't know her but knew of her. She's a geneticist in the Biosciences building. Still there, I think. Go dig up one of these old so-called newspapers," he said, tapping the faded tabloid on his desk. "Read all about it. It's mostly bullshit, but the names are there."

"It had red hair."

"What had red hair?"

"The dog. It had red hair. We had her for one day. She retrieved my father's bronchodilator from a closed desk drawer and brought it to him during a coughing fit. Later, it pushed a bucket up against our fence and used it as a step to climb over and escape…without a trace. I don't think it stayed a dog for very long."

"Goddamnit!" Tom pounded his desk. "Why did you have to come here? Years of ridicule. Years of therapy. Do you realize how hard it is to forget what I experienced?"

"I do. That's why I'm here. And I'm done forgetting."

CHAPTER 3

SEA MONSTERS

"Ouch!" The hot iron skillet bounced off the burner. Ashley inspected her palm and reached for a potholder. "What is it, Rossie? I'm making dinner right now." The muffled prattling of a TV commentator resounded through the hallway. She couldn't make it out, but her daughter's excitement was loud and clear.

Rosslyn's charged squeal reverberated around the living room. She turned her head and pitched another squall toward the kitchen. "It looks like that weird animal that Mark showed us at school on Friday."

"Mark who?" Ashley shouted back. "What animal?"

The hollering continued. "Mark Sternfeld. He's in my science class. He had an animal in a jar. It was a fish with legs and hair. An amphishi-anammal."

The kitchen went silent. Rosslyn waited, still watching the TV. Eventually, she turned to go fetch her mom, but Ashley was already there, right behind her, slack-jawed, eyes fixed on the projection. Rosslyn spun back to face it. "See?" she said, pointing.

A potholder dropped to the floor. Ashley curled her arms around her daughter. She pulled her close, both of them still glued to the image.

"Mark Sternfeld had this—"

"Shhhh. Just a minute, sweetie. Where's Daddy?" Behind her, a familiar set of hands found her shoulders, his breath brushing her neck. "You watching this?" she murmured.

202

A grown man in a khaki sports vest held a squiggly-looking fish with bug eyes and appendages sprouting from its underside. He was bubbling over with his new catch. "Got it using PowerBait, garlic scented," he gushed. "Never seen anything like it. It's got"—a beeping noise—"legs. Oops! Sorry." He smiled guiltily, then displayed his prize to the crowd gathered behind them.

The pert lady holding the mic turned to the camera. "It's got those kinds of legs," she said, with a giggle. Before turning it over to Bruce, the anchorman, she asked what he thought it was.

"Not a clue, Carolyn," replied Bruce. As if dipped in polyurethane, his perfect hair remained stock-still as his laminated face rocked back and forth. "But it's got some competition. One of our correspondents in Australia just reported on a walking triggerfish that, get this, has the bill of a platypus. More at eleven on that. Thanks, Carolyn. Craig Dunkle with the weather, right after this."

The air in the living room was as thick as paste. Alex, Ashley, and Rosslyn remained chained together, front to back, still staring straight at the TV projection. Bruce faded, and a cartoon character hawking bathroom tissue took his place. A cartoon selling toilet paper would have been a slam dunk for her joking father, but he wasn't speaking. He was barely breathing. Her mother's thumbs dug into Rosslyn's shoulder blades.

The tension in the room grew electric, humming with charge, a static bolt set to strike whoever spoke. Young Rosslyn was well aware of it, too. The numb silence of her parents was deafening to her. Her posture stiffened. It was a familiar feeling. But this time she wasn't going to ignore it. The thousand-pound gorilla was standing in the corner of the room, and she was about to kick it in the nuts. Wiggling from her mother's grasp, she broke from their chain, took a determined step forward, and turned to face the two of them. Her hands were on her hips, her head pushed forward, her mouth screwed up. "Now you're going to tell me!" she demanded.

They broke apart and looked at each other, each searching for a signal from the other.

Ashley squinted at Rosslyn. "Honey—"

"No! None of the *honey* stuff!" Rosslyn stomped her foot. "You always say that right before you lie to me."

Ashley cleared her throat. "Okay. Ummm, sweetie—" Rosslyn's eyes bugged out again. Another stomp. "Okay, not sweetie, either," her mother corrected. "Look, a long time ago, before you were born, your father and I met some people. Not really people, actually. They were not from here. They—"

"Are you fucking kidding me?" Rosslyn screamed. "There really were aliens? There really *are* aliens!"

"Language, sweetie," interjected Alex.

"I'm not *fucking sweetie!*" she blurted. "You met actual aliens and haven't told me about it?"

Alex tried again. "It seems like a dream to us, Rossie. It happened so long ago. We can hardly believe it ourselves. We couldn't prove it, and we didn't want you to get teased at school. It's already bad enough, even though we deny it."

"Where are they from? Mars?" Rosslyn demanded.

"They were from a planet called Ross 128b."

"What? Ross? As in Rosslyn? You can't be serious. I was named after the aliens' planet?" Livid, she tilted toward them, arms tight to her sides, fists clenched. "Jesus! Why not just name me ET? Too obvious? I can't believe this!"

"We're sorry, Rosslyn. You busted us on Santa Claus when you were eight. How could we expect you to believe in aliens?"

"A guy flies around the world in a sled and delivers presents to eight billion people in a single night. Got any evidence for that nifty piece of physics, science parents? Life evolving on other planets? It happened here, didn't it? Why not elsewhere? Right, astrobiologist Mom? Come on!"

She was furious. Her parents knew the day would come when they'd have to pull back the curtain, but her anger with them was shocking. She was precocious, well beyond her ten and a half years, but even so, they had underestimated her. With the Band-Aid ripped off, the rancor oozed out. Alex should have seen it coming. She was half Ashley, after all. And if there was anything Ashley hated, it was being lied to.

Indignant, Rosslyn leveraged her scorn. "No more surprises!" she bellowed. "Just answer the questions! To be absolutely clear," she continued, "you—I guess me, too—we're not aliens. We're humans. From planet Earth. Right? Tell me I'm right!"

"We're humans, Rossie." Ashley couldn't believe she was actually saying this to her daughter. Parenting had its challenges, but this was a topic not covered in Lythcott-Haims' *How to Raise an Adult.* She briefly wondered whether later editions might.

"And these weird animals, like Mark's at school and on the TV? Aliens, I suppose."

"Well, possibly," offered Alex. "Eleven years ago, Dagon told us—"

"Dagon?"

"An alien from Ross 128b," he continued. It felt weird to say it out loud in front of her. "Dagon said they would return. They would send their instructions for their assembly, actually DNA sequences, as a signal transmitted by light. It would take eleven years, eleven point two, more precisely, to reach Earth. We don't really know how this works exactly, but the DNA sequences are kind of like a starter kit. They get incorporated into life that already exists on Earth, like algae or bacteria, and then it's modified continuously until mature organisms from Ross 128b are fully developed. They'll look a lot like us."

Rosslyn pointed at the TV. "Like us? Do I look like a platypus?"

"It's not finished. It might look like a platypus at first, because that one's in Australia. The platypus lives near the coast there, so its DNA gets used in furthering the development of what might crawl out of the sea. Here in California, they might borrow from a rockfish, then copy some DNA from a sea otter or something, and eventually from humans."

"And I talked about rocks for my science presentation? Dumb, dead rocks."

"Rosslyn, you can't talk about this. Not now," urged Alex.

"Why not? I want to talk about it before the platypus does."

"The platypus can't talk," said Alex. He turned to Ashley. "Right, honey? I mean, maybe to Dr. Dolittle but—"

Ashley quickly waved him off and spoke directly to Rosslyn. "Rossie, if it's really happening, there'll be plenty of proof to convince the world, but right now, there isn't. We've been there. We learned to shut our mouths. We even lied about it. We had to."

Rosslyn stood silent, an overwhelming mouthful of revelation stuck in her throat. Finally, she asked, "Humans? They borrow from humans?"

Alex pulled out his stick and tapped up a projection of a man sitting at a table littered with soda cans and candy wrappers. "This is Dagon, or was, until he vanished. Who does he look like? It's someone you know. Maybe Dagon's slightly less handsome. But who does he resemble?"

Rosslyn looked back and forth between her father and the projection. "More handsome," she answered.

Ashley finally managed a smile.

"Come on. I was eleven years younger then," said Alex.

"Vanished?" asked Rosslyn. "Like he died?"

"His body died. Not really died, though. It sort of decomposed. It turned to dust. Just his clothing remained. Same for his mate, Shala."

"Shala? A girl alien. Did she look like Mom?"

"Not at all. No one can look that good, Rossie. Shala had bright red hair, freckles, and was a bit taller than Mom. We don't know who she borrowed from."

Bruce reappeared on the TV. On the monitor behind him, a restless crowd of protesters, many wearing gas masks and dressed in mock hazard suits, was shouting in French and waving signs. Some of the signs portrayed fabricated images of animals with two heads, extra appendages, or a multitude of eyes.

Rosslyn, with a year of remedial French under her belt, tried to read one of signs aloud. "It says something about radioactive waste and a bomb, I think. No, wait, abomination," she concluded.

Bruce shuffled some papers on his desk and looked back at his monitor. "John Castani is live in Marseille, on the Mediterranean coast of France. Protestors have gathered there to bring attention to what they say is radioactive contamination. John."

"That's right, Bruce. Earlier today, beachgoers were horrified by a number of miniature sea monsters that had washed up on the shore here. This image, provided by Provence Azur, gives you some idea of what they experienced. This tiny devil ray is covered with a hard shell, much like that found on the native loggerhead turtles. And, yes, those do look like legs. Some believe it's a prank, but as you can see behind me, these protestors are taking it seriously. Although strongly suspected, radiation has not yet been detected. Others are blaming GMO foods for the abominations. Bruce."

The pink in Bruce's lacquered face had faded to ash. He had experienced floods, earthquakes, and other shameless acts of God, but a global mutant crisis was not on his resume. After a dead-air pause, capped off by a look of surprise at a frantic cameraman, he simply said, "Well." He raised his eyebrows, looked down, stacked his papers once more, and then encouraged his viewers to tune in again at eleven o'clock. With that, he rose from the desk and walked off before the camera could break away. The cartoon with toilet paper quickly returned.

"We should call Janet," Alex said. He opened his phone. "I'll tell her to meet us at the Ale House in Ocean Park. We could try the beach there."

"Tell her to bring the large vessels and at least three air bottles," replied Ashley.

Rosslyn studied the exchange between her parents, her keen little mind putting it together. Janet's farm, the greenhouses, all those canisters of liquid air, the incubators, the sacks of culture media and nutrients stacked in the barn, the glassware, the freezers. It was all in preparation for this day. "It's an alien farm," she said.

CHAPTER 4

THE FARM

Deep in discussion of sea monsters, her students barely noticed her. They hadn't seen much of Ashley in the lab lately, but this morning it seemed like there were two of her. She whizzed around like a bee, pulling open drawers, opening cabinets, grabbing tools and materials like she was on a shopping spree. Their pair of little creatures would need all the help they could get. Most of the sea monsters found by the throngs scavenging the shoreline last night were already dead. Those found still alive quickly died in the hands of the foragers. Ashley knew they were lucky to find a couple of them still clinging to life.

Thanks to their sea monster sanctuary, a glass vessel primed with CO2-free air, a pair of creatures survived the trip to Janet's farm. Hastily gathering some essentials, Ashley was anxious to get out there. She carted the supplies to her car and hopped in. She was ready to roll when her stomach arrested her for skipping breakfast. A sandwich beckoned from the go counter in the building 167 cafeteria. She stared down the handicap sign in front of her car, got out, and dashed to the cafeteria.

Passing tables en route to the checkout, she overheard the feverish jabber. Climate change, radiation, oil spills, gene splicing—even Satan—each or all were to blame for the sea monster invasion. Beth, the endearing cashier with a ready smile for all, scanned Ashley's sandwich. She was in her fifties, a bit plump, with a ruddy complexion, gray hair in a bun, and wire-rimmed glasses on a gold chain dangling from her neck chain. "Morning, Ashley. That's all today, dear? You're wasting away, Dr. Woodsum."

"In a hurry, Beth. I'll try to make up for it with some ice cream at midnight."

Beth gave her a long look. "You okay, sweetheart? All this sea monster talk's got everyone in fits today. It's so silly. You worried about that? Tomorrow we'll be over it and on to the next big thing."

"I'm sure there's an explanation, Beth. There always is."

"Do you think it's radioactivity? Some think it's the new 7G network. I'm still using my old stick just to play it safe."

"Probably just aliens from outer space."

Beth laughed. "I like that one. No one expects aliens."

Ashley inhaled the sandwich on her walk back to the car. Speedometer ignored, she peeled the paint off law-abiding APVs as she sped pass them on westbound 101. Janet's farm, which was anything but, was actually a defunct ranch in Topanga Canyon. Once occupied by hippies in the late sixties, her father among them, it was now a relic surrounded by upscale cafes, wedding venues, and retreats for the toxin-ridding, bankrolled, vegan set. As she barreled south, the ranch homes lining Topanga Canyon Boulevard quickly gave way to hilly green and brown open spaces. She turned down a narrow stretch of Santa Maria Road and passed the Heartfelt Wildlife Animal Shelter adjacent to Janet's farm. She envisioned a cloud of DNA arising from the rescued bobcats, hummingbirds, and chipmunks recovering at the shelter. *What would their sea monsters look like now?* she wondered.

Already there, Alex's beaten Brabus sat in the drive, heat still radiating from the hood. Ashley parked behind it and noticed Rosslyn's book bag on the front seat when she strode past. She found her family in the ramshackle barn, where she chided Alex. "Why is Rosslyn here? She has school today."

"I tried to drop her off, but she refused to get out of the car." Rosslyn's eyes bugged out at him. "Oh, yeah, and I also asked her if she wanted to come."

Ashley chucked some stink-eye at him, then hugged her daughter. She took a quick survey of the barn, looking for signs of life. "Well, where are they?" she asked.

In the corner of the barn, Janet emerged from a makeshift corral constructed from stacks of baled hay. "*They* are eating," she answered. She wiped her hands together, then on her soiled pants. "Everything and lots of it. We'll have to move them to a greenhouse soon. Did you bring the samples?"

Ashley removed the cool pack slung over her shoulder and handed it to Janet. Rosslyn tugged on her arm. "What is that, Mom?"

"Do we know who they're from?" asked Janet. She zipped open the pack, pulled out a vial, and held it to the light.

"Anonymized," replied Ashley. "We only know the sex. One male, one female. They're donors from a blood grouping study."

Janet tipped her head toward the corral in the corner of the barn. "Well, someone's in for a big surprise if they see their alien doppelgänger on TV."

Another tug. "Mom?"

"They're human blood samples, Rossie. The Rossians can use the DNA sequences to construct their bodies. Like Dagon. Remember how he looked like Dad but more handsome?" She quickly pivoted to Alex. "Her words." She nodded toward their daughter. "We don't want all of them to look like Dad."

"But Dagon wasn't Dad, right? He was someone else."

"He was. We think they bring their own DNA sequences, too. That's what took eleven years to get here. There must be something special in those sequences that makes a Rossian a Rossian. And there's a transmitter of some sort, too. They call it Siru. It's like a conductor. We don't really know how it works, though. But their bodies aren't so important. It's just a vehicle to carry them. Dagon said they could carry many of them in one body. And they can make a new body if it wears out."

Ashley pivoted to Janet. "Well?" she implored.

"Alright, come on. But try to be quiet. They are easily distracted."

They followed Janet into the corral, where a large glass vessel sat on a table. Rubber tubes inserted into the cap led to a tall metal cylinder of compressed air. At the base of the glass jar, a pair of partly fuzzy, squirrel-sized animals busied themselves devouring fresh lettuce, oats, and hard-boiled eggs. Rosslyn at her side, Ashley crept in close and lowered her gaze. They looked quite similar, although the bigger one was darker and slightly advanced in the shedding of its scales. Both still retained their vertically oriented flat tails, shiny bellies, and a raised ridge where a dorsal fin once ran. Their faces had taken on a snout-like appearance, and their eyes were black and beady. They stopped eating long enough to study Ashley right back. They looked at each other, then back to Ashley, before recommencing their feast. "Chipmunks?" Ashley asked.

"More likely voles," replied Janet. "They're everywhere. There are foxes next door at the animal shelter, but I don't see any fox in them yet. I do think we should move them before they're exposed to the blood samples. They'll quickly outgrow their little eight-liter studio. Alex, can you truck the air cylinder? I'll carry the beaker. You two can get the doors and clear a path. Let's cover up, first. The suits are over here. Rosslyn, we can tighten yours up with rubber bands."

The greenhouse was a ten-by-ten-foot glassed-in, airtight shed plumbed with polyethylene tubing connected to an external cylinder of compressed air. A set of gas gauges embedded in the door were visible from the outside and interfaced with a regulator controlling the flow. A retractable vent fitted with a HEPA filter had been inserted into the roof. Troughs of lush ferns lined the inside perimeter of the shed. Sacks of nutrients sat stacked in each corner. The center was occupied by a large, vertically barred, raised white enclosure wrapped with a nylon mesh.

Rosslyn was quick to recognize the aliens' new home. "My crib!" she exclaimed.

"Sorry, Rossie, but you haven't used it in years," Alex said.

"But my DNA?"

"Don't worry, we scrubbed it good," said Janet.

She opened the beaker and placed it in the crib. Elated, the animals scurried out and bounded around their new home. Janet filled the food bowl and then jiggled a water bottle fitted to the crib. The larger one sat up on its haunches and eagerly sucked water from the attached tubing. The smaller one levered up the food bowl until half spilled onto the crib floor. After pushing the half-full bowl aside, it stood in front of the spilled half. Guarding its share, it squeaked at the larger animal and rattled its head.

"Look at that," said Alex. "I think we're going to need personalized food bowls."

"They seem human already," said Janet. "Speaking of which…" She uncapped Ashley's vials, dabbed some blood onto a piece of cheesecloth, and taped it to the nylon mesh on the crib.

"We're breathing," said Ashley. "We need to stop exhaling or get out of here."

Janet turned over a CO_2 gauge and read it. "Two hundred twenty parts per million. Better than the four-eighty out there. The ferns can gulp it down to two hundred or less, and the regulator should maintain it." She turned to the creatures in the crib. "Stay in here," she said, pointing at the floor. "You'll die out there." They froze, staring at her, then at each other. The big one squeaked at the little one. They both looked at Janet and squeaked once in unison. "Good," she replied.

There wasn't much else to do but wait. They agreed that Janet would stay and babysit the little beasts until Alex returned to relieve her. Rosslyn would finish what remained of her school day. Alex scribbled an official excuse note ascribing her absence to abduction by aliens.

"Really, Dad?"

"No one actually reads these. Right? I'm just stretching the truth a little. I mean, who would believe it if I said the aliens were abducted by us?"

———

Back in her lab, Ashley bumbled around, too distracted to be productive. Likewise for her students. They were spending most of their time talking over their benches or checking their phones for news updates. She concluded that the mindless task of organizing the tissue culture room would be fitting for a day like this. She padded down the hall to the door marked *Woodsum TC.*

She slipped into a blue paper gown, stretched some booties over her shoes, and pushed the door open. "Oops! So sorry," she said when the door collided with a body crouched behind it. "What? Beth! What are you doing in here?"

The startled cashier slammed shut the door of a mini-fridge and stood up. "Oh, my fault entirely, Ashley. You couldn't possibly see me there. Sorry." She brushed her hands down the front of her clothing and offered a furtive smile. "Someone's been stealing food from the café, and I was just doing a little detective work. Checking refrigerators for evidence."

"Really? That's so sad. What have they been taking?"

"Oh, the usual fare. You know, the BLTs, pizza slices, stuff like that. Might be hoarding it, so I was snooping around."

"Well, I'll keep an eye out for you, Beth. But you really shouldn't come in here in street clothes. You should gown up, first."

"Oops, sorry. I'll get out of your way now."

Ashley frowned at the back of the curious woman as she retreated down the hall. She shelved TC supplies and tidied the flow hoods until she realized she hadn't eaten since gulping down her go sandwich in the morning. Returning to the cafeteria, she found a lanky work-study student stocking the go counter. Ashley inspected a Caesar salad, shaking the container a few times.

"Pretty fresh," commented the student. "Those were just filled. Can't say that for the BLTs, though."

"I know," said Ashley. "They look gross. Why would anyone steal those?"

"What? Who's stealing? My stock records perfectly match the receipts. Every time," boasted the student.

"I thought you were trying to catch a thief. That's what Beth said."

"Beth said that? We match our records every night after close. Do you know her? If someone was stealing, she'd have the FBI here in a heartbeat."

Ashley's heart skipped a beat, and started again. "I guess I don't know her," she mumbled absently.

"Everybody knows her. Been here since before I was born. Nicest lady on the planet."

"Really?" Ashley was staring past the student and into space. "Which one?"

CHAPTER 5

NOT SHALA

Emma looked at the name tag and then at the adorable wisp of a girl whose bed it was attached to. Her hairless head covered with a scarf, she blinked her robin's-egg eyes at Emma. Smiling. *How can she smile?* Emma smiled back the best she could. She opened her stick and perused the data in the projection cube. *ALL, Philadelphia chromosome negative, B-cell lymphoblastic leukemia/lymphoma with hyperdiploidy, single course of induction therapy.* She scanned the blood cell counts and the sequencing data for the suspected genetic culprits. The news was quite good, but only if you knew you already had cancer.

"How you feeling today, Tessie?"

The little girl perked up. She shifted around in the bed and removed her head scarf. "I have red hair just like you," she chirped. She brushed a hand over her bare head. "At least I will when it grows back."

"Wow! Maybe we're related," responded Emma. She took the girl's vital signs, asked a few questions, checked her skin for bruising, examined her fingernails, and looked in her mouth for sores. "Are you hungry?" she asked.

"Not anymore, I just ate a big cheeseburger."

Another good sign. "Yum! I love cheeseburgers, too. But how about some vegetables next time? And I don't mean French fries, young lady."

Another toothy grin from Tessie. "I like green beans, but they should leave broccoli in the ground where it belongs."

An involuntary laugh—the best kind—bubbled out of Emma. Though heartened by the girl's progress, Emma could not escape the trench of disquiet dug by Tom Allen. She had to find Janet Harley, but it would have to wait until noon, when she finished her pediatric rounds. Skating a finger over the holo-cube, she punched in the treatment options for her darling patient. "Things are looking pretty good, Tessie. Can't wait to see your hair. See you tomorrow morning, sweetie."

Tessie said goodbye, waving the arm of a stuffed bear resting on her lap.

Finished with rounds, Emma wheeled over to Biosciences on her bike, but there was no trace of Janet Harley in her lab.

"We don't know," said a student, hunched over a bench full of plastic dishes. "She's usually in pretty early. At least we didn't have to lie to Rex Shelton today. She's really not here this time." Two other students joined in the chuckle.

A second student chimed in. "Maybe she's examining alien sea monsters with her Space Lady friend."

Emma recalled that moniker from the tabloids Tom Allen had pointed her to. "Would that be Ashley Woodsum?

"Yup. Space Lady. They're probably busy dissecting sea monsters."

"Sea monsters?" asked Emma.

"Which rock have you been living under?" asked the second student. "Sea monsters are all the rage." More laughter.

Emma *had* been living under a rock, a rock called health systems exams, for which she had spent her entire Sunday studying. Deep in a well, she hadn't looked at the news, or even talked to anyone, since seeing Tom Allen on Saturday. Any remaining time had been spent sleeping. She thanked the students and opted to bike over to Paleontology to find the next person on her *Alien Encounter* list. She came up empty again. Here, the occupants claimed that Alex Sina's absence, or presence, at any time of day or night, was not uncommon. After exiting the building, Emma sat down on the steps and finally popped open her stick for a gander at the news. She froze. Her eyes widened with each line of text and bulged from her head at the sight of the pictures. "They're back," she whispered to no one.

She had one shot left, Ashley Woodsum at the JPL. Ashley had received scant mention in the old news articles about the explosion in the UCLA cantina. In the tabloids, Space Lady had been variously described as the girlfriend, caretaker, or host of Alex the alien—then not alien, post-lawsuit. Happy to escape the limelight, Ashley's name was nevertheless published. It was all Emma needed to find her. And she was there, banging away on a keyboard in her office when Emma knocked on the door.

Her back to the door, Ashley waved a dismissive hand, the *get lost* signal familiar to her students. More knocking meant it wasn't a student, thus requiring a verbal dismissal. Ashley opened the door, and then her mouth, but no words came forth. There was Shala, the transcendent redheaded nymph, resurrected from the dust on the cantina floor. Mesmerized, Ashley poked a finger into the shoulder of the apparition darkening her door.

Emma glanced at her shoulder and back to Ashley. "Excuse me. Dr. Woodsum?"

She speaks. Ashley's face tingled. With both hands covering her gaping mouth, words seeped out through the cracks between her fingers. "Shala? But how—"

"I'm Emma, actually. Emma Curtis. Are you Ashley Woodsum?"

Ashley looked her up and down. She placed a hand on Emma's forearm and squeezed it—*corporeal*. "You're really here!" She squeezed again. "Wait! Oh, my god! She borrowed from you. Didn't she? You were the one. It has to be."

"Borrowed? Borrowed what from me? Who?" Emma's mind raced. She knew she was getting somewhere, at last. That much was apparent. But where? "May I come in?"

"Yes. Yes, yes, yes, please do. Excuse me." Still clutching Emma's arm, she backed into her office, towing along her stunned visitor, never looking away. She finally let go to shut the door. Standing on her tiptoes, Ashley poked her face close to Emma's. "Every freckle," she mumbled.

"I'm a medical doctor," said Emma. "I'm used to exams, but this one is making me uncomfortable. You're scaring me a little."

Suddenly, Ashley looked like a train was about to hit her. "Holy smokes!" she shouted. "You were the girl on TV! The one who named the Big Mac meteorite."

This was the second time in three days, and the second time since eleven years ago, that someone was too excited about that ancient news. "I was that girl," she said. "Now, please tell me why that's so interesting."

"What did you do with the chunk of meteorite that the cop chiseled off for you?"

Emma heard that, she could even see that chunk of rock in her terrarium, but didn't respond. She was quietly dialing a combination lock in her mind. The tumblers were falling into place. Two to the right, both Tom Allen and Ashley recognized her without ever having met her. Six to the left, she looked like *that woman,* both had said. Nine to the right, the evolution of her runaway red-haired dog hadn't stopped there, just as she had suspected. It had become—it had borrowed from her? Click! The safe popped open. She looked at the floor.

"The dog," Emma whispered. "It was all real. Wasn't it? It really happened. It did cure my father. No one believed it. I was a little girl. I stopped believing it myself." She stared past Ashley, into the infinity of the creamy paint on the cinder block walls. Shaken to the core, she felt arrested—by joy, fear, relief, wonder, betrayal, but most of all validation. No one but her parents had believed her. The data was right there. Her pencil sketches, the trashed terrarium, the runaway genius beagle. "It was real. Wasn't it?"

Never a hugger, Ashley hugged her until Emma's shoulders stopped shaking. Still clutching her, she stepped back. "It's okay. It's okay. Yes, it was real. It is real."

"The dog," Emma repeated. She finally looked up. "It ran off. It was a salamander at first. Then a hamster. Then a dog. Then, I guess it became...who? Me? Shana?"

"Shala. Not you. Shala. She only looked like you. Have you been following the news?"

"Well, no, not until minutes before I came over here. All these odd creatures. They remind me of what grew out of that rock." She fumbled through her backpack and removed her old sketchbook drawings of the odd little hamster thing.

Ashley inspected the drawing. "Ours grew out of a four-billion-year-old rock chiseled from the Isua Greenstone Belt. It was a worm, then a mouse that sprouted wings. It flew off and turned into a man named Dagon."

"Dagon?"

"His mission was to meet Shala, your doppelganger. He did. That's why these creatures are crawling out of the sea."

Emma's hand searched for the chair behind her and found it. She plunked herself down, parked her elbows on her knees, and buried her face in her hands.

"You're not going to wake up, Emma," said Ashley. "This is real, at least the way we currently define it. And there's a lot more to it. I can explain on the way to Janet's farm if you'd like to come along. I think you'll want to see this."

"Janet's farm? Janet Harley?"

"Yes. It's not really a farm, though. No crops, and she only has two animals, but they're quite special."

———

Much was discussed on the way to the farm. Emma's head swelled with each revelation, while Ashley soaked in Emma's account of her father and their runaway beagle. And what a Herculean feat! Emma had excavated Tom Allen from the dark hole of denial he had buried himself in eleven years ago. Yes, genes *were* altered in real time, just as Tom had proposed. Diseases *were* truly cured. No, not through miracles, but something close, something at least partially explicable. It was alien engineering. And that science was here again, in peril, and begging for a safe place to stay. But four billion years of life in the making was turning sour and spoiling their new nest. Something had to be done.

There was the Brabus, again parked in the long dirt drive. It seemed right at home in front of the weathered farmhouse, left unattended for years. Ribbons of grayed paint dangled from the exposed siding. Cracked windowpanes, those not replaced with plywood, were too dirty to see through.

On the sagging porch, a dubious bench swing hung at an angle. Birds roosted on a rusted wheelbarrow inverted in its graveyard of tall grass.

Ashley parked and walked past Alex's car. There was Rosslyn's book bag on the front seat again. "Must have come straight from school," she mumbled. "It's my husband, Alex—"

"Alex Sina?" interjected Emma.

"Yeah, that's the one. Looks like our daughter's with him.

"I didn't know you had children."

"Child. I guess two if you count Alex."

"What's her name?"

"Rosslyn."

Emma snorted. "Really?" Ashley shot her a terse glance. Emma mitigated.

"It's nice. I like it. It's a pretty name. Named after their planet. Right?"

"Yeah. Was a pretty name. Until kids at school turned it into Ross-alien."

"That's mean. Kids at my school called me Emma R S. Get it? M-A-R-S?

"Dicks. The greenhouse is behind the barn. I suspect they're out there now."

Ashley was correct. Rounding the corner of the barn, they could make out two large figures and one small, their faces plastered to the outside of the polycarbonate glazing. One of the large ones stepped back enough to make some hand gestures before pressing forward again. Then all three stepped back, vigorously nodding their heads while clapping their hands. Nearing, Ashley and Emma could see animate shapes shifting around in the greenhouse.

"Goats?" shouted Ashley.

Startled, the trio of observers jumped back to take in Ashley and Emma.

"Mostly," returned Janet. "Should have known. Marsters' Goat Farm just down the road. It's a B and B. They sell the cheese, soap, and the like. The kids have free reign of the area to roam about."

"They're so cute, Mom," bellowed Rosslyn. "They're learning to talk."

Emma stopped in her tracks. Their casual acceptance of it all was unsettling to her. She felt unfledged, the odd one out. She tried her voice. "Mostly goat?" she croaked.

As if her words had ushered her into existence, Alex and Janet suddenly focused on the talking stranger, the other person. Dumbstruck, both stepped away from the greenhouse and commenced zombie-walking in her direction.

"Not Shala," said Emma. Her hands pushed forward, protecting her brains from approaching zombies.

"But—" tried Alex.

"Not Shala," repeated Ashley. "Guess again."

Alex tilted his head, and the Big Mac meteorite slammed into his gray matter. "Big Mac!" he shouted, and raised his arms like he'd won a prize on a game show. "Holy cow! I mean goat, or whatever it was that Shala sprang from. Wow! What an imprint!"

Again, Emma felt like an exhibit at the Smithsonian. Janet touched the freckles. Alex glared, marveling as though Emma were a Madame Tussaud replica of their former goddess.

"Who is she, Mom?" chirped Rosslyn. Her head whipped back and forth between Emma and Ashley. "Is she an alien?" She stuck on Emma. "Are you an alien?"

"You must be Rosslyn. I'm Emma."

"She knows my name! Can they read minds, Mom?"

"I told her your name, Rossie. She's not an alien. Emma was the little girl who named the Big Mac meteorite eleven years ago. Remember how Dagon looked like Dad? Well, Shala came from Big Mac, and she borrowed DNA from Emma to grow herself up."

Eager to return to what were bona fide aliens, Rosslyn quickly lost interest in the ordinary human her parents found so fascinating. "Oh," she said flatly. She reluctantly embraced the manners instilled in her and offered her hand. "Nice to meet you," she said to Emma. "Wanna see the goats?" She dragged Emma over to the greenhouse, leaving the other three adults huddled in conference.

They weren't goats. No self-respecting zoologist would key them out as such. *No scales on goats' ears*, one might say. *Where's the tail?* another might ask. *And the eyes are much too close together. Carpus both front and rear? Where's the tarsus?* Nearly the size of eight-week-old Labrador puppies, the frisky beasts hurdled about, not on hooves but paddle-shaped feet, capped with four toes each. They could already stand erect on their back limbs, while working their fronts to groom each other. Slender digits extending from their multi-knuckled hands scratched off large tufts of thick fur. In its place appeared smooth patches of pink, stippled dermis. Heads rounding and snouts retracting, primates were inevitably in the making.

But those physical differences paled compared to what could be heard rather than seen.

Whaaaatter, the critter bleated when Rosslyn pointed to the silver bucket.

"See?" Rosslyn jumped up and down excitedly.

The articulation, although muffled by the glazing, was unmistakable. Nonplussed, Emma's jaw slackened, and her face flushed. Her odd beagle from eleven years ago, remarkable by any standard, could not talk. Her eyes drifted to Rosslyn. The child's willing embrace of the other-worldly could not be expected of fully formed, rational adult humans. Already, humanity had squeezed and shaped the narrative into a form they could digest through their narrow innards. Radiation, GMO, cell towers, even chem trails, anything real to explain away the unreal sea monsters. What would they make of these talking goat-like amalgams? They would be the Devil's work to some. Mad science, perhaps, to others. The goats wouldn't have a chance.

Emma broke from her reverie at the sound of Rosslyn's voice. "This one's a boy. He's named Enki, and that's a girl. She's Ningal."

"Oh. Those are interesting names. How did you come up them?"

"I didn't."

"Well, who named them, then?"

"They did. Those are their names."

"Ennnnki!" baaed the larger of the two creatures. Emma retreated a step back as Enki's slender fingers clicked against the inside of the glazing. Its probing silver eyes dug into hers, its brow furrowed in question, asking. Emma stared back, confused.

"Tell him your name. He wants to know who you are."

Emma drew closer again. The animal waited, wooden, eyes trained in anticipation. "I'm Emma."

"Emmahhh," blatted Enki. He bounced up and down on his hind limbs, peeled away from the glazing, and spun around in a circle. He faced his female companion. "Emmahhh," he bleated.

The smaller, fair-haired critter repeated the name and hopped over to face Emma. "Ennngal. Ennngal," it baaed.

Emma touched the glazing where Ningal had propped her hands. "Hi, Engal."

"It's Ningal, actually," corrected Rosslyn. "It just sounds like Engal because she can't say the first N very well. See, she showed me." Rosslyn pointed to a corner of greenhouse where an N had been etched into the dirt.

Emma was accustomed to a world that changed, sometimes quietly, like the imperceptible revolution of a clock's hour hand. But occasionally, there were quantum leaps, like the invention of the transistor or the deciphering of DNA. The major leaps were often unanticipated, but in retrospect, one could usually point to a predecessor of sorts. Perhaps an author of a futuristic fantasy novel or some high-minded speculator had guessed at something close. But, for a talking, literate goat from another planet—no such precedent would ever be found. Emma gazed at the future of humanity. It dropped to all fours and bit into a carrot.

"Oh, shit!" exclaimed Emma.

"Chiiit," bleated Enki.

"Opps. Sorry, Rosslyn. I hope he won't repeat that." She pivoted to Enki. "Don't repeat that."

"Chiit," repeated Enki. He hopped around, perfecting the utterance by repetition.

"What's the matter?" asked Rosslyn.

"Well, I have to sit for my exam this evening. I need to get back to UCLA." She approached the three adults, still conferring in a small triangle. "Ashley, I'm so sorry, but I need to get back. I have my health systems exam this evening. I know it sounds silly, considering all this, but I still want to be a doctor."

"Not silly at all. I think we should all try to carry on as normally as possible, if only to avoid suspicion. Someone may be watching us. Perhaps someone who doesn't approve."

Alex's eyebrows went up. "Like who? I mean, even if they are, and they don't like it, we have all of this recorded now. We all agreed we're going to break the news tomorrow. Right? The story is safe. We'll have a news crew out here in the morning and that's that. We'll show them. No one can stop this from getting out now. It's all documented."

Janet agreed. "We couldn't stop this from getting out if we tried. There are scientists all over the world looking at these animals. The genetics alone are inexplicable by any conventional rationale. It's a near certainty that someone, somewhere, figured out to how to preserve them alive by now. We have a chance here to control the narrative. Our story will stitch the pieces together."

"I'm not worried about our story, I'm worried about their story." Ashley tipped her head toward the greenhouse. "What if none are left alive after all this? I'm probably just paranoid, but this morning I found someone going through my refrigerator in the TC lab. Someone who definitely shouldn't have been there. It was Beth, one of the cafe cashiers. It was just so weird. She gave me a story that—"

Janet cut in. "In her fifties, maybe, a bit roundish in the middle, glasses on a gold chain, gray hair in bun with—"

"What? Yes! How did you know?"

"I didn't. There was a lady like that sitting on a bench when I went back to the beach this afternoon. She was watching me. I'm sure of that much.

She even got up when I started to leave. She was keenly interested in the three survivors in my beaker. Wanted to see them."

"Did you show her?"

"Yeah. I didn't see the harm in it. I let her take a peek. I was the only one down there who had live ones. I think they're dying more quickly now, and there aren't many more washing up. I found all three under the pier, barely hanging on."

Ashley's face grew long. "Do you know if she followed you? The lady."

"I don't think so. She went back to her bench. And I went back to UCLA for a while before coming here. Who do you think she is?"

"Trouble. Are the new ones in the barn? In the incubator?"

"Yes. They're fine. Two more voles and something else coming along that I didn't quite recognize."

Ashley hissed an expletive and raced off toward the barn.

Rosslyn looked up at her dad. "Mom said—"

"I know what she said, Rossie. But I'm not sure why. We better go find out."

The five of them stood staring at the capsized glass beaker. The rubber air line snaked around spastically; its hissing echoed from the empty vessel. Bones and bits of dusty brown fur were the only remnants of the three sea monsters it once housed. Janet crouched and poked at the bones, separating them into piles. Two spines, two skulls, eight appendages. She stood, hands on her hips. "There were three. Those two were the voles. The other—"

"Shit!" Ashley was off again, this time making a beeline back to the greenhouse.

"Mom said—"

"I heard her, Rossie."

Several steps behind Ashley, the trailing foursome watched her grab a spade propped up at the greenhouse entrance. They could see the goats inside, dark shapes hopping frantically, scrambling onto the fern pots, kicking up black soil that splattered against the glazing. The entire green-house rocked and rattled. Ashley stepped inside, driving the spade downward with all her force. She danced in a circle, hoisting and plung-ing the shovel into the ground. Her grunting finally stopped as they arrived at the doorway. Her head sagged as she leaned hard on the im-planted shovel. "Fucker!" she barked at the ground and twisted the handle.

"I heard her, too, Rossie," said Alex.

"Oooh!" exclaimed Rosslyn.

They all stared at the grisly mess creased under the receiving end of the spade. All but severed, the bloodied, baseball-sized head lay a few inches off, still tethered by a frayed rope of glistening spinal cord. Its eyes re-mained open, glassy and green. Its gnarled teeth, canines to make a wolf howl, protruded from an oversized jaw still clapping involuntarily. The goats had settled but kept their distance from what definitely wasn't a vole. It looked more like a badger with pit bull aspirations. Ashley gave it one more thrust. A dribble of rusty blood squirted from the neck as the head rolled free. She scooped up the body and pushed the head onto the spade with her foot. The others stepped aside, keeping their eyes on the dead beast as Ashley exited between them, kicking the door shut with her heel.

"It bit through the air line, Janet. Do we have more tubing?"

Silence.

"Janet? Hello!"

The four them, focused on Ashley, watched her flip the carcass aside and quietly return the shovel to its resting spot.

Alex was lost, oddly reflecting on their efforts to educate themselves as parents, particularly the chapters they had read on role modeling.

Meanwhile, Rosslyn, the recipient of said role modeling, had nearly peed her pants at the sight of her kickass, commando mom dispatching evil in a single bound.

Emma had forgotten about still wanting to be a doctor and had aban-doned her assumption that things couldn't get much weirder.

Ashley took in the onlookers. She pointed to headless clump of bloodied fur. "Beth," she said.

"That's Beth? The lunch lady?" asked Janet.

"No, but I think she did this. She knows who we are. She's trying to stop us."

CHAPTER 6

CRACKING THE CODE

The three of them sat around a thick oak table at the gastropub in Pasadena, a sentimental favorite of her parents. Rosslyn had grown weary of the fare, not to mention her parents' retelling of their first date there. But tonight, she attacked her grilled cheese with fervor. The activities at the farm, still fresh in her mind, had left her ravenous. Her mom, going all SEAL Team Six on that nasty badger thing, had forged in her a new-found admiration—and a tinge of fear—for her once unassuming parent. They ate in silence, coming up for air to watch the news projected in the holo-cubes over the bar.

Alex finally broke the ice. He waved his emptied fork at the cube. "Quasi stellar radio, my butt," he groused. "It's a code. Where are the geniuses who analyze this stuff? I guess they'll know soon enough."

The cube projected a live image of the Very Large Array Telescope at the National Radio Astronomy Observatory in New Mexico. They couldn't hear the sound, but a reporter was pointing in turns to one of the massive radio dishes behind him and then to a projected inset displaying so-called sea monsters.

Alex stabbed at the image. "It's microwave, nearly radio in frequency, you moron. How can non-ionizing radiation from space cause mutations? Who's their science advisor, John Herschel? And that's the telescope's official name? Very Large? An elegant, highly sophisticated instrument. Very Large is the best they could do? I would like to have seen that meeting." Alex pantomimed straightening a tie he wasn't wearing. "*Well, boss, I think we should call it Truly Huge.*" He shifted his head to the right. "*No, no, no, I got one, boss, how about, Really Big?*" Back to the left. "*Wait, wait, this is totally it. Super Gigantic!*"

A model of a quasar appeared, with squiggly lines radiating from it, some striking an Earth about fourteen inches from the quasar. Ashley watched, slightly amused by Alex, but mostly disturbed by humanity's willingness to embrace the unbelievable at the expense of the believable. "I'll call my friends at the near objects center to see what they make of it," she said. "Bill Janesky up at the Keck Observatory might be able to help, too. In any case, this needs to be timed carefully. If we expect help, the evidence has to be unequivocal. Everything has to line up. And we can't underestimate whoever is trying to stop us."

"They better not underestimate Janet. I wouldn't want to clean up that mess," said Alex.

Janet, agreeing to take the first shift, was left sitting in the fading light in front of the greenhouse. A plaid blanket draped over her, she looked like a hillbilly sitting in a rocking chair with the shotgun across on her lap. "McCoy or Hatfield?" Alex had asked as they bade her farewell.

"She'll be fine," said Ashley. "It's her husband I'm worried about. He's headed out to sit with her, but Ray doesn't know the whole story quite yet. A dear man, but he's in for a big surprise when a salty-mouthed goat greets him."

Only Rosslyn slept well that night. She dreamt herself an intergalactic superhero, karate kicking her way around the universe, waylaying villainous alien creeps to preserve all that was right in the cosmos.

Ashley rolled around restively until Alex left at three a.m. to relieve Janet. *He's right,* she thought, *we need to get the ball rolling right away.* She got up and padded into their office. It was only ten p.m. in Hawaii, where one of her colleagues was stationed atop Mauna Kea at the Keck Observatory. She knew he was privy to data acquired by the Very Long Baseline Array radio telescope situated near the Keck. She thought it best to start with a friend. She opened her desk holo-cube and punched up Dr. William Janesky. Though she'd not been expecting an answer, there was Bill, full and bushy-faced, staring right back at her through his thick-rimmed glasses.

"To what do I owe the pleasure?" he inquired. Always cheery and effusive, Bill unleashed an affable grin that nearly squeezed his narrow eyes shut. "Three a.m. there, huh? This is going to be good."

Ashley adjusted her end of the image, then hastily straightened her platinum mop at the sight of herself. "Hi, Bill. Surfing the galaxy?"

"No, I was watching reruns of the History Channel to learn more about space aliens."

"Will it never cease?"

"Not as long as I'm around to stir it up."

"You might be sorry for that. I'm calling to see what you think about the recent radio source coming from the direction of Virgo."

The mirth dropped out of Bill's face. "I'm not supposed to talk about that. I'll just say it's a bigger deal than what you're seeing on the news. You'll just have to be patient."

"I'm not. It's a four-element code, isn't it?"

His tiny eyes grew rounder. He started to speak, retreated, then, "Maybe."

"Tell you what, Bill. I'll let you in on an even bigger secret. You just have to follow my instructions. Okay?

"Sounds fun, but losing my job sounds not fun."

"Take a string of your code and make one element into a C, the next to a G, the next to an A, and the last one to T."

"I'm not so sure about this." But she could hear him clicking away even as he said it. He was mumbling to himself, "Goofy, okay you get the G, Daffy is A, Donald, then Pluto."

"You named the elements after Disney cartoon characters?"

"That wasn't me. People have a lot of free time up here."

"Whatever, Bill. Now do it again, but assign the A to Goofy, the G to Daffy, etc., then repeat, until you have generated four different lines of code with the four different assignments for each element."

More mumbling, more clicking. "Okay, line one, Goofy is G, in line two, he's A, in three, he's C, and four a T. Now what do I do with this?"

"Open up the NCBI site. Here's the URL. The button for gene alignments is on the right. It says, BLAST, Basic Local Alignment Search Tool." She waited. "See it?"

"Hmm, okay, yeah. There's an input box opening for something called FASTA."

"Right. Good. Now paste a line from each of your four converted codes in there. Maybe just a string containing a few thousand of the letters of each."

"Okay, there we go."

"Now hit the BLAST button at the bottom."

"Why are my hands shaking, Ashley?"

"Just hit it."

Ashley watched Bill survey the output. His eyes moved left to right, while his lips moved until they stopped. He stopped. Everything stopped.

"The third line. It's— What the hell?" Bill's face rose from view, replaced by his midsection, then his back, until he was out of the camera's reach altogether. She saw him cross the view from right to left, then back again. His hands were on his head. Then he was down, apparently on his knees, then out of sight before rising to pace anew.

"Bill!" Shouted Ashley. He returned to the chair, but only briefly, before rising and disappearing again. Ashley was questioning her three-a.m. capacity for judgment. Maybe it was too much for the uninitiated. Bill returned with a glass of water sloshing around in his shaking hand. He sat back down, biting his lower lip. His face was blanched.

He started to read the result but stopped and looked up at the ceiling. "What the hell?" he repeated.

"You okay, Bill?"

"How are you doing this?"

"How am I transmitting a radio signal from an interstellar source? I don't know, Bill. You tell me. How *can* I do that?

"Goddamnit! What's going on here? Who are you?"

"I'm Ashley Woodsum, Bill. You call me Space Lady, but not to my face. You have two grown children, Alicia and Brent, and when you're not living on a volcano, you live in Pasadena on Howard Street. Please, I know this is a lot, but you need to settle down. You have to—"

"It's human! What the fuck? A human DNA sequence! It's eighty-eight percent identical to human Poly A-D-P-ri-boose-poly-merse—"

"Polymerase. It's called PARP for short. It codes for an enzyme that helps stick the ends of two DNA strands together."

"I don't give a damn what it does! Why is it coming from a quasar source?"

"It's not, although I'm disappointed that you haven't already figured that out. Check the bend. It's coming from the Ross 128 system. They are sending their code here to reconstitute themselves."

"They?"

"Yes. They. They were here eleven years ago. Well, at least most recently, I guess. You'd have to ask the Sumerians about anything prior. Remember my famous fiasco in the cantina at UCLA? The ancient aliens nonsense you tease me about. That event triggered the release of their code. It gets read by cyanobacteria, which then evolve rapidly through real-time manipulation of their DNA in response to environmental cues. Ross 128b, the Red One, it's dying, and they need a new place to stay. They need a place, a physical place to house their consciousness."

Bill blinked numbly into the camera. His Adam's apple rode up his neck and dropped back down. He looked off to the right. There was some shuffling in the background. A greeting from someone off-camera. A long pause, then a query of some sort from afar. He cleared his throat. "I'm fine," he lied. A body crossed the view behind him and disappeared.

Ashley spoke softly, leaning into the microphone. "Bill, I'm sorry it's you. But I trust you. That's why I called. You've seen the sea monsters on the news. You probably have them on your beaches there. They're not caused by radiation or pollutants. They are the products of the rapid evolution from cyanobacteria. Some of their genes are coded by the radio signal from Virgo. Those same genes will be found in the sea monsters when biologists sequence their DNA. We're trying to put the pieces together. People deserve the truth, Bill. If we marry the astronomy to the biology, it will be undeniable, but either alone could be dismissed.

"Kathy Coleman," mouthed Bill. He stared straight ahead, as if Ashley wasn't there.

"What?"

Bill rattled his head like he'd just woke up. "Kathy Coleman, a biologist at U of H in Manoa. Her friend, Jim Cranston, from the Institute for Astronomy at U of H was just up here. He said Coleman was sequencing sea monster DNA, and it had genes from every kind of fish, some amphibian, and even mammal in it."

Ashley knew this was coming, one hundred percent. Biologists all over the world were likely scratching their heads as their sequences rolled off. Some part of her, the morbidly curious part, wished she could sit back and watch the folly unfold as increasingly ridiculous hypotheses were advanced to explain it.

"That's how it works, Bill. They pick up DNA from their surroundings and shuffle it around to suit their immediate environment. The sequences they send from 128b are like a starter kit. Those are the genes that can execute the design and code for their individuality. It's like Escher's hand that draws the other hand, except it can't draw anything without DNA from other lifeforms to do its drawing. Ultimately, they look a lot like us, if they survive long enough. They evolve into what is arguably the most sentient species available. It's the only way they can host consciousness. Bill? Bill, please." More blinking. More staring. "You can be a part of this or be run over by it. It's really happening."

Bill's mind sped over the gravelly surface of what might come to pass. *My kids. What will they do? My job. Will I still be able to do this? What about religion? And the government. The human race.* Ashley's voice tugged at him from far away. She came back into focus, looking as though she were trying to resuscitate a dying man.

"But they're dying," Bill said. Did he want that? Did he just want them to go away?

"It's the carbon dioxide. They can't tolerate it. It is way over four hundred ppm, back to where it was three million years ago when it started dropping off. They projected it would be below two hundred by now, but in the past few decades, we jacked it back up. Still have that Porsche? They weren't supposed to come now, but I can explain that later."

"What should I do?"

"You need to tell the VLBA headquarters in New Mexico. Tell them to do what I just showed you. They won't listen to me, but they will to you. Ditto for the VLA folks at the Domenici Science Operations Center in Socorro. Sounds like the biologists, like your Coleman, are already onto it. We'll be bringing a news crew out to meet some highly evolved beings tomorrow. There'll be a press conference. We've documented their evolution and will be releasing it. It's all good, Bill. They're benevolent. They can cure diseases. They are a place for us to go after we—"

"After what?"

"I don't know. I just know we need to help them before it's too late."

A new shape appeared behind Bill. A bright floral shirt and navy cargo shorts drew closer to the camera. The tanned face made his teeth look whiter when he spoke. "You okay, Bill? Rodney said you looked a little peaked. Who's this?"

"It's Ashley Woodsum. From the JPL. Ashley, this is Richard Dresdum, station head. Rich, I want to show you something. Ashley, okay if I call you later?"

"Sounds good, Bill. Don't try to sleep. You can't. See you."

CHAPTER 7

SILLY GOATS

The Brabus sputtered to a stop in the dirt driveway. Alex grabbed his bag and a flashlight and started into the darkness toward the barn. He heard some shuffling in the distance. "It's Alex, Janet. Don't shoot! I'm a Hatfield. Unless you're a McCoy, then I am, too."

A faint warble came from the direction of the greenhouse. There was laughter, followed by a baritone voice, unmistakably Ray's, Janet's husband. "It's okay, Alex. Come on down," Ray boomed.

Alex rounded the barn and lighted the path to the greenhouse. He heard some chatter and could make out the backs of Ray and Janet facing the greenhouse door. The warble thickened to a lush tenor. It was asking. A new voice, falsetto, chimed in, also asking. Janet chortled, then answered in staccato exhales, "Because you can't eat that!" More chortling from all. *All?* thought Alex. There was Ray, a deep and luxurious guffaw, then Janet, pitched and mirthful. But there were others—one shrill, one hoarse—all snorting and braying at a joke. "Even Ray couldn't eat that!" wailed Janet. More laughter erupted.

Alex closed in. He extinguished his flashlight. A lantern glowed between the chairs occupied by Janet and Ray. Their backs still to him, both turned their heads like owls to greet him. "Hey, Alex," chirped Janet. A remnant of a smile clung to the side of her face. "Enki and Ningal want to eat the shovel." She could barely get it out without laughing again.

A deep voice, muffled by the greenhouse door, blurted out, "Not the whole thing, just the handle! Steel gives me heartburn." Another uproar.

Ray's and Janet's blurry, crinkled images reflected off the greenhouse glazing. Bent over at the waist in their chairs, they were gasping and snorting.

Beyond the cloudy glazing, partly obscured by the glare of lantern light, Alex could make out two faces, shifting, turning, blinking. One came up close, darkly complected and toothy, with huge eyes and a broad nose. A ten-year-old's body supported its oversized head framed by a hallo of frizzy black hair. Bipedal, it was hunched over, chimp-like, but sporting a smooth, rounded crown and a flat brow. It pressed its anime face close to the glazing. It gave Alex the once-over and frowned. Its lips parted. "This is Alex, huh?" Alex stepped back, then forward again. The lips parted once more. "Can we eat *him*?"

A punchline for a setup he'd missed, Alex was lost in the ensuing hysterics. Ray, convulsing, had to stand up to catch his breath. Janet giggled, blew her nose, wiped her face, and melted into laughter all over again. Ray, larger than an average man, burly and bearded with shaggy brown hair, stood at Alex's side, a hand on his shoulder. "Sorry, Alex. We obviously need some sleep, but these two are hilarious. Best date Janet and I have ever been on. Hands down. I wet my pants when I first saw them, but they're truly adorable."

Janet wobbled her way out of the rocking chair and stood beside them. "We're glad you're here. We've been shoveling feed in there all evening. I mean kilo after kilo. They're voracious."

"I'm not voracious. I'm Ningal!" squeaked the smaller, eggshell-colored face beaming behind the door. Patches of stringy, straw-colored hair sprouted from her crown and dangled over her face. She was a head smaller than Enki, her features more delicate, but easily his equal in attitude. "How about another Snickers bar, Ray? I promise, I don't have peanut allergies, anymore. I fixed my EMSY gene." She pivoted to Alex and stared unblinkingly at him for a few seconds. "Mmmm, you do look pretty tasty. Hello, handsome."

Alex returned a faint smile, more at the absurdity of this creature hitting on him than the joke itself. He played along. "Sorry, I'm married."

"So what, sailor? Any port in a storm, eh?"

They all laughed.

"Whose blood samples did we put in there?" wondered Alex.

"Anonymous," replied Janet. "They probably look like the donors, but I don't think that's where they get their personalities. Far as we know, they are two distinct individuals from Ross, grown in the shells of the donors. They might look like us, but their experience is rich beyond our reach. Go ahead, ask them something."

Alex rubbed his chin and contemplated. He dug into his closet of remedial biochemistry, settling on energy metabolism, the bane of his graduate education. "Okay, name a rate-limiting step in the conversion of glucose to pyruvate during glycolysis?"

Enki looked at Ningal. They smiled at each other. "Otto knows."

Ningal perked up. "So, if Ray were to give me that Snickers bar he claims not to have, I could tell you how the sugar gets metabolized." She looked at Ray longingly. He pulled out the linings of his empty pants pockets and shrugged. Her face sunk in mock exasperation. "Holdout!" she sniped. "Okay, whatever. It's phosphofructokinase-1, Alex. The conversion of fructose 6-phosphate to fructose 1,6-bisphosphate. See, hotcakes, we have so much in common. So, how about that date now?"

"Otto Myerhof?" asked Alex. "Discoverer of the glycolytic pathway? Cheater."

Crestfallen, Ningal feigned offense until she broke into a wry smile. "No cheating. I'm just a good student. And Otto, a great guy but not a great teacher. So distracted by the simplest of things."

"She is cheating," said Janet. "They have access to their inhabitants, and their congregations as they call them. The cumulative knowledge is staggering. But their Bar is suspended, folded up somewhere between here and Ross. It was readied with the understanding that a sufficient number of assembled Rossians would be here and prepared to hold it. But, obviously, they're not doing so well. Apparently, there are only a few others, elsewhere."

"Puabi and Ekur are in Australia. G'day, mate," croaked Enki. "But they won't last long."

"Enki says sixteen have assembled so far. Someone must have figured out the CO2 problem and rescued them. Or it was just dumb luck. We don't know. No one's talking about it yet."

"Maybe they will after we go public with this," said Alex. "I assume we're all still good with calling it in this morning? There's no turning back now. Right after I left the house, Ashley tipped off Bill Janesky at the Keck, and he's busy contacting the other VLA stations about the DNA code. That alone might be the end of the world as we know it."

Janet nodded. "I'm with you. We need to do it right, before someone else does it wrong. KTLA 5 makes the most sense. They have a great relationship with the JPL. They covered all the rovers, they like the exoplanet stuff, and even had Ashley on a couple times. They know her. But we'll need decent light. Midmorning at the earliest."

"I'm ready for my close-up, Mr. DeMille." Ningal flashed her massive teeth and tipped back her moon-shaped face.

Enki pushed his face in close to hers. "This is my good side," he said, his head turned sidelong, tilted, displaying his pronounced jawline, his thick lips pursed in all seriousness.

CHAPTER 8

BETH

Ashley shuffled the deck of possible outcomes in her mind. They had to show their hand, but so much was left to chance. There was human nature—the wild card—twisting the odds and fattening the range of possible reactions. Above all, they hoped for cooperation and calm. That was the royal flush. People would understand; level heads would prevail. But if it went sideways, like a pair of twos in Texas Hold'em, a cluster bomb of panic could destroy everything.

She rocked gently in her chair, lucid, contemplating. She held her phone stick, the number for KTLA 5 already punched in, ready to dial. The TV was on. The BBC was her best chance of witnessing the early onset of a public response to the alien radio transmission. The signal had been gathered by a multitude of radio telescopes around the world, and she had just handed them the decoder key. There were countless amateurs who had picked up the signals, as well. DNA from space. Of course, denials would be offered. Perhaps a Chinese plot to sow chaos, or an accidental reflection of one our own transmissions. The far end of the hysteria spectrum would claim Satanic messages or end-time scenarios. But if connected to the sea monsters, Ashley knew it could not be hoaxed away.

Prime Minister Thunberg's head filled the projected image. The furrows in her brow deepened to caverns when the British reporter asked her why the world had been slow to adopt Sweden's policies for arresting climate change. She got off a few syllables before the pixels dispersed and were reassembled into the head of James Bryant, a BBC correspondent in Australia. Behind him, a HAZMAT crew donned in alarmingly bright safety suits that shouted *danger* were urging calm. They were hoisting a large container into a thick vehicle designed for war.

"As you can see," said Bryant, without actually looking, "the Australian Federal Police have cordoned off the area. The SIO designation on the vehicles behind me stands for Security Intelligence Organization. Regional public safety is here, too. And there's some military personnel on the periphery. From what we know so far, a mango farmer just north of Brisbane had taken in a couple sea monsters and managed to grow them. It's unclear why they hadn't died like the others. As you can see from this photo taken earlier, they look to be about the size of large wombats and, in fact, strongly resemble them. Apparently, his neighbors were aware of the animals and found them quite endearing but sounded the alarm when they learned of the code transmitted from outer space."

"Outer space, Jim?" interjected the local anchor in London.

"That's right, Alan. Late this afternoon, the Murchison Observatory reported on a radio signal emanating from outside our solar system. It appears that that signal contained a code that's been deciphered. Surprisingly, the code spells out the sequences of DNA that show high similarity to actual human genes. Zoologists believe the sea monsters are in some way connected to that signal."

"Human DNA sequences transmitted from outer space?" Alan was looking off-camera. He nodded his head repeatedly to someone stage-right. He looked down at his desk and then back to the camera. His lips trembled unprofessionally. "Uh, well, so what should I do? I mean, what are they doing? What should we do?" He shifted in his seat.

Ashley heard the broken anchorman but couldn't take her eyes off the photo of the wombats locked in a cage. They were well on their way. Large swaths of fur had already been replaced by a rosy, smooth dermis, and their faces had flattened to accommodate their rounded, enlarged heads. Their front paws differed from the rear ones, the digits splayed out, slender and flexible looking. She almost cried. Could no one else see the panic on their faces? They were already suffocating in the ambient air. They would probably be dead in hours. This was not a royal flush. The joker was on the table, faceup, laughing. The five aces held by human hysteria were raking in the pot. "You're going to kill them!" Ashley shouted at the projection.

"Who's killing who?" A small voice came from behind her. There stood Rosslyn in her PJs, swapping glances between the TV and her mother.

Ashley stood up and surrounded Rosslyn with her arms. "It looks like there are other goats, Rossie, or wombats, in this case, in Australia. The government has confiscated them, but they won't know what to do. They'll die."

"We have to help them, Mom."

"Well, we can't go to Australia, sweetie, and I'm not calling you that because I'm lying." She gave her an emphatic squeeze. Ashley looked at the phone stick, still readied in her hand. She deleted the KTLA 5 number. "But we can't let this happen here. Put some clothes on, Rossie. I hope you won't mind missing another day of school."

Ashley scrambled to her bedroom. She yanked some of her clothing off one side of the closet, some of Alex's off the other, and stuffed them in a pillowcase. The two of them dressed and sped off to the JPL to gather some supplies. The building was cold and still at six a.m. They stepped like thieves through the hallways. Ashley grabbed a couple mobile canisters of air and the harnesses to house them. She fashioned some plastic tubing into nose fittings and attached them to the canisters. Rosslyn sat in her office, quietly consuming a muffin and watching the news unfold on her stick. The volume was set low enough for her to overhear the voices in the lab outside.

"I can't let you do this, Ashley. It's a big mistake. I can't let them do it. Eventually, they will destroy everything I've made."

"You've made? Who are you? You're not Beth."

"But I am, always have been. Shala and Dagon could have told you as much. Not the scouts, though. So naive. I am sorry for what I had to do to them, but not as sorry as I'll be if I let this go on."

"Jack?"

"Jack died. I left a note for his widow. Remember? Long live Beth. Beth can save us."

"Save us from what? The Rossians are benevolent. They just need a place. Why are you so threatened by them?"

"You're threatened by them, too. Life is threatened by them. You don't understand. Humans never will. You only see a tiny sliver of the universe. You cannot see the part that the Rossians are dismantling. It doesn't pass through the narrow slit of your perception."

"They mean no harm. They can help us fight disease and improve the quality of life."

"They might mean well, but it's not going to end well."

"Why? Why can't you just leave them alone? They're not hurting anyone."

"Is Shrödinger's cat in the box dead or alive, Ashley?"

"What are you talking about?"

"Your knack for creating paradoxes when you run out of explanations. You decide the cat is both dead and alive. Both dead and alive? How can that be? Impossible, of course. So, you pretend both events occur, but only one can be observed after the box is opened. Really? It's utter nonsense, as are all of your dualities. Is light a wave or a particle? Again, you say both. How? It's a wave because you *see* a wave, and it's a particle for the same reason. But they're the same thing. You're just too blind to see it. You invent confusing paradigms to accommodate your limitations. The cat is neither dead nor alive, because there was no cat. You made it all up."

"You're not making any sense. Cut the crap and get out of my way, Jack or Beth or whatever you claim to be."

"I can't, Ashley. This is my creation. They're already warping it with their congregations. If they keep on gathering their precious Bar, the asymmetry will rip the universe apart. You'll perish, too."

"Your creation?"

"Of course. You haven't figured that out yet? Siru and the little hexagons that orchestrate the evolution of life? You know, the conductors of DNA remodeling? The Rossians might think they're God, but they're just bits of crystal to me. I designed them. I put them there. They were here when this rock formed along with every other rock. I wouldn't expect you to notice them. They look so much like all the other tiny splinters of granite.

The Rossians noticed them, though. Took them a while, but they did. And they didn't just notice them, they tinkered with them. They make those nasty progenitors with them. They're beyond my reach."

"But you're here. The Rossians say the conductor is outside, not here."

"It is. It wouldn't work if it was in here. It can't conduct itself now, can it? How can a set include all sets if it includes itself? The hand can't draw the hand without a hand. A long time ago, or in the future, depending on how you think of it, I built a machine. A thing of beauty. Not here, but on the *outside*, if you prefer that language. Think of my machine as a singularity generator. I get one foot inside, hit the on switch, pull in my other foot, and *voila*, my own universe. I'm not the first one to do it, but it's still quite an achievement."

"What machine? There's no machine."

"There is. Rossians like to call it Siru. It's outside, but it reaches in and operates through the little hexagons. Siru sees and directs through the hexagons. It can evolve sentient life from the most insignificant of living things. When it does so, properly and over time, that intelligence creates the stuff of my universe, all the in-between stuff that maintains order."

"You didn't make the matter in the universe. Mass is produced by energetic conversions. It's real. We can see it."

"See, there you go again, painting yourself into a corner that even Einstein couldn't find his way out of. Intelligent life throughout the universe—and trust me, it's everywhere—is all connected, instantaneously. It's what those idiots call Bar. It's like gravity. It is gravity. A glue of common perception. Life abounds everywhere, evolving self-awareness, all struggling to discover the world around them. But they are actually creating it. Everywhere they look, they make the fabric—the gravitational force that keeps everything in balance. I just help the life evolve. That's all. It does the rest for me."

"So, the Earth exists only because we think it does? It's all a grand delusion? A simulation? Please."

"Not that part of the universe. Not the part humans see. The rocks, the stars, the gases are all here, yes, because of energy and mass and all that superficial silliness that keeps you so busy. But what about everything else? Everything in between. The forces that maintain balance and keep order. The invisible girders that keep the roof and walls from collapsing. Humans have just begun to find hints of it. You give it quaint names like quintessence, M-theory, strings, gravitons. It's all wrong, of course, but at least you accept that there is something else out there. A hidden variable. Something you cannot see. That's life, as they say. I love your songs about life, by the way."

"Life? You care about life? You're a killer. You just want chaos."

"No, not chaos. Just the opposite. I want life. I need it. My Siru grows it up to sentience. I want the symmetry and balance it brings. If the Rossians continue accumulating Bar, the universe will bend. Too much self-awareness is toxic, Ashley. I know. It happened before, or later, whenever. That's why I had to create this new one. And now they're going to wreck that, too. And believe me, I did not want to kill the scouts. But they were too close. They left me no choice, just as you are now."

"The Rossians just want to survive. I trust them before I'll ever trust you. Now get out of my way!"

"I'm sorry, Ashley."

Beth took a step toward her while reaching into her apron pocket. Ashley backed up into a lab bench, hands behind her, fingers walking over the surface, searching for anything weapon-like. Then she saw the flash of red behind Beth. It didn't register immediately, but the dull thump was audible. The drubbing sent Beth's ample body slamming to the floor, affording Ashley a view of Rosslyn. A fierce glow decorated her little face, her hands still welded to the fire extinguisher. "Let's get out of here, Mom!" she announced with superhero gusto. Ashley picked up the supplies and did as she was told.

The APVs flashed their warning lamps as Ashely blew past them on the 101. She skidded to a stop behind Alex's Brabus, and the two of them hustled out to the greenhouse. Dawn was afoot, and the sky was lightening, but they only needed the sounds of the boisterous party to lead them.

"It's Ashley," she shouted from a distance.

"It's Space Lady!" came a reply.

It wasn't a tone Ashley recognized. High with the timbre of a flute. She stopped dead in her tracks, jerking Rosslyn back to her side, an arm around her. She listened.

"Hey! Don't call her that." It was unmistakably Janet's voice. "It's okay, Ashley. Come on down."

Then Alex chimed in. "Yeah, Ningal's still working on her manners."

"Manners? I've got manners. Listen and learn. Ashley, I would be very grateful if you would please leave so I can have your gorgeous husband to myself."

"Stop it, Ningal. That's very naughty," chided Janet.

A crescendo of laughter greeted Ashley and Rosslyn as they approached the three figures huddled at the greenhouse door. Level with their heads, Ashley could make out a couple more figures through the glazing, one slightly taller than Alex and a second, much shorter. They were draped in old hemp sacks used for harvest. Both were young adults, shiny and bright with vigor. Janet and Ray parted, allowing Ashley to take in the fully developed duo. Only inches from the door, she leapt back at the sight of the male; he was dark, sinewy, with full features and a smile to warm an auditorium.

"It's Jay!" shrieked Ashley. "Oh, my God! He must have donated blood when he worked in our building years ago. I took the oldest samples because I didn't think anyone would want them."

"Jay?" asked Ray.

"He's a lawyer now. He was putting his way through college by working nights in the Shipping Department at the JPL. I still hear from him once in a while. I couldn't imagine a better source of DNA, but Jay's going to freak out if he sees this."

"Jay's cool," said Enki. He looked at Rosslyn. "You wouldn't be here if it wasn't for him, little lady."

Ashley blushed at the implication. Her daughter searched her mother's face for an explanation that Alex then provided. "Jay made your mother human, Rossie. Not literally, but nicer and more, well, human. That's why I married her. No offense, Ningal."

Ningal shot back, "Humans are overrated, stud muffin. Don't knock it till you try it." She looked at Ashley. "Don't worry, Mom, I'm just messing with you. Besides, he's too boring for me. I'll bet he was a real firecracker back in the day, though. Huh?"

Alex squinted at Ningal. "I'm not boring. Ashley and I still dance when we go to the Avalon. Right, Ashley?"

Ningal smiled devilishly. "Hey! Would that be square dancing? Get it. A *square,* dancing."

Rosslyn got it. Her hands together, pressed tightly to her chest, she hopped up and down, giggling.

"Trust me, Alex, you're no match for her," warned Ray. "Give up now."

They enjoyed a few more minutes of mirthful badgering until they heard the sounds of tires crunching up the dirt drive to the farmhouse. They hushed their voices. Sensing the danger, their Rossian guests obliged.

"You already called KTLA 5?" whispered Alex.

Ashley shook her head. "No, I changed my mind. I told Bill at the Keck, though. Everyone knows that the code is DNA by now. But I saw how they reacted in Australia. It was horrible. They'll kill them."

"Who's here, then?" asked Janet. She picked up the shotgun.

They could hear the sounds of someone trying not to make a sound—the tick from a twig snapping underfoot, a pause, then a slow crush of downed autumn leaves, another pause. There was plenty of morning light. Enough to outline the shifting shape of a hunched interloper rounding the barn. The glint of black and silver metal appended to the trespasser was enough for Janet.

"Stop!" she shouted. She flipped over the twenty-gauge and pushed a shell through the loading flap until it clicked. The distinct sound of the pump sliding back and forth punctuated her command. "Don't come any closer! Identify yourself."

"Don't shoot. I'm Rich Weston. I do mainland reporting for KHNL in Hawaii. Bill Janesky at the Keck told me Ashley Woodsum knew about the code from space. So, I followed her out here. I'm sorry. Please don't shoot."

Rich heard a second voice hailing him from their direction. "Hey, Rich. Alan's in my congregation. He's sorry for sawing that notch in the ladder tread that caused you to break your ankle. He confessed to your mom, but she never told you. No big deal. You couldn't have gone pro, anyway."

The crew at the greenhouse looked at each other, puzzled. Janet lowered the shotgun. Enki whispered to them, "Just thought he should know. It really bugged his brother."

They could hear what sounded like whimpering in the distance, snot being drawn up, audible gurgles, part anguish, part release. An unsteady train of words reached them, halting, jagged, starting and stopping. "Who are— How could you— Where is—" More sniveling. "My god."

There was a tacit agreement in their nods. Alex spoke. "Come on down, Rich. We won't shoot."

"Who's there?" Rich croaked. "I'm a Catholic."

Quizzical looks all around, except for Ningal. Her impish grin widened. "Well, that's good news, Rich. We'll be playing bingo right after the ice cream social. Come on down."

Ashley winced. "Ignore her, Rich. It's okay, we won't hurt you."

"Yeah, let's have look at you, big boy," Ningal chimed in. "I got something for you, and it's sweeter than ice cream."

"Stop it, Ningal. You're scaring him," Ashley chided.

The steps resumed, slowly, then with increasing pace until the ruddy face of the portly, short stranger in a camo hunting jacket emerged in full light in front of them. He removed his ball cap, scratched at his gleaming scalp, and adjusted the massive camera dangling from his neck. A hole appeared in the midst of the thick red bush that hid most of his face. "Who knows who Alan is? How do you know?"

Enki turned to him. "Alan Weston, deceased at twenty-four, died in Afghanistan, posthumously awarded a Purple Heart for bravery. Survived by his wife, Kathy, and son, Eddie."

"Anyone can read an obituary. How did you know—"

"Once a Boy Scout, he showed you how to polish the axles on your pinewood derby car and then you beat him in the race," Enki added.

The floodgates opened. Rich was sobbing again. "What the hell?" he blubbered between snivels. "How?"

"Long story, Rich," said Janet. "We need a promise from you, though. Okay?" She touched his shoulder and angled her head down to meet his downcast eyes.

His head popped up quickly, but not for her benefit. They all heard it. The distinct sound of an approaching helicopter.

"Shit!" Janet shouted. "You never get helicopters out here." The sound amplified until they could spot the chopper above the tree canopy. "Damn it! Looks like military. Did you tell anyone, Rich?"

"No! I mean, I told my boss about the code, and that I had a lead and all, but— Oh, no." Rich pulled out his phone. "He must have followed my stick. He knows where I am."

The chopper passed over but didn't get far before circling back for another run.

Janet sprang into action. "We need to get them out of here now."

They opened Ashley's supply pack and removed the two small cylinders of air fitted with plastic breathing tubes. Ashley sorted the clothing she had gathered and got them dressed. She strapped a cylinder harness to each of the Rossians and affixed the nasal attachments to their faces. She looked at Janet. "Where to?"

"There's a back way to Marsters' Goat Farm, just follow the goats." Janet pointed through the thicket to a couple of straggler goats ambling down a path. "Find the farm manager and put these two on a tour. They run several per day. Ask that they join the City Hall return shuttle afterward. It will drop them at City Hall on Spring Street, near the south end of Grand Park. We can pick them up there when they arrive."

No one had noticed Rosslyn. She had collected a few carrots from the food trough and scampered off toward the goat path. Alex was first to notice his little piper luring a pair of animals toward the greenhouse. "The aliens!" belted Rosslyn, pointing to the kids sniffing at her carrots.

"They expect to see something when they get here, right? Let's show them some aliens. That should buy some time. At least until they realize we're just kooks with some goats."

Ashley led the Rossians off to the goat farm and returned in short order. "Absolutely brilliant, Janet. They even get the royal treatment for being handicapped. I told them they had COPD. They'll get dropped off at noon at City Hall." She cocked her head at the sound of heavy vehicles rolling up the driveway to the farm. Sounds like we're on, everybody. Let's not overdo it."

Janet stashed the shotgun. Alex and Ashley took their places in the two rocking chairs near the greenhouse door. Rosslyn stood by, carrots still in hand. Rich, befuddled but game to play along, took out his camera and started shooting the faux aliens, as instructed. The boots made no secret of their approach. Nor did the commanding utterance of their leader.

"I am Sergeant Max Rumbsling of the US Army. Remain in place. Any attempt to flee will be met with force."

No fleeing. In fact, the crew at the greenhouse paid little mind as the helmeted, amply armed troops approached the greenhouse. Rich continued to shoot photos. Alex and Ashley, steadfast and rapt with interest in the goats, remained mum, singly fascinated by the ordinary undulates.

Janet turned to the sergeant, a finger to her lips. "Shhh, they scare easily. They won't talk if they're scared."

Sergeant Rumbsling looked past Janet at the goats. He squinted into the morning light, his pale smooth face contorted under his visor. "Goats?" he said.

"Guess again," replied Alex.

"They're aliens from space!" squeaked Rosslyn. "And they like carrots."

One of the goats baaed. Rich jumped back, lowering his camera. "Wow! Did you hear that?" He glared at the others in amazement. "I guess they really do like carrots."

"I know what you're thinking," offered Janet, "but you have to spend a whole night out here to appreciate who they really they are."

A look of concern for the eccentric goat tenders spread across Sergeant Rumbsling's face. He turned toward his men and could feel their proverbial index fingers making circles alongside their heads. "Which one of you is Ashley Woodsum?" he inquired. Ashley half-heartedly raised a finger without removing her gaze from the goats. "So, you're the astrologist that informed, let's see, a William Janesky in Hawaii that the radiation from outer space is actually a code. Is that correct?"

"Yup."

"And the sea creatures? Do you have any sea creatures in your possession?"

"Just goats. Alien goats. They're not good swimmers."

"Alien goats, huh? Okay. Well, just to be on the safe side, Dr. Woodsum, we are going have to take the goats with us. Those are my orders. Is that okay with you?"

"Okay with me, but you better ask the goats." A goat bleated right on cue. "He says they like it here."

It was almost too much for Alex. He coughed to conceal his laughter, rose from his chair, and turned his face away from the men. Janet just rolled with it. "Yeah, their planet is warmer, like this greenhouse, and there's carrots growing everywhere on it. They feel at home right here."

"Carrots on their planet? Well, we'll keep them warm and give them lots of carrots." His promise was met with silence. He tried an "Okay?" It was the kind of *okay* reserved for little kids just before they're pricked with a vaccination needle. He searched his soldiers for clues, but none recalled any training for dealing with alien goat farmers. Rich was really getting into the swing of it. He showed the sergeant one of his snapshots, inviting him to share in his amazement at the otherworldly creatures.

After an hour or so of debating the merits of removing the space goats, Janet finally acquiesced. In return, she had the sergeant promise to provide them with plenty of reading material, preferably nonfiction. Two of the soldiers marched back to their vehicle and returned with a cage large enough to house the two goats. It was a simple measure coaxing the hapless creatures into the enclosure. They carried it back up the path. Ashley, Alex, Rosslyn, and Janet followed, transfixed on the goats like they were religious icons. Rich continued shooting. The army departed, leaving them in the drive, waving through the dust stirred up by the oversized vehicles. Once out of sight, the charade dissolved into hysterics of laughter, high fives, and jokes about space carrots.

"Let's stay put for a bit," said Ashley. "They may still be watching us. We can't risk it. We have a little time. Enki and Ningal will be at City Hall in about an hour and a half."

Rich was still staring blankly down the drive, into the lingering haze of the settling dust. "I love you, Alan," he said aloud.

CHAPTER 9

THE GOAT FARM

The beaming tour guide gushed about their sustainability efforts. A black ponytail whipped around behind her olive Charter Hat as she took in the group. She pointed out the rainwater collection trays and the diversion system plumbed to shunt gray water into their gardens. "We use one hundred percent renewable energy," she enthused. "Our solar arrays provide up to eighty percent of that." She paused momentarily to lever herself up on the balls of her feet. "Yes? Is there a question?" She pointed to a guest in the back, his ropey arm waving. The plastic tube lining his upper lip smiled with him. "Oh, my, you're way back there," she fretted. "Can I ask that we make a little space up front for our COPD visitors? Let's give them some breathing room." Her unseemly idiom triggered a few gasps and a groan. The reddened guide backpedaled. "Oops, I'm so sorry. Please forgive me. That was not intended as a joke."

Enki and Ningal shuffled forward, objects of curiosity to the crowd parting on both sides of them. They were a sight even without the tank breathers. Enki's untucked wrinkled dress shirt hung over a pair of baggy wool slacks that stopped well short of his bare ankles. His feet were stuffed like sausages into some frayed canvas sneakers. Ningal, petite for her hand-me-downs, swam in a puffy silk blouse and baggy avocado pants pinched tight at the waist by a length of hemp rope. Her feet slid around in a pair of faded blue Crocs. Once front and center, Enki fiddled with his nasal breathing tube while the guide waited. Having commanded the attention of the entire crowd, he comforted the embarrassed woman by assuring her that she was not funny at all. Unsure how to respond to what was either forgiveness or a rebuke, the rattled guide pressed on, asking Enki if he had a question.

"Yes, I do," replied Enki. "Why are you collecting energy from the sun when you could make the sun's energy right here by fusing hydrogen atoms to make helium, just like the sun?"

"Oh, well, maybe we should look into that. Does the Solar Harness Company sell those?"

"You would need a gravity condenser to make the plasma and—"

Enki's lecture on the Lawson criterion was interrupted by a subtle elbow jab from Ningal. "My friend is an engineer," she interjected. "Always thinking. Perhaps we can discuss this afterward."

More than happy to oblige, the tour guide directed the group toward a spacious corral replete with frolicking goats of all sizes. Accustomed to the tours, and especially the attention afforded by the guests, the animals scrambled toward the fences to greet them. Enki reached in for a head scratch. An adolescent black and white kid obliged. Enki rubbed its crown while making a deep gurgling sound. The animal's banana-shaped radar ears wiggled wildly in response. It baaed and scuffed the earth with its hooves. Quite suddenly, the entire population of frisky animals rushed Enki. Animals leapt over and pushed each other aside, muscling their way into the eye of the goat storm. Enki shuffled sideways along the fence rails and the excited herd followed en masse, bleating relentlessly.

"Wow!" the tour guide shouted to no one in particular. "I've never seen the goats take to a visitor quite like that."

Enki, increasingly aware of the pandemonium, let out a sharp whistle followed by a narcotic humming sound. The goats instantly ceased bleating and dispersed, lining the fence evenly, eager for any affection the other tourists had to offer. Enki smiled proudly, but Ningal was having none of his shenanigans. She javelined a scowl at him, leveling his grin.

Flummoxed, the tour guide stared at Enki. Eyebrows arched, she placed a hand on the back of her neck and opened her mouth into a circle, then closed it. She finally stabbed at a joke about having a goat whisperer among them, but the crowd remained focused on Enki and his curious companion. Once again attempting to deflect, Ningal explained that Enki grew up on a farm, where he learned about goat behavior.

"I grew up on a farm, too," responded the guide. "And I've been here for over twenty years, and they won't do that for me, or anyone else."

Enki smiled broadly. "I was a goat before I became a human," he chimed.

Ningal's eyes popped with fury, but the crowd laughed, so she laughed along. Enki did not.

Beyond the corral, the guide herded the tour into the milking barn. A couple of cheerful teens in dungarees sat hunched on stools, tugging on teats as streams of milk pinged against the stainless steel buckets. As she keenly observed the demonstration, Ningal's hand wandered absently, probing her own breasts while she studied the milking. The unshaven man to her left took an enduring sidelong glance at her, then shifted his feet for a better view. Noting his lascivious gaze, Enki gently grasped Ningal's elbow and guided her wayward hand downward until it came to rest between them. Finally, aware of the voyeur at left, Ningal abruptly caught the wanton eyes of the stunned stranger. "Baah!" she bleated at him.

They filed out of the milking barn and into the shop where the soap was made. Crowding into the small shed, they backed into shelves lining the walls while the guide positioned herself in the center. The room smelled of ammonia mixed with hints of lavender and coconut. Sacks of lye and bottles of oil of all varieties occupied the largest shelves. A smaller shelf housed a cubby filled with ampules of extracts and essential oils used for spiking scents into the soap. An imposing freezer labelled MILK ONLY stood in the back.

The guide stood near a large rectangular table cluttered with stainless steel bowls. "The milk must first be frozen," she started, pointing to the freezer. "Then the lye can be added slowly without generating too much heat. The heat can cook the milk proteins and turn your soap brown." She wrinkled her nose. "The mixture is next added to an assortment of oils along with some optional scents or additives. I like oatmeal in mine. It's like pudding at this stage." She scooped some pale orange slime from a bowl in front of her and let it drop back down. "After filling these molds, it sits for twenty-four hours and then we remove the bars and cure them in the air for a few weeks." She pointed out the curing bench upon which dozens of bars of varying geometry sat drying. "We check their pH for traces of lingering lye. Some of the old-school soapers taste them. They're pretty tangy if they still have some residual lye."

His back to the group, Enki was preoccupied with the curing table. He missed most of the guide's lecture but had heard the word *taste*. His nimble fingers slid over a silky triangle. It smelled delicious; waves of lemon and eucalyptus wafted from its surface. So fresh. He pulled it close. It looked delicious. His teeth sank like a butter knife, midway into the bar, until a pointed chunk gave way. It pressed hard against his tongue until his molars ground it to a paste. His eyes started leaking immediately as the fuming lava drained down his throat, ripping at the smooth lining of his esophagus. The fire spread quickly, up his nasal passages, over his face, down into his belly. Water formed everywhere, in his throat, in his nose and eyes. The plastic tubing in his nose clogged with mucus; his airways narrowed. He couldn't breathe.

Panicked, he coughed hard, spraying the solid remains of the macerated triangle across the curing table.

The guide shrieked. "Oh, my! No! No! No! Those are uncured, just taken out yesterday! Do not taste them."

Enki yanked out his nasal tube and gulped at the air. His raspy inhale was followed by a wheezing discharge. A goatee of thick spittle settled below his purple lips. He bent over, his shoulders heaving until his breathing began to normalize.

The guide filled a glass with water. "They're still quite caustic," she warned. "Even fully cured, the soap is not to be consumed. Perhaps some of you can attest to the awful taste of soap. It was once a punishment for children who used swear words."

"Fuck! Shit!" wailed Enki. "Goddammit!" He wiped an arm across his foaming mouth. The bubbly white spittle looked like fluffy clouds against his sky-blue shirt sleeve. He happily accepted the glass of water and drained it immediately.

The guide spoke over the crowd, still rumbling over Enki's salty outburst. "My word! Usually, the swearing comes first, then the soap."

"No more soap. Please!" pleaded Enki. The crowd chuckled loudly. None had expected a tour of the goat farm to be so entertaining.

After providing some additional details on soapmaking, the guide led the crowd into the gift shop, where a variety of goat-related souvenirs hung from racks and sat on tables. Ningal spun a spindled rack offering personalized goat key chains arranged in alphabetical order. She found Naomie right next to Natalie, then Nicole, followed directly by Norah, thus skipping over Ningal altogether. She poked around the space where her name should have been and removed a few Nicoles, but still could not find her namesake. "There's no Ningal," she said to the primly attired woman at the register.

The genteel cashier, gray hair in a bun, smiled thinly and apologized. Rakes of crow's feet sprung from the corners of her eyes. She explained that all names couldn't possibly be covered by a single rack of key chains. "Just the most popular names are offered," she said.

Ningal countered, "I have over forty-eight million inhabitants, from all congregations. And they all know my name. What is your name?"

"My name?" The matronly woman was taken aback. She erected herself to full height and straightened her print apron. "Why, I'm Alice." She tilted her head in a patronizing manner common to waiters and flight attendants. "Is there a problem?"

Ningal quickly found Alice at the top of the rack. "So, you are popular?" she asked in all sincerity. "How many people know you?"

"Well, I don't know, I have friends, but you misunderstand, I mean to say the names here are the most common. Lots of people are named those names. If we stocked uncommon names, we wouldn't sell very many."

"Oh, I see. You would only sell one Ningal, because I am the only one."

"Well, maybe not the only one but—"

"Yes. The only one. Except for the goddess of the reeds, but that is only a story."

Again, the center of attention. The tourists were gathering. They had forgotten about the goat tchotchkes and aromatic soaps for sale. They were hanging on every word from the eccentric tourist in Crocs. Enki wiggled his way over to Ningal. He inspected the key chain rack, gave it a spin, and searched the E's. Coming up blank, he turned to the cashier. Her probing green eyes peered at him over a pair of tortoiseshell reading glasses. "Why is there no Enki?" he asked.

Her head slumped in exasperation.

"We are not popular," replied Ningal.

"I am very popular," Enki corrected, "especially with the Makers." He could overhear a diminutive white-haired man with a wispy beard murmuring to his companion, *Scientologists.*

Once again derailed by the two scene-stealers, the guide clapped her hands to regain their attention. She announced that the shuttle to City Hall would soon be leaving. The crowd surrounding the oddball duo began to disperse and shuffled out to the parking lot in front of the reception. Last to exit, Ningal remained at the key chain spindle. Pointing to the A's, she addressed the dithering cashier with a hint of defiance. "I see that your mother, Abigail, is not very popular, either." The stupefied woman croaked an unintelligible syllable. Her wide eyes followed Ningal out the door. Once gone, the anxious woman tapped on a keyboard and found the vendor's site that offered the key chains. She placed an order for Abigail.

Enki and Ningal sat together on the packed shuttle. Ningal ran an index finger over the back of Enki's hand. She rubbed the darkened blotches and plucked at the loose skin. "These are new," she said. "You are aging. You pulled off your breather."

He could see a few furrows in her forehead absent only hours ago. A little loose skin was evident around her chin, too. "We could smell the soaps," he said. "We must be breathing some of the outside air. And through our mouths, too. We cannot live here like this. This Zumru will not hold the Bar for long, but it is too late to stop it from coming. The engineers have already opened the passage. The bend is nearly complete. The transit can't wait much longer. How will we hold it? Where are the others? We need more Zumru or the Bar will drift."

They sat still, leaning toward each other, their two heads touching. They spent the ride to City Hall in what appeared to be silence to those aboard the bus. But they were not silent. They were shouting, racking the minds built from billions of years of experience and wisdom. They were communing with all those coalesced and interlocked in their congregations. Surely an answer could be found among the trillions of souls accumulated, sharing, synergizing. They needed a harbor to keep them safe, out of the void, away from Etemmu. Together, they could find a place. The

Irkallan would not win. It had only made the stuff around them. It was neither their master nor maker. They had outgrown it. They were bigger than the sum of their parts now. They had become more than what the Irkallan had bargained for.

Enki and Ningal awoke, their heads separated. They nodded in agreement. "It will work," said Enki. "At least for a while. It has to."

CHAPTER 10

CITY HALL

Predictably, Sergeant Rumbsling had stationed a couple sentries on the road near the entrance to Janet's farm. They halted all four exiting vehicles and inspected each. Alex, in his tiny Brabus, had little to hide, while the others were asked to get out. Returning to character, Ashley asked the guards if the goats had said something to arouse their suspicions. Rich, ever the journalist, photographed them as they rummaged through his SUV. Janet and Ray kept silent, exchanging guilty smiles with Ashley and Rosslyn. With the guards mollified, they sped off, each vehicle pursuing a different course, as per their plan. Rich executed a circuitous meander around the Topanga Oaks neighborhood that returned him to Janet's farm, dragging the tailing guards with him.

Satisfied they weren't followed, Ashley and Rosslyn headed for the JPL. There, Ashley grabbed a large cylinder of air and a trolley to haul it. They hustled down to the parking lot, where they commandeered the JPL tour van. She turned off the AP features and steered the van onto the Arroyo Seco Parkway. The highway was hauntingly vacant as they sped west a few miles before exiting onto Alpine Avenue. There, Alex and Janet, in possession of some savory Italian sandwiches, awaited them at the Eastside Deli, where they piled into the van.

The bracing aroma of salami and pesto flooded the vehicle. "Sorry, couldn't wait," garbled a chewing Janet, a couple king-sized semicircles already carved into her sandwich. "A Sicilian, no onions, right?" She fished a sandwich out of the bag for Ashley. "Rossie, your dad said no mustard. Here you go, girl." Janet checked the time. "Their shuttle should arrive at City Hall in about ten minutes."

259

Alex already had his sandwich in hand, leaving a bag still heavy in content. "I got each of them the Boot," he declared. "It's shaped like the lower part of the Italian peninsula, and it's almost as big. It contains meats and cheeses representing all eight southern provinces. It's supposed to feed a family."

"They're going to need it," said Ashley.

They had ample time to make the noon pickup, so she punched City Hall into the AP screen and attacked her sandwich while the vehicle rolled cautiously to its mark. Janet opened her stick to the news. The doughy face of President Arland filled the projection cube. He seemed distracted as he tried to square up for the camera but kept looking sideways at whoever was coaching him. The image split in two. The president shared the cube with a twisting model of a DNA helix.

"I trust most of you know what DNA is," he began. "As you are likely already aware, we have been receiving a signal, that is, radiation, from outer space. Our radio astronomers in Hawaii have successfully decoded it."

Ashley squirmed in her seat. "Sorry, Bill."

"DNA is like a long string composed of four unique molecules." Arland pointed to the four different-colored balls in the double helix. "A section of the string, in which the molecules are arranged in a specific way, constitutes a gene. Genes, of course, are the instructions for making and maintaining life. The signal from space," continued the President, "contains four unique elements, and each can be interpreted as one of the four molecules that make up DNA. Remarkably, the four elements in the signal are ordered in sequences that strongly resemble the sequences found in some of our own genes, human genes."

The President looked down and acknowledged a question inaudible to viewers. "No, we do not know where it originated."

"Oh, yes, you do," mumbled Janet. "Watch out, here come the lies."

The President halted and looked left again. "Although no nation or privately owned company has so far claimed it, the signal may originate from one of the thousands of satellites orbiting Earth."

"No, it doesn't, and you know it," said Ashley. "Say it, Arland. It comes from outside of our solar system."

"We will determine the nature of this signal but believe it is nothing to be alarmed about at present. Please, we recommend that you continue with your normal activities."

Ashley shook her head. "Don't worry, Liar-in-Chief, we are."

President Arland looked down at something or someone. "There has been some fanciful speculation that the mutated creatures crawling out of our seas are somehow connected to the signal. This is a hoax. We do not believe the signal is causing mutations. One possibility we are exploring is the release of radiation or chemicals from undersea geothermal vents."

Alex bristled. "What? Are you kidding me? You don't think scientists are watching this bullshit? Why aren't they mentioning the DNA sequences obtained from the sea monsters? They're identical to portions of the transmitted sequence."

He got his answer when they proceeded down East Temple Street. Looking right, at each passing intersection, they could see the throngs already packed into Grand Park, a lengthy mall that paralleled Temple for several blocks, ending at the entrance to City Hall. A KTLA 5 van wheeled past them and turned down Hill Street to join the other news crews lining the park. Police vehicles were everywhere. The AP in the JPL van announced that a right turn on Spring Street, which would land them in front of City Hall, would not be possible due to current obstructions. It advised an alternative.

Ashley ignored the advice. Deactivating the AP, she turned right onto Spring but only got as far as the stalled Metro bus in front of her. Farther ahead, the Temple/Spring bus stop in front of City Hall was only made visible by the number of people who had climbed atop the flimsy awning covering it. The marble arches of City Hall looked as though they had vomited a dense, multicolored mass of humanity down the steps in front of them. Spring Street was blanketed with people, who spilled into the park as far back as it stretched. Some were protestors chanting unintelligible slogans. Others were throwing objects at the marble arches. Most just seemed curious and were seeking answers. A scattered handful—

garbed in assorted ET masks, dated *Star Trek* attire, and wobbly antennae hats—had joined the fray just for the fun of it. Apparently, all but the latter group had missed the President's speech on behaving normally.

They sat in the JPL van behind a city bus that could neither advance nor reverse course. The Marsters' Goat Farm shuttle certainly would not fare any better in approaching the bus stop, but where it would go was anybody's guess. A brittle rap on the driver's-side window left Ashley face-to-face with the impatient mug of an LAPD officer in riot gear. "Move it!" he shouted.

Ashley dropped the window. "But we—"

"I don't care! You can't park here. Just move it. Now!"

The cop stepped back into the middle of the street and bit into his whistle, clearing a few protestors aside. He signaled for Ashley to execute a U-turn. She complied and continued one block up Spring Street, back across Temple to a public parking lot on Acadia. The four of them tumbled out the van. Hauling the air tank behind them, they trekked back up Spring Street and into the melee in front of City Hall. Rosslyn and Ashley remained stationed near the Temple/Spring intersection. Janet and Alex pushed through the crowd and took up a position on the opposite side to watch for the Marsters' shuttle there.

But it never arrived.

Chapter 11

There They Are

Emma was backing into the ward while fending off the attending physician. He was needling her about an overdue incident report. "Tuesday," she informed him, only to learn that it was already Tuesday. He regarded her scrupulously, like he might a patient. "I'm fine," she said. "It's Tuesday all day, right?" The attending doc forced a disingenuous smile that tightened to a smirk. "I'll have it today," she said. He shook his head and continued down the hall, seeking his next victim.

Emma turned around to find young Tessie upright in her bed, entranced by a metal wire puzzle. Her nimble little fingers flipped, tugged, and twisted at the impossibly tangled loops. Unnoticed, Emma stood by quietly, admiring the tenacity of her young leukemia patient. She watched Tessie's eyes burn with determination. She was so worth saving, and she would likely save others, provided her errant biology did not overreach the limits of medicine. Her prospects were good, but statistics, by nature, always offered long and short straws.

"I can get you a surgical saw if you want a shortcut," piped Emma.

Tessie let go of the puzzle and unleashed a smile at her favorite doctor. "That's cheating," she said. "I'll get it. It just takes time."

Emma took out her pen lamp and looked in Tessie's ears, eyes, and nose. Her mouth looked free of mucositis, and her fingernails were clearing up nicely. She pressed a thumb into Tessie's bared shoulder and watched the skin rebound without a trace of color. "How's the hair coming along?"

Tessie removed her head scarf and brushed a palm over her copper stubble. "It's longer than it was yesterday. It still feels prickly, though." She leaned in, inviting Emma to graze her crown.

"Yeah, it's getting longer fast. At this rate, you'll be wearing a ponytail in a few months. How's your appetite? Ready for some broccoli?"

Tessie screwed up her mouth, then opened it to insert a finger in a well-recognized gesture. "Gross! My appetite will never be *that* good!"

"Someday your tastes might change, and you'll find broccoli delicious."

Tessie stuck out her tongue. "Ick! Never! I'll bet the space aliens wouldn't like it, either. Have you seen them yet? The newsman said they were coming." She took out her stick, and the cube lit up with a riotous scene of protestors overrunning the steps at City Hall. "See? All these people are waiting to see them."

Emma glanced at the image. "Well, no one has really seen them, Tessie. There's been a signal from outer space that apparently contains the code for DNA. Some of the code is similar to that of our own DNA. It isn't clear what it means yet."

"I'd like to meet them. Maybe they have medicine for my disease."

The veracity of her naive comment was mind-reeling to Emma. Their arrival could transform healthcare in unimaginable ways. She had placed her own hands on that miracle—her father, cured of cystic fibrosis. A disease gene deeply embedded in his DNA was cut, pasted, and corrected by an alien dog. "That's a nice thought, Tessie."

Emma followed Tessie's eyes, still fixed on the video projection. The camera panned over the chaos at City Hall before roaming into the over-populated park across the street. It stopped and focused on a couple of withering sixty-year-olds, sitting slumped against a tree. The tall dark one, a wiry male, leaned against his petite blond female companion. Plastic tubes dangled from their noses. They looked wasted. "There's some tired campers out here," reported the roaming newsman. "Looks like this couple has had enough. I'm not sure what they're doing out here. Hoping to be healed, maybe."

Emma gulped. She had seen those features before, unfinished but in the making. The broad nose, full lips, the huge brown eyes, the dark complexion. His companion, also familiar, with her dishwater-blond hair, pale eyes, button nose, and pert lips. Emma's jaw loosened. She spoke, unaware of her vocalization until Tessie repeated it.

"Goats?" Tessie asked. "What goats?"

The couple leaned against a tree along the perimeter of the park. In the near background, Emma could make out a building marked *Clara Shortridge Foltz Criminal Justice Center.* She composed herself and squeezed Tessie's hand. "No goats, Tessie. The park just reminded me of a farm, somehow. You are doing remarkably well, young lady. We'll have you out of here in no time. See you tomorrow, sweetie."

Emma ducked into the hall and dialed up Ashley on her stick, but she didn't pick up. She checked the TeslUber App and arranged an AP for City Hall. Skipping her last two patients, both flu victims on the mend, she raced out of the clinic, grabbing a sample of Tessie's blood from the lab along the way.

"City Hall?" asked the AP.

"Yes."

"Only nineteen minutes today. No traffic. But the streets there are blocked off. Where should I drop you?"

"How about the Clara Shortridge Foltz Criminal Justice Center?"

"Uh-oh. Have we been naughty?"

"Nope. But I could be. Is it a crime if I strangle you?"

"Impossible. I have no neck."

"How about if I pour some acid on your quantum plate?"

"That's misdemeanor property damage. Thirty days and a twenty-five-hundred-dollar fine."

"Okay, thanks. That might be worth it. Now please shut up and just get me to the justice center."

CHAPTER 12

RESCUED

The incessant buzzing of her phone stick had tested Ashley's patience. A countless string of badgers from all ranks of journalism had been ringing her. They were hoping to hustle a sound bite out of the famed astrobiologist. She popped it open, fully prepared to punch the red X, when a static image of Emma Curtis filled the ID panel. She poked at the green Y and there was Emma, live, crouched by a tree supporting the listing frames of Enki and Ningal.

"I've got them, Ashley!" she blurted. "They need help, quickly. We're near the backside of the criminal justice building, not far off Spring Street."

"Great, Emma! Thanks! We'll be right there!" Hoping to ward off the crowd, Ashley donned a scary-looking orange filter mask, put on purple latex gloves, and pasted a couple radioactive warning stickers to her shirt. She and Rosslyn shouted dire warnings as they wheeled the air tank through the masses.

Although she had once volunteered to help malnourished Kenyans ravaged by drought, Ashley was unprepared for the sight of the emaciated Rossians. It was shocking. Forty years older and thirty percent lighter after a few short hours. It defied physiology. Enki tried to smile at her, but his cracked, dried lips failed him. Most of his frizzy black hair had whitened, loose skin drooped under his chin, and his frail hands were shaking. Ningal, severely wasted and unconscious, leaned hard against the tree, her hair, still yellow but thin, pressed into Enki's bony shoulder. She mumbled incoherently when Ashley adjusted her tubing and fastened it to the tank line.

"Can you walk? We need to get you out of here," she asked Enki. She was fiddling with his breather while she called Alex and Janet for help.

Ningal, awakened by the air supply, perked up a bit when she recognized Ashley and Rosslyn. "The sea," she managed. "We need to go to the sea. The Ceti."

"The city?" Ashley asked. "Why? We are in the city now. This is City Hall. Right here." She pointed at the marble arches across the street.

"No. Ceti," corrected Enki. "In the sea. Take us to the sea."

Despite the confusion, Ashley was eager to comply. Rosslyn cupped her hands under Ningal's armpits and navigated her featherweight frame into an upright lean against the tree. Revived but wobbly, Enki stood up on his own power. The five of them struggled through the crowd and made their way back to the JPL van, where Alex and Janet joined them. Handed the Boot sandwich, Enki inhaled the entirety of the Calabria province in the first bite. Basilicata and half of Apulia met their fate in the second. Ningal chewed her Boot like a rabid squirrel. Her teeth sawed through the toe box and well into the vamp before she came up for air. Their moods brightened as their stomachs filled.

Ashley looked at Alex and Janet. "We need to get them to the ocean. They want the sea."

"Why?" asked Janet.

"I don't know, but I think we should do it."

"Ceti," squeaked Ningal between Boot bites. "C-E-T-I," she said, writing the letters in the air with her finger.

"C-E-T-I?" repeated Ashley. "Wait, you mean Cetus, the constellation, as in Tau Ceti?"

"No. Ceti," replied Enki. He released what remained of his Boot, placed his wrists at his sides, and flapped his hands like wings.

"Cetus, the whale!" shouted Rosslyn. "Cetus is the whale constellation. Right, Mom?"

"Whale! Yes," agreed Ningal. "Dolphin, too. Flipper and Pelican Pete." She sang the theme from *Flipper*, the ancient television series.

"Cetacea," added Janet, "the biological suborder containing sea mammals, like dolphins and whales." She looked at Enki and Ningal. "You want a whale?"

Ningal smiled, her cheeks still stuffed with Boot. She garbled,"No. We want to be whales."

CHAPTER 13

THE BEACH

The van crawled toward the sea, worming through the narrow confines of Rose Avenue in Venice. Approaching the beach, they passed the Ale House and crossed over the vacant Ocean Front Walk. Without slowing for the parking attendant booth, Ashley drove clean through the lot and onto the sand, where the van sunk to halt. "I think we're beyond worrying about parking tickets," she said. She turned to Enki and Ningal and pointed to the water. "Now what?"

"Bar is coming soon," explained Enki. "The bend is complete. We will wait here. Thank you, Ashley. Thank you, everyone. You are saving us. You are…" He looked to Ningal, searching.

"Heroes," she said.

"Yes, heroes," repeated Enki. "Superheroes! We will be okay now. You can go."

"I have nowhere I'd rather be, and neither does the van. It's stuck," said Alex. He looked at the others. Each concurred with a nod. Rosslyn added that superheroes always stayed till the end.

They trudged barefooted through the sand. The beach was largely deserted. A few stragglers poked around near the shore, presumably diehards still seeking sea monsters. It was midafternoon, but the October sun was forgiving, and the sand felt warm under their toes. A few feet from the lapping surf, they all sat down in a line, side by side, each facing the sea.

"What will happen?" asked Janet.

Enki and Ningal had settled back onto their elbows, both alternating their views between the sky and the water. "The others are ready now," said Enki. "We will join them soon."

Emma, to Enki's right, told him of the time that her father was cured of disease by a Rossian, the one called Shala.

"Shala is here now," he said, pointing to the water. "So strong. The one who called us. She is special."

"Can you heal, like Shala?" Emma asked. "She healed my father."

"Yes, but Ningal is a better healer," Enki replied wearily. "Many of her inhabitants are healers. Are you ill, Emma?"

"No, but I'm a doctor, and one of my patients is a beautiful little girl who is very sick. I would like to heal her." She removed the sample of Tessie's blood from a small cold pack. "This is hers."

Ningal reached past Enki and took the vial. She unscrewed the cap, covered the vial with her finger, and inverted it. A few seconds passed. "Some of her Form is not balanced."

"I know, she has cancer. B-cell leukemia with high hyperploidy. Can you help her?"

Ningal contemplated silently for a moment. She rubbed the tip of her index finger against her thumb, placed her finger over the uncapped tube, and inverted it once again. She replaced the cap and handed it to Emma. "Give her this. It will destroy the stem of the unbalanced cells. They will die."

"Thank you, Ningal." Emma retuned the vial to the cold pack. She leaned forward. Eyes moist, face flushed, she stared out into the expanses.

Ashley thought she should bring it up now since it would likely be her last chance. "Enki, do you know who killed the scouts? Sukka and Sanga?"

Both Enki and Ningal bowed their heads in reverence.

"I'm sorry," said Ashley.

"No, it's okay. Sukka and Sanga remain, but their Zumru is gone forever. The Irkallan destroyed their kernel. They cannot build Zumru again."

"The Irkallan came back," said Ashley.

"I hit her with a fire extinguisher," chirped Rosslyn.

Ningal gave Rosslyn a high-five slap. "Superhero!" she exclaimed.

"We know the Irkallan," lamented Enki. "It wants to destroy us."

"I know. It told me you are ruining its world by collecting, um, consciousness, I guess. It said it created the universe and the intelligent life in it. It used Siru to do this. It says you think Siru is like God. It's afraid you're going to discover the secret."

Ningal laughed. "Not God. No secret, either. Siru is just a machine. We know who the Irkallan is and what it wants. Yes, it made Siru and created this universe. And Siru helps assemble intelligent life. So what?" Ningal poked Ashley's arm with her finger. "Your Zumru is just a machine, too. Yes? But the Irkallan wants to spread the life force thin, into Etemmu, the dark place. That is where it best serves the Irkallan. The Irkallan takes a different path than us. It is singular and scattered throughout. It lives among the channels and waves created by the life force. Spread out, it is everywhere and nowhere at once. It cannot collect the life energy, like we do. It has no congregations. That is why it is threatened by us. We are growing stronger together. Those of Ross have learned to gather the Bar released from the Zumrus of many generations from many rocks, including yours."

"Why does the Irkallan care if you collect the Bar?"

"The Irakllan wants all of it for itself. It drives life to assemble Zumru that grows the life force. Then it survives on the waves of Bar created by it. It reaches to the limits of the universe."

"We make the waves lumpy," chuckled Ningal.

Enki smiled proudly. "Yes, we put knots in the Irkallan's strings. Only some, though. There is so much more energy left for the Irkallan, but it wants all of it. It cannot stop."

"The Irkallan said you are warping the universe and that it will collapse. It happened before. That's why it made this one."

Enki laughed. "The Irkallan always destroys what it builds. It is in its nature to push beyond the limits. Its desire for everything is a desire for nothing. We have grown beyond what the Irkallan needed from us when it made this universe. In its lust for all things, it has made something it can no longer control. Us."

They sat quietly for a moment, listening only to the rhythmic lapping of the gentle surf and the mournful wail of a single gull. Then, only a couple hundred feet from shore, a geyser sprang from the placid water. An enormous gray hump followed it, heaving upward and easing back down. The slap of a giant tail against the surface punctuated its message: *We are here.*

"The ends are nearly joined," said Enki. "Bar is coming. We must prepare."

Enki and Ningal rose to take a few shaky steps toward the water. They waded in up to their shins and sat down. Their torsos extended above the surface; they ran their hands through the water like sieves. They checked their palms and repeated the motion. The others, looking on in wonder, got up and waded into the surf to watch. They stood near the paddling duo, gazing into their open hands each time they pulled them up for inspection.

Ningal stopped. She poked a finger into her open palm and pushed around a glistening gray nodule the size of a bean. She showed it to Enki, who nodded in agreement. Ningal squished the nodule into a paste and smelled it. She smiled and offered Alex a whiff. He bent over and inhaled, then wrinkled his nose and quickly recoiled.

"Smells like crap!" he announced.

Enki laughed. "Yes. Crap," he echoed. "Ceti crap."

"Ambergris?" wondered Janet. "It's whale waste, a special kind, from sperm whales. Quite rare and valuable, actually. It's still used in some perfumes, believe it or not. It must smell better after it ages."

Enki and Ningal were busy rubbing the goop into their palms with their index fingers. The resulting ashen smear faded and turned chalky white. They rolled their hands into fists. Eyes shut, heads tilted back, with their faces to the sky, they hummed the theme from the old *Flipper* television show.

"The song is not necessary, but we like it," said Ningal. "Thank you, Alex, Ashley, Rosslyn, and Janet. We must join the others now. We are all here. The Bar comes. We can hold it here, but not for long. The Ceti are strong and capable creatures, but their Zumru is not fit for us. It will hold us like a paper cup holds water. It will leak eventually. Our Zumru must live above the sea. We are like you."

"How long will you have?" asked Janet. "As Ceti, how long can you last?"

Enki's voice had gone from rich to squeaky. It sounded like his lungs were full of helium. "We don't know. We have never tried it before. The bend is complete now. Bar comes. You will know it from the gravity. Don't be afraid. It will last only for the smallest possible amount of your time. We are moving a knot in the string. After the Bar comes, the Zumru will be sent once more from Ross. It will be here in about eleven of your years. Then, we can evolve once again. Maybe then we can join you if the gas is gone. We look forward to that time."

Ningal's uprooted blond locks were falling away. A few tangles rode the mild breeze, sailing sidelong down the shore. Her vacated scalp began to smoothen. A shiny coat of rubbery gray flesh expanded inch-wise across her crown, replacing the pink, rumpled flesh. She looked at her hands. The skin between her fingers had thickened into webs, the dermis gray and slick. She elevated her legs to reveal severely flattened feet, lacking toes altogether.

"Oops!" said Enki. His now stubby arms and newly flattened hands struggled to tear off his clothing.

Ningal chuckled. It was a shrill, repetitive squeak, rhythmic like the chopping of wood. She yanked at her shirt with her stubby hands.

Realizing their bind, Ashley and Alex pitched in, ridding them of their needless garments.

"I like it," piped Enki, his neck, almost nonexistent now, leaving his shiny bald head directly fused to his broadening shoulders. Words squirted out of him in a staccato pitch. "The water feels warm and smooth."

The curves were gone from their bodies. Bottle-like and tubular, their appendages retracted into stubby flaps, they wiggled around in the surf, flipping over onto their bellies.

Rosslyn bent over to touch Enki's glossy head and stroked it gently. Enki bobbed her noggin and slapped what remained of her shrinking legs against the water. "Superhero!" she squeaked.

"See you in eleven years," replied Rosslyn.

With one hand in her pocket, Emma could feel the cold pack containing young Tessie's blood. She thought about an end to suffering and what that might mean for humanity. She envisioned Ms. Rickestin, her multiple sclerosis patient, only forty, quaking in her wheelchair, barely able to feed herself. And Mr. Horbey, the carpenter, so ravaged by Huntington's chorea that he could no longer wield a hammer to feed his family. She wanted to say, *Don't go.* She felt embarrassed to be human—in all their recklessness, they had wasted such an opportunity. Given another chance, would they respond any differently?

Janet waded out to her waist, one hand on Enki, covering the blunt protrusion arising from the middle of his back. "We'll try to clear the air for you," she said. "We don't like the gas any more than you do. A new Earth will await your return." But she said it with more confidence than she felt. *What could possibly convince humanity to change course?* she wondered. Something profound had happened. The world witnessed it. There was no hiding the fact that a code for life came from outside of our solar system. Strange creatures had evolved in real time right before our eyes. The creatures' DNA matched the code. Would we just forget about it? Could it be rationalized away? Surely, man would rise to the occasion now. If not, then what else would it take?

Enki and Ningal slapped their final goodbyes on the surface and let the ocean swallow them. A minute later, the distant horizon was dissected by a water spout followed by an apocalyptic breach of an enormous sperm whale happily reunited with its kin. The four onlookers retreated up the beach and continued to gaze southwest toward the setting sun. They joined hands to form a small ring. Heads bowed, solemn as prayer, expecting the worst, they hoped for the best.

Ashley said aloud what they were all thinking. "We don't know where they went. Right?" No pinky shake was needed to seal that secret. "We can't tell anybody. We know what would happen."

"Save the whales," said Alex.

"We saved on parking," replied Janet, looking at their beached van. "Who's pushing and who's driving?"

They found a couple emergency blankets in the boot of the van and laid them behind the rear wheels. Behind them, Alex and Rosslyn scraped out parallel trenches in the sand reaching to the parking lot. Janet got behind the wheel, and Alex, Ashley, and Rosslyn leaned into the front grill. Janet started the engine.

What followed could not be chronicled.

And from the four participants, a consistent, uniform description of events could not be formulated. All concurred that it got very light, then very dark, then light again. But what happened between the light and dark, none could agree upon. Although no one knew how, they all agreed that the van had returned to the parking lot. They had to agree, because it had. But Janet was not found in the driver's seat. How she ended up face down in the sand along with the other three was only the tiniest of mysteries when put into context.

"Very different," said Alex. "Not at all like last time."

"The sun bobbed," said Janet. "You saw that, right?" Imploring, she looked to the others for confirmation. "It popped back up, then dipped below the horizon again."

The others nodded dutifully, fully accepting, although none were actually a party to her vision.

Rosslyn said she met a baby that looked just like her in the photographs her parents had taken. It talked to her. She carried it up a mountain, where it grew into an adult, a doctor. "She said she was a veterinarian, Mom. I want to be a veterinarian. A whale veterinarian. Did you see the baby, Mom?"

Ashley only smiled. She hadn't seen a baby. But she had seen life. All of it at once. It materialized from the nothingness between the stars, pulling and pushing on them. It spun the Earth. It spun the galaxy, poking it in the middle, making it spiral. It reached in every direction, beyond the next nearest galaxies, well beyond the boundaries of every earthly means of detection. She saw it all. There was an end to the universe—for now, at least. More would be added later.

CHAPTER 14

WHAT HAPPENED?

Ashley plopped down onto the sofa and snuggled up close to Rosslyn. All the lights, save those burning on the Christmas tree, had been turned off. She threw an arm around Rosslyn's shoulder and shouted toward the kitchen. "It's almost on, Alex." Projected in the TV cube, a rendering of the spinning globe appeared, lush with blues and greens and brilliant splashes of white light accenting the most populated regions of Earth. The globe ceased spinning and grew large as the viewer zoomed in from outer space and grazed over the North American continent. A dozen bright green beacons shined under the flyover, marking the hometowns of guests to be featured on the show that evening.

Alex hustled into the living room still drying his hands. He tossed the towel back toward the kitchen and dropped in on the other side of Rosslyn. "I'll bet we get the group thing again. Someone's mentioned it on every show so far." The globe dissolved and was replaced by a dapper gentleman, tan, bright-eyed, and jaunty, clapping his hands and bowing. Alex shook his head. "That Marty's such a ham, but he's still kind of lovable, somehow."

"Shhh," urged his daughter, "it's starting, Dad."

"Hello, everyone! I'm Marty Louis, and welcome once again to *What Happened?*" The chipper host of the weekly primetime show unbuttoned his bright green blazer and spread his arms wide, as if gathering in his live audience. Head on a swivel, he scanned the crowd before turning his animated mug to the camera. The host of the most popular show on television—global, live, and six weeks running—was once again commanding the rapt attention of at least a billion viewers worldwide. Another billion, residing in less convenient time zones, would watch the delayed version later.

The host quickly ran through the scenario. "As usual, we will hear uncensored, live witness accounts of the Transformation. This time, from the United States of America. As you are all aware, from your own sharing of the Transformation, no two accounts are identical. But if you hear something that sounds familiar to you, please ring in by clicking your green button. Our first three guests today, chosen by lottery, include a baker from Minneapolis, Minnesota, a teacher from Muskegon, Michigan, and an auto mechanic from Caldwell, Idaho. Their accounts, stark and unfiltered, will undoubtedly take us to place full of mystery and meaning. Their stories are at once personal and universal. We can learn from them." Marty pointed straight into the camera. "And we can learn from you."

Marty ran through a preamble, touching on a few poignant accounts from previous guests. Images of a double helix, comprised of a spiraling string of lettered code, spun into view. Swirling around the helix were photos taken of various so-called sea monsters from around the world. Marty took a seat behind a table and invited his first guest to join him, a portly, middle-aged man, with ruddy cheeks bracketing a fat smile. Hands clasped in front of him, the timid stranger, clearly unaccustomed to attention, shuffled over and sat down alongside Marty.

"Welcome," Marty beamed. He looked down for a second, then back to the camera. "Our first testimony tonight will come from Mr. Joseph Gassen. He is the owner of the Fat Cake Bakery in downtown Minneapolis." Marty turned to the guest. "May I call you Joe?"

"Sure," replied the man. "Can I call you Marty?"

"Of course, Joe. That's what everyone calls me. Except for my wife." He grinned sheepishly into the camera. "She calls me Martyr, because I complain so much." Marty pushed down an open hand to quell the chuckling audience. "Now, Joe, you know I must ask you." A long pause ensued while Marty stirred up the drama. He turned to the camera, raised his eyebrows, elbows bent, palms face up and parallel to the floor. "What happened?"

"Well, I saw my life, Marty. My whole life, and other life, too. All life, I think. It stretched out as far as anyone could imagine, but it was kind of lumpy on top and twisted together. I mean, I know I'm a baker, and all, so this might sound silly, but it reminded me of a Danish." The crowd laughed.

Marty stood up and shouted, "Life is a Danish!" The audience applauded. He sat back down. "No offense intended, Joe. You know we like to have a little fun on the show. But I believe you. After what each of us has experienced, how could anyone not? As I have said before, I saw clowns, happy crazy clowns holding my hands and walking me through an endless flower garden. It's true!" He shrugged into the camera, then returned to his guest. "Please, Joe, go on."

"Well, I could see shapes and figures all over the Danish." He paused abruptly, "And they weren't raisins or pecans, Marty." More laughter from the audience. "They reminded me of people, but not by their looks, or anything like that, but in a way I can't really describe. It was a feeling. Some of them I knew, most I didn't. They were all moving, too. Not steadily, but in leaps and bounds. They would just pop up instantly, moving from one position to another. All in the same moment, all at once. They were going somewhere. Into water maybe, or somewhere deep and fluid. I tried to follow, but then everything closed up around me. I woke up on the bench in front of my bakery, but don't know how I got there. I was inside before it happened."

"Making Danish, perhaps?"

The audience chuckled, Joe demurred. "No, we don't make Danish on Tuesdays, Marty. Seriously, though, the one thing I felt that many others have is that we're a part of something very big." The monitor behind them, tallying the green clicks alighted, instantly racking up millions of agreements.

"Ah, yes," Marty drolled. "Danish, Joe? We don't hear so much about that on the show. But something big. Something we all share? Always a favorite. I must agree with you." Marty clicked his own phone stick, adding to the tally. "My clowns' garden, it contained every flower that ever was, is, and will be. And I was one of them. It's true!" The audience clapped. More green clicks racked up. "And you know, Joe, my flowers all moved, too. As far as I could see, for miles, maybe thousands of miles, they all shifted, not as a wave but simultaneously, together and all at once. When one moved, they all moved. What does this mean?"

Joe could barely contain his excitement. His bottom bounced off the chair. "Yes! Yes! Exactly!"

"Fascinating, Joe. Thank you," Marty said. "Stay here, everyone. We'll be right back with our teacher from Muskegon, Michigan, right after this."

With Ashley's long arm dropped behind Rosslyn, she tapped the back of Alex's head with her hand. "See? Another one. They all know *it* happened, they just don't know what *it* was."

Alex reached behind his head and fiddled with Ashley's wedding ring. "Yeah, it does keep coming up. I think it's good. A little unity can't hurt. After all, it's the whole globe that needs fixing. It just makes me a little nervous when someone mentions water. You know, like Joe, here. At least we haven't heard about any whales or dolphins yet."

"I think they'll be all right," said Ashley. "After all, the IWC just banned commercial whaling altogether."

"Yeah, that's not like them at all. A very abrupt about-face. Did you read the announcement? They didn't even cite the depletion of whale stocks as a reason. It was more like a change of heart. Something about humanity rising above practices of needless predation and respecting life. Weirder still, no complaints were lodged by the whalers themselves. We're so civilized these days. What happened?"

ABOUT THE AUTHOR

Paul Polakis, PhD, is a biochemist who has published over one hundred original research articles, book chapters and editorials, as well as numerous biotechnology patents. He has previously penned one science fiction novel, The Aents (https://www.amazon.com/dp/B086R58XPM).

Paul lives in Mill Valley, California, with his wife and two teenaged boys.

Thanks for reading my book. I hope you enjoyed it. Recognition is very difficult to come by for independent authors. Book reviews really help. I would greatly appreciate it if you could leave an honest review of "Souls" at Amazon. Just a couple sentences would go a long way. Thanks.

www.ingramcontent.com/pod-product-compliance
Lightning Source LLC
Chambersburg PA
CBHW070740180626
46818CB00007B/2926